Dishonorably Interred

A Novel

by

Tommy Coletti

Published in the United States by HW Publishing, a subsidiary of House of Walker Publishing, LLC, New Jersey

Copyright © 2010 by Tommy Coletti
Library of Congress Control Number 2011925694
Cover design by Jennifer Harren and Tommy Coletti
Dishonorably Interred/Tommy Coletti
ISBN: 978-0-9834762-0-7

Dedication

For my children, Jennifer, Kimberly, Crystal and Michael, with thanks for all their encouragement to keep my literary dream alive.

And a special thanks to a good friend, Fred Thompson who took the time and had the patience to critique my work.

And to my editor and publisher, Michelle Nelson, without whose help, none of this would be possible.

Table of Contents

Chapter One   The Swimming Hole
Chapter Two   The Colonel
Chapter Three   The Shooting
Chapter Four   Loose Ends
Chapter Five   The First Clue
Chapter Six   The Fire
Chapter Seven   Iraq 2003
Chapter Eight   Family Business
Chapter Nine   The Stakeout
Chapter Ten   Chance Meeting
Chapter Eleven   Loose Plans
Chapter Twelve   Hit and Run
Chapter Thirteen   Interment Arrangements
Chapter Fourteen   Saturday Morning
Chapter Fifteen   The First Good Lead
Chapter Sixteen   Forensic Puzzle
Chapter Seventeen   The Interrogation
Chapter Eighteen   Attorney-Client
                       Relationship
Chapter Nineteen   The Key

The Swimming Hole

The water was cool and refreshing and awakened Bob Bryant's naked body from the hot and humid August afternoon. He swam slowly to keep himself moving but not fast enough to induce any form of strenuous exercise. He remembered when he was a kid and he and his friends would jump into the water as soon as they had completed loading up hundreds of bales of hay onto the Wilson farm trucks. The trucks would take a half hour or so to return before they had to reload them so they would use the time to cool down from the hot summer sun. This place had been their oasis during the hot and humid summers and their skating rink in the winter. The pond had been a popular place for teenagers for many generations. The creek that flowed through the farm that fed the pond had never stopped running as far as anyone knew. It was said that the Indians had used this area to grow crops and supply drinking water for their encampments hundreds of years ago. Every so often, someone would find an arrowhead and the story would be told again.

The Wilson farm had been around for over a hundred and eighty years. Winthrop Wilson settled here from Sheffield, England back in the 1820's according to the town records. He brought over his wife and son and started dairy farming with a dozen or so milking cows he purchased from the locals he met when he arrived. The Confederate Army had come through this portion of Frederick, Maryland on their way to Gettysburg during the Civil War. Nobody ever found any evidence that they used the creek and pond but the Wilson family passed the story down through their generations of how some dairy cows were stolen and butchered for meat by the rebels and a few cornfields were trampled by hundreds of soldiers marching through them.

Story has it that Winthrop's youngest son, Jeremiah, joined the Union Army right after that because he said the war was personal now because the Confederates had stolen property.

Jeremiah never returned to the farm. He was killed in one of the campaigns in the Wilderness the following year. Winthrop died a few years after that. It was said that the loss of his son was the cause of Winthrop's death, but most of the town's people said that the corn liquor that he made on the farm contributed more to his demise. There is a small headstone in the family cemetery that marks the existence of Jeremiah even though he's really not buried there.

Bob Bryant's grandfather, Jerry Bryant, had also worked at the farm and swam in the swimming hole when he was a boy before going off to World War I in 1917 with his best friend, Herman Wilson. Herman never returned alive. He was killed in France and the Wilson's requested that his body be returned to the family cemetery. It took five years before his remains were returned to the farm by the Army. Every year since his return, members of the American Legion Post in Frederick came out to the farm a few days before Memorial Day and placed a new little American flag near his headstone and one on Jeremiah's as well. Visitors could see the flags and the white headstones when they sat on the porch of the farmhouse, as told by Jerry Bryant. He continued to help around the farm after the war. Herman's mother requested that she be able to see the cemetery stones when she sat in her maple rocker on the porch so the grass was always kept short. She's long since passed away but Bob remembered his grandfather's story every time he saw those headstones while sitting on the porch many years later when he visited Amy Wilson. Those summer evenings in the 1960s were a great place to be especially when he was with Amy, the pretty grandniece of Herman.

Richard Bryant, Bob's dad, worked at the farm and swam there as well when he was a boy. He worked many summers with Stuart Wilson until they graduated from high school in 1940. After the summer of that year, Richard left to join the Navy to see the world and fulfill a two year commitment to the Navy while Stuart remained on the farm. Except for a few furloughs in 1940 and early 1941, Richard didn't return home for four more years after the attack on Pearl Harbor. Stuart left the farm and joined the Marines a few months later after the attack. He saw action in the Pacific Islands. He never talked about it but he'd sometimes treat the summer kids like they were in the Marines when they worked for him haying. He would have beaten Bob's buttocks to a pulp if he ever knew how much time his daughter Amy spent at the swimming hole in the evening's skinny dipping with Bob. He never asked about their long walks by the swimming hole. As long as they played by his rules and she was back at home before 9 o'clock, he was happy.

Bob could remember seeing Stuart driving the lead haying truck and shaking his head as he noticed all of the boys running out of the swimming hole naked, quickly dressing and getting ready to start loading hay bales onto the trucks. Amy's brother, Arnold, worked and swam there until the draft called him up in 1966. He drove trucks for the Army. Bob remembered sitting on the porch with Amy listening to her as she read one of his last letters home. He indicated that he would probably get a tour of Vietnam before his two years were up. He was killed while driving an ammo truck and was buried in the family cemetery on the farm. Stuart didn't talk about him very often after that. Occasionally he would say that the farm would have run much better if Arnold had returned home to run it with him and his other two sons.

The Wilson's continued to pass down the corn alcohol recipe to each generation. They all said it was for medicinal purposes. They shared it with their neighbors occasionally during festive events. Some of those neighbors thought the corn alcohol might have contributed to Stuart's death as well. He died in 1994 from complications from liver disease and was buried in the Frederick Cemetery.

As Bob finished his swim and began to gingerly walk up the rocky edge of the pond, he was startled to see his wife, Amy, smiling and looking at his naked body. She laughed and said, "I've almost forgotten the days when you exited the same way but at a much quicker pace. I guess you knew it was getting close to 9 o'clock and I had to be home." She somberly mentioned, "That was forty years ago."

"You want to relive those years?" he asked.

She smiled. "Get dressed you old fool. The attorney will be at the farm in less than an hour. You know we need to speak with her before the bank representative arrives." He smiled and began to dress quickly.

The farm was in foreclosure now from several banks. Amy's brothers, Bruce and Benjamin Wilson, had left the farm after the death of their father to pursue occupations other than dairy farming. They used the farm to finance these business pursuits. Their business failures were unbeknownst to the Bryants. Amy and Bob had only been on the farm once since they left the area thirty years ago to live and work in Connecticut after college. The farm had been rented out to prospective dairy farm buyers after 1995 but slowly declined in function and condition. That one unfortunate time was when the entire family returned to the farm for Bruce's son Todd's funeral. Four years ago, in August 2003, he was killed in Iraq and laid to rest in the family cemetery next to his great-great uncle Herman, uncle Arnold and the memorial to private Jeremiah of the Grand Army of the Republic.

Todd had a finance degree from Penn State. After graduating, he joined the Maryland Reserves and became an army officer. After 9/11, he joined the army and was assigned to a branch of Army Intelligence that dealt with the cataloging of money while he was stationed in Baghdad. He was given a commission and had a great job in the Army, everyone thought. He wrote home about his job protecting the tons of money that was being discovered by the Army and Marines in undisclosed areas throughout Iraq that Saddam Hussein had tried to hide. The Army reported that he'd been killed in a sniper attack. There were grumblings amongst some family members that his death was somehow tied to his protecting money but they had no reason to believe that.

It had been a very hot and humid day when the relatives and

4

friends of the Wilson family met to pay their respects. Bruce had decided that his son should lie next to the other family heroes; however, he never contemplated that if the farm was sold, a litany of legal matters would emerge. Amy and her husband Bob were now faced with those legal matters.

Bob finished dressing and slowly walked back to the farmhouse with Amy. He was sweating all over again by the time he reached the front porch. The temperature was exceeding 93 degrees according to the outside thermometer on the wall of the house even though it was under the shade of the porch. They stayed outside on the porch. There was no breeze anywhere to be found. It was a very hot Maryland August afternoon and Bob not only dreaded the heat, but the conversation that was about to take place with the lawyer that Amy hired. He could see the heavy white dust coming from the wheels of the lawyer's car as it exited the main road and made it onto the gravel road that began the quarter mile ride up to the farmhouse.

They wished the kids could have been with them on this day; not only to hear the proceedings that were about to take place but to walk the farm and listen to some of the old stories they could tell them about the place. Their daughter, Cora, was now teaching special education and their son, Bob Jr., was completing a student teaching program. Neither one seemed interested in their trip to Maryland so they didn't push it. Besides, they were grown now and had their own professions and lives to live. Bob and Amy were getting into the retirement mode anyway. Amy had one more year to go before she retired from teaching high school English. Bob had just retired this year after teaching college History and Political Science. He was contemplating going back for his doctorate in his retirement years but he had put that on hold to do some speech writing for some aspiring politicians in New England and around the Washington Beltway area. Amy was his teammate. There was nothing better than being married to an English teacher who edited and researched everything he wrote for his political clients.

The attorney's car approached the farmhouse and they could see two individuals sitting in the Ford Taurus Sedan.

"Honey, there are two people in the car. Who's the other one?" Bob asked his wife.

"I don't know. I only thought one attorney was coming."

As the car pulled up, they recognized that the passenger was one of Bob's old high school classmates. Bob hadn't seen him since Todd's funeral. Ed Manning was the lead attorney of the Law Offices of Manning, Watson and Breen. Bob thought he retired, but there he was, getting out of the sedan with a big smile on his face.

"For God's sake, how have you been, Ed?" Bob asked as he stood up.

"I'm just fine. I wanted to be here with you and Amy while Miss Terry Breen briefs you on the farm situation," he said as he reached over to shake Bob's hand. He then moved over and hugged Amy as Terry watched and smiled. Bob introduced himself to Terry who already met Amy a few days earlier to start the proceedings on what to do about the farm.

Terry Breen was the daughter of one of Ed's partners and new to the firm. After some brief conversation, Bob immediately summarized that Ed had probably placed her with them for her experience in foreclosure matters but also so that he could get out and mentor every so often on cases like these. Ed also confessed that this case was right up his alley and although he enjoyed semi-retirement, this gave him a chance to keep his fingers on the pulse of the firm.

Once they all sat down, Amy excused herself and went inside. She came back with both lemonade and iced tea to help quench their thirst. Bob looked out at the western hills and could see thunderheads developing. He knew that in a few hours they could get some relief from this heat with an old fashioned thunderstorm that usually cooled things down a bit. As the drinks were poured, Terry was poised to begin her presentation. She graciously waited for the small talk to end and for a sign from Ed as to when to begin. He acknowledged her professionalism and nodded for her to present the details of the plans and advise the Bryants of their choices. They could undertake to either salvage the farm or sell it. Both were being presented with enough time to forestall the foreclosure from the banks. She began her presentation.

"Mr. and Mrs. Bryant, three banks hold mortgages on the farm. Mrs. Bryant, your two brothers have defaulted on their loans and have apparently decided to walk away. The mortgages have almost exceeded half the worth of the farm. If a buyer can be found in time, which is doubtful because the three banks have run out of patience, then the loans could be paid off. There is also the amount of the compounding interest that is building which would also have to be paid. That is the simple solution, Mr. and Mrs. Bryant, to get the banks out of the equation."

"That would be good news for my brothers. They wouldn't continue to be hounded about the assets that they are barely hanging on to," Amy murmured.

Terry continued, "The reality of it all, Mr. and Mrs. Bryant, is that the banks want the farm as quickly as they can get it now because there has been rumors that a developer is poised to buy it to build a golf course and adjoining condos for, at least, half of the 200 acres. The remaining acreage is being considered for a water park where the creek would supply most of the water."

The four of them sitting on the porch realized there was money to be made once the farm was foreclosed on. Amy looked at Bob and then at Miss Breen and said, "I think I would like to pursue a buyer for the next 30 days or even try to get an extension if the banks would agree. Even though my brothers have defaulted, I still want to protect them from any further legal issues against property."

Bob stared over at Amy. He could have cared less about her two brothers who had almost destroyed the farm due to bad management of their investments and finances. She looked at him with a look that indicated that this was a decision that was not to be questioned until after the attorneys left and they could talk privately. Bob got the message and resigned to sit there and listen intently.

7

Terry concluded, "I will file your notarized intent with the banks immediately because the banks will take over the farm by default if the mortgages are not paid within 30 days."

Bob asked, "Miss Breen, what about the Wilson cemetery?"

"Mr. Bryant, the banks would remove the remains to the local cemetery. Any other requests for the location of the bodies to be interred somewhere else would be honored but the family would have to pay for it."

Amy looked over at Bob and said, "The local cemetery would be fine. I understand the reasons why the family had created their own cemetery but I never agreed with it. The local cemetery maintains the remains of all the military and civilian burials so why did we have to be any different?"

Ed spoke up with one point that was interesting to Bob. He said, "There is a retired army colonel, by the way, that has inquired about the farm and has offered to pay off the mortgages." Bob looked at him and couldn't resist asking, "Why didn't you bring this up at the start of the conversation Ed?"

"Bob, Terry needed to explain the history of the case first. Based on some research I did, I believe the colonel can come up with the money in the next 30 days. He indicated he is interested in buying the farm at the fair market price if you two are unable to hold onto the farm. He also said that he will pay to remove the remains of those gallant military men and place them wherever the Wilson family wants them interred to."

Bob looked at Amy and said, "Then all we need to do is get in contact with this retired army colonel and sell it to him for the balance of the mortgages and interest before the 30 days are up." He looked at everyone and continued, "Or, we can get an extension on the 30 days and then sell it to him under the fair market price and be done with it. It's a piece of cake either way if this guy is really serious."

Terry cut in and reiterated, "Mr. Bryant, the banks are adamant that there will be no extensions for any reason and this ex-Army colonel has a conflict of interest. He is also the Vice-President of the Colony Bank here in Frederick, Maryland. The bank holds one of the liens. I suggest that if you both are willing to pay off the farm, then the extension would not be necessary, the colonel could then be contacted under normal real estate conditions at a later time and the cemetery matter could be worked out with the local cemetery authority or even better, if you prefer, the Arlington National Cemetery authorities. All the Wilson men were killed in action so they fall under the authorization by Congress and can be interred at Arlington." She looked at Ed Manning for his nod and said, "The best thing of all in this type of payoff would be that the both of you could deal with the real estate market directly and probably realize a considerable profit."

Bob looked at Amy and then asked Terry and Ed, "What is the amount of money required to pay off the three mortgages and the attorney fees?" Ed looked to Terry for the answer. She rumbled through several papers in her briefcase and came up with the exact amount.

"The banks will require a total of $534,440 including compounded interest and our firm would require $2,100 for legal fees and filings."

"Wow, over a half of a million dollars!" Bob exclaimed. But then he realized that they were talking about 200 acres of prime farm land with a house that, even though it needed a lot of work, was surely worth more than what the banks were demanding.

"Terry, have you done a market analysis and value research on the property yet?" Bob asked.

"My research indicates that the farm is worth about $900,000 in its present condition. It could go for as high as $1.1 million if the Maryland real estate market continues on the growth path that it is presently on. I believe that an investment to fix the home up could increase the value of the total property to $1.5 to 1.7 million."

Bob looked at Amy and said, "Our home in Connecticut has approximately $30,000 left on the mortgage and the house is worth over nine hundred grand on the present Greenwich, Connecticut market. We could save the farm but only if we could sell our home in a very short time. We should consider re-mortgaging our home to save the farm from foreclosure, but could we borrow 500K or even 600K against it for a short time?" Bob was thinking out loud that they could make a few bucks on the farm before they sold it around the fair market price to that colonel or better yet, for a price that Terry indicated, after fixing it up. They could actually make a minimum of five hundred thousand bucks on this deal or as much as a million or better now that he understood all the numbers.

Amy seemed pleased but still concerned as Bob started running numbers by both attorneys and her. Amy stopped him. "Bob, we'll talk about the details later. I need to feel comfortable about this option." Bob saw the concerned look on her face that she had exhibited for the second time. But the possibility of financing this deal became stronger and stronger in his mind. He looked away after Amy's comment and noticed the bank representative's car pull off the main highway and onto the gravel driveway of the farm. The car stopped in front of the farmhouse. Two men exited and approached the four of them sitting on the porch. Bob and Amy didn't recognize either one of them but Ed and Terry knew them both.

They were introduced to the Bryants as they all sat at the old farm kitchen table on the open porch. Mr. Hank Jarvis began to talk while his associate, Mr. Sean Quinn, stood by and listened. He began with a simple question.

"When will the family be able to vacate the farm?" The Bryants thought that was rude at first but they waited to see how Terry, would react.

She quickly said, "The Bryants, not the Wilsons, are discussing their options and there wouldn't be any decisions until they review all their options. One would be to pay off the mortgages and claim complete ownership of the farm through release from the Wilson brothers."

Mr. Jarvis smiled and said, "The bank I represent would welcome a complete payoff. The other two I cannot say. It's a reasonable solution to the problem, but time is running out.

Unless the Bryants have that kind of cash to pay off the loans, 30 days wouldn't be enough time, in my estimation, to receive a loan of that nature from any bank."

Terry shot back, "Mr. Jarvis, you are in no position to conjecture on anything of what they can or cannot do within the next 30 days. If your bank or any of the others are not offering any solutions as to an extension of time or a reduction of interest on the overdue payments, then your business here is completed. Now if you would be so kind and leave the farm, I would like to continue my private talks with my clients."

Hank Jarvis was speechless for a few moments but then recovered enough to make a semi-apology to the Attorneys and the Bryants.

"I'm sorry, but my tone and statements were possibly misunderstood. I did not mean any disrespect. I'm just stating facts, Miss Breen. Mr. Sean Quinn here represents the interest of a developer who does have the cash available to buy the farm within minutes of the loans defaulting. He can also offer his services to the Wilsons, excuse me, the Bryants, with any other arrangements they are considering to pay off the mortgages."

Terry nodded and said, "I understand your explanation and your associate's proposed services, but I will remind you that you've been invited here to meet Mr. and Mrs. Bryant who still may want to right the wrong that has occurred concerning mismanagement of the mortgages and property. Good day gentlemen. I will present my client's position tomorrow morning when the bank opens and I have filed their intent concerning the foreclosure."

Both men smiled. Neither extended a hand. They turned around and exited the property as fast as they could. In a very short time, their car was entering the main road with a fine trail of white dust following it.

The Bryants sat speechless as they watched the car leave. Terry fixed her paperwork on the table, padded some sweat gathering on her nose and forehead with a pink handkerchief and looked at Ed for some signal to continue on. Ed smiled at

11

Amy and Bob and said, "That is why I hired this young lady. She is as sharp as a razor in case you hadn't noticed. Both of those gentlemen have been cut very deeply and they didn't even feel or see the blood coming from their throats when my girl here finished with them. Good job, Terry."

Terry blushed and then turned to Amy and Bob and asked, "Mr. and Mrs. Bryant, can you produce that kind of cash in less than 30 days?"

"We can Miss Breen, but we need the rest of the day to confirm our net worth and borrowing ability as well. We still have to decide whether we are really going through with paying off the mortgages. That doesn't include what response we are going to get from my brothers-in-law when they have to agree to give up their ownership of the farm once it is paid off," Bob said.

"Mr. Bryant, I will contact both of them and inform them of the tentative proposal. I'm pretty sure they will agree with it and I expect they would cooperate in signing over the farm to you both with relative ease." Terry believed that she could have all the answers in the morning and hoped that the Bryants would make the decision to save the farm. She finally said, "I have some personal reasons why I want you to keep the farm and eventually sell it to someone who wants to maintain it."

Bob said, "Miss Breen what might those personal reasons be, may I ask?"

"Well, first of all, Mr. Bryant, I do not like Mr. Quinn. He represents the developer who probably will never get a golf course or a condo complex built because most of the area residents don't want to entertain any zoning changes and I'm pretty sure they wouldn't welcome that type of industry into the area. Secondly, I hope that the farm would be maintained as a dairy farm and participating again in that industry. A producing dairy farm is a good thing for the future of the property and the community." She looked at Amy, "I personally do not care who owns the farm but I do hope whoever becomes the new owner continues to run it as a dairy farm. This area of Frederick has always been the center of the dairy community."

Amy and Bob seemed pleased as they looked at her and each other. They affirmed their respect for Terry's opinion when Bob told her he hoped that they could oblige. Both of them thanked the two attorneys for their time and advice. They told them that they had some decisions to make but they would have their final answer first thing in the morning in time for Terry to file and notify the bank on their behalf. They saw them off and watched their sedan exit the farm road onto the main highway.

Bob looked at Amy and asked, "Would you care for a swim in the pond?"

Surprisingly she accepted. They stepped off the porch while holding hands and headed to the swimming pond like they had done many times before a long, long time ago.

The Colonel

Jarvis looked back at the farmhouse as he drove his car and entered the main road leading back to town.

"That lawyer is an arrogant bitch. The only thing going for her is her looks."

"Yeah, she's got a great ass and a fine rack, but that's it," Quinn responded. He then looked out the passenger window.

"I've been working this shit job for almost a year now. I wish I was still in the army. Maryland is worse than Iraq in the summer because the humidity makes everything seem hotter."

Quinn continued to look out the window until Jarvis asked, "Are you listening to anything that I'm saying?" Quinn looked over at him and simply said, "No." That simple statement angered Jarvis, but he knew better than to pick a fight with his passenger who had served under him in Iraq.

Quinn was a martial arts expert, sniper and had been a Staff Sergeant in the Army. Both men were familiar with the farm but only Jarvis had visited the farm with a few other men that were assigned in the Maryland Reserves before they left for Iraq. The officer that had invited some reservists to share a few days at the farm before they shipped out was none other than First Lieutenant Todd Wilson. Jarvis spent those days swimming in the Wilson pond, drinking beer and got a taste of some of the corn liquor that was still kept on the premises. He even paid tribute to the Wilson cemetery and was told the history of its occupants. Jarvis brought Quinn and several other reserve members as the lead military honor guards to pay their respects at the military funeral for Captain Todd Wilson almost two years later.

Jarvis said, "I'm going to have to contact the Colonel and update him on the Bryants. I'm not sure yet if they are going to attempt to save the farm." He hated to have to update his boss of that potentiality.

"I want to listen in on the conversation because I have a few ideas that I want to run by the boss to try and stop them from raising the cash they need to save the farm," Quinn said. Jarvis didn't ask him what his ideas were as he continued to drive. Quinn continued to sit and stare out the window but only nodded when Jarvis said that they should call the boss immediately when they got back to the Colony Bank in town.

Bob and Amy lay next to each other half submerged in the water on the bank of the pond. It kept their lower body cool and they could feel the strength of the sun on their exposed backs.

Bob asked, "Was our little escapade at the swimming pool anything like the ones we had here years ago?" She rolled over onto her back while squinting from the brightness of the sun and said, "You were quicker in those days but I'm very pleased that you learned to slow down and pace yourself."

"I guess that's a compliment," he said while he kissed her left breast. She smiled, stood up and plunged back into the pond to cool her already reddening shoulders. Bob followed and they both spent a few more minutes in the pond, avoiding the conversation that they knew they would have to have about finishing the business they had both come to Maryland to settle.

They quickly dressed and began a slow walk back to the farmhouse. By the time they reached the porch, they had discussed most of their assets and liabilities. They also could see and hear the approaching thunderstorm that was quickly heading towards the farm. They closed up the farmhouse and headed back to the hotel in town where they were staying. While Bob drove back to town, Amy made an Excel spreadsheet on his laptop and began entering data that could help them make a reasonable decision whether they were going to risk their livelihood to pay off and save the farm from foreclosure. Amy kept stating figures and numbers on various stocks, CDs, insurance policies and investment plans they had acquired over their 30 plus years of marriage. Bob listened while he concentrated on his driving.

They reached the hotel parking lot about 30 minutes later. The storm was passing and the rumbling of the thunder was fading.

The rain had been very heavy during the ride to town, but it was now just sprinkling on the windshield of their rented white Ford Taurus. The parking lot was steaming from the rain hitting and cooling the hot asphalt. The air was thick and humid now, but a little cooler as a result of the storm. Still, they welcomed the cool dry air when they entered the hotel lobby. It actually felt cold at first until their bodies adjusted to it. They walked past the pretty desk clerk who smiled and greeted them on their way to the elevator. They rode the elevator up several floors and didn't speak until they entered their hotel room.

Amy pulled the laptop from its case and set it on the table near the couch. The spreadsheet was instantly back on and in view. She sat in front of the screen to double check her entries and commented with inaudible sounds. Bob sat opposite her and began with the 64 thousand dollar question.

"Can we save the farm without too much risk to everything we have accomplished in the last 30 years?" She sat back, looked straight at him and said, "We can Bob, but do you really want to do this?"

"Do I really want to do this? You must mean do we really want to do this, Amy."

She rose and walked to the balcony window that overlooked the park across from the hotel. She didn't move for a minute or so as Bob sat there allowing her time to think of what he'd just said. She turned with the most serious look on her face and said, "I want to keep the farm." He acknowledged her decision and said, "That's fine with me, but we need to begin to make serious arrangements once we have verified that your figures are accurate enough to pull this off."

"No, I mean live on the farm. Retire here and have our future grandkids visit and share in the experiences we had here as kids. You could write your speeches here. You would be a lot closer to your clientele and Washington is just a short drive away. I could retire one year earlier and the reduced retirement would only mean about one hundred dollars less a month income."

Bob was about to argue and explain all the reasons why they couldn't or shouldn't do this then simply said, "Alright then." She looked at him with what looked to be confusion and said, "Alright? A simple alright is all you can say?"

"Yeah, it's just a simple alright. What else would you expect me to say?" he answered smiling. "I don't know what the kids are going to say, but I'm sure they will get over it. I do know that we have a lot of work to do in the next few days and I don't know if we can pull this off," he said.

She slowly moved over to him and wrapped her arms around his neck. "I love you and thanks for being the man that I married." He looked into her eyes and told her that he loved her too, but he was sure the incident at the swimming pond influenced his mood and decision. She pushed him away kiddingly and said, "You are a real jerk, you know that? But thanks anyway for being that jerk," she bantered. She looked at the time and said that she was going to call Cora and break the news to her. She also needed Cora to go over to their house and look up some information in their financial files that she kept in the den. Cora would need to give her some figures to make sure her spreadsheet was accurate enough to talk things over with Terry about their decision to not only save the farm, but to live on it as well.

Bob asked, "Do you still know how to milk a cow?"

"I never planned on milking any more cows in my lifetime. I want to fix the farm up and make it a working dairy farm again. We could hire someone to run it for us. There has to be an ample supply of experienced dairy farmers who live in this area that could make the place functional again. If there aren't any, then it would just be a great place to live."

John Moore's cell phone rang several times before he picked it up. He read the caller ID and immediately recognized Hank Jarvis's name and number. He continued to let the cell ring as he closed his office door at the Colony Bank and assured himself that the pending conversation would be very private. "Moore here," he answered.

"Colonel, we may have a problem."

John Moore immediately corrected him. "Mr. Jarvis, my name is Mr. Moore, John or just plain Moore but not Colonel. Do I make myself clear, Hank?"

Jarvis corrected himself mentally and just said, "Yes, Sir. I understand." Moore acknowledged his reply and began to ask what problem Jarvis thought could be at hand. Jarvis explained his meeting with Terry Breen and the Bryant family. Moore stopped him and asked who the Bryant family was. Jarvis, realizing his haste, began to slow down and explain who they were. Moore listened to the details Jarvis presented and said that he would check out their finances and assets. Moore instructed him to sit back and wait to see what Attorney Breen would be filing in court as to their intent for the farm. He also instructed him to continue to work behind the scenes getting to know members of the zoning boards as well as the inland and wetland commissions in town. He wanted Quinn to complete the land search on the farm to assure him that there were no other liens on the property except the three banks he knew of so far. He explained one more thing he wanted Jarvis to accomplish.

"When Quinn finishes with his tasks today, I want him to go up to Connecticut and do some research on them," he said at almost a whisper. "I want any information he can get on them as soon as possible. I will do my part on this end to get information through my contacts as well as through the bank." He didn't wait for an answer. He closed his cell phone and then reopened the door to his bank office. He returned to his desk to see that his phone was blinking. His secretary said that the call he requested was waiting on line one. "Thanks Ms. Clemens. John Moore speaking," he said as he picked up the line.

Jarvis was a little irritated that Moore had ended his conversation with him so abruptly but he didn't give it a second thought because he was use to the Colonel's ways. He had served under his command for four years and despite the condescending tone the Colonel sometimes used, he would have followed him anywhere. In the twenty two years Jarvis had spent in the Army, Colonel John Moore was the best commander he'd ever had. He also made a mental note to stop irritating the man by calling him Colonel and get use to calling him Mr. Moore.

"I wanted to talk to him before you hung up." Quinn said. Jarvis just looked at him and shook his head. Quinn ignored his gesture and left the office. He already had several plans in his head that would interfere with the plans that Amy and Bob Bryant were contemplating. He had already decided he didn't need to tell Jarvis or get Moore's permission.

Amy called Cora from the hotel room after dinner to update her on what they were considering. She kept the speaker phone on during the conversation so Bob could listen in and comment if needed. She asked Cora to stop by their home in the morning to obtain some information they needed to validate the figures she had put into the spreadsheet she created. She was planning to discuss them with Terry Breen in the morning before the court filing was to take place. Amy and Bob had gone over the figures during and after dinner and felt sure they could pull off this plan to save the farm. Cora answered the phone and the two of them conversed for a few minutes; small talk about the weather, how each was doing, what the farm looked like and the condition it was in.

"Cora, please go into the house and unlock the file cabinet in the den next to the desk top computer." She detailed where she had hid the key to the cabinet. She explained what files and papers she wanted Cora to look at. "I need you to write down the exact figures from those files." Cora listened intently, wrote down some more of the detailed instructions and acknowledged all the instructions she had been given. Then the obvious questions began.

"Mom, why do you need all this stuff? It sounds like you are doing some high finance planning. What's up?"

"Cora, I fell in love with the old place again and realized that I wanted to save it from the bank. Also, your father and I plan to fix up the house and move back to the farm and retire there.

Amy waited for some type of an explosion from Cora as to why would she want to do that or what would happen to the house in Connecticut, but there was none of that to be heard.

Cora surprised her and said, "I think that is a great idea! I'm very happy to hear that you'll retire early."

"Wow! I expected more opposition from you."

"Hey, it's not my decision to make. I'm happy for you both. Anything else I can do to help make your transition to retirement and to Maryland any easier, just let me know. In the meantime, I'll get the information you need and get back to you first thing in the morning. Oh, do you want me to tell Bobby?"

"No. I'll call him tonight and tell him myself."

"Ok, I understand," Cora said. The conversation ended and they both hung up, Amy turned to Bob before dialing Bobby's number and said, "That was easy. Do you think Bobby will take it as well?"

"Let's hope so," he said as she dialed Bobby's number.

He softly hung up the phone, slid a folded fifty dollar bill to the hotel desk clerk and smiled. As he walked past her, he gently brushed her buttocks and simply said, "Thanks. There will be more for you each time that phone is used and you can tell me what the conversation was and with who. Do you understand?" She blushed at the sensation she felt from his touch, looked around quickly and then just nodded. Quinn left the hotel lobby and went directly to his car. He picked up his cell phone and called Jarvis. Jarvis answered his cell and listened to the details of the conversation Sean heard between Amy Bryant and her daughter.

"Are they really going to try to stop the foreclosure on the farm and pay off the debt? Are you sure they are going to live on the farm? Shit, that will make our task even more difficult," he exclaimed to Quinn. Jarvis remembered Moore's instructions and ordered Quinn to leave town this evening and drive directly to the Connecticut address listed by the Bryants when they had signed into the hotel.

Quinn said, "Not yet, I still have some more research to finish."
"Forget that," Jarvis fired back "The Colonel wants this job completed by tomorrow."
"It's going to take eight to nine hours to drive to Connecticut. That means that I will get there between three and four in the morning if I drove all night. Are you nuts?"
Jarvis looked annoyed and said, "I want you to leave now. Quinn, it's more important to get to their home before their daughter does. You need to get that key they talked about and get into all the files." Quinn didn't like what he was hearing, but he obeyed orders from his former Sergeant Major. He acknowledged his task and said that he would keep in touch when he was in Connecticut and after he had searched the house. Jarvis ended the conversation and immediately dialed Moore. He listened to Jarvis and only reacted with, "Good job Hank. Keep me informed of what Quinn is doing in Connecticut." He immediately ended the conversation again before Jarvis could respond.

Moore finished his last sip of wine and looked over at his dinner companion.
"Tomorrow I will have some information for you to research at the bank. The time has come to initiate the project and for you to earn your share." Former First Lieutenant Marilyn Porter, now a Colony Bank loan specialist, smiled and held up her wine glass to make a toast. She sipped the remaining wine from her glass as she thought of Captain Todd Wilson. She briefly remembered the tall handsome farm boy from Maryland that she had been in love with who had been killed. He was a great lover too, but his love could never fulfill her desire for wealth like the man sitting across from her could. She placed her wine glass down and moved her hand over to touch his. He smiled and enjoyed the tender touch and the moment. Marilyn withdrew her hand and began to get up and leave the dinner table.
"Where are you going?" She looked seductively at him and began unbuttoning her sheer blouse.

21

"I'm going to put on something more appropriate for the evening. I'll meet you in there in a few minutes." Moore followed her gesture which indicated the hallway to the master bedroom of her apartment. He smiled but continued to think about what the conversation with Jarvis had indicated as Marilyn left the room.

The Bryants called Bobby several times. He apparently wasn't home, so they left messages for him each time to call them at the hotel when he returned. They thought they had some great news to tell him. As Amy hung up the phone on the last message, the desk clerk hung up softly and wrote down the time of the call. The desk clerk realized that there was no reason to contact Sean until she heard what Mrs. Bryant had to say to her son. She reviewed and noted the times and lengths of the calls just in case that meant a few more dollars would be added to the tip Sean would be giving her.

Quinn finished filling his tank with fuel for his drive to Connecticut. He looked at his watch before entering the Mustang. It was 7:15 p.m. He calculated that the earliest he would arrive in Greenwich would be 3:15 a.m. He hoped not to be there no later than 5:00 a.m. because he figured Cora Bryant would be getting to the house around 7:00 a.m. He had decided he needed time to see what kind of neighborhood it was and what type of security system he would have to deal with at the house, assuming they had one. He didn't want to be noticed by any of the neighbors while he was getting in and out and didn't want to wait for Cora. He knew where the file key was hidden. His task was to accomplish the task cleanly and with no problems. He felt under the passenger seat of the 2005 black Ford GT Mustang and reassured himself that the .9 mm automatic pistol with a silencer was still there. The pistol, along with a couple of full clips, was covered by a handkerchief and was available, if by some slim chance he would need it.

The weather was clearing from the recent thunderstorm as he

entered the ramp for Interstate 70. He headed east to Baltimore and then north on Interstate 95. He set his cruise control for 75 miles per hour and let the 5.0 liter engine do its job.

The Shooting

Amy and Bob were awakened a little after midnight when their son, Bobby, called to ask in his usual tone, "what's up?" They thought that he would have called a little earlier but Bobby had been nocturnal since birth. He kept them up as a baby, kept them up through the high school years and would call them very late at night when he was up studying in college. They never saw him before 11:00 a.m. on weekends and when they did, they usually had to wake him. He would always leave them a message to wake him early declaring that he didn't want to sleep too late. But he never would get up even when they did wake him early as he requested.

"Hello," Amy sleepily whispered into the phone.

"It's me, Mom, Bobby. What's up?" He asked again. "Are you awake?"

"I am now," Amy replied as she cut on the light on the bed stand. She felt no need to ask why he was calling so late. She already knew.

"Bobby, we have something to tell you."

"Cool." Amy paused to consider his English diction but refrained from commenting.

"Well, your father and I have decided to save the farm, fix it up and live on it in our retirement years."

"That sounds like a good idea."

"Have you talked to Cora already?"

"Nope, should I have?" Amy relaxed a little knowing it was his true response.

"No, but I expected a little different answer."

"Why? You guys can do what you like without asking for my permission. I think it's great. Go for it Mom." Amy talked to him for a few more minutes to get caught up on how he was doing and to give him a few ideas on what they had planned for the farm. He wished them well and asked them to keep him updated. He volunteered to do anything they needed done to assist in the transition and said good night.

As soon as he entered Connecticut on Interstate 95, he was ticketed for exceeding the speed limit by 15 miles per hour. Quinn was upset that he had been pulled over by a Connecticut State Trooper. The Trooper said that he would have to appear in court if he wanted to contest the speeding ticket. He explained that he had ten days to either pay the $300 fine or send in the ticket contesting it. Sean glanced at his watch. The trooper noticed and asked, "Where are you going in such a hurry?" as he moved his flashlight back and forth in the Mustang after handing him the ticket.

"I'm heading to Boston to see some relatives and I want to get there soon so I can spend more time with them." The trooper said that he better slow down or he would never make it there. He flashed his light in the back seat again and only noticed a dark blanket. Quinn looked at his watch. It indicated that it was 3:22 a.m. The trooper shook his head and said, "Just slow down and have a safe trip." Quinn did slow down as he entered Greenwich. He made very good time but was tired and needed a cup of coffee after his long drive. He saw an all-night café open and decided to grab some refreshment before checking out the Bryant's home.

Marilyn woke to the snoring of Moore. She slowly got out of bed and put on her robe. She contemplating going to the couch and getting another hour of sleep but realized she had a lot of research to accomplish today. The earlier she could be at the bank the better she would be with no one around looking over her shoulder as she checked out the Bryant's financial credit scores and anything else she could find out about them. She decided to forego the extra hour of sleep and take a shower instead. Anyway, she had to be sure she wasn't seen with Moore when she came to work. They had made sure no one knew about their sleeping arrangements.

As she turned on the shower, he awoke and decided to lie in bed until she returned from the shower. He was always more aroused in the mornings than evenings and he decided that she would have to re-shower again after he was through with her.

Quinn finished his quick breakfast of toast and coffee and entered the men's room of the diner to wash his face and freshen up a little. He noticed another man standing at one of the sinks splashing water on his face. Both men nodded to each other and a conversation commenced.

Quinn asked, "Are you from Greenwich?"

"Yep, born and brought up here."

"Is Round Hill Road close by?"

"Yeah, it's about a fifteen minute drive to get there. Follow Lake Avenue out of town and bear left when you see the road sign, about 4 miles from here. Do you have relatives here?"

Quinn nodded and said, "I have some friends I am going to surprise this morning. It's been awhile since I've seen them after getting discharged from the Army."

"How long had you been in the Army?"

"Too long, Bro, too long".

They both laughed and Quinn thanked the man for his directions and left. Within a few minutes, he was on Lake Avenue and, keeping within the posted speed signs, looking for Round Hill Road. He found it and began counting off the house numbers looking for 412 Round Hill Road. By the looks of the numbering system, he would have a ways to go. So far, all the houses indicated single digits. He continued on for about five minutes until 412 came into sight. The houses were openly separated by nice rolling lawns and manicured shrubbery. The colonial home was lit by outside lights and a few lights strategically placed inside to indicate activity in the household. *Good job,* Quinn thought. Mrs. Bryant was conscious about burglary and had set up a convincing charade. Quinn drove up the street and turned around about a quarter mile up the road. He returned to observe a very quiet, upper middle class neighborhood. He observed that there were no parked cars on the street so he decided to pull very quietly into a neighbor's driveway several houses down, where there were no lights on at all. Either the occupants were really asleep or no one was home. As his luck would have it, he saw a real estate sign on the lawn and realized there was no one there. The place was for sale. He donned some cotton gloves he had in his jacket pocket. He reached under the seat and felt for the .9 mm pistol. He removed the handkerchief and placed the pistol in the small of his back under his light jacket. He then reached into his glove box and retrieved his small digital camera. He exited his car and walked quickly back to the Bryant house. He cut across the manicured lawn to the rear of the house and hid in the shadows of the trees. No sounds of cars coming or even a dog barking could be heard. He pulled out his pen light and checked the window sills for any signs of an alarm system. None could be seen through several of the rear windows he had checked. He tried the back porch screen door and found it unlatched. *Good luck so far*, he thought, as he entered the screened in area and felt the door knob of the rear door. It was locked, but it was a standard brass door knob that he could probably pick it in ten seconds or less. He strained to see inside. He tried to see if there was any type of security panel near the rear door to indicate some type of alarm system was present. He couldn't see anything. He picked the lock and in less than ten seconds, was standing in the mud room, prepared to exit as quickly as possible if an alarm sounded. All he heard was silence.

As he searched for the den, described in the eavesdropped phone conversation, he saw the security alarm panel. It had not been activated. The Bryants were paying good money to protect their home, but Quinn was amazed they were too lazy to activate it. As he passed the security panel, a cat scampered by him. He laughed to himself. It must have been the fault of their daughter, who, upon leaving the house after feeding the cat, forgot to reset the alarm. *This couldn't get any easier,* he thought. He found the den and located the key to the financial cabinet. He opened the file cabinet and began taking pictures. Social security numbers, banking account numbers, credit card numbers, the Bryant's 401K plans and other retirement accounts and even medical records were photographed. Quinn placed everything back in the exact order he had found them and closed and locked the file cabinet. He exited the home through the same door and locked it. He again stayed close to the rear of the house within the shadows. He quickly walked to the Mustang when he saw a car approaching from the same direction he had entered the neighborhood. He did not get into his car but waited in back of it for the other car to pass. The car slowed and he recognized what the black and white sedan was. The Town of Greenwich Police lettering was illuminated as the policeman driving lit up the red and blue strobe lights of the car. Quinn remained standing directly in the middle of the rear of the Mustang partially hiding the Maryland plates. He had planned that move just in case. His other move was to make sure the .9 mm pistol was loose enough to be drawn before the policeman could draw his pistol. Quinn knew he needed to plan his move expertly especially with a silencer attached to the pistol hindering his draw.

Officer Jake Bishop noticed an outline of a person standing directly near the rear of the car parked in the driveway at 408 Round Hill Road as he approached the scene. He knew the house was for sale. He had passed it while on patrol for several weeks since it had been on the market. The owners had left the neighborhood for a new home and employment in Houston, Texas. The owner's employer was selling the house as part of the relocation deal that had been arranged. Jake Bishop prided himself in keeping very informed of the citizens in the neighborhoods he patrolled. His police cruiser's lights enabled him to make out a man standing and looking directly at him. He looked for the license plate of the car so he could call it in while he investigated the situation but he couldn't see the number, letters or State it was from. He knew it wasn't Connecticut based on the light color of the plate. He called his dispatcher that he was stopping to check on a parked car in the driveway of 408 Round Hill Road. The dispatcher acknowledged and said that he would be on standby waiting for Bishop to report on the developing situation. He stopped the car, put the shift lever in park, unlatched the pistol strap of his holster, grabbed his flashlight and exited the car. Officer Bishop shined the flashlight in Quinn's eyes and called out to him, "Step away from the car and keep your hands away from your body where I can see them." Quinn knew the drill and kept his eyes lowered so as to not get blinded by the flashlight but kept his hands in view of the officer. His peripheral vision kept him aware of the policemen's position and able to see what he would probably do next, so Quinn calmly stayed still as Bishop approached. Officer Bishop warned Quinn for a second time, "Step away from the car." His intent was to get the license plate number so he could call it in and get information on the dark Mustang he now recognized. Quinn didn't move but did state to the officer, "I was looking for the Bryant's house and I realized this wasn't it, officer. I was about to get back into my car when you arrived." As Officer Bishop walked closer to Quinn, he relaxed a little when he heard the suspect's explanation of why he was in this driveway in Bishop's patrol area. Quinn saw that the officer had taken the bait as Bishop moved his right hand away from his pistol in an attempt to call into his portable radio to the dispatcher, while still holding the flashlight on Quinn with his left hand. Bishop stopped his forward motion when he spotted the gloves the suspect had on his hands. He began to move his hand back towards his pistol. Quinn dropped to a crouched position, reached behind his back, pulled out the .9 mm pistol, aimed and shot the officer. The noise was muffled by the silencer. Officer Bishop fell back onto the driveway's edge and partially onto the street. He had a .9 mm bullet hole in his chest and was unconscious. Quinn heard the sound of the expended shell rolling on the cement driveway. He quickly picked it up and placed it in his pocket. He entered the Mustang, shoved the warm pistol under the passenger seat, started the car and slowly backed up. He didn't have enough space to get around Bishop or the flashing cruiser but had enough space to turn the Mustang around and exit over the lawn. He kept his headlights off as he slowly exited the scene and glanced quickly from side to side while driving away to see if any lights had come on or doors had opened. He didn't see anything as he slowly picked up speed to exit the neighborhood.

He reached the center of town and followed the signs to Interstate 95 and south. He looked for signs of police cars with lights and sirens, ambulances or any type of emergency vehicle heading for the area of town from where he had come from. There were none. An occasional delivery truck or lone car could be seen, but nothing indicating an emergency. He entered the ramp for I-95 and headed back to Maryland.

The Greenwich Police Department dispatcher waited a minute and called Bishop.

"Officer Bishop, respond as to your status." There was no response. He waited another ten seconds and called in again.

"Officer Bishop, respond immediately." No response. He immediately called for the closest police car to proceed to the address given by Bishop earlier. The responding cruiser approached the scene to find Bishop's cruiser parked in the middle of the street with the lights still flashing. To the horror of the responding policeman as he stepped out of his cruiser, Bishop lay still in a pool of blood. The officer, drew his pistol, crouched as he approached Bishop and checked the pulse in his neck. Bishop was barely alive. The officer screamed into his radio, "Officer down, I repeat, Officer down and wounded. Send backup and an ambulance. I repeat, send backup and an ambulance."

He stayed with Bishop and waited for emergency help and police backup to arrive. Lights came on in a few of the adjacent houses as the sun rose on the neighborhood and sirens and flashing lights could be seen approaching.

Quinn began to shake. The adrenalin high was subsiding and he was beginning to get nauseous. He always felt that way every time he had killed someone with his sniper's rifle in Afghanistan and then a few years later in Iraq. He was having the same feeling now but with a little more intensity. It was the same intensity he felt the time he had killed an Army Captain for threatening the Colonel he worked for. He needed to pull over somewhere, get some coffee and relax a little. He would have to call Jarvis and inform him of the shooting incident soon, but the former Staff Sergeant would wait until he felt normal and could see what the local news had to say about the shooting. He exited I-95 at Port Chester, New York. He was only a few miles from Greenwich. He found a coffee shop on North Main Street and stopped for that coffee he so desperately needed. The place had a TV and it was tuned on to the morning news. He ordered coffee and waited to see what the news would report.

Amy and Bob woke up early. Neither one of them could really sleep well considering they didn't get to bed until after 1:00 a.m. They discussed the mid-night call they had with Bobby and both felt very good that both their kids were one hundred percent behind their decision. They showered, dressed and were down in the hotel dining room for breakfast before 6:00 a.m. They had several hours before they had to meet with Terry at her office so they decided to spend the time having a leisurely breakfast, wait for Cora's call, and then, walk to the Manning, Watson and Breen Law Office. They figured they would have a little time to check out the town and get a little exercise in as well.

Cora turned onto Round Hill Road and immediately found it blocked by several State and Greenwich Police cruisers. As she approached the roadblock, a State Police Trooper indicated for her to stop. She lowered her window to converse with the approaching officer.
"I'm sorry miss but the road is blocked due to a shooting incident of a Greenwich Police Officer. What is your business here?"
"I'm house-sitting my parent's home at 412 Round Hill Road. They're away on business and I am responsible for the house and feeding their pet cat."
The trooper instructed her to proceed slowly and stay clear of the roped off investigative area. She proceeded as instructed and arrived at her parent's home. She checked the house to make sure it was still locked and that no burglary had occurred. She noticed that the alarm had not been activated and realized

she had forgotten to set it when she had left the house yesterday. She made a mental note not to do that again. Cora thought to immediately call her parents and let them know what occurred a few houses down from theirs, but she decided to get the papers and information her mother had requested first before calling. She found the file key and proceeded to gather the information. Within a few minutes, she was calling the hotel in Frederick to speak with her mother. The phone rang until the desk operator picked up. Cora left a message to have her mother call her at her home as soon as she returned to her room. The desk clerk acknowledged the message and both parties hung up. The desk clerk noted the time and message in two places. One place was her skirt pocket. She too had been bribed by Sean Quinn to keep track of the Bryant's messages.

Quinn ordered his second cup of black coffee when he saw the news flash with a bulletin stating that a Greenwich police officer had been shot and was in serious condition at Greenwich Hospital. There was more information to follow in a few minutes. He could feel his pulse accelerate and his chest tighten as he sipped the hot black coffee. It seemed an eternity before the commercials ended and the news anchor was back on the screen. Several people stopped eating as the news anchor began to describe what had happened on Round Hill Road in Greenwich. Some of the waitresses stopped serving to listen as well. The news anchor explained that an unidentified person had shot and seriously injured an officer of the Greenwich police department around 4:40 a.m. this morning, August 23rd. The news anchor switched over to an on the scene reporter who repeated almost the same information the news anchor had just said except that she had flashing lights and people standing around near the roped off crime scene. After the report, the news anchor said that the Greenwich Hospital surgeons were working to remove a bullet from the chest of the officer. Sources in the hospital said that the bullet had just missed the policeman's heart. No other information was available at this time concerning the shooter. A news conference was to be held in a few hours by the Greenwich Police to give an update on the progress of the investigation. He relaxed a little knowing that he had not killed the officer. He was almost sure that the officer never got a detailed description of him, his car or license plate number. The one thing he did know was that the police would have the .9 mm pistol bullet to match up against his pistol if they apprehended him with it. He decided that he would field strip the pistol and discard the pieces on his way back to Maryland. He was a little angered that he would have to purchase a new one and that would set him back around seven hundred dollars not including a silencer; but that would be peanuts compared to what the Colonel would be giving him for his share of the prize. He contemplated staying longer to hear the news conference but figured the officer would probably make it and he should get back to Frederick as soon as possible and report in. Whether the officer lived or died, didn't make any difference to his main objective which was to get the photos back to Jarvis so that he could give them to the Colonel. He paid his check and left. Within minutes he was cruising down I-95 and heading south again.

The Bryants finished breakfast and headed towards their room. They planned to use its facilities before they walked to Terry's office. The desk clerk recognized them and alerted them to their room key box where a message had been left for them. The clerk at the desk handed the letter to Amy. She read the note and said, "It's from Cora. She wants us to call her right away." Bob nodded and immediately headed in the direction of the elevator. They reached the room and Amy called Cora. A few rings went by until Cora answered. She explained what happened and how close it had been to their home. Amy asked if they had mentioned the name of the officer.

"Mom, I heard some of the policemen on the scene talking and they were saying that it was Officer Bishop but it hasn't been confirmed yet."

"Oh my God, Cora, how is he?" she asked as she put the phone on speaker so Bob could hear. Bob and she knew Jake Bishop very well. He had been a policeman in their town for many years and Amy had taught several of his kids. She was relieved to know that he was still alive.

"Cora, please let us know as soon as the police or the hospital release more information."

"OK. I'll keep you both informed."

She then asked her about the financial information she found in the den cabinet. They went through all the figures and information. Within a few minutes, the financial conversation ended and Amy had double checked her figures and in a few cases, altered them on the laptop spreadsheet.

"Cora, keep us updated, please," she said again, very concerned.

"I will Mom. Good luck to you and Dad with the attorney today.

Bye," Cora said. Amy hung up.

Amy turned to Bob with a concerned look on her face.

"Bob, how secure are these phone lines in the hotel?"

"They are as secure as the desk clerk or operator wants them to be. Why?"

"I am pretty sure that I heard another hang up before I hung up from Cora."

"Amy, there is no reason why the hotel clerk or operator would be listening in on your conversations with Cora," he said with a perplexed look on his face.

"Yeah, I guess you are right."

She began to talk about the shooting as they exited the hotel room. The desk clerk heard and noted as much information as she could remember on another piece of paper that she put in her pocket next to the other message she had noted earlier. She smiled at them as they exited the hotel lobby to the street for their planned walk through town.

She faked another orgasm as she felt the Colonel go limp on her. *He took forever,* she thought. He'd actually been a decent

34

lover the night before, but two times in less than eight hours was too much sex for a man his age. She smiled as he rolled over and told her how much he loved her. She responded with a weak, "Love you too, sweetie," as she quickly got out of bed and headed for the shower for a second time. Marilyn needed to douche and get his mess out of her. She didn't want anything oozing out of her and onto her panties while she sat at her desk at work. The thought of the Colonel's semen in her, disgusted her. The only man that she never felt disgusted with had been Todd. He always made her reach the height of passion. She compared her sexual trysts with Todd to the experience she had with the Colonel last night. She felt grief as she recalled those earlier days and put them out of her mind as she finished dressing. She needed to say good bye to the Colonel and get to the bank so that she could begin the research she needed to complete before too many people arrived at work.

Loose Ends

Jarvis called Quinn on his cell phone. The call went immediately to voice mail. Jarvis seemed irritated that he would have to leave a message. He was use to people responding immediately to his calls. When the Sergeant Major called, everyone responded. All the junior NCOs and even the lower ranking officers had responded to his calls. He never really liked Quinn, but he put up with his poor attitude and lack of respect for rank because he could always get the job done quickly and efficiently while under his authority in Iraq. Jarvis left the usual sarcastic message for him to report back to him as soon as possible. He didn't like having to leave messages for someone who should have called him regularly to update him on the task he had been given. He never took into account that maybe the cell service was poor in the area that Quinn could have been driving through on his way back to Frederick.

The Greenwich Police held a news conference at 9:00 a.m. The local, state and even some national news agencies had arrived and set up microphones for the Greenwich Chief of Police to release the latest news statement on the investigation of the shooting. After several minutes introducing the FBI and State law enforcement participants assisting the Greenwich Police in the investigation, the Chief said, "Our officer, Officer Jake Bishop, has successfully come through the operation to have a .9 mm bullet removed from his chest. Officer Bishop is still unconscious, but once he's awake, he will be questioned by local, state and federal investigators. I have no additional details to give you. I will now introduce the surgeons that removed the bullet. Let me present Dr. John Pease and Dr. Richard Mellow." He looked at them and said, "Gentlemen." He then turned the microphone over to them to answer questions from the reporters.

Quinn picked up the news from a local radio station that carried CNN which had a crew at the Greenwich Police news conference. He was relieved knowing that the officer was going to make it but still felt a little uneasy because he still didn't know what the officer would remember and be able to tell the investigators. He decided it was time to call Jarvis and let him know what happened and that he had successfully obtained the information he was sent to retrieve. He noticed the missed call on the phone and recognized Jarvis's number. He listened to the sarcastic message and quickly responded to the number. Jarvis came on the line in a matter of a few seconds.

"Jarvis here."

"I retrieved the information you wanted from Connecticut." Jarvis questioned him for more details on the information he had obtained. Quinn responded with the types of files he looked at, numbers he photographed, dollar amounts he remembered, and previously unknown personal information on both Robert and Amy Wilson Bryant. Jarvis seemed pleased as he sarcastically asked, "Why'd it take you so damned long to report back on the status of the trip?"

Quinn casually said, "There was a slight problem."

"What kind of a problem, Sean?"

"Well I had a slight run-in with a local Greenwich cop while I was leaving the Bryant's home."

"To what degree was the run-in" Jarvis cautiously asked.

Quinn paused and said, "I'll give you the details when I see you in about five hours or so. Turn on CCN. There should be some more information on the shooting. I guess I'm the unknown assailant." He immediately hung up.

Jarvis was irritated and wanted to shoot Quinn himself as he heard the line go dead. He wanted to contact the Colonel but hesitated, realizing he should get as much information as possible before alerting Moore. He knew Moore would drill him for specific details and ask what actions had he instituted to resolve potential problems that could arise from the incident. He worked for Moore too long to not know exactly what the old man would ask and expect of him. Jarvis switched on the TV and selected CNN. Several minutes went by as different news items worldwide were presented and discussed. He read the ticker tape messages on the bottom of the screen which didn't indicate any news coming from Greenwich, Connecticut. He kept listening and occasionally reading the bottom screen as he fixed himself a cup of coffee. Ten minutes went by and still there was no news on the Connecticut shooting. He couldn't call Moore until he had something concrete to tell him. He finished the coffee and decided to finish dressing when the news anchor said that there had been a shooting in an upper class neighborhood in Greenwich, Connecticut. *That was a typical news lead in*, he thought. People get shot all over the country but when a shooting incident happens in a white upper class neighborhood; the press glorifies it and makes it world news. He patiently waited for the anchor to finish the lead in. The story switched over to the pre-recorded Greenwich Police Chief's remarks and the questions and answers that were given by the surgeons who operated on the police officer. Jarvis was alarmed, but he did not see any incriminating evidence that the authorities had or any leads on the shooter. Of course he realized that they wouldn't reveal any leads until they had a suspect in custody. They didn't have a suspect because he was miles away from the crime scene. He decided to not tell Moore anything yet. He figured, by the time Quinn returned and they had printed out the pictures he had taken in the Bryant's house, they would have received more information on the police officer's condition and maybe the Greenwich Police would have more information to divulge to the press and public. *Maybe they would have a drawing of the suspect or a description of Quinn's car*, he thought. If they did and were getting close to identifying Quinn, then he would take more action by informing Moore of what had happened. He finished dressing and called Moore to inform him only that Quinn was on his way back to Frederick with the information he had requested.

Moore had just finished his shower and was drying when his cell phone rang. He recognized Hank's number and answered it. He listened while Hank gave him the details of Quinn's trip to Connecticut and was advised that he was returning with the information he had requested.

"Hank, get the information to Marilyn at her office at the bank as soon as it is available. Call her first to alert her that your email will be coming. You did well Hank." He ended the conversation and closed his phone. Jarvis actually felt guilty that he did not tell him about the shooting but did enjoy the fact that Moore had taken a few seconds to commend him on a job well done. He was also pleased with himself that he had gotten up enough courage to lie to the Colonel which he had never done, except about his personal life style.

Jake Bishop could hear sounds. He didn't know if he was dreaming or not. He became aware that something was in his mouth and it was expanding his lungs and chest without his control. His eyes were blurry for a few seconds and then he realized he was in a bed. He focused and read the clock. It was on the wall near a desk that had people wearing surgical gowns moving about. He felt a hand on his and looked over to see a woman smiling at him. He heard her say, "Officer Bishop, you are in the hospital and you are going to be just fine." He went to talk and couldn't. The nurse explained, "You have a breathing tube in and I will remove it as soon as I get better oxygen readings from you. Just relax, Jake, and I will take the tube out very shortly." He saw her leave for a short time and return with another person. He focused again and realized it was his wife Susan. He smiled and didn't realize that he had fallen off to sleep again. It would be another hour before the breathing tube would be removed and his mind was clear enough to answer some questions from the investigators that were waiting outside the recovery room.

Quinn was becoming sleepy as he drove his Mustang through Philadelphia on Interstate 95. He realized he had been up for over thirty hours now and needed to stop and get an hour or so of sleep. He figured that an hour would not make any difference in his return to Frederick with the information he possessed. Jarvis wouldn't know whether he had traffic problems or he was just keeping within the speed limits to not draw any attention to himself. Sean recognized a truck stop up ahead and turned off to mingle among the big rigs. He found a suitable shaded area, pulled over and stopped. The Mustang looked out of place alongside the Mac and Peterbilt trucks idling while their drivers either were in the diner eating, or sleeping in the overnight cabs. He remembered the .9 mm pistol and silencer that he needed to discard. He decided to disassemble the pistol. He realized that this place presented a good opportunity to get rid of both. He reached under the seat while holding a handkerchief looking to make sure no one was observing. He quickly released the clip and disassembled the .9 mm in less than a minute. He put some of the smaller parts into one of the cotton gloves he had used when breaking into the Bryant's house. He wiped every piece of the pistol and the silencer with the handkerchief. The frame of the pistol and silencer were too large to fit into the other glove so he decided to go into the diner and order something that would have to be put in a take-out bag. He figured the take-out bag would accommodate the remaining pistol parts and silencer that he needed to discard. He dropped the first glove with the small pistol parts in it into the first available trash can he saw on his way into the diner. He entered the diner and sat at the first open seat he found at the counter. A waitress approached him and asked him for his order.

"Can I get a take-out order?" He asked. "I'm in a little hurry."

"Whatever you want is available in take-out."

He ordered a ham, cheese and egg sandwich with a large black coffee. In about ten minutes, he was back in the Mustang eating the sandwich. Upon finishing it, he placed the remaining parts of the pistol and the silencer into the take-out bag making sure not to leave any prints on any piece. The clip and the remaining .9 mm bullets were placed in the remaining glove. He walked to another trash barrel and dumped the take-out bag, the other glove and the handkerchief in it. With that task being completed, he returned to the Mustang, set the alarm on his watch for an hour and proceeded to try to get some sleep. He was still a little upset that he had to dispose of a perfectly usable pistol and now needed to get another silencer, but it was something he had to do to distance him from the incident.

Bishop woke up and within a minute or so his mind was clear enough to motion to his wife to have the nurse come over. The nurse understood Bishop's request to remove the breathing tube. She had already recorded the oxygen percent in his blood stream and was just waiting for him to wake up and request that it be removed. Within minutes, he had his voice back. It was hoarse, but he could be understood very well. After ten minutes of privacy with his wife, he agreed to have the investigators come in and question him about what he could remember and tell them about the shooting. The first person he greeted was his Chief. Two other gentlemen were introduced but Jake didn't concentrate enough to remember their names nor did he care. He was still a little groggy and his chest was very tender from the surgical cut he had on his chest. He would have to wait a few more days until he found out how really tender it would become.

The Chief began slowly, "Jake, can you try to reconstruct the incident as best that you can remember?"

Bishop began, "I noticed a car and a man standing directly in back of it in the driveway of the Henderson house. I knew the Hendersons had moved away and their house was empty; that's why I stopped to investigate why this guy was parked in the driveway." He tried to clear his throat then continued.

"I radioed in, and then got out of my cruiser. Chief, I used caution and I was trying to get the numbers off the license plate. It wasn't a Connecticut plate but I couldn't see what state it was from."

"Okay, relax. Please continue," the chief remarked.

"I remember requesting the suspect move away from the car but he wouldn't move. He just stood there. The guy did not speak to me at first but, then said that he realized he was in the wrong driveway. He said he was looking for 412 Round Hill Road and realized he was at 408." He coughed and grabbed his chest to ease the pain.

"I guess I relaxed just a second too long when he said that. I thought the guy was harmless and then I remember being hit. I got winded right away and was trying to catch my breath when I blanked out. The next thing I saw was Marty Berg standing over me with a lot of lights and people around me. I guess Marty had to be one of the first officers at the scene to find me."

The Chief nodded and asked, "Jake, can you describe the suspect's face or the type of clothing he was wearing? Did he have an accent? And what was the make of the car the suspect was standing near? Anything you can remotely remember Jake, could be helpful in catching this guy." Bishop said several things that he knew were facts they could use.

"His voice was not that of a Connecticut Yankee or the New York borough type. He sounded southern." He took time to think and then explained that it did not sound like a person from Georgia or the Carolinas. He paused and said, "I'd say he was from Maryland, Delaware or even the DC area. It was a Mustang and the color was either dark blue or black. I remember the shine from the chrome wheels and the dual exhaust pipes." He also remembered, then explained that the suspect had dark hair, but he hadn't been able to get a good look at him because he never once looked up. Bishop admitted that the suspect was smart enough to keep from getting blinded by his flashlight. "Chief, I was attempting to hinder the suspect's line of sight to me. That didn't work very well on this guy." He started to get a little drowsy again but did manage to state that the suspect had a light jacket on that concealed his pistol which he realized the suspect had pulled out from his back. He suspected that the shooter was some kind of professional. He looked at the Chief and said, "This guy had to be probably ex-military. I'm glad his shot was a few inches left instead of right if you know what I mean." Bishop's eyes were becoming heavy now and all three men realized it as the nurse asked them to come back after he had time to get some more rest. Each man wished him well and left Mrs. Bishop and the exhausted police officer alone.

Sean Quinn woke up forty five minutes later. He was still tired but the power nap was enough for him to feel comfortable that he wouldn't be falling asleep at the wheel on his way back to Maryland. He called Jarvis to see if anything had popped up on the news concerning the Greenwich shooting. Jarvis was now at his office at the bank and felt his cell vibrate in his pocket. He viewed the number and quickly answered it. He heard Quinn say, "Hey, Sergeant Major. You're glad to hear from me, aren't you? Did you hear any more on CNN?" Jarvis controlled his answer. He replied that he had not heard anything new. He told Quinn to stand by while he checked CNN on-line. Within a minute, he returned on the phone and said, "Sean, the authorities are searching for a dark blue or black Mustang being driven by a white man, average in height and weight and wearing a light colored jacket. He was presumed armed and dangerous." There was silence on the other end as Jarvis waited for a response. There was none, as Quinn drove along on the Interstate. Jarvis directed him to get off Interstate 95 and follow the secondary roads. He instructed him to get on Route 1 to Baltimore, go around on the beltway and find Route 26 to Route 550 into Frederick. He raised his voice and said, "Stay off Interstate 95 and Interstate 70. I don't care if it takes you a few hours more. Did you make a disposal?" Quinn acknowledged the instructions, answered the question and then closed his cell. Jarvis looked out the opened door of his office to make sure no one had seen or heard him use his cell phone. He emailed Marilyn to say that the information that Mr. Moore had requested him to forward to her was going to be delayed.

Jarvis knew Quinn could email the photos and information to him from his phone immediately but didn't instruct him to do so. He thought it was better to view the photos and information together when he arrived. He figured if the authorities caught Quinn and confiscated his phone, all he would be implicated for was a phone call from his employee. Jarvis was becoming more scared and very cautious now. Quinn was becoming a larger liability to the overall plan Moore had initiated.

Marilyn had completed her research on Bob and Amy. Their credit was outstanding. They owned a house that had been assessed at $450,000 by the Town of Greenwich. The value of the house was at 55% of the market value. They had banking accounts exceeding $300,000. She couldn't estimate their 401K accounts, but both of them had contributed into them for over 20 years. Based upon their salary history and a guess that they had contributed 5% of their income into the 401K accounts, Marilyn estimated that there had to be about a million in the accounts. They had no debts except $29,400 remaining on a $250,000 mortgage that would be paid off in less than three years. The history of the parent loans that they needed for their kid's college education was excellent. They had several Master and Visa cards that had excellent histories and they had no outstanding liabilities to be found. She gathered all the information and entered it on a spread sheet and forwarded it to her banking vice president, Mr. Moore. She also said that Mr. Jarvis of the Outstanding Loan department was delinquent in forwarding some field work that Mr. Quinn had been assigned to provide.

Amy and Bob finished their meeting with Terry. They instructed her to file paperwork of their intent to pay off the mortgages on the Wilson farm with the county court clerk. They acknowledged that they would have certified checks for the banks holding the mortgages within 30 days of the filing. Terry was tasked with contacting Amy's brothers to sign paperwork acknowledging their forfeiture of any claim to the farm in return for a clean slate of their defaulted notes. Amy and Bob felt confident that they would return to Greenwich in a few days, see the loan officer at their local bank and re-mortgage their home for the figures Terry would forward to them to completely clear the farm from all claims. Amy planned to write a letter to her superintendent and explain her change in retirement plans and say that she would resign her teaching position immediately at the high school before the start of the fall semester. She knew her boss would actually be happy for her as she had discussed retirement with him several times in the last year. Amy and Bob both felt that their children seemed happy that they were retiring and the idea of them living in Maryland while they were living in Connecticut didn't bother them at all. Most of their relatives, they thought, would be pleased that they were returning to Maryland. All seemed good in the world as they stepped out of the law office. They planned to do some shopping and sightseeing in Frederick which had changed just a little in the past 30 years.

Quinn exited Interstate 95 and had gotten onto Route 1. He was irritated that he had to spend more time on the road and hit every stoplight and stop sign on his way back to Frederick. Jarvis sat at his desk and was fuming as he re-read the email that Moore had sent him concerning the information he had failed to give to Miss Porter. He thought of how that bitch had almost cost him his Sergeant Major's stripes one time before when she was screwing Wilson and Moore at the same time in Iraq. Now she was again becoming a pain in his ass. He remembered that he put the fear of God in her back in Baghdad when he hinted to her that Captain Wilson would be very upset if he knew about her more than friendly relationship with Colonel Moore. She was about to threaten him that day with a court martial as she screamed at him for what he had insinuated but she stopped cold in her tracks when Jarvis politely handed her a picture of her with her head buried in the Colonel's lap performing oral sex on him. Jarvis smiled to himself as he sat in his office thinking about that day. It was a way to fend off the irritation he felt from Moore's recent email. He smiled again remembering the satisfaction he received when Quinn used his high powered camera with night vision to clearly indicate her indiscretion with the Colonel. Jarvis knew Porter hated him ever since that incident and she always loved to zing him every so often to remind him of it. She did it again today.

45

Quinn was within 20 miles of Frederick when he called one of his two friendly girls at the Frederick Hotel lobby desk. Christina Mitchell answered in her usual business manner and heard Sean ask if she had any new messages for him to retrieve.

"Yes I have several messages for you and I would be more than happy to make sure they are placed in your room key mail box in the lobby," she said. He understood exactly what she meant. She must have had a customer or an associate with her and needed to act as professional as possible in her reply. He thanked her and said that there would be a few more dollars in her piggy bank as he closed his cell. He decided to drive by and pick up all the information before meeting with Jarvis. He always knew that any good additional information Jarvis received from him could probably lighten the ration of shit he was going to receive from the Sergeant Major when he saw him in an hour or so about the shooting incident.

Moore was in his office looking over all the information Marilyn had just provided him with on the Bryants when she walked in. He smiled at her and said, "These people are very financially sound and very capable of paying off the farm debt. I guess I will have to pay the fair market price for the farm and be done with it, Marilyn." Quietly he thought that it was an investment that would pay off eleven million times as he watched the shapely woman begin to exit his office. He looked up at her and said, "Any word from Jarvis or Quinn yet?" She turned around and shook her head negatively.

Sean arrived at the hotel and quickly approached the lobby desk. Christina Mitchell saw him coming and politely, but loud enough for some people in the lobby to hear her say, "Mr. Quinn, I have taken the liberty to extract your messages for you. I saw you coming and thought that you would want them as soon as possible based on our last phone conversation." He smiled.

"Thank you Christina." He slid another $50 bill in her hand during the exchange of the messages. Sean went over to the lobby couch and read them. He again smiled as he passed her at the lobby desk and headed for his car. Within ten minutes, he arrived at the bank. He approached the bank clerk at the reception desk.

"Is Mr. Jarvis in his office?"

"Do you have an appointment with Mr. Jarvis? Sir, I am unaware of any appointment Mr. Jarvis has with you." Quinn did not respond to her question or answer but brushed past her desk and headed into Hank Jarvis's office but murmured as he passed by, "He does now, sweetheart."

Jarvis's first statement upon seeing him was, "I hope you took care of all the loose ends."

The First Clue

Quinn closed the door to Jarvis's office. No other words were exchanged until he attached his camera to a USB port leading to Jarvis's desk top computer. Within a few seconds, images of the papers and files were available for viewing. Facts and figures of the Bryant's personal finances and accounts put a smile on Hank Jarvis's face. He continued to review the information for a few more minutes. He spoke in a whisper to Quinn.

"Make sure you remove all this information from your camera as well as your cell phone." Quinn paused and then smiled before he answered back even softer, which made Jarvis strain to hear him.

"Are you getting a little paranoid, Sergeant Major?" Jarvis did not respond at first, trying to understand what he had just said.

"Look, call me Hank or Jarvis and cut out the sarcastic Sergeant Major shit," he said speaking louder. "The Colonel," he corrected himself, "Mr. Moore has reminded me several times about calling him Colonel. The last time he chewed my ass off for it." Quinn laughed out loud which irritated Jarvis. Quinn eased off of Jarvis a little and said softly, "I have already taken everything off my phone except what I had as backup, so watch me delete this shit right in front of you." He completed erasing the images from the camera and smiled at Jarvis and said, "See, Hank, it's done." Jarvis looked at Quinn and said, "You did a fine job but I want you to tell me what occurred with the authority figure you met?"

The men spoke in a tone and language that could not be readily understood by a casual observer if one had been eavesdropping outside his closed office door.

"The authority figure asked me some personal questions and I responded with the appropriate answers. As far as I'm concerned, the matter is closed and no further questioning or concerns should be forthcoming." He then smirked at Jarvis and rolled his eyes.

"Thank you, Mr. Quinn for your professionalism. You

completed your task admirably."

As the conversation ended, Quinn handed Jarvis the notes the desk clerks had written of the phone conversations between the Bryants and their children. Jarvis's face turned red as he understood that not only were they going to free up the mortgages on the farm property, but they were going to live there as well. He said, "I will forward this information to the bank vice president. I want to thank you, Mr. Quinn, for your services. By the way, are you still going to sell your black Mustang?"

Quinn stopped in his tracks and looked back at Jarvis and said, "I have been thinking about it for a while now that the fuel prices have rocketed up again. I was thinking of a sporty foreign car with good gas mileage but if you are interested in it, I can give you a good deal on it."

"No thanks, but good luck with that. I know you'll find something soon. That Mustang should fetch a good trade-in price."

"By the way, have you informed the Colonel of my meeting with the authority figure?"

Jarvis just shook his head negatively. His stomach immediately turned thinking about it. Quinn noticed the changed expression on Jarvis's face and smiled as he departed. Jarvis forwarded the prints of the documents to Marilyn as attachments to the polite email he sent. He left his office and walked to the other side of the bank to Moore's office. He told the secretary that he needed two minutes with Mr. Moore on an urgent matter. The secretary buzzed Moore and announced Jarvis and his request. Moore saw him immediately. He read the notes that Jarvis had presented to him and scowled. He now had a more difficult situation to handle. He looked up at Jarvis and said, "I am calling a meeting at my residence tonight to discuss this matter with the entire group." Jarvis controlled his urge to inform the Colonel that Quinn had been involved in an incident in Connecticut. He was upset enough and nothing had come of it so far, so why bring it up and irritate him any further. He left his office feeling that he had made the right decision not to inform him yet.

Trash collection at the truck stop was done daily by the truck stop staff. Bottles and cans were separated from the trash with well-marked containers for the public to use. Those containers for recycling were picked up weekly by a contracted sanitation company. It was Tony Sposato's duty to empty the truck stop's parking lot recycle and trash containers. The signs placed on the trash cans indicating, 'We recycle', were ignored sometimes which forced the truck stop management to institute a trash check policy to ensure their sanitation partner would continue to pick up the waste. Tony Sposato hated searching through the trash containers for cans and bottles that should have been discarded into the proper recycling receptacles. He always left that duty to be performed for last. He finished loading the recyclables into the designated receptacles provided by the sanitation company and looked at the eight or nine bags of trash he would have to inspect to make sure no bottles or cans had been discarded in them. After five bags were inspected, he noticed a cotton glove with what looked to be a pistol bullet clip partially exposed, hanging out of it. On further inspection as he picked up the clip, he saw that it was empty but some live ammunition was left loose in the glove. The attendant brought the glove, clip and several bullets to his supervisor. His supervisor immediately called the police.

Several hours later, the Pennsylvania State Police and FBI had combed the remaining truck stop parking lot trash and found the remaining pieces of the .9 mm pistol, a powder soiled handkerchief, a pair of cotton gloves and a silencer. Within hours, the ballistics lab of the Pennsylvania State Police had re-assembled the pistol and silencer, fired it and compared the bullet's ballistic characteristics sent by the Connecticut State Police to the bullet that had been removed from Officer Jake Bishop. The ballistic lab confirmed that both bullets had been fired from the same gun, but only partial finger prints had been lifted from the pistol. The serial number on the pistol had been filed off. The investigators confiscated the video surveillance tapes from the truck stop's four cameras, but those were not aimed in the direction of most of the trash receptacles in the truck stop. The investigators had hoped to be able to identify a dark blue or black Mustang based on the wounded officer's description, but only large rigs were seen on the tapes with some cars parked near or partially out of view of the cameras.

After leaving Jarvis's office, Quinn realized that he needed to get rid of the black Mustang. He thought of trading it in and also worried that someone could have identified part of the plate number or caught a glimpse of his features. He thought of the cliché *a, good defense requires a great offense*. He would draw attention to the car by involving it in an accident then reporting it as stolen. He emptied his pockets as he undressed to take a quick shower when he saw the name and number he had written down on a hotel note pad of Christina Mitchell, one of the two cute receptionists he had solicited to spy on the Bryants at the hotel. He immediately called her to get some more information as to what she could find out about the Bryant's schedule for the rest of day. After a little banter with her on the phone, he said, "Thank you very much for that information you gave me earlier, sweetheart. By the way, Christina, you looked great when I saw you." He could hear her giggle and then she said, "You're welcome and thank you." He asked about the Bryant's whereabouts.

"Oh, they are out touring Frederick. They probably will be returning in the next few hours or so for dinner. They made arrangements for room service after 7:00 p.m."

He thanked her and said, "You can expect a big tip the next time I see you, sweetie. Do you have the make and plate number of their car, by the way?" She took a few moments and searched her desk register computer and said, "Yes, a white Taurus with plate number, 445 BDD." He thanked her, hung up and looked at his watch. He had to find them and execute his new plan quickly.

Amy and Bob finished their tour of Frederick and the outlying countryside. They agreed to head home the next day and begin the task of re-mortgaging their home to free up the farm. As soon as the farm was free and clear of any claims, they would seek out some recommended construction contractors from the Frederick area to update the farmhouse. They also planned to put their home on the market after they felt the farm was in decent enough condition to support their present lifestyle. Everything now was beginning to come into place but they needed to agree to a list of priorities. They planned to use some of their savings to immediately get things going when they had complete ownership of the property. They felt comfortable with their plan as they discussed some more details on their drive. They began to see it as almost fool proof as they drove towards their hotel and their last night in Frederick.

Quinn took several white vinyl covered magnets from his apartment refrigerator on his way out to his car. He walked to the rear of the Mustang and strategically placed the three by five inch magnets on the white license plate to change the appearance of the plate's number configuration. His Maryland plate, at a distance, now looked like 81 CD instead of 681 CDA. Even though he was going to report his car stolen after he completed his new mission, he thought a little misinformation with the plate was needed to make things work better just in case someone did witness what he was about to do. He placed his black wool service cap low on his head to lessen the chance that anyone would recognize him. He bitched to himself that the cap was too heavy to wear in the Maryland heat they were experiencing, but he needed the added disguise. He immediately headed out of Frederick and for the highway leading to the farm. He kept the top up and the air conditioning on high as he slouched in the driver's seat. It was a fifteen mile trip to the farm and the route the Bryants would most likely be returning on from their tour of the countryside. He reached the farm in less than fifteen minutes and had not seen any white sedan of any kind passing in the opposite direction. He continued on for several more miles when he noticed several cars approaching. He saw a red pickup truck passing a white sedan on the straight away in front of him. He slowed and hoped to quickly identify the occupants in the white car. He allowed the pickup truck enough space to complete the pass and get back on the right side of the road. He concentrated on the white sedan and spotted the plates, 445 BDD, and recognized it was the Bryant's rental car. He stood on the brakes and did a controlled spin around and was heading in the same direction as his prey in about fifteen seconds. The powerful Mustang roared as he power shifted the gears. In a short time, he was several hundred yards behind the white rental car. The Bryants never noticed or heard the black Mustang's tires screech or see it do an emergency turn around. They continued to drive but slowed as they approached the farm entrance. Quinn realized they were slowing down and he slowed the Mustang to keep his distance. He thought they were going to turn in but then realized they were just slowing down to look at the place as they passed. They began to accelerate and continue on to Frederick. He knew the road very well and waited for his opportunity. He accelerated at a predetermined straight away he knew would support his speed and the maneuverability he would need to push the Bryant's car off the road. He came up behind them. Bob Bryant observed a black car approaching in his rear view mirror. He assumed that the car was going to overtake and pass him. They continued their conversation until both of them realized what was happening. Quinn hit the Bryant's rented Taurus in the rear left corner of their bumper with the right front bumper of his shiny black Mustang. The glancing blow at the higher speed he was traveling was enough to cause the white Taurus's rear end to skid inward towards the shoulder of the road. Bob attempted to keep from losing control of the Taurus but the 60 miles per hour the Taurus was traveling caused him to over steer. The rental flipped over onto its roof. The car continued to slide for several hundred more feet until the friction of the roof sliding on the pavement ceased, causing it to right side itself again. The inertia was still too much and made the car flip several more times until it hurled itself into the roadside and rested upside down. He managed to keep control of his car as he drove away watching the accident unfold in his rear view mirror. As his luck would have it, no cars were in the vicinity to witness the crash. It was several minutes later that he came upon the red pickup truck that he had observed passing the Bryant's car earlier. His heart was racing as he had not figured that the accident would have been so dramatic. He didn't want to kill the Bryants but the sight of their car over turning made him wonder if he had succeeded in accomplishing that. He started to feel a little guilty until the realization that they were hindering his group's plan to get the farm, replaced his guilt with satisfaction.

He stayed behind the red pickup until he reached the outskirts of Frederick. He pulled over on a side road, parked the Mustang, and left it unlocked with the keys in the ignition. Before he returned to the main road, he removed the magnets from the plate and the black wool service cap he had worn many times while he was in Iraq. The cap was soaked with sweat as he wrung it out and stuffed it into his back pocket. He then walked to the entrance of the road where he had turned off and casually walked for a few minutes hitch hiking. A few cars coming out of some of the side roads passed him until one stopped and gave him a lift back to within a block of his apartment. He entered his apartment, put the magnets back onto the refrigerator and called the police to report that someone had stolen his black Mustang GT.

Amy was dazed and realized she was upside down in the car. She was able to release the seatbelt and fell onto the roof of the Taurus, banging her head harder than she expected. She checked Bob, who was also hanging upside down and unconscious. She gently touched him and attempted to speak to him, but he only mumbled. She noticed a large cut on the left side of his head. She tried as best that she could in her cramped quarters not to bang his head as she had just done. She made sure to protect his fall to the roof as she released his seat belt.

He continued to mumble as she began to panic that she would not be able to get him out of the car. She heard a noise and realized someone was attempting to open up Bob's door. The person who had come to rescue them was finally able to open the damaged door, which caused Bob's twisted leg to fall out of the opening.

Marilyn arrived at Moore's apartment around 6:15 p.m. She arrived early so that no one would notice she had come with an overnight bag. She carried a fresh suit for tomorrow's workday and some groceries that she would prepare for Moore after Jarvis and Quinn left. As soon as she arrived and deposited her articles, she fixed herself a stiff scotch drink. She knew she needed something to calm her nerves before meeting the two goons as she sometimes described them to Moore. She also needed to be in a more relaxed mood in case the Colonel became aroused and wanted to make, what he thought, was love to her. She could hear Moore in the bathroom finishing up with a quick shower. She slipped off her shoes and sat on the couch. She flipped on the remote and began watching the local news. Moore finished his shower and exited the bathroom to see her sitting in the living room. He acknowledged her presence and said that he would be right out after he had dressed. Several minutes later, he appeared. He approached her and bent down and kissed her on the cheek. She did not respond as he expected.
He asked, "Is there a problem?"
Realizing her unresponsiveness to his affection, she said, "No, I'm just a little tired." She made the effort to kiss him back and even squeeze his left buttocks with her right hand and pull him slightly towards her. That pleased Moore enough to believe everything was fine between them. He began to explain to her why he wanted this meeting with the team.

At 6:55 p.m., Jarvis rang the doorbell for Moore's apartment. Moore greeted him and invited him in to make himself comfortable in the living room. As Jarvis entered the room, he acknowledged Marilyn with a simple good evening. She only nodded because she hated this guy and couldn't bring herself around to even look at him never mind speak to him. He sensed her irritation but quickly sat down, hoping that Quinn would be on time. He kept glancing at his watch every thirty seconds or so. *That renegade is always late,* he thought. At 6:59 p.m. the doorbell rang again. Jarvis relaxed knowing that his subordinate was exactly on time. Moore greeted Quinn in the same manner that he had greeted Jarvis. He showed him to the living room and Quinn, seeing Marilyn alone on the couch, sat right next to her. He smiled and acknowledged her first while he checked out her legs, breasts and face, in an obvious sweep, with his blue eyes.

"Hello, Marilyn." She responded with a smirk but no verbal recognition. Quinn looked over to Jarvis and said, "I decided to buy a BMW convertible." Jarvis smiled and said that was a good idea and they could talk about that after the meeting.

Quinn looked back over to Marilyn and asked, "Maybe you would like to go for a ride when I buy it?"

"Perhaps, sometime, Sean."

Deep down inside she would have liked to take him up on the ride. Even though she didn't like him, she had fantasized about him a few times while the Colonel had his way with her. It made the time go by during the sometimes revolting sex.

The Colonel took the floor now that everyone was present and quickly got to the point for the meeting. Marilyn already knew his plan, but she was here for dinner and sex unbeknownst to the other two members of this little group. John Moore began, "We need to come up with a plan to discourage the Bryants from living on the farm." They all knew the reason why it was so important to keep them off the farm. Eliminating them was out of the question, although the thought had entered Moore's mind when he heard that they were planning on retiring on the farm. He never had the slightest clue that Quinn had already taken it upon himself to try to do just that about an hour ago. Moore explained, "I thought of interfering with their ability to get the needed funds to pay off the farm debts, but that

56

wouldn't keep them from being able to use their savings. Marilyn has informed me that their savings exceed $300,000 and they could possibly acquire a home equity loan on their house to come up with enough cash to accomplish what they need. We need to discourage them from wanting to live on the farm so I am tasking you two to accomplish that," he said as he looked directly at Quinn and then glanced at Jarvis. Jarvis immediately felt uncomfortable because he did not have a clue as to how to plan what the Colonel was getting at. Quinn smiled and said, "We could burn the farmhouse down or damage it enough to render it useless. I know the other two banks have been bitching to the Wilson brothers that they did not have enough fire insurance on the place anyway, as they thought it was becoming a fire trap." Moore smiled and said that he had that exact idea in his mind. Jarvis relaxed knowing that Quinn's idea was doable even in the Colonel's opinion. Quinn volunteered to accomplish the task. Jarvis did make one good point when he said, "Sir, they could always rebuild on the land. They could put a smaller and more efficient home on it in a very short time."

"That's a very good point, Hank, but what if the water supply was not fit for human consumption," the Colonel suggested.

The two men he was addressing looked at each other. The Colonel continued on with some more details of his plan. "That well is an old dug well, if I recall." He hinted, while looking at Quinn, "Someone could introduce enough lead granules down there to spike the readings that the county health agency would insist needed to be taken in case of a house fire had occurred." He hinted again, while looking at Jarvis this time, "Someone could make sure that the appropriate boards and agencies in Frederick were aware that these precautions would be needed to be enforced and carried out." He then looked around the room, "I would hope that Mr. and Mrs. Bryant would become discouraged enough to accept the offer Mr. Quinn's developer, which is us, of course, or me as a private person, are presenting. We're both offering a fair market price for the farm now aren't we?" He smiled but no one said anything for a few

57

moments.

Quinn piped up and asked, "Sir, what is your timetable for these tasks to commence?"

"Let's commence them immediately so as to save them the aggravation of having to move their money around. I want us to take ownership of the land as soon as possible," he said as his smile turned into a stern look that both men were familiar with when they had served under him in Iraq. Marilyn enjoyed watching both of them react to the seriousness of Moore's expression. She especially enjoyed watching Jarvis's reactions when he was uncomfortable. Moore looked around at them and asked if there were any more questions. Marilyn shook her head negatively and the other two remained motionless. Moore dismissed the two men, thanked them for coming and reiterated his instructions that he wanted the farm in his possession as soon as possible. Both men nodded in agreement and exited the apartment. Quinn headed with Jarvis to his car

"Apparently you decided to trade in the Mustang for a BMW?" Jarvis asked.

"No; I'm going to buy one outright." Quinn didn't even ask what Jarvis thought about his choice in automobiles. Jarvis didn't care what he bought as long as he was not driving the Mustang.

"How did you get here?"

"I used a taxi and now I need a ride back to my apartment."

Jarvis was a little annoyed that he needed a ride. He always acted too nonchalant in Jarvis's opinion and he dared to ask him, "Where's the Mustang?"

Quinn smiled and said, "Can you believe it? Someone stole it. I reported it to the cops. That's why I was almost late for the meeting."

Moore turned to Marilyn, "Are you going to prepare something for us to eat?" She remained motionless on the couch for a few seconds which surprised Moore who expected his ex-lieutenant to respond instantly to his request. Marilyn wanted to say, but kept her thoughts to herself, that the old bastard could fix his own god damned dinner for all she cared. She smiled and rose from the couch and headed for the kitchen. As she passed, he caressed her right breast and asked, "What did you plan for dinner?"

"Stuffed chicken with rice and vegetables. I also brought a nice bottle of chardonnay to go along with the dinner." Moore was pleased with her choice.

They finished dinner quietly. Very little conversation had transpired. Marilyn excused herself.

"I'm going to bathe, John." Moore raised his wine glass in sort of a salute to acknowledge her statement. She left and entered his bathroom. She undressed completely and began drawing water in the tub. As she bent over to test the water, she became aware of the Colonel standing directly behind her. She slowly looked back over her shoulder and noticed that he was naked from the waist down and aroused. As he walked slowly up behind her, she said, "I'd like to be able to bathe first and be as clean as possible before we make love. I'm a little sweaty. I'll be more appealing to you in a little while." Moore never acknowledged any of her requests and penetrated her from behind. He was rigid and she had not seen him in that state of arousal in a while. She thought of moving away but dared not disappoint the Colonel because she knew how enraged he could get when he was disappointed, especially if his performance wasn't good. He pumped her for what seemed like an eternity. She concentrated on tightening her vaginal muscles as much as she could in order for him to climax quickly. She made noises of pleasure to accompany her hopes that it would aid him in finishing with her quickly. She could sense his climax coming so she talked dirty to him in order for him to complete his work with satisfaction. His legs shook and he became weak as he ejaculated and groaned like an animal. He finished and backed up smiling at her. He was going to say something but he was too winded and chose to remove some tissues from the dispenser on the sink counter, wipe himself and then asked, "Did you enjoy that lovemaking, Marilyn?" She smirked and said, "I haven't seen you that hot in a long time." She ignored his question whether it was good for her because it wasn't. She needed a bath more now than ever. The good thing was that the old man wouldn't be bothering her tonight for another bout of quick and bad sex.

Officer Jake Bishop had been out of his hospital bed and walking on the ward hallway. He was talking to his wife when he stopped and remembered something. He looked at her and said, "Damn, there was some kind of a seal on that plate. It was like a crest or something." He walked slowly back to his room and used the phone to contact the Greenwich Chief of Police. After a few moments of bantering with the Chief's secretary, the Chief came on.

"Chief, I remember that there was a seal, or crest, or shield of some kind on the license plate of the dark Mustang. I remember that I could see it between his legs before he shot me.

"That's good Jake. I'm going to check it out. I'm glad that you called. I'll get back to you."

The Greenwich Police Chief instructed one of his detectives to search the National Department of Transportation data base for States issuing white or lightly colored license plates with seals on them. Within a few minutes, the Chief had the answer he wanted. Based on what Officer Bishop had reported on the type of accent the shooter had and the color of the plate with a seal, he guessed that Maryland was probably the issuer of the plate. There had to be a lot of Mustangs in Maryland but it was a start. *Maybe some of the owners had rap sheets,* he thought. He called Bishop back and explained what he found, assumed, and what they were going to look for. Bishop was pleased that he had remembered something useful for his department to use. He hoped that more bits of his memory would come back and aide his department in getting the bastard that had tried to kill him.

Jarvis returned Quinn to his apartment. He didn't ask Quinn anymore questions about what he had said about his Mustang being stolen and Quinn never offered any further information. Quinn entered his apartment and quickly changed into less casual clothes for his planned expedition later in the night. He called the local car rental agency and requested an automobile for several days until his car was hopefully recovered by the Frederick Police. He managed to complete all the paperwork over the phone using his credit card and Maryland driver's license number. About an hour later, two Enterprise cars stopped at his apartment address. One rental agent rang his apartment intercom and informed Quinn that his rental was available outside his apartment. He signed the paperwork, tipped the agent and took delivery of the keys for the car. The agent left in the other Enterprise car. He didn't tell Jarvis what he was planning because the man would only hound him for every detail on how he was going to accomplish the task. He didn't need a plan. He would improvise like he always did and the task would get completed without any strings attached. He thought of the plan on his ride back with Jarvis to his apartment. He figured that he would go up to the farm late tonight and see what there was in the basement that could be used to disguise the main cause of the fire he was going to set to burn the farmhouse down. He thought that he would wait until later to work on the well in order to get a hold of some material that he knew would temporarily ruin it. He thought about Marilyn Porter and the nice legs she had. He had almost been able to see her crotch while she sat on the couch in Moore's apartment. He wondered how the old man managed to keep her satisfied at night. He knew Todd did, but he never knew why she occasionally blew and screwed the Colonel while she did Todd. He fantasized that she must have been one horny bitch. Too bad he couldn't get her interested in him. He knew he had the essentials to please her. Maybe after he had a little more money in his pocket she might see him in a different light. That idea quickly faded because he realized she'd probably have more money than him based on her relationship with Moore.

Jarvis returned home after dropping Quinn off. He planned

to call and maybe get with him later and work on the Colonel's request and ask him about the Mustang being stolen. He made some mental notes on what he thought would be the best way to make the fire look convincingly like a case of an unattended old place that developed an electrical problem or something of that nature that the investigators would all agree on was the cause. He didn't know that Sean had a plan all his own already and would be implementing it in a few hours.

She was in bed when the Colonel decided that he still had a little lovemaking left in him. He slid under the sheets and spooned Marilyn. She could feel his arousal and dreaded that he would want to take her again. She turned to him and said, "John, I'm a little tired and I really enjoyed the lovemaking in the bathroom earlier." He ignored her plea and requested, "How about some oral sex then?" as he pulled her hand to his groin so that she could feel his rigidness. She obliged his request. In order to complete her task, she fantasized about the only man she enjoyed performing oral sex on. As the Colonel climaxed, she kept from gagging as she thought of Todd.

Amy Bryant was cleared and released from the Frederick Hospital Emergency Room. She was banged up, but her small cuts and bruises were no comparison to her husband's injuries. Bob had a concussion and his twisted and broken leg needed to be set in the operating room then operated on. She managed to call Cora and inform her of what had occurred. Cora advised that she would inform Bobby and they would come right down together. Amy assured Cora that her father would make it through the operation and that she didn't want her children racing down to the hospital as fast as they could. She would expect them sometime tomorrow evening. Amy thought that would assure them enough time to safely get to Maryland and for Bob to recover from the effects of the anesthesia he was about to be given.

The Fire

He exited onto the Wilson farm road at 10:30 p.m. as indicated by the digital clock on the dashboard of his rental. About half way up the driveway, he shut off his lights. There were no other houses within two miles of the farm and Quinn didn't need another inquisitive cop interfering with the task he needed to complete. He approached the farmhouse and noticed that some lights must had been left on by the Bryants after their meeting with the lawyers, Jarvis and him. He quickly devised a plan in case someone was babysitting the place for them. He would simply knock on the door and ask whoever answered if Amy or Bob Bryant were available because he represented a client that was willing to meet either one as soon as possible on a new deal for the farm. He even had a few business cards ready in case he needed to identify himself as a representative of an interested client. His other excuse for being there so late at night was that his client was in a hurry to get the first bid on the place. He got out of the car and walked directly to the front door and knocked as if he was being expected. After many attempts knocking, he picked the lock and entered. He quickly checked over the first floor looking for any type of alarm system. He laughed at himself knowing that no one had lived in the place for the last three years and the Bryants wouldn't have had time to get one installed in the five days they had spent in Frederick. He wondered if they survived the accident. He figured that someone had to be injured by the way he saw the car roll over and over. He checked upstairs and then the basement. Clear of anything except dust and stale air, the place was still very hot from the week's heat and he would be happy to get out of there as soon as possible. There were flammable materials in the basement next to a 500 gallon oil tank that was about a quarter full. The tank was old and had some signs of rust on the bottom near one of the front legs. Sean found some tools in the basement and decided to see if he could rupture the oil tank enough to make it look like that was the cause of the fire he was about to set. The oil tank was close to the gas hot water tank which had a pilot light that was continuously lit despite the house being unoccupied for a long time. He surmised that he could place some old wood furniture next to the hot water tank. He would have, at least, a creditable case for the fire marshal to contemplate that the fire was a malfunction of the oil tank in which fuel oil came in contact with the pilot light. With all the wood furniture placed close to the source of the ignition, Quinn thought he had a good plan. He worked on the tank enough to get some oil to drip out of the bottom and onto the concrete floor. He still needed more of a flow so he used an old pipe he found, as a pry bar to open up a slightly larger, but inconspicuous hole in the tank. The smell from the fuel oil was strong and Quinn gagged a little but stuck it out long enough to see the oil reach the hot water tank. He found some paper and lit it with a match and helped the combustion begin. The oil began to burn slowly from the lit paper, but when the wood furniture caught fire, the flames quickly engulfed the dry old furniture and raised up high enough for him to see the rafters of the first floor begin to catch on fire. He thought he would stay in the basement as long as possible to ensure the fire would burn hot enough to burn down the entire house but realized he didn't know how the gas hot water heater would react to the fire. He knew he had to leave the basement in case of an explosion from the gas bottle that fed the gas heater and also because the black smoke of the burning fuel oil was becoming thicker and it was difficult for him to breathe. He worked his way to the front door as he watched the smoke and flames follow the cellar stairs to the first floor and then to the kitchen. He left out the front door and even locked it. No finger prints would be detected because he had been wearing leather driving gloves he had purchased immediately after he rented the car. He entered the car and started it. The flames had engulfed the entire kitchen area now and they were quickly spreading to the other first floor rooms. He turned the rental car around and slowly headed down the farm road and away from the fire as he heard an explosion. He realized the flames must have reached the gas bottle of the gas water heater. He didn't have to worry about seeing the farm road since the glow from the farm house illuminated his way to the main road.

He noticed the headlights of a car coming from the direction of town. He decided to turn away from the approaching car and hoped that its occupants would stop, slow down or even approach the farmhouse to investigate the blaze. He figured that they would, at least, hesitate on any account before driving away. He kept his lights off and drove quickly away from the scene. He watched in his rear view mirror and could see the car turn off to the side of the road. They didn't go down the driveway but he expected that they must be using a cell phone to call in the fire. Quinn could see the engulfed farmhouse very well before the rolling hills cut off his view. He put his headlights on and proceeded to run at a reasonable speed away from the farm.

Norma and Ed Walsh watched from their car as the farmhouse burned in the night. They called 911 from their cell phone and reported the fire. It took 25 minutes before the first fire truck reached the farm. By then it was completely destroyed. The Walsh's gave a statement that they were heading home and they saw the farmhouse on fire. They didn't see anyone or any vehicle in the vicinity of the farm. The fire police began an investigation as soon as the fire trucks were able to extinguish the fire. They used two tank trucks and had to draw additional water from the pond to finish the task. They determined, during their preliminary investigation, that the fire started in the basement. Based on evidence, experience and some educated guessing, they surmised that something had caused the hot water heater to ignite fuel oil. They also could see remains of wood furniture and other stored items that only fueled the fire. The farmhouse was a complete loss.

Quinn dialed Jarvis on his cell phone at 11:25 p.m. as he drove along. Jarvis was up watching television when he answered the call. Quinn simple said, "The building everyone is interested in is no longer available for viewing. The building will never be listed on the market again. Check the morning paper for the story. Oh, yeah, check on a car crash that took place earlier for me, will you? It involved the Bryants."

After he hung up, Jarvis understood that Quinn had just gone off on his own to execute part of the Colonel's plan. He became concerned about what he meant about "the accident" he indicated the Bryants were involved in. He decided he would check the paper first thing in the morning, view the news he said would be in it and inform the Colonel to check the exact section of the paper where the article about the fire was. He was becoming more uneasy about the crash Quinn mentioned and wanted to read about it before the Colonel did just in case he needed to inform him of what he had done on his own. He realized Quinn had used the excuse that his Mustang had been stolen to cover the accident involving the Bryants. He was doing too much without specific orders. He worried about what the Colonel's reaction would be when he informed him. He also didn't want to bother the Colonel tonight while he was probably doing Porter again at his apartment. He decided to wait to inform him about the accident as well.

Quinn stayed away from his Frederick apartment for the night. He found a motel just outside of Thurmont, Maryland and stayed there. He decided he would return to his Frederick apartment in the morning and see Jarvis at the bank a little later to inform him that he would take care of the well water in a few days.

Terry Breen finished dressing and attempted a phone call to the Bryants at their hotel about 7:00 a.m. concerning some questions she had about their financial information. As she dialed, she scanned the morning paper and quickly read about the fire that took place at the farm last night. She now needed to know if the Bryants were aware of this. There was no answer at the hotel room phone. She hung up and dialed the front desk. The desk clerk informed her that the Mr. and Mrs.

Bryant had not returned to the hotel last night nor had they checked out. Terry thought it was odd that they would have not returned to the hotel. She thought that, maybe, they had stayed at the farm. She froze thinking that they had been injured or worse at the farm. She quickly left her apartment. She never turned the next page of the paper to see the article about a Connecticut couple that had been involved in an accident just outside of the city limits.

Jarvis called the Colonel at 7:15 a.m. He knew he was an early riser and chanced that he would have probably showered and was ready to sit for breakfast by that time. The Colonel answered his cell phone on the second ring.
Jarvis asked, "Sir, have you read the morning paper yet?"
"No, but I will in a few minutes."
He politely asked the Colonel, "Sir, please, when you do, turn to the third page of the first section and look for an article concerning a fire that had taken place last night. Mr. Quinn has brought the article to my attention and I thought that the bank would be interested since they hold one of the three mortgages on that property. I'll see you, sir, at the bank in a few hours."
Moore closed his cell and said, "Marilyn, hand me the paper." This irritated her a little because she was preparing breakfast for him and the paper was closer to him than to her. She responded and brought the paper over to him while she thought about how self-centered this man was. She was beginning to detest him for his crude mannerisms, self-satisfying love making and general chauvinistic attitude towards her. She would be so pleased when she received her share of the money and would be able to tell this son of a bitch where to go. She deposited the paper right in front of him as requested. As she turned to go back to the stove and attempt to make a decent breakfast for the man, she had to pass by him. As she did, he reached under her robe and fondled her bare buttocks. She faked a smile as she moved away. She would have liked to smack his face but kept with her plan to treat him nicely until it was time to leave with her share. The Colonel smiled as he

67

read the story about the fire in the morning news. He showed the paper to Marilyn who asked, "When will the well water plan be executed?"

"Soon, my girl, soon," was his answer. She was irritated by that statement as well but she didn't show it. Neither of them saw the story of the Connecticut couple injured in an accident on the next page of the paper.

Quinn was in town by 8:00 a.m. and returned to his apartment to shower and change. He smelled a little of smoke so he immediately put his clothes into the washing machine. He completed all his tasks and was at the bank parking lot a few minutes before Jarvis reported to work. He stayed outside in his car until Jarvis's Ford Taurus turned into the parking lot. He walked to Jarvis's car and waited for the man to get out so he could give him a message.

"I'll be back at the property and I'll handle the well within a day or so," he said. Then he turned and walked away before Jarvis could say a word.

Quinn noticed Marilyn's Honda entering the parking lot and waited for her to park. As she exited her car, he approached and said, "Good morning, Marilyn." She smiled but did not return the greeting. Ignoring her lack of response, Quinn pursued his quest.

"When would you like to take a ride in my new BMW convertible I'm going to buy today?" She ignored his question so he repeated it. "When, Marilyn?" She stopped and turned to look at him. She was ready to cut him down verbally but remembered her disgusting evening with the Colonel and her irritation just this morning when something came out of her that was even surprising to her.

"Maybe this afternoon you can give me a ride, that is, if you really do buy one. After work, you could treat me to a ride with the top down," she said. Quinn was very surprised but reacted coolly.

"I'll be waiting here for you when you get out of work."

"No, meet me outside my apartment around 5:00 p.m. or so. I

would like to be able to change into some casual clothes.

"5:00 p.m. sharp it will be," he said, as he turned and left. Marilyn was pleased and a little excited. She looked around to make sure the Colonel wasn't in the parking lot yet to see the verbal exchange. If he was, she could cover herself by saying she was just being polite to him. He'd heard Quinn invite her for a ride yesterday evening when they were at his apartment for the group meeting. *No harm done* she thought, but then she realized Jarvis had seen them talking and probably heard the conversation. She made a mental note to mention her ride to the Colonel if Quinn actually did buy the car and arrived to give her a ride this afternoon.

Terry Breen concluded her meeting with the fire marshal at the firehouse. She was relieved that there had been no one in the house. She explained that she had not been able to get in touch with the Bryants yet. The fire marshal explained that the fire did not seem suspicious in nature and that the fire department would furnish their report in a few days with copies to her, the banks that had holdings on the property, the Wilson brothers, and the Bryants. They considered the matter closed except for having demolition crews bulldoze the charred remains of the farmhouse into the hole left by the stone cellar. The bill for that would be sent to the present owners. They wanted complete assurance that the area would be free from any dangerous conditions to the owners or the general public.

Moore, Jarvis and Porter were all at work by 9:10 a.m. Their task for the next few days would be to wait out the Bryants to see what their intentions would be now that the farmhouse didn't exist anymore. Quinn was still completing a list of duties he had been assigned. One was to call to make an appointment with Breen to discuss her client's position on their plans for the Wilson property that his clients were still interested in. He was curious what Breen would say about the fire. That is, if she knew already. There was no answer. He left a message on her answering machine while he drove around completing his remaining assignments for the bank before he purchased the new car.

Benjamin read about the farmhouse fire and he immediately notified his brother of the incident. They discussed what their sister and brother-in-law might do now about paying off the mortgages on the farm. Bruce was especially interested in their intent for the family cemetery. Benjamin said that they should both get together and call Amy and get her intentions directly. They both agreed to meet later and call her to discuss all matters but especially the cemetery. It would be several hours later before they were informed of their sister and brother-in-law's accident.

Quinn walked into the Frederick BMW Dealership. He was greeted by an over enthusiastic salesman who asked if he could be of any assistance.
"Yes. I'm looking for a deal on a new BMW 3 Series convertible. I like the silver one I noticed on the lot and was curious as to what type of a deal I could get?" Several hours later, Quinn drove his new silver BMW convertible out of the dealership and onto the highway. The BMW handled better than the Mustang GT did. The only thing he missed was the tone and the brute power the Ford had but he was relieved a little that he had distanced himself from the shooting in Connecticut and the accident with the Bryants now that he didn't drive the Mustang GT anymore. He wondered how long it would take the police to locate his Mustang. He laughed to himself that Jarvis had insisted that he had to do something with the Mustang. He never gave Jarvis any timetable as to when he would be getting rid of the car but he smiled to himself because he knew Jarvis would be ragging on him about the car as soon as he saw him again. He was pleased knowing that he had the upper hand again by just teasing the ex-Sergeant Major and saying, "What Mustang?" when he asked him about it again. He didn't know that Jarvis had figured out what he had used the Mustang for.
Frederick Police Officer Dan Hayes was on patrol when he

noticed a black Mustang pass him in the opposite direction. The car was being driven by some kids who had the top down and were cruising a little too fast, in his judgment, this morning. He quickly slowed down and turned the black and white around. He pushed a display button on his laptop for the latest list of automobiles reported missing or stolen. A black Mustang GT convertible was the third automobile on that list. He put on his police lights and began to pursue the Mustang. He quickly approached the car and the kids were smart enough to pull over, stop and run from the stolen vehicle. They all disappeared before the elderly policeman could stop, get out of his cruiser and go after any of them. Hayes reported the license plate number and confirmed the car had been reported stolen the day before by its owner, Mr. Sean Quinn.

Terry Breen finally got in touch with Amy through information she had received from the hotel receptionist after calling several times to get a location on the Bryants. Amy found time while waiting for Bob to fully awake from the effects of the anesthesia he had been given, to inform the hotel receptionist that she needed an extension on her hotel room. She advised the receptionist that she would be staying in Frederick longer than they originally anticipated. She explained the details to the receptionist who recorded some of the finer points on a note paper that she later put into her pocket. Terry was informed of what had happened on the highway by the receptionist on her third attempt to contact the Bryants. She immediately dialed the number Amy had given the receptionist to call her at the Frederick Hospital.
"Hello Amy. I heard what happened. How are you two doing?" Amy explained the details of her husband's condition. "Bob sustained a fracture of his left femur and will require convalescence and therapy. He's in stable condition now. I'm waiting for our children to reach Frederick this evening. They'll be staying at the same hotel with me for now." Terry was very concerned as she listened to Amy. How was she going to tell her about the fire now after what they had been

through? Unfortunately, she had to do it.

"Amy, I have terrible news to tell you. The farmhouse burnt to the ground last night. I just returned with a copy of the investigative report. It indicates that the gas water heater malfunctioned and caused the oil tank to catch on fire. With all the combustible articles in the basement, that only contributed more to the intensity of the fire. By the time the fire department arrived it was total loss. I am very sorry." Amy did not say a word for a few uncomfortable moments.

She eventually responded, "Terry, have you filed our intent this morning yet?"

"No. Not after having been informed of the fire."

"Well, continue with the filing. The land and the barn still have value. We can build a new house on the property. There is some insurance to claim, I'm sure. I know Bob will be in agreement on what I have instructed you to do. Continue on as we planned and check on any insurance claims we can make."

"I will Mrs. Bryant, and give my best to Mr. Bryant."

An hour later, Attorney Terry Breen filed the Bryant's intent at the Frederick Courthouse.

At 5:00 p.m. Quinn was waiting outside of Porter's apartment. He was dressed casually and brought along a small picnic basket that was placed in plain sight on his rear seat. Marilyn appeared from the open door of her apartment in white slacks and a pink halter top carrying a matching pink sweater and a pink purse. Upon seeing her, Quinn quickly jumped out of the car and scurried over to the passenger door to open it for his very attractive guest. She smiled and quickly sat in the black leather seat. He didn't say one word until he was out of the city limits heading out towards the Wilson farm. Marilyn was content to let his eyes glance at her every so often as she relaxed with the wind blowing through her hair and the warmth of the sun on her exposed shoulders and arms. She enjoyed catching Sean glancing at her. She became a little aroused knowing that he wanted her in the worst way just by the way he was glancing. She felt in control. That was a feeling she hadn't had for a while with her grotesque relationship with the Colonel.

She finally asked him, "Where are you taking me?"

"I have a nice place picked out that I've been to before that is quiet and relaxing. It's a good place for me to get a chance to get to know you better. I have taken the liberty of picking out a wine that you might enjoy." He pointed to the basket in the rear seat. "This basket contains the essentials for a good conversation that may entice you to have dinner with me later."

She smiled and said, "I'm very impressed, Mr. Quinn, that you have taken the time to do all of this for my benefit." She stared at him a little longer than he expected which aroused him and made him think that she was really interested in him. He had to turn away to concentrate on his driving and reposition himself behind the wheel as he felt his loins stir. Marilyn commented on how different the property looked without the farmhouse on it as they passed the entrance to the property. Quinn only smiled and never commented. He came to a dirt road and turned off onto it. Marilyn had recognized the area and knew they had passed the farm but she wasn't familiar with this road. She casually asked, "Where does this road lead?"

He smiled and said, "It's the other entrance to the property." As he slowed down on the dirt road, they both could see the green hay field and the pond. She'd heard Jarvis and Moore talk about the water that was available on the property that a developer was interested in for a possible condo development and a water park. She was impressed by the beauty and serenity of the water and surrounding area. Two maple trees were near the pond and Quinn pulled his convertible directly under the smaller of the two trees. He opened the door and grabbed the picnic basket. He quickly rounded the car to her side but she had already gotten out on her own. He asked her to follow him as he headed for the larger maple tree. By the time she felt the cooler temperature from the shade of the maple tree, he had already spread open a thin blanket and was beginning to open up the wine he brought. She noticed that he had also brought a small container. He handed her a glass half full of white wine and asked her to please hold his glass because he needed his hands free to open up the container. She was impressed when he opened up the container and saw that he had brought some white and red grapes with some light cheddar cheese and crackers for them to munch on while they conversed and sipped their wine.

Officer Bishop sat on a soft chair in his hospital room. As he tried to read a book his wife had purchased for him to get his mind off the shooting experience, something occurred to him. Out of the blue, he remembered that the shooter had said that he was at the wrong address. The shooter said he needed to be at 412 Round Hill Road instead of where he had parked his car. He remembered it now because that was the Bryant's house and he knew both Bob and Amy very well. He called his wife and repeated the fact he had just recalled. She told him to call the station to talk to the Chief. Twenty minutes later, two FBI Agents knocked on the Bryant's front door. There was no one there to answer.

Sean was a real gentleman and Marilyn was very happy that she had taken the chance to become more familiar with him as a person and not just a part of the plan the Colonel had. He began with some good small talk and she relaxed. She was also aware of how he looked at her and appreciated her beauty. They finished the first glass of wine and he immediately poured her a second.
"I'm surprised that I am enjoying your company. I also congratulate you on your choice of wine."
"I knew you would enjoy it. I've seen that many times in the past you have had similar wine. This is one of my favorites as well."
"I'm impressed that you would have taken the time to notice my taste in wines."
"I always take the time to make sure beautiful women like you are given the proper respect and treatment while in my company."

She blushed as she looked directly in his blue eyes.

"Would you care for some more wine?"

"If you are you trying to get me a little tipsy, you are succeeding, Mr. Quinn."

"It's Sean, Marilyn, please call me Sean. Would you be interested in having dinner with me later this evening?"

She looked at him while she placed her glass on the blanket.

"I would like to have dinner with you, Sean, but I can't tonight. I have a dinner date with Moore. Maybe in a few days we can arrange to have dinner some place away from Frederick."

She could see the disappointment in his eyes but she had a little treat in store for him that he couldn't have imagined in his wildest dreams. She stood up as if she was ready to leave. To Quinn's surprise, she asked, "Are you as hot as I am from this late afternoon's heat?"

"Yes, but the ride back to your apartment will cool you off unless you want me to put the top up and the car's air conditioning on?"

"The top down sounds better because I will need to dry off quickly on our way back." She untied the pink halter top and dropped it on the blanket. He gazed at her perfectly shaped breasts and dark pink erect nipples. She unzipped her white slacks and dropped those onto the blanket as well exposing her thong panties. She kicked her sandals in his direction and turned to expose her back as she slid off her panties. She walked casually towards the water but stopped right before the edge. Quinn was still motionless.

"Are you going to swim with me or not?" she asked seductively looking over her shoulder. Quinn fumbled a bit to get his pants and shirt off and almost tripped as his underwear caught around his ankles. He was aroused before he got into the water which amused Marilyn but also made her aware of the size of his erection. He grabbed right before she reached the water.

"Please wait a little until I cool off in the water. We'll return to the blanket in a few minutes. We have plenty of time. Please, be patient. I really want to enjoy your company," she said as she looked him up and down. He obliged and became even more excited. They cooled off in the water for a few minutes as they both enjoyed moment.

As promised, she returned to the blanket and waited for him. He approached her like a gentleman, first kissing her and asking, "Are you comfortable on this thin blanket?" She just nodded while he began kissing her mouth and gently fondling her erect and hardened nipples. He worked his mouth between both of them occasionally touching her between her partially opened legs. He worked the same areas until he could see and hear her rapid breathing. He slowly began to kiss her pubic area and slowly kissed down each inner side of her now open thighs. He teased her for a minute or so before he buried his mouth between her legs and worked her sensitive area for several minutes. She gently pushed him away and moved her hands around his throbbing manhood. She performed oral sex on him for just a few minutes until she couldn't stand it any longer.

She told him softly, "I want you now, Sean," and he obliged. He entered her slowly and cautiously. He commented, "I'll be gentle, Marilyn, I don't want to hurt you in any way." She responded by pushing against him more until she completely engulfed his manhood.

He began a slow rhythm and increased it as she responded more and more. She almost screamed as she climaxed time and again before he exploded inside her. They remained locked for several more minutes appreciating their surroundings and her giving of herself so unselfishly. She looked at him as he dismounted but stayed in eye contact with her.

She smiled and said, "I really need to get back into the water for obvious reasons." He smiled, assisted her off the blanket and into the water. He held her after she had bathed and freshened up. He told her, "I'll be waiting for your call for dinner later in the week and I hope that you will consider a longer evening at my apartment or somewhere you choose after our dinner."

"I will call you very soon, I promise," she said.

It was obvious that he wanted her again but he settled for the anticipation of seeing her again. She really liked him and her fantasies about him were far exceeded. She had never been made love to like that before. Even Todd never performed like Quinn just had. Her disgust for the evening ahead increased as she thought about her relationship with Moore. She knew she needed to keep to her plan. Now, she had Quinn to fantasize about while Moore grunted and sweated over her in his quest to please her.

The FBI agents found the Bryants on the Frederick Hospital surgical ward answering questions about the accident from the Frederick Police. The agents were considering, as they heard the conversation about a black Mustang with Maryland plates being involved, that it might be the same Mustang involved in a shooting in Greenwich, Connecticut. Amy answered all the questions the FBI Agents asked about the incident in Greenwich. Cora and Bobby had arrived a few hours before the agents and they indicated that there had been no break-in at their house.

Amy said to the agents, "Cora was the house sitter and was at the house the morning just after the incident and she checked all of our documents, files and valuables. Nothing had been stolen or disturbed."

"Could the assailant have arbitrarily used 412 Pound Hill Road while he was conversing with Officer Bishop?" Bobby asked.

The agents did not answer his question. They left the hospital after noting all the information the Bryants had given them. So far, the authorities had a gun and silencer with no further clues as to its owner, a Maryland plate on a black or dark blue Mustang with not all the characters noted on it, and a conversation that included a house close to the crime scene. A similar Mustang was described by the Bryant couple in a hit and run accident that almost killed them. The agents surmised that this could not be a coincidence.

Quinn dropped Marilyn off at her apartment about an hour

before Moore arrived. She hustled to get dinner ready for him and try to look presentable. She also hoped that Jarvis had not told him about the impending ride during the day to piss him off and put him a shitty mood. She didn't know where Jarvis had been this afternoon but she was sure Quinn was smart enough to keep away from the man when he took her for a ride. She didn't need a picture of her doing Quinn at the swimming hole like the one that had been taken by someone and presented to her by Jarvis when she was giving the Colonel oral sex. The only thing that she was going to bring up in casual conversation this evening with him was that she really liked Quinn's BMW convertible and she was thinking about getting one when she could afford it. That would give her a little time to relax and she could pick up on any irritation or negative body language that indicated Moore knew more about what had happened besides a casual ride in a new BMW.

Moore arrived at Marilyn's apartment for dinner and sex around 7:30 p.m. He entered the apartment using his key to find Marilyn rushing to prepare food in the kitchen. She smiled at him and said, "I'm sorry I am late with dinner but I went for a longer ride than I expected with Quinn." John Moore didn't react but she felt that he would question her a little more. He did just like she expected and his body language indicated some irritation. She quickly, and with the most casual tone in her voice, said, "I really liked his BMW and I'm going to get one as soon as I can afford it. Maybe you might buy me one before we are rich?" She could see him relax a little knowing that the interest in Quinn was his car and not him.
"How was your experience with Quinn?"
"He was a real gentleman and is more polite when he is away from that idiot Jarvis." It was her way of throwing a shot at Hank Jarvis just to remind the Colonel that she didn't like the man very much. Moore ignored her comment but did accept her explanation of why dinner was a little late. *No harm done,* he thought. He'd rather have most of them getting along than having to hear all of them grumbling a little about each other.

He remembered when he was in Iraq and was their commanding officer. He had developed a team that had pulled off the biggest heist still not known by the Army or any law enforcement agency. If his plan worked, they would never suspect or know that it ever took place

Iraq 2003

Colonel Moore's office was in a concrete building protected by sandbags that had been stacked three quarters up the side of the building. It was located in the Green Zone in Baghdad, Iraq. He had entered the city several days after it had been occupied by the American Forces. He commanded one of several Army Intelligence offices that dealt with real, and counterfeit, United States currency that had been found in many locations by both the Army and Marine Corp during their thrust into Iraq. Moore had been reassigned from the Maryland Reserves and put in charge of an Army group quickly formed to support the U.S. Treasury Department to assure that the currency was documented and kept under guard in several areas in the Green Zone until properly determined by the American Government, as legitimate property of the new Iraqi Government.

Most of the currency that had been stored by Hussein and his Republican Guard henchmen needed to be returned to the United States and exchanged for gold. Gold would then be moved into storage vaults at Fort Knox for the new Iraqi Government to use to eventually restart their economy and pay for the reconstruction of their country. It would take many months for Colonel Moore's group, temporarily located in a former Baghdad meat packing building, to catalog and pack the currency to be flown back to the United States under tight and heavy security.

Under Moore's responsibility was approximately $100 million in one hundred dollar bills that had been cataloged. He also had members of his team examining another $20 million or so in counterfeit bills in twenty, fifty and one hundred dollar denominations. Treasury representatives had been assigned to his command to assist in the identification of some excellent grade forgeries. Those that were determined as counterfeit were burned in special furnaces constructed by the Army Engineers within the former meat packing building.

Moore commanded recently promoted Captain Todd Wilson,

who had been transferred from the Maryland Army Reserves into his group due to his financial background. He liked Wilson when he first met him because he was very thorough and a good officer. The men and women he assigned under him liked and respected him as well. Wilson had been put in charge of one of Moore's groups to count and document the legitimate currency for shipment back to the U.S. Treasury department.

Colonel Moore had hoped to retire as a Brigadier General after his completion of the task he had been assigned to in his tour of Iraq. He missed that promotional opportunity when it was revealed that some men under his command had conspired to sneak some of the good grade counterfeit money out of Iraq to the United States. It was a slap in his face that he was unable to foresee the attempted heist and he paid for it with a letter of reprimand in his record that affected any consideration for his one star promotion before he retired. He was grateful that he did not become a scapegoat for the Army to blame and be demoted to Lt. Colonel for the heist attempt. It was determined during the investigation and trial that the individuals responsible had acted on greed. Moore still remembered that after the four greedy individuals were court-martialed and given five to ten year sentences in prison, it had still cost him his star.

His marriage had also come to an end a year earlier and that had cost him a very heavy financial settlement. He had two fairly young children that were accustomed to the very best and his ex-wife insisted he provide them even more because of his infidelity with a young woman he met before his tour in Iraq. Moore's monthly net income after his divorce rivaled that of a First Lieutenant and he found himself embarrassed that he was unable to live like he had been accustomed to. His tour of duty to Iraq fulfilled his need to get out of the United States for a while to save up some money. His attraction for women continued on while he was in command in Baghdad. He noticed Second Lieutenant Marilyn Porter the first day when he observed her standing at attention in the group welcome for their new commander. Despite her desert fatigues, she still was very attractive. He was disappointed to learn, within a few days, that young Captain Wilson and she were lovers according to the scuttle butt at the officer's club.

The Colonel also met Sergeant Major Hank Jarvis and Staff Sergeant Sean Quinn the first day he took command. The Sergeant Major was a typical stern kiss-ass which meant he thoroughly supported the company commander and his wishes to such an extent that he was sometimes irritating not only to the troops but to the commander as well. On the other hand, Moore realized that Quinn was a combat veteran who tolerated Jarvis and could be relied on to perform any task he was instructed to do. He was temporarily assigned to Moore's financial group while he was recovering from combat shrapnel wounds he had received while on a sniper mission. Quinn was on his second tour and his former commander was a friend of Moore's who didn't want the young staff sergeant to be recycled home and out of the Army too early. Quinn had clearly said he was done with the Army after his second tour of Iraq was completed. His former commander wanted the sniper available if he needed him so he arranged with Moore to utilize him until he was healthy and he required his services. The arrangement assured both officers that Quinn would complete the ten months of his remaining tour.

Colonel Moore ran a strict command and those under it realized that fact after only a few days. That strictness was consistent until the scandal broke out that counterfeit money had been stolen but prevented from being shipped back to the United States. Those several weeks during the investigation were the hardest Moore had ever had to endure in his twenty years in the Army and ten years in the Reserves. With the possible promotion to Brigadier General lost, and a letter of reprimand on record in his army career file, Moore felt betrayed by his only real love, the Army. Compiled with his recent divorce that put a financial strain on his lifestyle and his urge to date and fornicate with any woman, the need to earn extra income was overwhelming.

Within weeks of the closing of the investigation, Moore had

devised several plans to sneak money out of Iraq and to the United States even though the others had tried and failed. One thing Moore learned from the investigation was where the chink in the Army amour was in investigative procedures. He determined that the others got caught because they were careless and had not thought through the entire process carefully. He needed several accomplices that he could trust and he began his search to seek out a few close subordinates to help him with several plans he had developed in his mind.

The first individual he undertook to be a potential accomplice was his Sergeant Major. Jarvis had never married. Moore suspected that he was a homosexual because there had been rumors by some of the enlisted men that the Sergeant Major liked to abuse young recruits and had been seen in places in the States that were known hangouts for gay men. No one could prove it, but Moore planned to make Jarvis think that he knew and had proof that the top sergeant was gay. Anyone in the Army accused of homosexuality knew that considerable harm to their career, including demotion, expulsion and financial ruin, could happen. Moore watched Jarvis by using the covert experience of Staff Sergeant Sean Quinn. He approached Quinn and made it clear to him that he suspected Jarvis as being a homosexual and wanted Quinn to confirm his suspicions. He knew that Quinn disliked Jarvis because he was a true warrior and Jarvis was a lifer hiding in an alternate life style. It didn't take Quinn long before he observed Jarvis watching some men taking showers in the open facilities in the field. He would act as though he was reading and resting, but all the while, he was observing the naked men going into and out of the field showers. Some of the men acknowledged his presence but he acted as if he was ignoring them. Sometimes he would even scold them for not covering up with a towel as they passed him. He would make rude remarks to them based on the size of their penises or shape of their buttocks. After a while, some of the men began thinking that this guy was a blatant queer.

Quinn continued to watch Jarvis for several weeks. One day, a young PFC was going to complain that Jarvis reached up and grabbed him while he was dressing in a nearby tent after completing a field shower. The Sergeant Major's excuse was that he should have covered up when the senior sergeant was touring the tent area. Quinn convinced the PFC that he would get into more trouble than it was worth challenging the Sergeant Major on the alleged inappropriate act. What Quinn did, was report to Colonel Moore that the incident confirmed that Jarvis was a potential homosexual and that he should be made accountable for his actions. Colonel Moore ordered him to be silent about the matter until he had time to address it with the Sergeant Major. Quinn remained silent, but returned to caution the PFC again, who continued to make slanderous remarks to other soldiers about Sergeant Major Jarvis.

The PFC continued, despite Quinn's warning, to make remarks, until one evening, the PFC was a victim of a sniper shot to the right shoulder in the Green Zone. He was shipped out of Iraq for medical recuperation.

Colonel Moore never knew Quinn had acted on his own to wound the PFC to protect Jarvis from an investigation. Several days later, as a command meeting was ending, Colonel Moore asked the Sergeant Major to take a walk with him. He immediately obliged. The Colonel informed the Sergeant Major that he had some ideas that he wanted to pass by him for his thoughts and maybe suggestions to assist him in resolving them. During the walk, the Colonel hinted that he was seen committing some pretty suggestive and lewd acts. Those lewd acts were construed by some of his staff members, both senior NCOs and junior officers, as homosexual in nature. The Colonel couldn't prove that he was a homosexual but he threatened that he would remove him from his command and court-martial him if it was proven. The court-martial would end in an undesirable discharge from the Army as well as the forfeiture of all retirement benefits. Jarvis denied everything. Moore gave him particular incidents that he had been involved in both stateside and in Iraq that caused Jarvis to stumble in trying to answer and defend himself. The Colonel knew he had

84

him. He told him that he would keep these incidents confidential as long as the Sergeant Major behaved himself and controlled his urges. Jarvis never mentioned one word of the conversation again.

Moore slowly let Jarvis into his inner circle, but each time, he had an incident to discuss with him. Jarvis got deeper and deeper into Moore's web due to his uncontrollable urges. When he felt the Sergeant Major was too deep in trouble, Moore arranged to shelter Jarvis if he participated in the big heist.

The next individual he needed on his side was Quinn. He was getting out of the Army, had come from a broken home, and had been dirt poor until he made some rank in the Army. He wasn't attached to anyone as far as Moore knew. He could be brought into the group, but Moore had to play it very cautiously with him. He would use Quinn's past commander as a bad guy who was trying to get him to stay in Iraq to finish his second tour. He knew Quinn wanted out and he would use his position to keep him in his group for a favor in return that would also make the sniper very rich.

When Quinn's old commander requested that he be returned, Moore held off until he could speak to Quinn about staying in his group. Moore promised to keep him in his command for several more months until he was relieved to return back to the States six months sooner than his tour with his old commander would be. Moore just asked for some allegiance that would pay off very profitably for Quinn if he agreed. Quinn knew that Moore was up to no good. He decided to stay on and see what was going to happen. It was better than shooting bad guys and most of all, being shot at by them. Moore told him that Jarvis was involved. He said that they both would keep the homosexuality issue as an albatross on Jarvis to keep quiet, participate and help them make a fortune as well.

Second Lieutenant Porter was the next individual that Moore wanted into the group for several reasons. One was his lust for her, as well as the hope that her greed for wealth would make her start giving him sexual favors for a long time to come. He fantasized every night when he tried to fall asleep in the heat of

Iraq in the summer months. He encouraged her daily that she was a credit to the Army. He told her many times that her work was impeccable and that, at his first opportunity, he was going to promote her to First Lieutenant. He would pay as many complements to her as possible without going over the edge to be construed as sexual. He knew she had been mistreated by Captain Wilson who had spent time with her but never treated her as a serious partner. He had a girlfriend back in Maryland that he dated through college and was probably going to marry when he returned. Marilyn Porter was a clean and pretty young woman that filled his needs so many miles from home. Moore didn't care that she loved Wilson as he just wanted the companionship of a younger woman to make him feel young again. He didn't realize that eventually, he would fall in love with her.

Moore had been humiliated by his ex-wife, not only financially, but sexually, because she always complained that he was an animal and she would not make love to an animal anymore. He had gone without a woman for a long time until he got involved with a woman in Maryland and his wife's private investigator caught him cheating on her. The more Wilson ignored and frustrated Marilyn Porter, the more Moore worked on her to build up her confidence again by saying that she was a special woman.

His plan and charm overcame Marilyn one evening when she actually kissed him during a sad story he was telling her about his evil ex-wife. He reciprocated by kissing her back. One thing led to another as Marilyn let him pet her a little until he actually had her believing that he was embarrassed because he thought he was impotent. He confessed that he didn't want her to think of him poorly because of his inability to perform. Marilyn felt pity for the man and told him that she had a cure for any impotence he thought he had. She unzipped his fly and performed oral sex on him until he became as rigid as ever and climaxed. All during her act to please her Colonel, the couple was being observed by Quinn, who had been ordered by Jarvis, to keep an eye on those two because he suspected Moore's intentions. He ordered him to take pictures of the young lady with the Colonel if something presented itself. It did that night, and he took the best shot he ever took with an infrared camera, with Marilyn's head buried in the Colonel's lap. Jarvis now had something on him in case he exposed his homosexuality. So began the four individual's relationship in the next stage in their loose partnership.

Colonel Moore's group continued to monitor, count, record, pack and ship hundreds of pounds of U.S. and foreign currency monthly as Army and Marine troops would find stored money in palaces, houses and other buildings they came across, sometimes accidentally. There was more than one incident when troops of various ranks would store a few thousand dollars in one hundred dollar bills in their shoes, canteens, duffle bags or anywhere they thought they could hide the cash to get it home. They usually got caught. Some did manage to get the cash home but Moore's group did a fine job keeping most of that from happening.

Captain Todd Wilson was the charge officer of one of Moore's groups who daily inspected the currency and ensured that the proper protection and procedures were being carried out. Wilson did his job well, and Moore felt sure that he would maintain the group's integrity and effectiveness. It was a hard job protecting Iraqi money that had Franklin's and Grant's pictures on them. Todd was irreproachable in his procedures, follow-ups, investigations and the shipment records he maintained. He had never been off as much as one dollar in the months he was in charge. He had never been involved in the money scandal that ended Moore's chances of receiving his star. Captain Thomas Banks, the officer in charge, had run Moore's other section very loosely and not up to the standards Moore had set. Moore was his own undoing since he never followed up in detail on some of the reports or scuttlebutt about loose money in Bank's group. Banks was court-martialed and shipped back to the States. His career was ruined and he was expelled from the Army. He was sentenced to five years of prison with probation possible after serving three years for his involvement in the attempted theft. As Moore's reputation declined after the scandal, he devised several plans to pay back the Army and brought in the three accomplices to execute those plans. He also started his quest to get Wilson involved. He first tried to befriend him, which never happened. Moore became frustrated and decided to devise a plan with Jarvis and Quinn. Moore ordered Quinn to have his sniper rifle ready one evening when Moore ordered Jarvis and Wilson to a meeting. At the meeting, he hinted, and tried several approaches, to get Wilson on board until Wilson finally realized what the two men were up to.

Moore said, "Captain Wilson, we have several fool-proof plans that we want to run by you and get your professional opinion. We think we can ship $9 to $11 million in cash out of Iraq and later split it up five equal ways. That means a little over $2 million that each of us could have to use for the rest of our lives."

He couldn't believe what he was hearing and yelled, "Are you two out of your fucking minds?" He emphatically told Moore and Jarvis, "This conversation never took place and I want to be immediately transferred back to my Maryland reserve unit. Baghdad patrol and the chance for combat were better choices for me than this crazy plan."

Moore tried to calm him down and told him, "None of the plans can be instituted unless you are a part of them."

"I won't be part of anything," Wilson yelled back.

"Captain Wilson, your request for transfer has been denied. You will continue with your present duties and this conversation never took place. You do understand, don't you?" he said slowly and precisely, while staring at him. "Besides, no one would ever believe you. An accusation that the Sergeant Major and I made a joint suggestion to you to steal money would seem trumped up and ridiculous, especially after what we all just went through. Captain, your career would be over."

Moore dismissed Jarvis and Wilson from his office. Outside, Quinn waited for the signal to either kill Wilson, or let him live. The signal was for Moore to turn off his office light if

Wilson was to be killed or leave it on to indicate the young Captain was on board. Jarvis had not been informed of that part of the plan. Both men stepped out of the office and onto the active street as other soldiers and marines moved about. The light in Moore's office went out. Quinn aimed at Wilson's head through his night scope and squeezed the trigger of his 50 cal. single shot sniper's rifle. The bullet went through Wilson's head and killed him instantly. Quinn quickly reloaded and shot a second shot that hit Jarvis's upper thigh in an attempt to make the shooting look like a random sniper attack. Jarvis was screaming that he had been shot. He didn't know how badly he had been hit because he was covered in blood from Wilson's head shot. His leg was burning and he was panicking that he was going to die. Quinn laughed to himself hearing Jarvis scream when he had been hit with only a grazing flesh wound. Quinn felt he deserved some pain for forcing him to have to wound that PFC that he had groped. He quickly disassembled the rifle and put it in its case and escaped off the roof of the building he had fired from. To draw attention, he used the M-16 he was also carrying to shoot bursts of fire into the side of a building to make it seem that he had fired at the sniper. His plan worked. He explained later to the investigative team that he had seen a person carrying something coming off the roof and had shot at him. He said that the sniper was never found by the 20 or 30 troops that followed him in his search. His descriptive hunt for someone who never existed, worked. He returned later to retrieve the case containing the sniper rifle from under the rubble and debris that was everywhere in the city.

Jarvis eventually received a purple heart for being wounded in Iraq. He found out a year later from Quinn, during one of their disagreements, that he had been the victim of Quinn's ingenuity to execute Moore's plan to eliminate Wilson after he had rejected their plan. Jarvis never felt comfortable after that knowing that Moore had confided only in Quinn about the assassination. Marilyn wasn't told until months later that Wilson had become suspicious and nosey about the heist but was unfortunately killed by a real sniper. She never knew that he had been approached and asked to participate and was purposely killed for rejecting Moore's plan. Marilyn believed the Colonel and never knew that Quinn had killed Wilson. Immediately after Wilson's body was taken to the mortuary at Graves Registration to be prepared for shipment back to the United States, Moore arranged for Jarvis to accompany the body to Frederick, Maryland despite his flesh wound, to ensure that the coffin was not opened for any reason. He revised his plan and sent Quinn with him when he found out that the Wilson family was going to bury him on the family farm. He wanted Quinn there to begin to plan the logistics. Moore was now able to make a better plan and things changed. He took personal charge of the arrangements for Wilson's metal coffin to be loaded onto an aluminum shipping case to be flown by the Air Force transport plane stateside. His command at the Iraqi meat packing warehouse still had a functioning cold storage and freezer section which only aided further in his plan. Wilson's body was stored in the adjacent cold storage facility next to the packing room where palletized money was being prepared for shipment out of the country. Moore arranged for the service to be held for his command to honor Captain Wilson prior to his body being shipped home. Because of the cold storage facilities available on site and Moore's insistence that a service be held at his command, his body was allowed to be held overnight, unbeknownst to Graves Registration, for the heist that was to follow.

Twelve hours prior to the shipment of the body, an identical metal coffin and aluminum shipping case were requisitioned by Moore. While the four thieves performed their task filling the metal coffin with $100 bills late at night, Wilson's body lay in the other one. They calculated what the weight of one gram of $100 bills were. They worked out the math and realized that $1 million weighed approximately 22 pounds. They multiplied it by Wilson's 210 pound embalmed body along with the ten pounds of his clothing which equaled to be the weight close to $10 million. To make it a more profitable venture, they stripped the interior fabric off of the metal coffin and were able to add an additional 22 pounds of money. They now had just a little over $11 million in cash stuffed into it. Moore ordered Quinn and Jarvis to remove Wilson's body from the other metal coffin and place it in a body bag. Porter was never given the details of how the money would be shipped out until she put two and two together that night as the body was being removed. She was, at first, alarmed as it was removed, placed in a body bag and carried out. Moore recognized her alarm and explained to her that he had made proper arrangements with a local Iraqi crematory for a secret disposal of Wilson's remains. She never knew that Quinn just buried Wilson in an undisclosed location only known to him and two local Iraqi civilians he had paid $100 apiece to assist him. The metal coffin and aluminum shipping case Wilson was originally placed in was returned a few weeks later as not needed. No one ever questioned the reason for the additional coffin and shipping case order which were eventually returned and supposedly unused according to Lt. Porter's signed report. Lt. Porter also arranged the books to not include $11 million for shipment back to the United States.

The metal coffin filled with $11 million and in the aluminum shipping case, arrived at Andrew's Air Force Base to full military honors with the other eight bodies that had been returned with it. Captain Wilson's coffin was never opened at the flight line when it was removed from the aluminum shipping case due to Sergeant Major Jarvis's insistence that he was accompanying the body and was the other victim of the hideous assassination. Standing with a crutch on the flight line in full military dress, Jarvis did not have to inform the military inspection officer again that the coffin was not to be opened. The stern look on his face and glare in his eyes overwhelmed the junior officer assigned to check all returning coffins. His metal coffin was loaded into the hearse of the Frederick Funeral Home, to be taken away for the wake and funeral to follow. The coffin was never opened at the funeral parlor either due to the accompanying paperwork that identified to the recipient undertaker that the body was not to be viewed. It explained that a partial decapitation had occurred due to the wound received and all embalming was completed to U.S. mortuary standards. The paperwork had been signed by a Major in Baghdad Graves Registration and Colonel Moore, and was presented by Sergeant Major Jarvis to the Frederick Mortuary. All seemed in order as the wake and funeral were carried out. The metal coffin was put in a cement vault and then laid to rest at the Wilson farm. The spirits of Jeremiah, Herman and Arnold Wilson had guarded the $11 million until the time to claim it would occur. The burning of the Wilson farmhouse signaled the arrival of that time.

Family Business

Amy answered the phone at the hotel. The voice on the other end hesitated for a few seconds before he spoke.

"Amy, this is Bruce and I have Benjamin on the other extension so we can have a three way conversation. How are you and Bob doing?"

"Hi guys," she answered. "We've had a rough run but we're okay now. Bob is doing much better. I hope you two are well."

They both answered that they were fine but were more pleased to hear Bob was doing better after his surgery.

"We needed to make sure that everything is okay with you two before we talk about what you and Bob are doing to buy the farm." Bruce said.

"Thanks for your concern," Amy said as she motioned to Bobby and Cora to go into the bedroom extension in the hotel room and pick up the phone to listen in.

"Bobby and Cora are on the other line as well."

"We were informed by a Miss Terry Breen of the accident and of your intent to pay off the loans and take over the property," Bruce said. "She also said you were probably going to live there. Is that your intent?"

Amy was going to be a little sarcastic to her brother by first stating that they could at least thank Bob and her for bailing their asses out of the jam they were in, but instead, she said, "Yes, we are keeping the place in the family, at least for now, and we are still going to buy the farm despite the accident and now the fire." She kept her cool and slowly said, "We wanted to make sure that both of you were okay with what we are doing."

"Benjamin and I have no choice but to take this offer, which is being almost jammed down our throats." Bobby piped in.

"Uncle Bruce, you are way out of line. You two should be pleased that the farm will remain in our family. If my parents hadn't stepped in, this place would go under along with your credit." Bobby reminded them. "It's just property now. The farmhouse is gone and anything of value or sentiment is gone as well. You both need to act mature and just say, thank you, and let it go at that."

There was silence on the other end for an uncomfortable several seconds. Finally, Benjamin said, "Okay, everyone calm down. We are all under pressure here and taking shots at each other isn't going to accomplish anything."

Bruce spoke up. "He's right, I was out of line. Bobby, Cora and Amy, my concern is Todd's grave."

Amy said, "I can leave it alone or have it moved with the others to Frederick or even to Arlington if that is what you wish. Bruce, it's yours and Joyce's choice and I will accommodate your wishes."

"Amy, Joyce and I agreed that we want Todd interred at Arlington," Bruce said chocking up.

"Arnold and Uncle Herman should be at Arlington as well then," Benjamin said. "Do you agree?"

Amy responded, "Yes and I am pleased that you both do." Both of them acknowledged that they did.

"Look, I'll contact Miss Breen and have her inquire on the movement of the graves on our behalf. I will also have her contact the local funeral parlor and the Arlington Cemetery administration. Once she has the information we need, I will get with the both of you and your wives, to plan the arrangements."

"We want things to be kept simple to make it easy on all of us," Bruce said.

"I understand and I hope that I can get everything done that is required in the next 30 days to secure the farm from foreclosure," Amy said.

"Amy, we'll come to the hospital once Bob feels well enough to receive visitors," Bruce said. "I'm pleased the farm will remain in the family. If you two ever choose to sell all or part of it, I would want to be contacted."

"Me too," Benjamin said.

"Ok. I'll let you both know if that ever occurs but we have no plans to sell it. However, I promise to give you both the first option to buy it back. I'll keep you both informed of Bob's recuperation and our progress in stopping the farm foreclosure."

Jake Bishop was gaining more strength by the hour. He kept going over the shooting in his mind but couldn't remember any new details he could give to the Chief of Police. He kept trying to remember the license plate. He could picture the crest or seal but not what the numbers or letters were. *Just one number or letter*, he thought, *could assist them in narrowing in on the black or dark blue Mustang that was from somewhere in Maryland.* He kept picturing the scene over and over in his mind and concentrating on the partially exposed plate in between the assailant's legs. He guessed that the portion of the letter or number he saw to the right of the seal was either the letters 'C or G' or the number '0'. Based on the position of the legs of the shooter, it had to be one of those three. Maybe that could narrow it down just a little more. He called the Chief and explained what he thought he remembered. The Chief said he would request some computer printouts from the Maryland DOT. He'd also request the FBI to work with the DOT to sort the data so that they could eliminate the obvious registrations that didn't meet the criteria they were establishing now.

Quinn spent most of his day in Hagerstown and away from Frederick. He shopped most of the gun shops there and gathered as much lead shot he could legitimately buy for the next phase of his task at the farm. He planned to use the lead shot as the catalyst to alter the chemical makeup of the well water at the farm. He gathered about twenty pounds of the metal before doing a little shopping for some other items he required. One was a new .10 mm pistol he always wanted that was similar to the one he was used to in the army. He already had a .10 mm silencer lined up that he could pick up hot from an acquaintance he knew. He placed the order for the .10 mm pistol and knew that he would have to wait awhile before he would be able to pick it up. He understood the Maryland law was to have a security check completed by the State Police before anyone acquired a new pistol. He thought about the ticket he received in Connecticut but realized that wouldn't hold up a security check to buy a pistol. Upon completion of his purchases, he called Jarvis to tell him his timetable to begin his next phase of the task. Jarvis was in his office. He was always over-cautious about conversations with Quinn. He called Moore's office and informed him of Quinn's intent to finish the second phase of his instructions. Moore did his usual and hung up without ever so much as a goodbye. Jarvis ignored the Colonel as he was used to the arrogance of this man. He also relaxed, knowing that he did not have to do anything for the second phase. He had already inquired about whether a well inspection was mandatory by state statues when the property that contained a well was exchanged during a sale. He was advised that it was. The contamination in the well would show up a few days before the closing and slow down or even stop the purchase of the farm. He also relaxed knowing that the Colonel didn't need to be told about the shooting or the accident yet. Things were running smoothly so far.

She called Sean on his cell phone. Sean was cautious these days about answering unknown calls to his cell. He took a chance and answered. He was delighted to hear Marilyn's voice.
"Nice surprise. Have you decided to have that dinner with me?"
"I'm calling you from a pay phone across from the bank for obvious reasons. I'd like you to stop by later this evening when you are free. I want to see you and yes, I would like to have dinner with you, but not tonight." She explained that a few drinks and some small talk was all she had in mind if he wasn't too busy. "If you can't make it, I understand. I didn't give you much notice." Sean was very excited about her even suggesting that he come over for a drink or two. He maintained his self-control.
"I have some business for the Colonel to complete before I can stop by. Let's say 10:00 p.m. if that is fine with you?" He

hoped that it wasn't too late for a drink. He said, "It would be like having a night cap."

"10:00 p.m. is fine and if you don't mind, can you park down the block from my apartment so that I won't have to explain to either of our two associates why your car was at my apartment?"

Sean said he understood completely and would call her on his cell phone when he was nearing her apartment.

"You should have been in the spy business," she laughed.

"You are a very secret commodity and I need to carry out this assignment with precision," he responded in a deep dark tone. She laughed again and hung up the phone. As she was returning to the bank, Moore eased away from the window. He was curious as to why she would be using a pay phone.

Joe Walker was an ex-army intelligence officer and a two year veteran of the FBI. He served in Iraq in 2003 and again in 2005. Upon completion of his six years of active duty, he chose to apply to the FBI instead of staying on in the Maryland Reserves. He looked over the Maryland DOT report that he had put together for the Greenwich Chief of Police who had contacted him less than an hour ago. He was a little skeptical when the Chief explained the motive for his request. Walker felt that the Chief was pushing the envelope a little based on the reason given. He had faxed the list to the Greenwich Police as requested and was casually looking over the twenty five hundred registered Maryland license plate numbers that fit the criteria. He did another sort on the numbers associated with only Mustangs listed as the auto registered. He sorted again to focus on black and blue colors of any shade. He still was at two hundred and twelve but that included vintage Mustangs. Based on the description given by the officer, he sorted again and eliminated all Mustangs older than 1999. He was now looking at thirty one registered automobiles that fit the criteria Officer Bishop described. He began to look over the names of the individuals and was considering deleting the female registrants but chose to maintain them on the list. None of the registrants were wanted by any State or Federal Government agency. He bounced traffic violations in Connecticut against the list and waited a few seconds for the computer to respond. He had three hits. A 2005 black Mustang with Maryland plate number 681 CDA and registered to a Sean Quinn of Frederick, Maryland came up on the computer as the most recent. The other two were over a month ago so he immediately concentrated on the Quinn ticket. Mr. Quinn had been ticketed for speeding in Greenwich, Connecticut at 3:05 a.m., August 23rd, the morning of the shooting incident. He was employed by the Colony Bank of Frederick, Maryland. He was Caucasian, fit the height and build that Officer Bishop could remember, and had a Maryland pistol license. He was an Iraq War veteran and at one time, had been in the Maryland Reserves. Walker didn't remember him but he looked up the suspect's Army record and reviewed his assignments to Afghanistan and Iraq. He noted his sniper and finance experience. He thought it was odd for a soldier to be assigned to two totally different service groups as Quinn had been. He continued reading his army record and noted Quinn's decorations and service profile as written by his commanding officers. Colonel John Moore and Lt. Colonel Richard Brenan were the two individuals who praised him highly and frequently. Walker was now very interested in Mr. Quinn.

Walker reviewed Quinn's employment history and noticed that he was employed almost immediately upon his discharge from the Army. His immediate supervisor was a Harold Jarvis and the bank VP they reported to was a John Moore. Walker went back to Quinn's Army record and noted Moore's write up. He contemplated whether they could be the same? He thought Quinn was becoming more interesting as he read his Army record. Walker decided to investigate Quinn. He contacted his immediate supervisor and detailed what he had found. He was given permission to find Quinn and bring him in for questioning. No accusations, just information as to why he would be in Greenwich on the 23rd, which was the same day and almost the hour that the shooting incident in Connecticut took place. Both men agreed that Walker would proceed with caution based on Quinn's military record. With permission to find Quinn and question him, Walker decided to pay him an unannounced visit in the morning, before the man headed off to the bank.

Quinn was notified by the Frederick Police that they had recovered his black Mustang and he would have to report to the Police Station as soon as possible. He told Jarvis that he was leaving to go to the police station to claim his car. Hank Jarvis began asking questions as Quinn prepared to go to the station. Quinn became irritated and closed the office door. He spoke softly.

"Look, you idiot, I have to go to the station and identify my Mustang. They probably figured out by now that it was involved in the accident with the Bryant's rental car." Jarvis's face seemed to drain of color as Quinn expected it would. He smiled as he noticed the grayish color and anguished look on Jarvis's face when the reality of the Mustang being involved with the accident was finally spoken.

"Shit. The accident. Fuck!" Jarvis mumbled.

"That little nudge I gave the Bryants off the road, paid off, didn't it?" Quinn said. Jarvis couldn't speak for a few seconds until he regained his composure.

"What the hell are you going to do now?"

"I'll take care of it, Sergeant Major. You just keep the Colonel from worrying about little things like this now, okay?" Quinn remarked casually as he opened the door and left the office.

The Frederick Police had taken Quinn's car into the investigation area and was combing it over for evidence or any kind to tie it to the hit and run accident that had occurred. Officer Hayes was unable to apprehend any of the kids that had been joy riding in the hot Mustang. Based on a recent phone call from the Connecticut authorities, Walker, by then, had traced the Mustang to the Frederick Police link of stolen cars that had been found. Through Walker, the Frederick Police

99

were now also aware that a black Mustang was suspected of being involved in a shooting in Connecticut on the 23rd of August. Based on information exchanged with the Frederick Police, Walker was pleased that he didn't have to wait until the next morning to meet Quinn. He was alerted that Quinn had been asked to come down to the station to identify his car. Walker immediately drove to the station and waited with Officer Hayes for Quinn to arrive.

Quinn was taken into an interrogation room and realized something more than a routine questioning on the identity of his car was being planned. He figured that some further questioning was in store for him. He concentrated on remembering the details of the story he was going to tell. The apparent waiting was the first sign he recognized. He waited in the warm room for approximately twenty minutes while Agent Walker and Officer Hayes watched him in the adjacent air conditioned room. Quinn recognized the tactics and remained calm. Eventually Officer Hayes entered.

"Do you own a black GT Mustang with Maryland plate number 681 CDA?" he asked.

Quinn said, "Yes, that's my car."

"How'd you lose the car?"

Quinn faked embarrassment and said, "I parked the car at my apartment parking lot and when I came out to use it, it was gone."

"The keys were in the ignition when it was recovered from a bunch of kids that were driving it, Mr. Quinn."

Quinn had forced himself to turn red and look really embarrassed.

"I left the top down and the keys in the car. I was in a hurry and just assumed that it was safe there."

"Why were you in such a hurry, Mr. Quinn?"

He explained that he had to be at his boss's house for a meeting that evening that was mandatory and he was running late.

"Look, I changed at my apartment before I completed my last few chores for the bank. I figured I'd be ready for my meeting if I finished up across town close to my boss's house instead of having to come back to my apartment and then back again. It was a dumb thing to do but shit happens. I didn't see any kids around when I left the car in my parking lot. I had to rent a car until I bought a new one."

Officer Hayes signaled for Agent Walker to come in and continue with the interrogation. Quinn anticipated something like that would happen so he mentioned his new wheels to see what would happen. Walker heard the statement when he entered and immediately asked him about buying a new car before he even knew what happened to his old car. Quinn played it smooth. He looked at Agent Walker and asked, "Officer Hayes, who is this guy?" Walker slammed his fists on the table and shouted. "You don't need to know who I am. I want you to answer my question." Quinn paused and began a well thought out explanation.

"Whoever you are, I do a lot of research for the Colony Bank. I get paid real good money if you care to check my tax records. I'm single and can afford several new cars. I paid cash for it. Based on the cheap suit you are wearing, I guess you wouldn't understand that, now would you?"

Walker was angered and a little embarrassed by Quinn's comments. Officer Hayes said that he was going to keep the car for a few days for the FBI and his department to look it over. He explained that the car had some damage to the right front bumper and fender.

"Shit, that Mustang was cherry. It didn't have a scratch on it," Quinn said in disgust.

"Well, Mr. Quinn, it has more than that on it now and...," Agent Walker interrupted Hayes and told Quinn, "You will need to stay in the area in case we need to contact you. We may have some additional questions for you to answer."

Quinn coolly looked at Agent Walker and said, "Agent, I will be either at my apartment or the Colony Bank. You can reach me at these numbers," he said as he handed his card to Officer Hayes. Officer Hayes thanked him for coming into the station. Agent Walker did not say a word to him as he left.

Walker called his supervisor and told him what had happened

during the interview. He asked permission to continue investigating Quinn. He wanted to pay him another visit, but he wanted to tail him first. The agent's supervisor agreed. As Walker hung up the phone, Hayes asked, "Agent Walker, why didn't you question him about the Connecticut shooting on the 23rd?"

"Quinn is only a possible suspect at this time and I want more information before I begin pressuring him during another session. I also don't want him running to an attorney if he thinks we are accusing him of something more."

Dusk came and Quinn set out to complete the second phase of Moore's plan for the farm. He checked to make sure he wasn't being followed by the smartass agent he had run into at the Frederick Police station. He thought that he owed the agent for the shitty way he had been treated when he was being questioned. He'd work out something for that guy some other time. He had more urgent business at hand. Satisfied that the authorities were not interested in him, he drove to the farm. He was able to access the well and remove one of the old boards that covered it. He poured lead shot he purchased down into the well and then replaced the boards carefully and was out of the farm in less than ten minutes. The farm well poisoning was completed just after dark. He had some time to kill, so he headed for his apartment to freshen up before his late nightcap with Marilyn. He thought of her at the pond and expected the same type of experience when he reached her apartment. Why else would she call him from a pay phone, and then agree to such an odd time to meet him for a late drink at her apartment? She had to like him and was going to like him some more tonight, he anticipated. He drove up to his apartment and decided to check his mail slot in the apartment atrium. He opened it and found several utility bills and one envelope from the Superior Court of Greenwich, Connecticut. He immediately opened up the envelope and read the contents. The letter notified him that he had five more days to contest the speeding ticket he received on the 23rd of August and be assigned a court date or pay the fee said before the date indicated. He contemplated telling them to go to hell by not responding to either, but decided that he would pay the three-hundred dollars.

As Quinn washed and changed shirts, he thought about the ticket and began wondering if the Connecticut State Police ever reviewed violations that had occurred in the vicinity of the shooting on that day. His ticket was on record and he couldn't be sure that he got away as clean as he originally thought he had. Was there any description of his car in Greenwich that morning? He couldn't be sure. He wondered why the sarcastic FBI agent never asked him about the ticket. He was sure the FBI knew. Quinn also thought about the guy he had asked for directions to Round Hill Road. That guy probably didn't know or suspect anything, but he couldn't be sure that the cops hadn't combed every inch of Greenwich and the surrounding towns looking for someone in the early morning hours of the 23rd just before or after the shooting. He wasn't even sure if they were ever going to catch the kids that actually took the car. He knew that the police would realize the kids didn't do anything, but he was thankful that the old officer wasn't fast enough to catch the kids. His realized he was still pissed about Agent Walker and a little payback was in order when he had time. He decided not return to the apartment and hoped Marilyn would invite him to stay the night. It would also give him a chance to be away from the apartment if the FBI did come looking to ask him more questions. He packed several bags and would return to Hagerstown later that night if his visit to Marilyn didn't include a sleep over. He called Jarvis on his cell phone. Jarvis didn't answer so he left a message that he would be away from his apartment and phase two of his task had been completed. *The ball was in Jarvis's court now*, he thought, as he closed his cell phone.

Hank Jarvis had finished climaxing and was cleaning himself off in the back seat of his car. The young University of Maryland college student quickly stood up and pulled up his pants. He held out his hand for the $20 he agreed to this time

103

for Jarvis to have anal intercourse with him. He told Jarvis, "It will be $40 the next time you want me. You'll also have to wear a condom next time." Jarvis grumbled.

"You bring them with you. I'm not carrying any."

The college student reminded him that he had told him to bring condoms but Jarvis said, "I want the real thing not some latex cover up." Jarvis was becoming annoyed as he grabbed the man.

"I'll decide if I want to wear a condom or not."

"Then the price will be doubled to $80 if I have to risk getting any diseases from someone like you."

Jarvis slapped him. The blow startled him and he felt the sting on his left cheek. The young man recovered from the blow. He retaliated quickly and struck out at Jarvis. He hit Jarvis in the face and the force caused a cut to the inside of his mouth. Jarvis held up one hand in defense and the other to his face. He could taste the blood.

"You cut my fucking mouth you little bastard. Look at me. I'm bleeding."

"Take me back to campus now," the student said.

Jarvis said nothing as he pulled out a handkerchief and dabbed his mouth and exited the rear seat. He opened the driver's door, climbed behind the wheel and started the car. The student followed cautiously and entered the front passenger seat. He watched Jarvis for any further signs of aggression as he buckled his seat belt. Jarvis turned the car around on the old back road and headed back to the campus. Neither man said anything for several miles until Jarvis apologized for the incident.

"Look. You're going to have to change your ways and adhere to my rules if you are going to be a steady customer," the student said. Jarvis agreed, then apologized again and said that he enjoyed his company and was hurt that they had an altercation.

"It's only business," the student said. "I'm sorry for the punch. It was reactionary. Remember, you slapped me first."

"And I apologize again," Jarvis said. "Can I call you

tomorrow?" The student paused.

"The day after tomorrow will be better. I have another appointment tomorrow night." Jarvis drove the car up to the campus entrance and stopped. His voice became higher as he almost pleaded that he would pay double and wear any type of condom if he could have him tomorrow night. The student looked at Jarvis and thought for a moment and then said, "Okay. I'll see you tomorrow at the same time and place. The price will be doubled anyway to $80 because of the schedule change I am making with my other client." Jarvis smiled and agreed but held out his hand across the chest of the college student to stop him from exiting the car. He asked, "Please stop seeing other clients because I want to have a steady relationship with you. I really like you and want to be your companion and not your client."

"Look, I need a steady income and I really don't want any type of relationship with anyone until I finish my art degree next year," the student replied. He departed but turned as he left to reconfirm the same time and place tomorrow. Jarvis nodded and smiled. He stayed for a few extra moments as he watched the student walk back on campus. He turned on his cell phone and immediately heard it beep. He realized that he had missed a call. He recognized Quinn's number and began to dial it.

The phone rang as Quinn was heading to Marilyn's apartment. Quinn answered and said, "I finished what I needed to accomplish and I am heading out of town tonight. Watch my apartment before and after work for a day or so while I'm away."

Jarvis remarked, "I heard the message you left. I'm not your fucking employee Quinn, you are mine, remember? I don't like being ordered to watch your apartment." Quinn became angry.

"Look you stupid idiot, if the police are on to me because of that traceable speeding ticket or some description the cop I shot gave them, or the Bryant accident, then you, me and the Colonel are fucked. They can easily find a record of all the calls on my cell records between the three of us you imbecile." There was silence on the other end of the phone for a few seconds.

"I'll watch your place for an hour or so in the morning and after work to see if there is anyone casing your place out."

"That's better Sergeant Major. Also, tell anyone that does come looking for me that I have taken a vacation day and will be back after that. You got that?" Jarvis responded that he would keep to that story if he were questioned, but maybe both of them were getting a little too paranoid and were having too many second thoughts.

"I have spent most of my adult life being over cautious. It helped me survive, Afghanistan, Iraq and my association with you. Call me if anything develops."

He closed his cell phone as he approached Marilyn's apartment complex. Jarvis was going to say some more before he realized Quinn had ended the call. That always irritated Jarvis about Quinn but he realized that he had to follow the man's instincts and do what he had asked.

Quinn parked his car away from Marilyn's apartment as she requested. He casually walked up to her apartment complex's main door and pushed the ringer for her apartment. He looked around but didn't notice a man sitting in his car in the parking lot. Marilyn quickly responded. She pressed the button to unlock the downstairs door. A few moments later, he knocked on her apartment door. She welcomed him in and quickly closed the door behind him. He noticed the lights were turned down low and it was a little difficult to see her. He observed she had a terry cloth bathrobe on.

"Welcome to my apartment, Sean." He was about to speak when she disrobed and stood before him naked in the dim light. She looked at him and said, "Well, do you like?" She approached him and kissed him very gently. He grabbed her tightly but not forcefully and responded, "Yes, very much," as he pulled her close to him. He felt the smoothness of her back and then buttocks as she slid her tongue ever so slowly in and out of his mouth. He picked her up and slowly walked towards the dim light in the bedroom. He entered the bedroom and gently laid her on the drawn sheets. He began to undress as she positioned herself on the bed. He made a motion as to shut the light off when she said, "Keep it on. I want to see you naked." He obliged. He knew she enjoyed looking at him in his aroused condition. He teased her a little by taking his time slowly removing his socks before removing his boxer briefs. He turned sideways so that she could observe the extent of his manhood that had swollen to its maximum at the sight of her waiting for him on the bed. He slowly walked to the light switch and turned off the light. Colonel Moore watched the bedroom light go off from his car. He had seen enough. He now knew why Marilyn called someone from a payphone and acted and sounded nervous when she refused his invitation to spend the night with him earlier. He always knew when she was nervous. He headed home to make some alternate plans for Ms. Porter and Mr. Quinn

The Stakeout

Joe Walker and his partner were outside Quinn's apartment complex at 8:00 a.m. Walker was still pissed the way Quinn had embarrassed him in front of the Frederick Police Officer. He purchased two coffees and a couple of bagels from the shop down the street for Craig Thompson and himself. They were preparing to sit and watch Quinn's apartment until he exited for work. His plan was to approach and ask him some more questions. Thompson would stay back in case Quinn was uncooperative or even worse, if he decided to get foolish and run because he was guilty of something. The fact that they had not located Quinn's BMW concerned them, because that could mean that maybe Quinn had left earlier or had not returned to his apartment. They decided to wait until 8:30 a.m. and if Quinn wasn't observed coming from, or going to the apartment, they would find and question him later at the bank.

Hank Jarvis sat in his car and watched the two men in the black Ford Taurus sedan sitting across from Quinn's apartment. He'd been at the street corner since before 6:30 a.m. anticipating the worst and now he had reason to believe the worst had come to pass. He continued to watch the men until a few minutes after eight and called Quinn.

Quinn had left Marilyn's apartment a few minutes after one in the morning and headed for Hagerstown to spend the night. He was asleep in his motel room when his cell phone rang. He answered it on the second ring to hear the panic in Jarvis's voice as he explained that there were two men, he thought, casing out his apartment. Quinn calmed Jarvis down a little and asked for some more details of what he had observed.

"There's a black Ford Taurus sedan with two guys in it, sipping coffee across from your apartment."

"Remember to tell whoever comes looking for me that I am on a one day vacation and that I can be reached on my cell phone. If it's the authorities, they have my cell number. Tell the Colonel what's going on so he can think about any damage control we might need." Quinn emphasized that he did not want Jarvis covering up anything so that the Colonel had a clear picture of what was going on. He repeated his instructions to Jarvis and asked emphatically if he understood. Jarvis was calm by now as he acknowledged his instructions while pulling into his parking space at the bank.

"I will call and explain the situation to Marilyn and even use her as an alibi if I have to. I'll make up a story that she was with me on the trip to Boston if the authorities have connected me in any way with the incident in Greenwich to the ticket I received on the same morning and are watching me or, worse, going to arrest me. Run that by the Colonel while I call and tell Marilyn to stay out of the office for a day until we can figure out what the authorities have in store for me."

He ended the call with Jarvis and hoped that he could catch Marilyn before she left for the bank. Jarvis was not relaxed anymore. He almost vomited thinking of what he had to say to the Colonel.

Marilyn was about to leave her apartment when Quinn called and laid out the situation. She obliged his request, but told him that she was disappointed that he hadn't told anyone about his escapades and that she would call the Colonel immediately.

"I'll make sure that that idiot Jarvis doesn't screw up the story. By the way, I enjoyed last night and I want to continue our relationship in secret until we both have our share of the rewards we will be getting soon," she said.

He acknowledged the request and said, "I look forward to our next meeting. I have a few things in store for you." He also said that he wanted her to double check to make sure everyone's story was in sync and that the Colonel was aware he might have to come up with an alternate plan now that he was being tailed. Marilyn ended the call and dialed Moore's cell. Moore let the cell ring for a while when he noticed it was Marilyn's number. He was angered that she was now screwing Quinn. It was like when she was screwing both Wilson and him in Iraq again. That had also infuriated him, but this hurt even more because he loved Marilyn and thought she, at least, cared for him based on the relationship they had been having for a while. He finally answered the phone and listened to what she hastily had to say about the pending situation that could be developing. He was angered to hear that he had not been informed of the shooting in Greenwich or the stealing of Quinn's car. Marilyn said it was the first she had heard of it too, when Quinn called her this morning. She wanted Moore to make sure Jarvis informed him of everything so that he could make decisions based on good information. While Moore was on the cell with Marilyn, he saw Jarvis quickly walking towards his open office door. He closed his phone and cut her off and waved Jarvis in. He motioned him to shut the door. Marilyn realized in mid-sentence that Moore had disconnected. She decided to wait at her apartment until he planned his next move for the group.

Jarvis looked nervously at Moore after he completely divulged to him every bit of information he could remember on what had occurred to date and the developing situation. Moore walked back and forth a few times in his office and then turned to Jarvis and yelled, "God dammit." He lowered his voice at the cowering Jarvis, "We'll go with Quinn's plan that Marilyn was with him when he went to New England. It will be a simple story of Quinn getting a speeding ticket in Greenwich on his way to Boston. I'll call Marilyn back and tell her to get with Quinn to iron out the details. I'll tell her to come to work now since I will need her here today anyway. I will instruct her to tell Quinn that after their return to Maryland from the Boston trip, she remained at work while he continued on a few more days of vacation to do whatever he can come up with if someone questions him about that time. Quinn's presently off today on some private business as far as we know but he can be reached. There is no harm in that story." Jarvis asked about the Mustang. Moore looked at him and said, "Quinn took care of that by saying someone had stolen it. That's the story. Do you have that Mr. Jarvis?" Jarvis expected more belittlement from the Colonel for his cover-up of the shooting but it did not

110

happen. He simply nodded and remarked that he would return to his desk and get back to work as if everything was normal. The Colonel smiled and said, "I will be talking to you a little later. We need to straighten out some communication problems you and Quinn have developed over the last few days with me." Moore was about to open up his office door but he stopped in disbelief as Jarvis began telling him a few more details of Quinn's stolen Mustang story. He confessed that he did not tell him about the accident with the Bryants. Jarvis left Moore's office several minutes later like a scolded school boy after a visit to the principal's office.

Quinn listened to the instructions Marilyn relayed to him from the Colonel and thanked her.

"I like having you as my girlfriend and knowing the Colonel likes the story about you being with me in Connecticut on the way to Boston." "The Colonel doesn't need to suspect anything more than just that story. I have to try to protect you now, she said.

" Quinn laughed and agreed and told her that he'd be in touch.

Jarvis returned to his office and tried to look busy. John Moore fumed inside but tried to remain calm as he decided he would concentrate on the Bryant's accident later if the authorities accused Quinn on that charge. Right now he needed damage control for the trip to Connecticut and to find out more about the FBI's next move. He kept thinking of the Wilson graveyard and needed to get to it as soon as possible before the whole plan fell apart.

Joe Walker and Craig Thompson walked into the bank and asked for directions to the office of Mr. Sean Quinn. The receptionist explained that Mr. Quinn worked out of his supervisor's office and that was Mr. Henry Jarvis. She directed both gentlemen towards Jarvis's office. Hank became nauseated when he saw the two men approaching. He remained calm since he didn't know if the two men were the authorities or on banking business. He knew the whole plan rested on his ability to remain calm as possible with anything that came up in the next week or so. He continued to hope that the two men were not authority figures, but he developed an instant headache when they identified themselves and displayed FBI identification credentials. Jarvis smiled and welcomed the two men into his office. He acted very calm and courteous and made sure both men were comfortable before he entertained any questioning. Walker began.

"Is Mr. Sean Quinn employed at this bank and is he available for us to talk to?"

Jarvis said, "Yes, Mr. Quinn is one of our best employees but he is unfortunately away for a day of vacation. I can get in contact with him for you or I can even give you his personal cell phone number if you like. Agent Walker, is there a problem that I need to know about as Mr. Quinn's immediate supervisor?"

"We just need to ask Mr. Quinn some questions about an incident that happened in Greenwich, Connecticut on August 23rd as well as some other questions about his Mustang that he reported stolen the next day," Thompson said.

Jarvis didn't inquire about either incident as he passed over the bank business card with Quinn's personal cell number written on it. Walker said that he already had his number, but both men thanked Jarvis for his cooperation and left.

Jarvis dialed Moore's cell and quickly updated him as he watched the two agents leave the bank. Moore said, "Be at my apartment tonight at 6:00 p.m. sharp," and hung up. Marilyn was aware of Quinn's questioning by the authorities and Moore's requested meeting a few moments later as he relayed the information to her as she drove to the bank. He told her to also call Quinn, wherever he was, and inform him of this evening's meeting so that he could call in.

Quinn saw the call on his cell phone screen from the agent and let it go to voicemail. He decided to wait a little while and finish his breakfast at the diner he was at before returning the call. He went over the dates and events in his head first but then decided to write them down so that he could answer any questions as smoothly as possible if he was questioned over the phone. If they wanted to see him tomorrow at the Bureau Office, he would have more time to substantiate his alibi with the other members of the group. He also knew that they might want to see him immediately and he was prepared to go, but only after he personally conversed with Moore.

Quinn waited about fifteen minutes before he returned the call to Agent Walker. Walker was more pleasant this time and inquired if Quinn had been in Connecticut at the time and dates he asked him previously. Quinn confirmed both.

Walker asked, "Was it business or pleasure?

Quinn answered casually, "Just passing through Connecticut a little too fast on my way to Boston with my girlfriend." Walker asked about the ticket he was given for speeding and Quinn laughed, "Is this all about that? I haven't turned in the $300 yet but I plan to do so in a few days. I'm sorry that I failed to mention that yesterday when you were interrogating me." Quinn had emphasized interrogation but Walker ignored the sarcasm.

"Are you available to come in for some further questioning later on in the day?"

"Well, I'm sort of on a little day vacation in Hagerstown. I could stop by the bureau office tomorrow and answer a few more questions, but I would prefer we talk over the phone now and get it done with." Agent Walker said that he needed to talk to him in person at the bureau office today but later this afternoon would be fine. Quinn tightened inside but casually said, "I can be there approximately at 4:00 p.m." Both men agreed on that time and Quinn ended the conversation.

Walker looked at Thompson and said, "What do you think?"

"I'll give you my evaluation once I see him and observe his body language during the questioning."

Moore listened to Quinn's update of the phone call he had with the agent.

"Sean, you haven't been forthright with me lately concerning the shooting, the accident you had with the Bryants, and now, your relationship with Marilyn. Is there anything else you haven't told me about yet?"

Quinn apologized for the shooting incident. He explained he thought it was necessary not to get caught by that cop. He also said it was necessary to run the Bryants off the road in order to slow their quest to free up the farm. He didn't apologize or even address the Colonel's mentioning of Marilyn since she was fair game and nothing more. He did say that he expected the Colonel to support his alibi for the sake of the task they still had to complete. He calmly told Moore, "Colonel, if I end up in jail, then you all end up in jail."

The Colonel was disgusted by Quinn's statement and hung up the phone. He decided that he would deal with that at another time. Quinn realized that the Colonel had ended the conversation. He headed back to Frederick to keep his appointment with the FBI later in the day.

The Bryants finished their business over the phone with the Connecticut bank representative. The conversation had gone very well and they decided to refinance their Greenwich home for the amount of money they needed to free up the farm. They had been convinced to use a lesser percentage five year variable loan instead of a traditional 15 or 20 year conventional mortgage. Their plan to sell their home within the 5 year span of the loan before the percentage changed seemed the right choice. They were informed that it would take approximately five working days to confirm their qualification and another week to ten days to research both the Greenwich property and the Wilson property in order to close and receive a check from the bank. The whole process would be completed within the next few weeks. They were also informed that Bob would have to sign the papers at the Connecticut bank when they were ready. They called Terry and gave her their banking contacts and the remaining information she needed to protect their interests in acquiring the Wilson property. She, in turn, was to notify the banks that held the mortgages that payment was imminent.

Moore and Jarvis received notification from Breen's office that afternoon that the Bryants were paying off the loan that their bank and the others held on the Wilson property and expected to close prior to the time period the bank had agreed on for foreclosure. That was the second bit of bad news Moore and Jarvis had received today. Several minutes later, Moore called Jarvis to tell him that Quinn was on his way to the FBI Bureau Office to be questioned on a matter that had occurred in Greenwich, Connecticut. Jarvis thought of the old saying, *three strikes and you're out*. The thought of the whole plan coming apart caused him to have to relieve his bowels in the bank men's room. He thought of spending time in prison and almost vomited as he sat on the toilet. Moore sat in his office and tried to keep calm as he devised a tentative plan in his mind. He would go to his apartment at the close of business today, withdraw the cash he had on hand in his safe, and be ready at a moment's notice to disappear if so required. He reconsidered that plan. No one was accusing him of anything and so far, Quinn was just being questioned. He knew Quinn was competent enough to withstand any serious questioning by the authorities.

Marilyn worried about Sean and now began to think of the possibility that she might end up in prison. She was aware of the money in the coffin on the farm but she could always turn evidence that she was forced by Moore to keep quiet under the penalty of bodily harm. But she also knew Sean and Moore were very efficient at adapting to changing situations. She would sit back instead and support any of their decisions that they made. Jarvis, on the other hand, was an idiot and she cared less about what would happen to him. But she knew that if one fell, they all would fall. She realized that she still had to tolerate Jarvis.

Sean arrived at the FBI Office approximately five minutes early. As he asked for the office of Agent Walker, Agent Thompson greeted him and asked him to follow him to

115

Walker's office. The agent thanked him for coming in. Quinn remained calm and polite and said, "I always follow orders and I'm here as requested." Walker slowly opened a file as he noticed Thompson approaching. He wanted to keep Quinn's anticipation as high as possible. Quinn didn't follow his lead and knew the agent was going to play a head game with him. He had observed the best Army interrogators in Afghanistan and Iraq query suspected terrorists and saboteurs. Walker wasn't in their league, but he would remain relaxed to see what the other guy, Thompson, was going to be like. Quinn thought, *was this going to be the hard questioning good cop – bad cop scenario or just two inexperienced agents trying to get lucky?* Quinn enjoyed games better when they were either life threatening or sexual in nature. This one wasn't on either of those scales so he sat back and decided to enjoy their game. Thompson began with the same questions Walker had asked over the phone hours before about his Mustang. Quinn didn't complain and answered as he had done previously.

"I haven't decided yet whether I am going to keep it or to sell it outright." Quinn casually remarked that he wasn't sure how much he should ask for it. Thompson quickly butted in.

"Do you own a pistol?"

"I have a pistol license and I just ordered a brand new .10 mm pistol. I had one in the service and wanted another one similar to that one. I should be able to pick it up as soon as I have been checked out by you guys and the State Police."

Walker asked, "Where is your .9 mm pistol?"

Quinn looked up at Walker and said without losing eye contact, "I don't have a .9 mm pistol and if I did, agent, you'd be asking me to produce the pistol with the recorded serial number on it now, wouldn't you?" Quinn looked at both agents and asked what the intent of the questioning was. Walker said that he was here to answer questions not ask them. Quinn stood up but was immediately calmed by agent Thompson.

"My partner was out of line. Please, Mr. Quinn, sit down and relax a little." Thompson even offered him a soft drink. Quinn realized the good cop-bad cop approach had started and relaxed. *These guys were amateurs for sure,* he thought.

Walker asked Quinn, "What was the intent of your trip to Boston on the 23rd of August?"

"I took my girlfriend to see the Orioles play the Red Sox, take in a few sights and restaurants and show her where I had grown up before I moved to Baltimore. I have some relatives there that I was going to look up but never did because my girl was called back to finish a bank deal that Mr. Moore needed completed, so back we came. I took a little time to look around at different auto dealerships to trade in my car, which was very expensive to fuel on my New England trip, by the way. And then it got stolen." He also said that he needed to take some time to take care of some personal business. One was to buy a new pistol that he planned to shoot at the rod and gun club where he often spent time. He looked at both agents and said, "Check that out and if there are no more questions, I would appreciate your permission to leave. You both realize that you ruined my one day of vacation. I still have time for dinner with my girlfriend unless you two plan to ruin that too." Walker excused Quinn but told him to stay in town in case they wanted to ask him some more questions. Quinn looked at both agents again and said, "I'm not going anywhere and if you need to ask any more questions, you can contact the Bank's legal office and ask their attorney's permission to talk to me." Quinn then informed them, "I will consult with the bank's legal counsel early tomorrow morning."

Thompson said, "You don't need an attorney. We only needed you to answer a few more questions."

"You two look, and act, more like inexperienced keystone cops." Quinn rose from the seat and exited the office casually. He never waited for any remarks from either agent and took his time walking out of the building. Walker turned to Thompson and asked, "Well, what do you think? Is he lying?"

"He's a cool customer; I'll give him that, but let's see what his girlfriend has to say in the morning."

At exactly 6:00 p.m., Jarvis and Porter were sitting in John

Moore's living room. No one said a word until Moore's cell phone rang. He answered and immediately put it on speaker so all present could hear and be heard as necessary. Sean detailed the experience he had with the two agents and knew that he would be under surveillance but the two agents didn't have anything on him except to hope that he was the guilty suspect. Sean even gloated a little on how he had handled the agents.

Moore asked, "Did you gloat as well when you were with Marilyn last evening at her apartment."

"You are out of line Colonel." Quinn paused, "excuse me, Mr. Moore. I don't appreciate your tone and my personal life being discussed by you for any reason."

Moore began to act as if he was still the commanding officer chewing out an enlisted NCO and wanted to embarrass Marilyn in front of Jarvis on her indiscretion when Quinn told him, "Knock it off. Your fucking Army days are over and I need your advice and intelligence to get us past this situation in order to complete the task we all are involved in."

Moore was both impressed and a little embarrassed by Quinn's response. He said, "I want you to update Marilyn on her role as the girlfriend who accompanied you on your trip. I don't know how we are going to account for her being in the car when you were stopped. I'm sure the arresting officer noted you as a single person in the car." Quinn was silent as he contemplated an explanation.

"I'll swear that I was asleep in the back seat and never stirred when Sean was stopped and given the ticket," Marilyn said.

Moore looked over at her and said, "Again Marilyn, I'm sure that the trooper double checked the back seat looking for another occupant."

"I could have been under a black blanket that Sean had in the Mustang and the trooper could have missed me. I could have kept still as to not alarm the trooper. I could say that I was just plain asleep in the early morning hours."

Moore started to shake his head negatively but stopped.

"It might work. Sean, do you have a black blanket in the car?"

"I do have a navy blue blanket that looks almost black that I

118

took out of the Mustang. It's in my apartment."

Moore instructed Marilyn to be at work on time and be prepared to answer questions tomorrow. He instructed Quinn to visit Marilyn's apartment tonight for dinner about 8:00 p.m. and stay there until eleven or so and return to his own apartment for the night. Moore wanted any authority figure following Quinn to realize that Porter was really his girlfriend. He instructed Jarvis to watch the apartment to see if Quinn was still being tailed by the agents.

Jarvis said, "Sir, I can watch until 9:00 p.m. and then I have to leave for a personal engagement I have planned." Moore looked over at him sitting on the couch and stared with an angry look on his face.

"Hank, I need you to be there until Quinn leaves at 11:00 p.m." Quinn spoke up and said that Jarvis would only be needed for an hour or so to see if the agents were actually tailing him. He only needed Jarvis to confirm the tail. Quinn continued, "I don't want Jarvis being caught observing the agents watching me at Marilyn's." He began telling Marilyn what the story was going to be if she was questioned by the agents. Moore interrupted and said he could do that later. Quinn insisted that all the parties should listen in and evaluate his story to make sure it passed the litmus test. He also feared they would be tapping Marilyn's phone soon. He cautioned Moore and Jarvis that they could be at risk as well. After approximately five minutes, all of them were in agreement on the details of the Boston trip. Moore ended the call with Quinn. It was 6:40 p.m. He looked at Jarvis and told him to case Quinn's apartment area and be sharp when he did it. Jarvis left on cue. Marilyn began to move as well when Moore touched her arm gently and said, "I forgive you for your indiscretion with Quinn."

She looked at him and said, "I like Sean Quinn but I didn't screw him so I don't need your forgiveness."

Moore was surprised and somewhat delighted to hear her statement. He let her leave and told her to put on a real good act for the agents if they questioned her tomorrow. She left without saying a word. Moore contemplated what she had

119

said. Maybe Quinn hadn't made love to her yet or maybe she was lying but he didn't pick up on it. *Whichever the case, he thought, when the money was in her hands and she saw the amount he possessed, she would be sticking around him more than Quinn.* He knew Quinn wouldn't be taking her with him anywhere. He was too free and would never be tied down to her kind. *She was just a trophy to Quinn,* he thought. She was something very serious for him and he was going to make sure he didn't drive her away. He would handle her as he did when she was involved with Wilson. She'd be back in a short time. In the meantime, he needed to get through this crisis with the help of all of them.

Walker and Thompson observed Marilyn enter her apartment shortly after 7:15 p.m. A few minutes later, Quinn approached in his new silver BMW and parked on the street. He rang the doorbell and within a few moments, disappeared into the apartment building. Several lights went on and off as the men watched Marilyn's apartment. Jarvis slowly drove by and immediately recognized the government sedan parked on the opposite side of the street, but close enough for the two agents to have an unhindered view of the apartment building. He didn't need to stay now since he had just confirmed the surveillance was happening. He was relieved because he didn't want to be late to his appointment with his college student. He had thought about it all day. He became aroused just thinking about the sweet young man he had fallen for the first time he had sex with him. Jarvis called Quinn and simply said that he was right. Quinn closed the cell and asked Marilyn for something to drink. She offered dinner but he declined because his stomach wasn't really up for an evening meal.

They both went over the story several times as instructed by Moore. They then just kept telling stories and getting to know each other better. Neither one of them indicated any desire for sex or dinner, but were content just talking. Eventually, Marilyn made a few sandwiches later in the evening with some soft drinks. Quinn was observed by the two agents leaving at 11:00 p.m. They followed him until he arrived at his apartment. He exited the BMW and entered his apartment, went to the window overlooking the street and observed the FBI agents slowly drive by and leave the area. He returned to his BMW and set out for the college campus. He didn't know what Jarvis was up to, but he had an idea where he would be this evening. He knew Jarvis hung around the campus and figured he had found someone to fulfill his needs. He hoped it wasn't another homosexual fulfillment but the way Jarvis had been acting recently, especially telling Moore he had other things to do, he figured he was up to something. He didn't need the spineless queer getting picked up for any lewd acts. He was concerned that Jarvis would spill his guts to the cops if he was ever hard pressed by the police who knew his association with him.

He cruised around campus but concentrated on circling the main entrance looking for Jarvis's car. Around midnight, he saw a car he recognized approaching from the opposite direction. He passed the car and observed another man in the car with Jarvis. He watched in his rear view mirror until Jarvis pulled over and stopped. He immediately pulled over and exited the BMW. He observed a figure leave the car and begin to walk back on campus. Jarvis quickly drove away. Quinn concentrated on the figure and began to quicken his pace until he was within one hundred feet from the college student. He noticed several other students walking and talking in the vicinity but kept his attention on the student that had left Jarvis's car. The student turned down a side street and began to pull out his electronic key to enter the common door to the quad apartments he was apparently assigned to. The area was poorly lit. Quinn quickly overtook the student. He hit him from behind, which winded the kid. The student fell forward and landed face down. Quinn put his knee to the back of the student and then grabbed his hair and jerked back his head. The college student was completely pinned. The student began to yell when Quinn applied more pressure to his back while pulling his head further back, encouraging the student to be quiet. The student immediately obeyed. Quinn spread the student's legs with his other hand and grabbed his groin from behind and squeezed. "Leave Jarvis alone, he's mine. Fuck him one more time and your dick will be in the river. Do you understand?" The student remained quiet until Quinn squeezed harder. The student groaned and whispered he understood. He instructed the student to remain on the ground face down. He threatened him with death if he turned over and tried to recognize him. Just to make sure he understood his last instruction, he performed one quick and last move. He pushed hard and quick on his back, jerked his head a little further and squeezed his groin one more time before he released his grip. He quickly exited the campus and returned to his apartment hoping there would be no sign of the FBI at his place. Upon entering his apartment, he called Jarvis. Several rings later Jarvis answered and began to complain to Quinn about the hour. As he rambled on, Quinn stopped him short and simply said, "I banged up your student bitch tonight so don't go into any story about how I woke you up. Stay away from that little shit before you get caught on campus by security or worse yet, the local cops. If I catch you doing it again before we finish our job, I will kill your bitch, fuck you up and get Moore to cut you out." Jarvis began to protest but Quinn hung up the phone.

Chance Meeting

At 9:00 a.m. the two agents had requested the bank receptionist give them directions to Miss Marilyn Porter's office. Within a few minutes, they had identified themselves to Porter and were sitting in her office. They were very cordial to Marilyn as they began their questioning.

Agent Thompson asked, "What's your relationship with Sean Quinn?"

"We have been dating for a few months." Thompson asked where she had been on the morning of August 23rd. Marilyn paused and then replied that she had been in a car with Sean on their way to Boston.

Walker said, "Miss Porter, Sean Quinn was reported alone according to the report filed by the Connecticut State Trooper who stopped him for exceeding the speed limit on I-95 in Greenwich." Marilyn blushed and smirked a little at Walker's statement. Walker and Thompson picked up on the blush and the smirk.

Walker asked, "Have I said something funny or embarrassing to you, Miss Porter?" She smiled and slowly began to answer while glancing back and forth between agents.

"Well, Agent Walker, if you must know, I was sleeping in the back of Sean's car when he was stopped by the police officer. I was partially clothed and was covered by a blanket and surely didn't want to pop my head out and, first alarm the trooper and secondly, have to explain why I was in my bra and panties in Sean's back seat. I had undressed to keep from wrinkling my clothes and I did feel comfortable doing that in his car. That is until the policeman pulled us over."

Both men looked at each other and smiled which further made Marilyn blush. Marilyn had convinced them so far by the cute blush and embarrassing look she had engineered for the agents. Thompson pushed a little further when he asked about the game at Fenway Park in Boston.

"Oh, the Red Sox won and the place was going wild because they had come from behind." He asked her what the score was.

"Oh, it was six to five or something like that."

Thompson was an avid Orioles fan and remembered the score and the game when Boston had pulled off a ninth inning win. He looked at Walker and nodded in agreement. Walker had one more question. He asked who could confirm their presence in Boston.

"The only two persons who knew of our trip were Mr. Moore and Mr. Jarvis."

"What about the people you were going to visit?" Thompson asked.

"We never visited anyone. We ate lunch, saw the afternoon game and had to return to Frederick right away. Mr. Moore called me on my cell and informed me that he had an emergency task for me," Marilyn said and smiled. Both men thanked her for her time and left the bank. She called Moore and Jarvis to inform them of her statements to the FBI agents. Walker and Thompson talked as they drove back to their office.

"I wish that she would sleep in my back seat sometime." Thompson said.

"She acted legitimately and she almost convinced me but I still want you to check further into her background. I'm going to do some more checking on Quinn and also call the crime lab that was checking out the Mustang at the Frederick Police Station. I'm prepared to look elsewhere should the Mustang be found clean, Walker said.

Moore called Terry Breen's office to ask her if she was free for lunch as he had a proposition for the Bryants that he would like her to present to them. She asked, "I'm curious, Mr. Moore. Can you give me some details of your proposal?" Moore declined. He admitted that his people were finishing up the proposal and that it would be prepared around 12:30 p.m. "Is Hayward's Pub acceptable to you if you would be so inclined to honor me with your presence for lunch?" She accepted his lunch invitation and hung up. She immediately called her clients at the hospital and informed them of her

124

impending lunch appointment. They wondered why one of the banks would be attempting to contact their attorney concerning a new offer for the property. They questioned Terry who said that it would not hurt to listen to Mr. Moore's offer, even though she knew they were set in freeing up the land and building a new retirement home once Bob had healed. She reminded them that she had hoped the farm would have become a working dairy farm again and she was very pleased that they still strongly intended to live on the land and keep it a dairy farm. She also joked that she hadn't had a business lunch date in weeks. Amy told her to get back in touch with them at her earliest convenience to inform them of Mr. Moore's offer.

Agent Walker finished talking to the forensic lab technician on the phone who indicated that the Mustang they had investigated was clean. The gun powder residue Agent Walker had hoped to find in the glove compartment, trunk or floor was not present. The only items found were some missed food particles and a few human hairs that were Quinn's. Walker asked the lab technician if he had found any women's hair and if he had noticed anything out of the ordinary in the Mustang. The tech said that he came up with nothing. Walker had one other lead that he needed to follow up on which was Quinn's military record. He requested his file from the Army records administration and had the file in his computer within the hour. Upon review, he could find nothing out of the ordinary and was impressed with Quinn's accommodations and write ups. He was still interested in Moore's recommendation in Quinn's record and would follow through with that to see if the two Moores' were connected. Further requests to the Army for an electronic copy of Colonel Moore's military record satisfied his suspicion that the two men were in fact the same man. Further review of Moore's records detailed his position and the groups he commanded in Iraq in 2003 and 2004. He was further intrigued when he viewed some more army records that listed the members that had been assigned to Mr. Moore's command. Two individuals that stuck out in his review were First

Lieutenant Marilyn Porter and Sergeant Major Henry Jarvis. Walker called Thompson into his office and identified the four individuals he had researched in the Army records database. Thompson was given the task of researching each one's entire military history to see what other commonalities could be construed from the records. The search would take the rest of the day as Thompson systematically did his research on the four individuals.

Terry entered Hayward's Pub and approached the reservation desk. She identified herself and said that she had a business lunch with Mr. John Moore. The hostess had been alerted earlier by Moore and escorted her to his table. Moore rose and greeted her ever so politely. They entertained some small talk concerning the hot weather they had been having and discussed the various soft and hard drinks that were available from the menu. Both ordered lunch and shortly, their drinks were delivered to the table. During lunch, Moore conveyed some interesting information to Terry. He first asked her to inform the Bryants for him that he was sorry that they had been involved in an unfortunate accident. He wished Mr. Bryant a full and speedy recovery. Then he got down to the business at hand. He informed Terry that he had done some further research and that the farmland, immediately around the burned out farmhouse, would have to be inspected by some Maryland State agencies to confirm that there were no environmental issues with the property. Terry stopped sipping her wine and asked, "What type of environmental issues are you referring to, Mr. Moore?"

Moore explained with a concerned tone in his voice, "The soil and water in the immediate area of the farmhouse will have to be tested. That means if any contaminates are found like lead, arsenic or others, then building a home in the immediate area would not be approved by the city agencies until those readings were corrected. They would be unable to get building permits. That would mean, Miss Breen, that your clients would have to consider either cleaning up the location, which can be very

126

expensive and time consuming, or building on another location on the property which would mean further costs for testing the new area being considered as a building site for their retirement house. It could further cause delays because each test takes many weeks to complete. It could sometimes take months I'm told, because of the different agencies involved and commissions required to approve them meet monthly and sometimes, as I was further informed, miss a month or two delaying it even further." He smiled as he said that the Frederick and State agencies were very slow handling procedures such as these. Terry controlled her urge to tell him that his tone and facial expressions were very irritating as she sat there listening.

"The cemetery is another issue. Even though I understand that the individuals interred there are family to the Bryants, I am prepared, if they so agreed, to pay all the expenses to intern the veterans at Arlington or any cemetery of their choosing as part of the deal to purchase the land. I believe that is a generous offer, Miss Breen." Terry looked at him as their food was delivered.

"What are the figures you are offering to my clients?"

He looked her straight in the eye and said, "I am initially prepared to offer your clients $900,000 for the property including moving their hero relatives to any cemetery with full military honors. I would consider it an honor, as a retired Army Colonel, to be able to offer my services to them."

"And what will you be doing with the property if my clients agree to accept your offer to purchase it, Mr. Moore?"

"I always thought that I wanted to live on it myself. Maybe even turn it back into a dairy farm again. Of course, I'd have to hire someone to run it for me, but that is what I was thinking, Miss Breen."

"That is a very generous offer but didn't one of your employees, Mr. Quinn, as I remember, represent a developer that wanted to purchase the place for the foreclosure price?"

"That's true, Miss Breen, but when I investigated the land further and had the opportunity to view it myself, and I really fell in love with the place. I did consider trying to buy it for the foreclosure price, but I feel that is a conflict of interest with my bank and I have waited until I knew your clients were serious about paying off the lien on the farm. This is strictly a real estate offer and it can be negotiated with them if they are interested," he said as he signaled for the waiter.

"Miss Breen, all I ask is that you take the offer I am making as an opportunity to save your clients the aggravation that is bound to develop now that the land has to be tested and not yet recertified for new construction."

"Mr. Moore, are you prepared to go through the same ordeal to get the property recertified?"

He smiled and said, "I have all the time and the money to accomplish it, Miss Breen." The waiter approached the table and stood by Moore. He reached into his suit jacket, drew out his wallet, picked out a $100 bill and handed it to the waiter.

"Take care of this young lady and serve her anything else she so desires. Miss Breen, please excuse me. I have another engagement to attend to. Please pass my offer on to your clients and call me at your earliest convenience with their response. I have enjoyed you company very much. Have a good day." Moore quickly stood up from the table, leaving his untouched meal and exited the pub.

Terry Breen sat there a little perplexed due to his quick departure. She looked at the waiter and said, "I'll have another glass of wine and would like to view the dessert list, please." The waiter nodded while Terry sat there contemplating why Moore was so interested in the property and what was he really up to. She spent some time with Ed Manning on the phone and also directing several law clerks to do some research on specific points Moore had brought to her attention before she called her clients.

She called them a few hours after her lunch with Moore. She explained what had occurred and that Moore's suggestive manner made her curious as to why he was so interested in the property. They listened and responded that they would discuss the matter and get back to her before the close of business tomorrow. They wanted to make sure that they still felt passionate about living on the farmland during their retirement years. Mr. Moore's offer was tempting to them but not within the real price of the land as compared to current real estate listings they had been informed of and had researched themselves.

Amy sat in the hospital room and quietly contemplated what had just transpired. She wasn't upset, but had second thoughts as to her previous feelings about getting back to her roots in Frederick. Bob sat up in the hospital bed and told her that Moore must know something about the property that they were unaware of.

"Did your brothers have any geological tests performed on the property or has there ever been any serious commercial business offers made to them or even your father before he died?"

Amy couldn't remember any but she said, "I'll call Benjamin. I don't want to call Bruce because I don't want to get into the cemetery issues right now. Benjamin should have more information on the farm. He handled most of the books and organized the mortgages against the farm."

She called Benjamin and explained the recent interest in the farm by Moore and said, "I want to know if you had done tests or had commercial offers when the farm was working and even before Dad died?"

"Amy, the farm's value was based on the land and its ability to support dairy farming or crop growing. There is no hidden, oil, gold, silver, copper or any of those types of items on the farm. If there is, I don't know about it. We'd never requested any testing. Are you still going to keep the farm despite all that has happened to Bob?"

"Both of us are still in agreement to keep and live on the farm."

She realized, at that moment, that her phone call to Benjamin convinced her of that. She didn't wait until the next day. She called Miss Breen and told her to inform Mr. Moore that they weren't interested.

Craig Thompson had spent several hours researching the four individuals Walker asked him to investigate. He compiled four file folders of the information he had gathered and placed them on Walker's desk.

Joe looked up, "What'd you find?"

"I found some interesting associations between the four of them and I think that we should bring all of them in for a questioning session."

"Show me what you found."

He began, "Moore was the commanding officer of the others. He was in command of a special financial group that cataloged captured money for shipment to the U. S. Treasury Office. Colonel Moore was very efficient and a good officer according to the report, but there was one letter of reprimand in his military file for allowing several soldiers to almost get away with stealing counterfeit money. The men were caught but Moore took a hit for it. It probably cost him a promotion. Marilyn Porter was a First Lieutenant in Moore's command and she now works at the bank for him. Sergeant Major Henry Jarvis, better known as Hank Jarvis, was the top sergeant in Moore's command and guess who was a Staff Sergeant temporarily assigned to Moore's group while he was recuperating from some minor combat wounds? None other than our boy Sean Quinn," he said while smiling at Walker.

Walker pondered and looked at Craig Thompson.

"All of them here in Frederick, Maryland and employed at the local bank. He corrected himself and said, "They are running the bank. Is this a coincidence or should we be looking for something else?" he mumbled to Thompson.

"I would like to have them rounded up and all brought in for questioning," Thompson said. Walker told him he did too, but they couldn't, because they hadn't done anything wrong. Walker told Thompson to check on the military records of Frederick residents that had been in the Army from 2001 through 2007.

"Maybe he should look at the Maryland Reserves. I'm sure there are Frederick residents on that list."

"I'll have the back shift administrative people run off different sorts so both of us can review them in the morning," Thompson said.

"And I'll contact the Greenwich Police in the morning and tell them that we have some interesting information, but they cannot make a collar just yet unless the picture I'm going to send can be identified by the officer that had been shot," Walker advised.

"Well," Thompson said, "I didn't have anything planned for tonight, so I'll stay at the office to do some more research."

Walker said, "Okay, go for it Craig," and left him to his task.

John Moore was about to leave his office for home when his secretary informed him that Miss Breen was on his phone. Moore immediately picked up.

"Miss Breen, I'm glad to hear from you so soon."

"Mr. Moore, I just finished talking with my clients and unfortunately they have declined your generous offer."

Moore said, controlling his tone, "I'm very disappointed but I am prepared to offer them $1 million for the property. I'll await their response on that offer, Miss Breen. It was very nice talking to you." She heard the phone go dead. Terry was perplexed by his abruptness and slowly hung up the phone. She decided to call the Bryants in the morning as she began to prepare to leave the office. Moore was irritated and that had caused him to quickly hang up on Terry. He called Marilyn and asked if she would care to have dinner with him. She did not hesitate because she felt she needed to keep in close contact with Moore now that there were some difficult problems ahead of them to solve. She agreed to meet him at a local restaurant they both enjoyed. Moore was pleased that she accepted, but would have rather had her back at his apartment for dinner. He thought that maybe she would grant him some time at her apartment later after they had eaten.

Craig Thompson worked until 7:35 p.m. His eyes were strained by all the data he had read over the past several hours.

131

He looked over the four sets of records he had compiled earlier. Quinn and Jarvis both had received purple hearts in Iraq. Quinn had received another in Afghanistan with a Bronze Star. Jarvis had been hit by sniper fire. He felt a little guilty checking out these veterans who had definitely done their duty. All four files indicated that the individuals were raised up in other states. Quinn was brought up in Boston, Porter in New York, and Moore in Philadelphia. He searched a little more and found that Jarvis had been brought up in Cape Cod, Massachusetts. The bank employment records indicated that Moore had been offered the VP bank job right out of the service when he retired. Craig guessed that Moore had hired every one of them. He was tired now and decided to get a bite to eat and a beer. He had also almost completed compiling a list of soldiers alphabetically, 'A through V', who had seen active service between the dates requested by Walker. No one in particular stood out so far as an associate of the four individuals he was concentrating on. He figured he'd complete the review of soldiers with last names starting with 'W through Z' quickly in the morning. He left the office and headed to one of the local watering holes.

Terry finished her work at the office and decided that she needed some dinner and maybe a cocktail. She left the office and headed for the first quiet looking bar and grille she could find before she went home. She decided on a quick bite and a drink at Hayward's Pub. She'd been there for lunch and really didn't want to drive across town to find another place for a quick meal. She entered Hayward's and sat at the bar next to a gentleman who she hadn't seen before. He didn't acknowledge her presence at first as he drank a tall beer and munched on a sandwich. She ordered a margarita and asked for the bar menu. "You shouldn't order the sandwich supreme; there isn't anything supreme about it," he said.
She looked over to see the young man smiling as he sipped some more of his beer. She smiled and acknowledged his advice. She held out her hand and said, "I'm Terry Breen and

who might you be?"

"My name is Craig Thompson, FBI."

"Wow, I'm just a local attorney. I never met an FBI agent before," she said as she laughed in mockery. Thompson laughed as well.

"I guess you're not impressed as much as I am that you are an attorney."

Terry looked at him to see if he was mocking her, but he looked generally sincere.

"I'd recommend the chef's salad," he said.

"Good pick, I'll go with that," she said as she turned to the bar attendant who took the menu from her.

"So what brings you out to Hayward's Pub at 8 o'clock at night besides a beer and a sandwich?" she asked while taking another sip of her margarita.

"I was investigating some files and was wrapped up in them until my stomach growled and my eyes started hurting."

"I'm in the same situation," she said as she relaxed more looking at this pretty good looking guy. She paused and said, "Are you really an FBI agent?" He opened his sport coat enough for her to see his concealed pistol as he pulled out his shield and identification.

"Yep, 100% FBI." She felt a bit embarrassed that she had asked and began to explain when he cut her off and said, "You have the right to see my identification and you were smart to ask for it." She reached into her purse and handed him a Manning, Watson and Breen Attorneys at Law Business card with her name on it. He examined it and made a comment, "Wow, you are a full partner in the group. I'm impressed." She laughed and said, "Unfortunately no. I have worked for the group for almost a year now and my father is the full partner."

"So you're the son your dad didn't have," he said and laughed.

"No, I have a brother who didn't like law and he is a surgeon in Baltimore. He's got a son and another kid on the way so my dad is all set with the name carry on thing and all."

He laughed and said, "My mother was a secretary for the FBI office in Richmond and my dad was a truck driver for a local

delivery service, so I guess I followed my mother's career."
They both laughed.

"Would you like to sit at a table so that we could have a better conversation?"

"Agent Thompson, are you hitting on me?" He quickly looked both ways as if acting like a secret agent and said, "Yes, but I need to interrogate you first for more information."

"Why would you need to interrogate an attorney," she giggled.

"Because I need to know a lot more about you so that I can build up enough courage to ask you out some evening for dinner," he responded as she observed his bright blue eyes that seemed to go right through her.

"Okay interrogate me."

The evening went well for the two of them until she looked at her watch.

"My, my, it's almost 10:30 p.m. I have to get up early tomorrow," she said and then frowned. He smiled.

"I've really enjoyed your conversation and company, Terry. I would like to ask you out for dinner some night soon. Maybe I can call on you?" She looked at him for a second too long until she thought she made him uncomfortable. She realized that she was quickly looking though her mental appointment book and started to laugh.

"What's so funny?"

"The look on your face." She explained her pause and said that she would be delighted for him to call on her and she would enjoy having dinner with him anytime. She began to pull out some cash to cover her tab when he put his hand on hers and said, "No, let me pay. I appreciated your company and the tab is on me." She liked the touch of his warm hand on hers. She thanked him for his gesture to pay. He held her hand until she said, "If you don't let my hand go Craig, I won't be able to get home, go to work tomorrow and wait for your phone call." He was embarrassed but she loved every bit of it. He stood up as she did, to leave. He kissed her on the cheek lightly. She could smell the scent of his cologne and she stirred inside like she hadn't done in a long time. She smiled as she turned to leave and thought that this had been a very good evening. She wanted more of Agent Craig Thompson. He watched the slim beauty as she walked away. He also stirred inside and planned to call her first thing in the morning at work to set up a real dinner date. He wanted more of Attorney Terry Breen.

Loose Plans

Marilyn finished her last morsel of the late dinner she had with Moore. He stared at her as she finished. He'd been quiet during most of the dinner making Marilyn very uncomfortable.

"You must have been hungry the way you finished your dinner in such haste," he said. He'd hardly touched his as he was concentrating more on how to convince the Bryants to accept any of the many offers he was prepared to make to get the property in his name.

"Do you care for dessert?" She declined.

"Do you want to be dropped off at your apartment or would you care to stay the night at mine?" She looked up in disbelief that he would have even considered sleeping with her again after he suspected her involvement with Quinn.

"Are you surprised that I would ask you to spend the night at my apartment, Marilyn? You must understand that I love you and will always love you."

She smiled and was beginning to say something when he cut her short by calling the waiter over for the check. She realized he did not want to talk about her involvement with Quinn and he was ready to go back to his apartment. She didn't really want to make love to him tonight, but she resolved herself to it to keep within the inner circle of the game they were in at the moment. They left for his apartment.

Quinn left several messages on both Marilyn's apartment and cell phones. He realized that she must be with the Colonel and he would have to share her occasionally. He knew he wasn't in love with her, but she was very good at love making and a nice person to be with. He also knew that if she found out he had blown Todd's head half off in Iraq, she would probably blow his alibi and jeopardize the whole operation to get the $11 million stored in the Wilson cemetery. Quinn was a little hungry. He closed his cell phone and spotted the sign for Hayward's Pub. He pulled over up the street and was about to exit his car when he spotted Terry leaving the pub. He stayed in his car and watched her drive off. He then noticed Agent Craig Thompson walk out and open a car door a few cars down from where she had just been parked. He wondered whether they had been together, or was it just a coincidence, as he waited for Thompson to drive off.

Amy left the hospital with her children after spending the entire day there. She had a lengthy conversation with her son and daughter during their drive to the motel. All three talked about Moore's offer and definitely agreed that there was no amount of money he could offer them that would change their minds. Amy also planned to call Bruce first thing in the morning to find out any last requests for the re-interment of his son's remains.

Agent Joe Walker had turned in for the evening. As he laid there wide awake and watched his wife fall off to sleep, he thought about all the possible connections between the four people he had Thompson investigating. He wondered if he could find a link to tie all of them together. He thought of his days in the Reserves and some of the friends he had lost in 2003. He also thought that he should make an effort this Veteran's Day to pay tribute to his fallen comrades at the local cemetery.

Moore didn't approach Marilyn when she got into bed. He laid there until she made the first move by gently touching him. He forced himself to keep from being aroused until she performed oral sex on him. He became rigid and mounted her quickly. He actually performed well enough for Marilyn to enjoy part of the experience until he climaxed, which was almost as soon as he mounted her. He fell asleep in just a few minutes after that as Marilyn stared at the ceiling and thought of all that money she would be getting and how everything would soon change. She looked over at him and thought to herself that it couldn't change soon enough for her, especially after what she had just endured.

The next morning, Amy talked with Bruce and informed him that Mr. Moore from the Colony Bank was still very interested in the property. Bruce didn't care very much and said, "Amy, I don't know the guy. He isn't anyone Benjamin and I ever dealt with. My immediate family has agreed that Todd should be interred in Arlington. Please have Attorney Breen finalize the arrangements for that to take place soon." Amy explained that she would do as they all requested and also confirmed what the family decided for the other relatives in the family plot.

"Amy, we would all like to see Arnold and Uncle Herman buried next to Todd. You know, a headstone for Jeremiah should be placed in the Frederick cemetery alongside the Union and Confederate soldiers that are buried there. Does that sound alright with you?"

"Yes that would be fine, but what about Benjamin?"

"I already talked to him and he is in agreement with me about Arnold and Herman and he liked the idea of a headstone in the Civil War section of the Frederick cemetery for Jeremiah." With that settled, Amy called Terry to inform her of the family's decision and to instruct her to finalize the arrangements.

Terry returned the call as soon as she received her message. She informed Amy that she would have the Frederick Funeral Home arrange all the necessary court orders, permits, contacts with the appropriate cemetery administrations and transportation requirements. She also said that the entire movement would be under the observation of an Army Honor Guard assigned from the Maryland Reserves. Amy thanked her and now felt comfortable about the final interment arrangements and schedule she knew Terry would carry out in the next few days so that the family could make arrangements to attend if they so desired.

Moore called Terry's office from his cell to get an update on whether the Bryants were interested in his latest offer. Terry took the call immediately.

"Hello Mr. Moore. I'll get to the point since I know why you called. I want you to understand that the Wilson property isn't for sale and that my clients are set on building on the property in the near future." He graciously accepted her information although he wanted to explode inside.

He asked, "Miss Breen, are they going to keep the cemetery as it is?" Terry thought that question was odd for him to ask so she pursued a little more for him to explain his question.

"Why would you ask that, Mr. Moore?"

"Well, Miss Breen, I am a military career Army officer and I am curious if they have decided to move the soldiers to another cemetery."

"Mr. Moore, I am making arrangements for the three bodies to be interred at Arlington and a headstone to be placed in Frederick for the civil war veteran as a memorial." Moore responded cordially.

"Thank you for telling me. I'm pleased to hear that news." Moore sounded pleased to Terry but inside, he was panicking since now he needed another plan. He tried one more time.

"I would also like your clients to know that I am prepared to go higher if they change their minds. I would also be honored if I could attend the removal and witness the shipment of the Wilson men to their final resting place." Terry thought that also was a little odd for him to say.

"Thank you Mr. Moore, but this is going to be a very private ceremony only attended by the family and the Maryland Reserve Guard of three to four men." She advised that the offer of his personal services wouldn't be required or requested. She bid him a good day and hung up. Moore slammed the phone down hard enough for it to crack, rendering the receiver useless. Marilyn heard the noise from her desk several offices away. She casually walked over to Moore's secretary and remarked about him slamming down the phone. The secretary said that Mr. Moore had been talking to an attorney in charge of the Wilson property. Marilyn knocked on the open door to Moore's office and asked to see him on a private matter. Moore signaled for her to come in and close the door behind her.

Marilyn looked at him and asked, "What happened? Why did you slam the phone down like that?"

"I just finished a conversation with Attorney Breen. I want the group to meet tonight for dinner. I want to be out in the open in case the FBI is still observing Quinn's place or your apartment. I plan to buy dinner and use the noise of the restaurant as a cover while I ask all of you to contribute to a plan on how we are going to act quickly to get at that coffin in the Wilson Cemetery. I want you to make the reservations somewhere out of town for all of us at 7:00 p.m. in my name. Do you understand?" She nodded, turned and opened the office door and thanked him for his time as she smiled and walked past his secretary.

Quinn and Jarvis were in Jarvis's office pretending to be working. All the time they were waiting for news of Moore's success on getting a bid on the Wilson property. Marilyn called Jarvis and informed him of the dinner plan and advised that the Bryants had declined the offer. Jarvis turned to Quinn as he hung up.

"The bid was rejected. We meet at 7:00 p.m."

"Shit, that's bad news. I wonder what the old man has up his sleeve." Quinn asked, and shook his head knowing that it was going to get ugly now. He knew he would more than likely be the spearhead to carry out the plan Moore had probably already conceived for him.

Joe Walker and Craig Thompson went over all the information both men had gathered since they had last met to discuss Moore and his group at the bank. Thompson had more information than Walker expected. Upon hearing all the facts he had gathered, Walker was sure there was something more than just coincidence that connected the four individuals. While looking at the data Thompson had supplied, Walker noticed some names that he had forgotten to review in his list from "W through Z" of reservists that had served in Iraq. One of the names that he observed was Todd Wilson. He had known him vaguely now that he remembered. Walker remembered the large military funeral that was held for him in Frederick before Walker shipped out to Iraq. He recalled that he was buried on the farm where he grew up and next to family members that had died in other wars. He remembered the twenty-five or so active duty soldiers that paid tribute to the fallen Captain at the farm.

Thompson asked, "Why are you staring into space?" He quickly explained and moved on to the rest of the names and information on the list but he felt that Wilson's name would give them some clues as to what these people all had in common.

Terry was thinking about Craig. She decided to call him instead of waiting for him to call. As she dialed his number, she thought, this was the 21st century and a woman could call a man and set up a date. Thompson had just entered his office when he heard the phone ring. He picked up and was delighted to hear her voice. He acted official and said, "Hello Miss Breen is there a problem? Do you need the help of the FBI?"

She laughed. "Yes Agent Thompson, I do. I need to take you out to dinner tonight if you are available?" Thompson was taken aback. He responded, still trying to act official.

"I will have to check my calendar and get back to you." He realized that she might hang up on him for being an ass. He quickly laughed to lighten the mood and said, "I would be very happy to have dinner with you. I look forward to seeing you tonight or any night for dinner for that matter."

"Good, you can pick me up at my home address at 6:30 p.m. I made reservations for 7:00 p.m. at a restaurant that I am sure you will enjoy. It's my treat and I do not want to hear anything more about it." He laughed.

"Okay, I will be counting the minutes until I pick you up." She gave him her address before saying goodbye. Terry looked around the office to make sure no one heard her conversation. She felt good and looked forward to seeing her blue eyed cutie tonight.

Jake stood up and welcomed the Chief as he entered his room. He was doing better than the doctors had expected and was determined to be sent home sooner than later. Everyone, including the Chief, encouraged him to get better quickly, but also cautioned him to not overdue it.

The Chief said, "Jake, take a look at this photo the FBI in Maryland has sent me." He handed the picture to Officer Bishop who stared at it for several seconds and shook his head slowly.

"Chief, I never saw this guy before." The Chief patted his shoulder as he looked at the picture with Bishop.

"Take your time and try to compare this guy to the features you remembered just before the shooting." Jake sat down and looked at the picture and simply said, "This does not look like the guy who shot me." He reminded the Chief that the subject kept his head down all the time and he didn't get a good look at his face. Jake said that the picture didn't match with the angle of any features he remembered in his mind. The Chief thanked him for the effort and began to leave.

Officer Bishop said, "Chief, I have to be sure. I never want any innocent man to be harassed by the police due to a mistaken identity caused by me." The Chief left and Bishop became upset that he couldn't contribute to the case again. His wife reminded him that he had done a lot to put the FBI and the department on track to find this guy. She began to tear up.

"Jake, they wouldn't have any clues if I had buried you." He realized he had upset her and promised, "I'll act more like a police officer and stop feeling sorry for myself because I can't contribute more to the investigation."

Amy was in the hospital talking to Cora in the family lounge. The usual conversation was underway when Amy had a thought and asked, "Did anything unusual happen at the house the day Officer Bishop was shot?" Cora was, at first, confused until Amy redirected her question. "Did you notice anything out of the ordinary that day after you found out Officer Bishop had been shot?" Cora retraced the events in her mind which took a few moments and then began talking. She detailed seeing the police cruisers, the yellow crime scene tape, talking with the State Trooper and explaining that she was house sitting her parent's house while they were away. She remembered unlocking the back door and looking for the cat. She stopped talking and Amy asked, "Cora, what is it?"

"Mom, I forgot to activate the security system and made a mental note to re-arm it when I left." She immediately saw the look on her mother's face of concern and reacted quickly.

"But the house looked fine and I fed the cat and got your information from the files you asked me to get."

Amy asked, "Did you notice anything else?"

"No, everything seemed in order, Mom, and I armed the security alarm when I left after I called you from the house."

Amy later explained what Cora had described, to Bob. She thought about calling the FBI Agent. Bob discouraged her from calling.

"Amy, nothing was stolen and thank God Cora realized it before anything could have been stolen. The incident with Officer Bishop is isolated. I'm sure that the assailant was interested in our neighbor's house that is for sale and obviously unoccupied." Amy listened to his remarks but wasn't sure that she shouldn't run that by the FBI.

The Neapolitan was one of the nicest restaurants in the area. Terry had always enjoyed the food there when she entertained big clients for the firm. She knew the owner well and had gone to college with his daughter. The daughter had a successful career in medical research and occasionally would invite Terry for dinner when she was in town visiting her parents. Terry knew she would get great service and food so she booked dinner for two at 7:00 p.m. for her and her new friend Craig.

Marilyn Porter enjoyed the restaurant as well and planned to have Sean take her there for dinner some evening. The restaurant was far enough out of Frederick and relatively expensive to keep the local nightly Frederick crowd from

143

packing the place. It was also too far away from Hagerstown for the locals to endure the ride to get there. She figured that the place would be an excellent spot to hold a business meeting and enjoy a good meal. It would help relax the members of her group which was needed to devise new plans to implement.

Terry and Craig arrived ten minutes before their scheduled dinner reservation. The restaurant wasn't crowded so they were seated at a table for two in the rear of the building which offered a little more privacy. That pleased her because she wanted everything to be perfect this evening. The place had a great atmosphere and the selection of wine was incredible according to Terry during the small talk she and Craig were engaged in as they looked over the menu. He relied on her to pick the meal based on her familiarity with the place. The wine list was presented and Craig picked a smooth merlot to go with whatever Italian dish she suggested. He felt very good that she approved of his selection and the small talk continued.

John Moore entered with Marilyn, arm in arm. Following directly behind the couple were Quinn and Jarvis. All four were escorted to their table and sat down without noticing Terry and Craig sitting in the rear of the restaurant. Terry noticed the group first and tried to look away. Knowing that she had not been seen, she attempted to conceal her disgust and aggravation from Craig that Moore had picked this restaurant, which dampened the atmosphere for her. Craig noticed the difference in her look as she tried to concentrate on his small talk.
He asked, "Is something wrong?"
"It must be very obvious."
"Your beauty is overwhelming, but I saw something in your expression that either reminded you of a past problem or you remembered something that is affecting your ability to concentrate." She apologized. "It's just that I observed an individual that came in that irritates me."
"Oh, some ex-boyfriend? You know, I could arrest him on the

144

spot for upsetting you."

She smiled and said, "You are very gallant but it isn't an old boyfriend. It's a banker that I really don't care for." Craig casually looked over and recognized Sean Quinn, Hank Jarvis and Marilyn Porter.

"Holy shit", he exclaimed to Terry's amusement. It was the first time he had used foul language in front of her. She smiled and said, "You know those people over there?"

He nodded and quietly said, "I'm presently investigating them." He realized he was talking to an attorney and quickly said, "I am doing some research on them that had been requested by the State of Connecticut and the FBI Bureaus in Pennsylvania, New York and Connecticut." He realized he had already said too much.

She said with a little concern in her voice, "Agent Thompson, please tell me more."

"I apologize for my unprofessionalism. Please ignore what I just said and forget my previous comments. Can we just change the subject?" Terry was too interested now and a little more concerned by the way he acted to let the matter drop so she began to give him more information on her association with the group hoping that he would divulge more details to her. She explained her involvement with Mr. Moore yesterday, and the two other gentlemen several times in the past week. Craig stopped being evasive and listened.

Terry explained, "I represent two clients that are attempting to pay off three mortgages on their family farm. The Colony Bank, here in Frederick, is pursuing foreclosure on the property and they have several supposedly interested parties that want to develop the land. I've had several meetings with Mr. Moore, Mr. Quinn and Mr. Jarvis." He listened very quietly as Terry detailed the Moore involvement but never once mentioned who her two clients were that she represented. She almost finished her story about the fire when she stopped and asked, "Am I boring you?" He was caught off guard for a few uncomfortable seconds until he regained his composure.

"I apologize, but I do have some questions I need to ask you but it would have to wait until I officially have you in my office and can record what you have just said to me." At first, she thought this was a game to get her to his apartment, but then she realized this man was dead serious. Their dinner was delivered and they ate quietly as Craig occasionally glanced over at the table where Moore was very busy in conversation with his dinner guests. Terry pursued some more questioning but Craig became more evasive as questions were asked which began to put a damper on her planned perfect dinner.

John Moore waited until all his guests were well into eating their meals. He quietly said, "As you all know, the Bryants are keeping the farm. They have also made arrangements to move the three Wilson men to Arlington National Cemetery as soon as possible." Moore paused and looked at all three of them individually before continuing. "I have information that three to four Maryland Reservists will accompany the vaults. I assume that they will be loaded onto or into some type of truck and escorted from the farm to Arlington because of their weight and size. There will probably be a day where the vaults will be kept somewhere in Arlington until the grave sites have been designated and prepared." He said that the information was pretty vague right now until he received more details. He explained that he needed to plan a way to get to the flatbed or delivery trucks or storage location at Arlington and exchange Todd's vault with another one. He looked at Quinn and asked, "Do you have any ideas on how to make the switch quickly and quietly?"

"Your switch idea could work better at the farm but it would involve overnight guards of the flatbed or delivery truck and having enough time to break the vault seal, open the casket and remove its contents. The guards for the event will, of course, be Jarvis and me." Moore listened and said, "Okay, continue."

"Well John," Quinn loved calling him that, "I would expect that the Reservists wouldn't want to have to spend the night guarding the three dead veterans. That is, if the truck to deliver the vault was in need of repairs or, better yet, replacement." He continued while glancing at Marilyn and Jarvis. "If the truck that was to carry the vault was damaged by us while the grave diggers were busy at the grave sites, and I had a truck and another empty vault nearby stored in, maybe the barn that is close by, we might be able to pull this off." He looked at Moore and continued. Quinn's quick mind began to reveal his thoughts as Jarvis wondered to himself, how does he think up this shit?

"We would have to buy a vault and rent a flatbed truck with a portable crane heavy enough to handle the vault. I could probably be able to rent one of those from Delaware or Pennsylvania so as not to be associated with the Frederick re-interment business. It would take some brass balls, but I feel I could handle it. John, what do you think?" He smiled as he looked at the Colonel's expression when he called him John again. Moore liked the idea.

"Sean, begin to make arrangements immediately. Marilyn, you will need to make contact with the Frederick Funeral director that is handling the re-interment. You will need to figure out a way to get all of the detailed information, even if it is personal, from the funeral people."

Marilyn stopped sipping her wine and said, "I'll go to the Funeral Director, himself, and inquire about some fictitious relative of mine that needs to be moved from somewhere to Frederick. I'll work out the details and get back to the group on how the locals could help solve the problem I present them." She was sure that they would use the Wilson move as a basis for her information.

Moore smiled and said, "Good." He looked over at Jarvis, "Hank, your job will be to find out who is the Maryland Reservist contact that assigns Reservists to support re-interments." Jarvis looked a little uncomfortable but nodded in acknowledgement.

Moore said, "The money will be taken out of the casket, put in some duffle bags I have and divided up at my apartment. I have moving storage boxes we can put the money in. I have devised a marking system and they will be put in with other storage

147

boxes I already have in my apartment. None of you will be able to receive your money until you resign from the bank. That will occur in weekly intervals before I finally resign." He paused to make sure everyone was attentive, lowered his voice and said, "Porter will be the first to resign. Jarvis, you will be a week later and Quinn, a week after him. I will remain in Frederick until all of you have resigned and have been paid. After that, all of you will be on your own as I will stay on for a while to make sure all seems normal until I retire under normal circumstances." He said that this was their last chance to complete their quest. "It has been a long four years and we are six feet away from our goal." He looked around the table and said, "I expect everyone to report back with your assignment plan by tomorrow evening." He realized that everyone, except him, had completed their dinner. He asked, "Anyone care for dessert?" No one cared to eat anymore. Quinn noticed Terry leaving the restaurant with the FBI Agent he met. He waited until the couple left the building when he brought the observation to Moore's attention as the others listened. Moore looked at all of them and said, "Your assignments have just been accelerated."

Terry and Craig quietly exited the restaurant hoping that no one in Moore's group had seen them. She laughed when they were seated in Craig's car.
"Wow, that was like being really sneaky," she said. Craig was a little more serious when he started to drive off towards Frederick. He asked, "I hope you do not mind going to my office to make a statement."
"You are really serious about this, aren't you?"
He looked over at her and said, "Until tonight, the FBI had no clue that you were in any way involved with these people and before you or I compromise our relationship and professionalism, we should get this questioning session out of the way."
She felt a little embarrassed and awkward by the way he turned so professional with the cold tone in his voice. She didn't want

to jeopardize her new relationship with her new friend, but she also wanted to find out what was the interest the FBI had between her clients and the Colony Bank group they'd seen at dinner.

Quinn left the restaurant just in time to see Thompson escort Terry to his black sedan. He knew the car from Jarvis's description as the one that staked out his apartment. He threw his keys to Jarvis who had followed him out of the restaurant. Quinn asked for his keys in return. Jarvis was confused as usual until Quinn said, "I don't want to tail the FBI Agent in my silver BMW. I want your car to follow them." Jarvis asked Quinn to return his car to his place after he was finished with it. He never acknowledged Jarvis's request as he quickly left the parking lot in hot pursuit of the FBI Agent's black sedan.

Thompson pulled up to his office and escorted Terry inside very quickly and quietly. Within several minutes, she was sitting at a table with a video camera positioned on her. He offered her a soft drink. She moved her head negatively as she was a little annoyed but also a little intrigued on what was about to happen.

Craig asked, "Are you ready to make a statement?" She looked at him and paused for a second but then the suspense was overwhelming. She nodded in approval.

"Please say yes, Miss Breen."

"Yes, I am ready." He began with the questioning of name, address, occupation and ended with the remark that she was making this statement under her own free will. She responded to all the questions with precise details of the facts as she knew them to date. The questioning and answering session lasted approximately fifteen minutes. Upon completion, Craig was a different man again. Terry noticed that as soon as he had turned off the video camera.

"Terry, I must apologize for being so abrupt. As soon as I realized there could be a conflict of interest in our relationship until this session was completed, I had to act according to FBI policy. Do you realize the implications if I had presented this information to the Agency after several days of involvement with an attractive, young attorney who represents clients that are involved with a group that is under investigation by the FBI?" he asked, while holding her hand to soften his words. She looked at him and tried to regain her feelings for the hot date she landed that turned into a professional interrogation in less than two hours. She felt that she was in the old Hollywood movie, "Dr. Jekyll and Mr. Hyde", by the way he had acted towards her. She looked down at his hand holding hers and was going to pull it away until she realized that this guy was really a professional. She regained her composure and said that she had some questions for him now that she had cooperated with his office.

"Why do you think the Colony Bank", she corrected herself, "the Moore group, is so interested in the Wilson farm? Besides the obvious worth for development or private use, what is the connection? Is there something on that land that has forced these people to be so interested in it? I need you to give me some information so that I can protect my clients as much as I can, legally, without interfering with your investigation of this group." Thompson paused on every question and then began to answer slowly.

"Terry, the group has a history that has been substantiated by their Army records. Their interest in your client's farm is still a mystery to me, but there is a connection in that Sean Quinn is under investigation for being in Greenwich, Connecticut at the same time a shooting of a police officer took place. That location is several houses away from your client's house. Mr. Moore, alias Colonel Moore, is Colony Bank's VP and was Sean Quinn's commanding officer in Iraq. Mr. Jarvis, alias Sergeant Major Jarvis, is a bank supervisor and was Sean Quinn's old top sergeant there. Ms. Porter who works for Moore was a First Lieutenant in Moore's command. The group was a financial specialty group that counted money for the U.S. Treasury Department that was confiscated from Saddam Hussein's hiding places during the Iraq Invasion. Information I received just prior to our dinner date indicated that Captain Todd Wilson was a member of Moore's group before he was killed by sniper fire in the Green Zone. We both know what Captain Wilson's connection is to the farm. There are too many coincidences to not continue to gather as much information as possible. That is why I needed to question you before we had any more of a personal relationship."

Terry sat there for a few more moments until she looked up at Craig who continued looking directly at her. She noticed that his eyes looked bluer now that he had relaxed. He was her date again and not the interrogator.

"I understand completely and I am very pleased you remained professional." She looked at him and asked what they should do next. Craig said that he would follow up with his boss tomorrow on her statement and make further inquiries about the group. She smiled and said, "No, I mean, what shall we do with the rest of the evening now that we are sitting in the FBI Office?"

"I'll take you home. I know I have I ruined your evening." She said that he could take her home, but asked if he would he be interested in having a drink or two at her apartment when he dropped her off. She informed him that she made a great margarita. He smiled, grabbed her hand and gently, but firmly, escorted her out of the office and into his car.

Quinn watched them get back into his black sedan and drive away. He followed behind in Jarvis's car at a safe distance observing them until Thompson stopped at a small apartment complex that wasn't very far from Marilyn's place. The two occupants left the car and headed inside the building. Quinn observed some lights going on and decided that the occupants would be busy for a while so he had time to implement a plan that had just come to him. He left and headed to find something else appropriate to drive back with.

After several margaritas and some small talk, Craig looked at his watch. It was 11:45 p.m. Terry noticed his quick check on the time and internally felt a little dejected. She thought that maybe he would make some type of advance towards her, but he was checking his watch as if he was worried that his mother was waiting for him or something; or maybe he was a real gentleman and wasn't going to push himself on her on the first date. She decided to take a chance.

"Agent Thompson, I assume you live alone. Do you?" He was a little perplexed, but realized that she picked up on his checking his watch a few moments ago.

"I do live alone, Terry. You probably noticed my checking of the time, didn't you? Well, based on your statement this evening, I figured I would get into work early, talk to my boss about it, and do some more research on our friends at the Colony Bank. I really have enjoyed your company and I would love to take you out again soon. I will call you to make some plans. Maybe this weekend we could spend some time together?" he asked as he rose from his seat on the sofa. He slowly moved over to her as she rose and put his arm around her waist. In a very quick, but smooth move, he kissed her on the lips long enough for her to react. She responded, as he thought she would, by relaxing and letting him make any other moves he desired. He stopped kissing her and looked into her eyes.

"I really did enjoy this moment and I will call you tomorrow at your office." She could feel his arousal and didn't move. She enjoyed his manhood pressing against her but she respected his gentlemanliness.

She said, "I was beginning to worry that you didn't care for me but I can feel that you really do." She backed away and smiled, took another look into his eyes and leaned forward and kissed him again. "You better leave now and I look forward to your call tomorrow." She walked him to the door, they kissed a third time and she bid him good night. As she locked the door, she felt like a school girl again and couldn't wait until he called her at the office tomorrow. She began to think of the investigation that Craig had talked about and decided she would talk to the Bryants first thing in the morning. As Craig left the apartment complex, he thought about Terry and calling her tomorrow. Would 8 o'clock be too early he thought. He realized she didn't get to the office until 9:00 a.m. 9:15 a.m. would be a good time to call her and ask her out this weekend. He didn't want to be too forward. Then he laughed to himself, maybe he should force himself to wait until noon to call her. He contemplated that again and decided 9:15 a.m. was a better time. He missed her already as he walked to his car. Terry watched him from her apartment window. She liked what she had experienced so far. She was a little embarrassed that she had an urge to jump him as soon as she felt his arousal. She didn't feel very ladylike getting that urge, but then she smiled because she hadn't had that urge in a few years and several bad dates ago.

Quinn returned with a black Dodge pickup truck he had hotwired several blocks down from Terry's apartment. He kept the motor running and the lights off as he waited for Thompson to leave Breen's apartment. As he recognized the man slowly walking to his car, he began to move and align the front right fender with the anticipated open left front door of Thompson's black sedan. As Thompson walked in back of his car in anticipation of getting into the FBI sedan, Quinn accelerated to 30 miles per hour and headed directly for the impact point he had planned. Thompson did not hear or see the dark truck until Quinn put on the lights and blinded the FBI Agent as he was opening up the driver's door. The truck had now exceeded 40 miles per hour and headed for Thompson. Thompson froze for a second too long with the door open. He began to dive for the seat as the Dodge Truck hit him and completely ripped the sedan's door off of the car. The impact threw Thompson and the car's door some 50 feet from the impact sight. Quinn kept a low profile in the driver's seat in case some neighbor was able to see the hit and run incident. He kept a steady speed as he drove away in case there were police patrolling the area from the recent auto theft he had just been involved with.

Terry watched in horror as she saw Craig catapulted with the detached car door from the hit from the black truck. She knew it was a bad accident. She called 9-1-1 and screamed into the phone to send an ambulance. She ran to the scene where Craig was lying still in the street. She thought the worst, until he moaned enough for her to hope he would survive this terrible accident.

Quinn returned to the area where he had hotwired and stolen the black Dodge pickup. He looked very cautiously to see if anyone was in the area as he rolled to a stop without the lights on. He doubled checked the cab to make sure he had not left any incriminating evidence in it. He knew his cotton gloves protected him from any finger prints being left behind. He made sure not to disturb any fingerprints from the real owner of the truck which would be dusted by the investigators. He sprinkled some whiskey on the driver's seat and the front floor mats from a half pint of Rye whiskey he had purchased earlier as part of his plan to get Agent Thompson off his back. He quickly left the truck and within minutes, he was driving back to Jarvis's undetected.

Jarvis noticed the lights of his car pulling into his parking place. He met Quinn outside and caught the keys as Quinn tossed them to him. He reciprocated with Quinn's keys. Jarvis began to ask questions and Quinn simply said, "One of the FBI agents that have been harassing us won't be anymore." Jarvis froze thinking his car was involved somehow. Quinn realized his expression and quickly said, "You don't have to worry about anything. Your car and your ass are free of any involvement." Jarvis began to ask more questions as Quinn was getting into his convertible. He stopped and looked at Jarvis and said, "Hank, just read the paper tomorrow morning." He started the BMW and left quickly.

Joe Walker got the call from his supervisor that Craig was in surgery to repair a broken right hip, right femur and ankle from the hit and run crash he had survived. He immediately told his supervisor that he would meet him at the hospital in 30 minutes or so. Upon arrival, Walker found an attractive young woman holding a cup of black coffee and sitting in the waiting room of the surgical suite. The charge nurse identified her as the woman that called in the accident and accompanied the ambulance to the hospital. Walker's supervisor entered the waiting room a few moments later.

Jack McManus had been a Special Agent for 20 years and hadn't had an agent under his command hurt in any way in more than 13 years. Both men descended on Terry Breen and in almost five minutes, had gotten more information than expected. Terry discussed how she met Thompson, their dinner date, the questioning that she'd undertaken to clear up any conflict of interests she might have representing clients that could be associated in an ongoing investigation the FBI was performing. She became very upset and began to cry as she described the hit and run incident and how she thought Craig was dead when she first approached him lying in the street. Both agents calmed her down and occasionally asked questions while they all waited to see how Craig Thompson was going to be after the surgery. At 5:15 a.m. the lead surgeon appeared in the waiting room and asked to talk to the next of kin. Seeing there weren't any present, he agreed to talk with Special Agent McManus. "Agent Thompson is a very lucky man and fortunately for him, he will make a full recovery from his injuries. The hit was more of a glancing blow than a direct one. Mr. Thompson must have been partially in the car when he was hit, evading a full impact. He will need some physical therapy, but he should be back to work in four to five months. The young agent is in fine physical shape and that contributed to his survival. Most people would have probably been in worse condition or possibly dead."

Joe Walker found Terry hugging him and crying on his shoulder as she reacted to the news of Craig's condition and prognosis. After a few moments, the agents asked when Craig would be able to talk to them.

"It could be several hours before he recovers from the anesthesia and pain medication he is receiving. Come back in a few hours or, better yet, go to the cafeteria which is just opening up. I promise that if you go to the cafeteria, I will page you as soon as I think he's coherent enough to be questioned."

Hit and Run

Terry remained at the hospital. She walked over to the Bryant's hospital room at 10:30 a.m. to inform them of her chance meeting with Agent Craig Thompson and the hit and run incident. She updated them on all the information he divulged, but couldn't give them the next course of action concerning Moore's group. Agents McManus and Walker would be handling that now based on the conversation she had with them earlier. She asked them to be prepared if either of them were to call. She wasn't sure that they would, but she wanted them prepared for that eventuality. She also explained that she would finalize all the arrangements for the re-interment by the end of the business day. She was also going to call and give them the contact person at the Frederick Funeral Home. Upon completion of her conversation with them, Amy and Bob looked at each other in amazement on what had happened and what was developing. As Terry left, they both realized that they must mention the story Cora had told them about the alarm being off on the day of the shooting. They agreed to tell the agents when they came to talk with them.

Amy also told Bob that she couldn't remember much about the day the family buried Todd on the farm. Bob agreed and said that none of these people rang a bell to him either. They decided not to call Bruce to see if he had any recollection of these people. It was bad enough that he and his family would have to relive this tragedy all over again and they didn't need to complicate it anymore with the Moore group. They assumed that the FBI would figure it out and it would be better that way.

Despite being tired, Terry decided to visit the records room at the Frederick News Post before she went home to shower and change clothes from the evening before. She wanted to view what had been recorded for the burial of Captain Todd Wilson on August 30th, 2003. She planned to return to the office and do some work before she returned to the hospital to visit Craig.

She knew the director of the research area very well from previously working as a law clerk for the firm prior to completing her law degree. She first headed for the microfiche area and began to search articles published in August 2003. She first found the notice of the death of Captain Wilson on August 21st, 2003 in Baghdad, Iraq. She viewed several articles that were published a few days prior to his interment at the Wilson farm that covered the hometown boy's short life. There was an article about his sports accomplishments, both in High School and at Penn State. Another article mentioned his short career in the Maryland Reserves when she came upon the funeral details of the 30th of August. There were a few pictures of the distraught parents and family. She was able to recognize Amy with what must have been Mr. Bryant following behind the parents of Captain Wilson. She couldn't make out his features from the photo, but assumed it was him. There was another photo of the Wilson cemetery with the honor guard presenting arms while the casket was being put into position for burial. She couldn't make out the faces of the honor guard until she enhanced the size of the picture. Then, there it was. A link to Moore's group had attended the funeral of Captain Todd Wilson. Mr. Hank Jarvis. He was standing at attention with an aid of a crutch and saluting near the rifle squad. The next picture was him alone with a somber expression on his face. The caption below that picture said, "Wounded comrade pays respects."

She read the article that mentioned that Sergeant Major Henry Jarvis had been wounded when Captain Wilson had been shot and killed. The article mentioned the flesh wound that Jarvis received did not keep him from attending the funeral of his group's Captain. The article went on to explain how both men had been gunned down in the safe area of the Green Zone by a Sunni sniper. It also went on to mention that the local Soldiers and Marines, who had orders to go to Iraq, had attended the service in honor of the Captain. She thought that she would mention this to Craig when she visited him later in the afternoon at the hospital.

McManus was in Walker's office for nearly an hour reading the update Thompson had left for Walker the night before with information about Moore and his group. The Terry Breen video was the icing on the cake. McManus viewed the video as Walker was becoming more confident now, that a link was developing between Quinn and the Greenwich shooting. Walker also had a link to the Wilson farm and the Moore group, but why? What was the link? He couldn't keep harassing the group by bringing them in for questioning. He knew he'd have a lawsuit to contend with if he did that. He discussed his options with McManus who was still contemplating if the FBI had enough evidence.

Jarvis initiated his inquiry at the Maryland Reserves. He called and talked with First Sergeant Willard Smyth who he realized was an old acquaintance of his in his early Army career. They both remarked to each other about those days and asked questions about the status and locations of common friends and acquaintances they both knew. Eventually, Jarvis got to the point and asked, "Will, do you know anything about a request for any reservists to attend a re-interment of a 2003 Iraq war veteran?"

"None that comes to mind Hank but I will let you know if something comes up."

"My ex-CO is interested in the re-interment for an officer that was under his command. This captain served under my ex-CO Colonel Moore in Iraq. Colonel Moore was unable to attend the funeral because he was in a command in Iraq at the time and couldn't leave. You know, the old man wants to pay his respects to the young Captain before he is finally laid to rest in Arlington now that he is being re-interred."

"I understand completely, Hank. I will let you know what the arrangements are when and if I am contacted." Jarvis thanked the First Sergeant and hung up. He opened up the newspaper and immediately read the story on the front page about the hit and run incident that had seriously injured Agent Craig Thompson. Jarvis's stomach turned and he immediately reported back to Moore, who was also not pleased to be told about it.

Quinn entered the Hagerstown Monument Company office. He found the concrete department foreman.

"Excuse me sir, but would it be possible to purchase a concrete vault? I have a client that wants one for a private cemetery."

"That's an unusual request, but I can sell you one for $800. The vault is a heavy piece and you will need special equipment to load it onto a flatbed."

"I figured that, so I'm prepared to rent a flatbed with a portable crane to perform the task for my client at his expense." He rolled his eyes in a form of mockery and said, "My client is a very eccentric individual and money is no object."

"Well, in that case, I'm sure the owner will not mind your proposal. I have portable crane equipment available and I would be happy to rent the truck and crane to you for an additional $1,000. When would you need it?" Quinn smiled.

"I can pick up the truck and crane with the vault right now. I'll need the truck for as long as," he paused, "Let's say three to four days." He could see the foreman beginning to balk at the request.

"I don't think the owner will want his truck and equipment tied up for that length of time." Quinn eased his apprehension. "I'll offer an additional $500 a day for any day past the three day rental. I'll pay you directly so that you can cover the inconvenience you might incur explaining the whereabouts of the truck to the owner if I am a little longer than what I planned." The foreman was not quite convinced yet. "What does your client really need this for?" Quinn cut him short.

"This is a private matter but I assure you that nothing illegal is being done here that would involve you or the owner. I explained that my client is a very rich individual and complete privacy is all he asks for at a fair price." The foreman still hesitated until Sean handed him $500 in cash.

"This is just a little extra right now to be discreet." He then pointed over at his new BMW. "I will leave the keys for that beauty with you, until I return with the truck. The BMW is a gift from my client just to let you know how rich he really is." The foreman nodded as he shoved the $500 into his pants pocket and gave Quinn a receipt for the $1,800 cash for the vault and three day truck rental. Quinn smiled again and reminded the foreman, "Remember, if I'm late after three days, I will give you $500 for each day and you get to drive the BMW a little longer. You work out the details with your owner. Now point me to where the truck and equipment are." The foreman never smiled but just nodded and then pointed to the truck Quinn was to use.

Marilyn Porter arrived at the Frederick Funeral Home dressed in a conservative black dress with shoes and a purse that matched. She rang the funeral director's doorbell and waited for a response. Mr. Thomas Atkinson answered the door and, to his delight, observed a very attractive young woman that obviously looked a little distressed.
"Is the funeral director available?" Atkinson immediately identified himself as the director and showed the woman into his office. Marilyn hesitated for several moments and looked like she was trying to control her emotions before she said her name and the reason why she had come unannounced.
"Mr. Atkinson, my name is Marilyn Porter and I work at the Colony Bank here in Frederick. I am sorry to bother you but I need some direction on how to handle a most difficult situation for my family that I was just informed of this morning."
"Ms. Porter," he emphasized Ms. because he did not know the woman's marital status, "I am here to help you in any way that I can." Marilyn realized that she would have to act like the single woman in need of dire help. She knew that her act was working by his reaction so she continued, "It's Miss Porter, Mr. Atkinson. I have," she sobbed and corrected herself, "had, a brother who was killed in Iraq a few years ago you see, and my mother is moving from New York to stay with my other brother. He lives in Thurmont, Maryland and has invited her to live with him and his family because she is ill now and doesn't

have many years left, if any at all." She paused and tried to control herself.

"Miss Porter, I don't quite understand what you are trying to tell me," he said as he sat next to her and tried to comfort her by holding one of her hands. Marilyn moved her hand to her lap so that his hand could feel the softness of her upper thigh as he still held her hand.

"I'm sorry for babbling, you must think that I am an idiot."

"I can see that you are under considerable stress and maybe you should start over again and explain what I can do for you to help solve the apparent stressful situation you are in." Marilyn looked directly into her his eyes and smiled.

"My mother is moving and she is distraught because she will not be able to visit my brother's grave anymore on a weekly basis." She stopped for a few moments to show a little emotion as she wiped away a small tear.

"My mother walked to the cemetery until her health made it too difficult to do that anymore. Now, she has friends drive her there weekly to visit my brother's grave." She began to tear up again and finished with her last punch line. "But now that she has to move to Thurmont. Would it be possible to move my brother from New York to Thurmont or Frederick?" she asked as she squeezed the man's hand. "It would make it so much easier for mother to visit his grave,"

"It can be arranged to re-intern anyone, Miss Porter." Marilyn smiled.

"How could that be done? And have you had any experience doing that sort of thing?"

The director fell into the trap as he proudly explained, "My establishment is presently in the process of arranging for several soldiers to be moved from Frederick to the National Military Cemetery at Arlington, Virginia. I see no difficulty in moving a soldier from New York to any city in Maryland at the request of the family, but it is very expensive, Miss Porter, I must inform you. However, I can make arrangements when your family is ready to proceed with such an undertaking."

"How much time is needed? How would the casket be moved?

162

Will there be procedures to protect the remains of the deceased? Will I need an honor guard? Is that mandatory?"

"Miss Porter, I can assure you all that will be taken care of when your family wants to move your brother."

"I'm so relieved, Mr. Atkinson. Thank you for so quickly putting my mind at ease."

"As I referred to earlier, it just so happens that the day after tomorrow, I will be at the cemetery of a family to begin the re-interment of several family soldiers that were killed in action during different wars. My staff has made arrangements for the transportation of the vaults containing the caskets on several trucks capable of handling the loading and unloading of the vaults. A three to four person honor guard will be present at all times during the removal, movement and re-burial of the soldiers. I have arranged for a small funeral service to be held for the family of the deceased at Arlington."

"I am so relieved that you have experience with these types of arrangements." She asked for his card and gave him her cell number in return so they could contact one another. He wrote her name and number down. She shook his hand and thanked him for his time. As she started to leave, she turned, and asked one more question, moving very close to the director. He could smell her perfume and feel the warmth of her breath as she spoke slowly.

"Mr. Atkinson, what do you do if there is any equipment failure while removing the vaults?" He looked at her a little perplexed as he took in her aroma and warmth.

"That has never happened in the 22 years that I had been the funeral director." She looked at him as she faked a look of apprehension.

"But what if it happens?"

"Well, if something like that happened I would have the honor guard stand by at the site for as long as it took for my staff to replace the faulty equipment and continue on with the process."

"Even if it took all night to replace what was broken?"

"Miss Porter, even if it took all night, the guard would be on duty watching over the vaults until my staff returned."

She smiled, shook his hand again and said, "You have been very helpful and you will be hearing from me very soon. I will have to coordinate all this with my brother who will be acting for my mother."

"I understand and I look forward to serving your needs."

Marilyn laughed to herself and thought that this guy had been very nice, but he couldn't keep his eyes off her and she was sure he would have liked to service her. She knew the low cut dress and short skirt helped with his pleasantries and information. She gave the director one more thrill. She gently kissed him on the cheek turned and headed for the door. She paused at the doorway, as she saw the director recover from his surprise at the kiss and scurried to open the door for her.

"Your people take care of everything including equipment, staff, arrangements and any paperwork involved right?" He smiled and nodded as he opened the door. She smiled back but couldn't control her feeling of success as she approached and hugged him. She made sure to hug him enough so he could feel the woman that he could clearly see she was. She left, returned to her car and drove away. The funeral director watched her drive away. Marilyn had brightened his busy day. She waited until she was out of sight to call Moore. He answered, listened and told her she had done well. He instructed her to call Quinn and Jarvis with the details she uncovered.

Sam Lombardo heard the knocking on his front door. He ignored it, since he was still trying to get a little more sleep before he would have to report back to his job at the small machine shop in Frederick. He'd been working fourteen hour days on a rotating schedule and today was his last day before he would have two days off. He needed some sleep and he wasn't about to get up for anyone unless they smashed the door down. Several moments later, he heard the door crack as it slammed against the wall. He jumped out of bed when several policemen screamed at him to get down on the floor immediately. Before he was awake enough to realize what was happening, he'd been thrown on the floor in his underwear and cuffed with his hands behind his back. He lay there confused as to what had just happened and why these cops were in his bedroom. Agent Walker ordered the policemen, "Get him some pants and a shirt and have him put them on before he is taken downtown." Lombardo was wide awake now and started asking questions as to what was happening. Several policemen ignored him until he started raising his voice. One policeman assisted in silencing Lombardo with a shot to his diaphragm with a night stick. Lombardo lost all his air and was speechless for several minutes. He didn't say a word to anyone after that experience, remaining silent even as his rights were read to him and until his interrogation began at the FBI bureau with Agent Walker.

Terry entered the step-down room next to the intensive care unit to find Craig awake and sipping some iced water through a straw. His bruised face lit up as soon as he saw the young beauty at the doorway.

"Hi," he said.

"Hi yourself," she quickly responded. He motioned for her to come in as he attempted to put the plastic cup with the straw onto his serving tray. He misjudged it and it fell off onto the floor where the water and ice went everywhere. He was obviously frustrated and winced with pain as he sat back on his pillow after trying to catch the plastic cup. She smiled and bent down and placed the cup back on the serving tray. She poured some fresh water and ice and then looked for something to pick up the spilled fluid. One of the nurses had seen it happen and was by Terry's side in a few moments to clean up the spill.

"How do you feel now that you're awake?"

"Pretty shitty actually, if you must ask." He realized his remark was uncalled for. "I'm sorry. My ankle and leg hurt a little but my hip is driving me crazy. The medication they're giving me for the pain makes me a little on the edgy side so please accept my apology for being a little flip with you." She smiled.

"I just wanted to come by and check to see if you needed

anything. I hoped that you would be feeling better."

"Terry, I am going to be here for several weeks, but I look forward to seeing you every so often."

"I'll be at the hospital every day or as often as you can stand my company." He attempted a smile and his eyes drooped a little because the medication was still affecting him. She began to talk when she noticed that he had fallen back to sleep again. She sat down and prepared to wait for an hour or so to see if he would awake. She felt responsible somehow for this mishap.

Sam Lombardo sat at the interrogation table alone. He'd been sitting there for ten or fifteen minutes, he guessed. He was scared and couldn't remember all the details of why he'd been read his rights. He knew he was being suspected of being involved in a hit and run which he knew was something very serious. He was smart enough to keep quiet and wait to see what more would be asked of him. He hadn't asked for a lawyer even though he realized he probably needed one, but he had all his faculties now and planned to be polite, direct and sincere. He knew the cops were pissed about a hit and run or something they thought he'd done, but he was really confused as to why the FBI was also involved.

Quinn was several miles away from the vault shop with the gear he needed to open up the Wilson vault. He answered his cell phone and heard Marilyn's voice. After a few minutes of small talk and flattery to entice her to have dinner and much more with him, he received the information she had acquired from the Frederick Funeral Home. He realized he had an extra day to prepare for the task.

Hank Jarvis received the information that he needed as well. His contact at the Maryland Reserve Unit had called him back to let him know that he was sending three reservists to accompany the three vaults to Arlington and gave him the name of the Sergeant in charge. Jarvis informed his contact that he and several other retired soldiers would be there as well

166

and to let his man know that they would assist in any way they could. He also wanted to remind First Sergeant Smyth that his ex-CO would be attending and that he should understand that the Colonel was a stickler on proper military procedures and protocol. He emphasized that his men should be sharp at all times.

Walker and McManus entered the interrogation room together. Lombardo stiffened when he saw both of them. No one said a word until Walker asked Lombardo, "Why didn't you stop after you hit the man?" Lombardo didn't answer because he knew as soon as he denied anything; the situation would get really rough for him. He let the interrogator go on. Walker asked him again, "Why didn't you stop?" Lombardo began to slowly speak.

"Sir, my name is Samuel Lombardo, Jr. I don't know who either one of you gentlemen are since you haven't given me your names. I know I'm in an FBI interrogation room but I don't know why." Walker became a little irritated and put his face close to Lombardo's.

"I'm Agent Joe Walker and this is Special Agent Jack McManus. You are here because you hit an agent last night with your truck and kept going. Based on all the booze we found in your damaged truck, I'm surprised you can even remember your name this morning, Mr. Samuel Lombardo, Jr."

"Agent, I had not been drinking last night and if you cared to do a blood alcohol on me you will find out two things." Walker sarcastically asked, "And what would that be?"

"You will find that that I have no alcohol in my system and that I am a type one diabetic who will need his insulin in less than an hour."

Walker looked at McManus who immediately left the room to send a squad car to Lombardo's apartment for the vial and needles. Walker eased up on his interrogation and asked Lombardo to detail where he had been last night. Lombardo verified his place of employment and the exact time he punched out. He detailed his stopping to get fuel in his truck and had the charge slip in his wallet to prove his purchase. He said where, and at approximately what time, he parked his truck and even detailed the TV program he watched from 11:00 p.m. until mid-night. He explained that he went to bed and was there until he was yanked out of his apartment this morning by the police. Walker asked, "Have you ever had an accident with your truck?"

"I just purchased the truck five months ago and it was clean, black and shiny as of last night."

"Where is my truck? I didn't see it when I was dragged from my apartment." Walker explained that it had been parked on the street when a black and white spotted it and noticed the damage to the right front bumper with blood on it.

"My truck was parked in the apartment parking lot in the #4 slot which is my assigned spot. I have both sets of keys. One is on my keychain and the other on the cork board in my kitchen if you care to check it out. I suggest you all hurry up with my insulin before we all have a problem." Walker released the handcuffs and told Lombardo that his medication was on its way. Walker knew that this was not a case of a drunk driver. Someone had stolen this guy's truck, attempted to kill Thompson and cover it up.

Interment Arrangements

Quinn arrived at the Wilson farm with the flatbed truck, new vault and attachable vault winch crane. He approached the barn where Jarvis had been waiting for him to open up the barn doors so that after he drives the equipment in, he could close them up as quickly as possible. They figured that no one, including the family, would be interested in going to the barn after the re-interment. The barn was not visible from the cemetery anyway. It was close enough for Quinn to retrieve the equipment at the precise moment he would need it, after he sabotaged the Frederick Funeral Home's equipment. Jarvis looked very irritated and nervous to Quinn as he exited the truck. He ignored it because he thought he was just scared as shit about what they were going to do tomorrow. Jarvis asked him where did he leave his BMW. Quinn detailed his exchange with the vault company foreman and told him that he would return for his car after he had used the truck and the equipment. He smiled at Jarvis and said that he needed another favor. "What now?" Jarvis barked. Quinn ignored the nervous sarcasm and reminded him that he had followed Breen and Thompson home after they both had dinner with Moore. He enjoyed watching Jarvis's face turn gray and then red as he detailed to him how he'd stolen a truck and hit Thompson with it while he was leaving Breen's house last night.

"I think he's dead, but I haven't seen the newspaper yet to confirm that. Did you read the paper yet?" he asked as he buckled his seat belt in Jarvis's front seat. Jarvis almost became sick. He glared at Quinn and then yelled, "You son of a bitch. You almost killed the FBI Agent?" Quinn laughed.

"Well I guess he is tougher than I thought, but he'll be out of our hair for a while. The favor is for you to call Moore and tell him to make up another alibi for me."

"I won't call Moore and you shouldn't. Are you fucking crazy? Call Porter instead and ask her to make one up for you," Jarvis angrily said.

Quinn actually agreed with him and quickly dialed Marilyn to update her on the situation that had developed and to request another alibi from her. Marilyn was immediately upset with him.

"Why in hell would you do something as crazy as that, Sean? You were just supposed to follow them and see if there was something more between them than just a dinner date."

Moore was listening to Marilyn chastise Quinn to his delight. He reached for her hand and indicated, by nodding, that she should agree to the alibi he had requested to keep things running smoothly. He actually approved of Quinn's act but kept from informing Porter as she worked out the alibi with him. He thought it would keep the FBI busy looking for the hit and run driver and not concentrating on them during tomorrow's re-interment. He hoped that Quinn had not been sloppy pulling off the hit and run with anything that could incriminate him. They worked out the details while on the phone so all four would have the detailed information. She hung up on him and looked at Moore.

"Do you think the FBI will link Quinn to this or will they treat it as an unrelated incident?"

"Until they have a witness, or unless Quinn has been careless, the FBI wouldn't do anything. They will probably come looking for him after their leads lead nowhere just because of his association with the agent. They can only hope he will make a mistake during questioning that is probably going to happen very soon." Moore noticed the two agents coming into the bank as he left Marilyn's office.

An hour later Quinn and Jarvis returned to the bank to find Joe Walker and Special Agent McManus waiting for Quinn in Jarvis's office.

"Where were you last night?" Walker asked Quinn as he stood and walked to within inches of him and glared.

"Damn, Agent Walker, you are a real pain in my ass these days. Now what is it this time?"

McManus could immediately see anger come over Walker's face as Quinn ended his remark with a smirk. He anticipated

Walker's attempt to grab Quinn but was too slow to react to the speed of the younger agent. By the time he could react, Walker attempted to jack Quinn up but the ex-army Staff Sergeant defensively evaded Walker's aggression. Walker counteracted and was about to attempt his second move when McManus had enough time now and stepped in between both men and told Walker to back off.

"Good move on your part for his sake Agent."

"Shut up Quinn." He then looked quickly at Walker. "Joe, please stand down."

McManus ordered both Walker and Quinn to move further back from each other. Both men obeyed his order as Jarvis's office phone rang. Jarvis listened as Moore told him that Audrey Wilkes was on her way to his office. He was relieved a little that Moore had called in the bank's legal attorney. He informed Quinn and the two agents.

"The bank's attorney is on her way gentlemen."

Special Agent McManus said, "An attorney is not needed here, Mr. Jarvis."

"Excuse me Special Agent McManus, but I think one is needed here now and Ms. Wilkes will be interested in the Gestapo tactics I have just witnessed."

McManus ignored Jarvis.

"Where were you last night?" he asked Quinn.

"I had dinner at the Neapolitan with Moore, Porter and Jarvis, Agent McManus. You should check with your own people," he said as Walker glared at him. "Thompson saw me there. Ask him."

"I can't right now. He's in the hospital. He's recovering from some major surgery after someone tried to kill him in a hit and run incident," McManus said as he still kept watch on Walker. Quinn actually changed his expression and said, "Holy shit, I'm sorry to hear about that." He paused, then continued, as he saw the attorney entering the office. "After that, I spent the rest of the time at Marilyn Porter's until I went to work early this morning on an assignment for Mr. Jarvis." Audrey Wilkes heard the last remaining remarks from Quinn. She introduced herself and said, "This interview is over unless you agents have something to charge Mr. Quinn with. Otherwise, I expect you both to leave the bank as soon as possible. Please contact me before asking Mr. Quinn or anyone at the bank any further questions. If you have any questions in the future, I will accompany Mr. Quinn or any other bank employee to your office where you can interview, not interrogate them. If you come here again, other than within the conditions that I have just set forth, I will personally see that you are reprimanded by your superiors."

Neither of the agents acknowledged her introduction or statement and just turned and left. As the agents left the bank, Audrey turned to Quinn and Jarvis and began to question them, in detail, of what had transpired since Quinn's first questioning session with the FBI. Both men detailed what they wanted the attorney to believe as the absolute truth. Moore passed Jarvis's office to observe both subordinates in detailed conversation with the attorney. McManus and Walker knew they had made a mistake by confronting Quinn at the bank. They now had complicated things by involving the Bank's attorney.

Audrey completed taking notes from the two men. She was conscious of Quinn's constant staring at her breasts and thighs. Her short skirt made it difficult to hide her thighs and, thanks to the air conditioning in her office, her erect nipples. Quinn enjoyed the entire conversation but Jarvis looked concerned and listened to every bit of information Wilkes gave them about dealing with the FBI and other authorities. Upon completion of the session, Jarvis thanked Audrey and left the room. Quinn stayed on for a few moments to become more acquainted with the brunette beauty and attempted to start some small talk. Audrey was cordial until Quinn asked, "Maybe you might like to have dinner with me?"

"I don't think that is possible, Mr. Quinn," she said with a slight agitation in her voice. "You are now my client and I do not mix business with pleasure."

Marilyn Porter peeked in to ask Wilkes some questions when she noticed that Quinn was still with her. Marilyn excused herself and began to leave when Wilkes stopped her. "Please come in Ms. Porter. Mr. Quinn and I have just finished." Quinn, realizing that he had been professionally dismissed, winked at Porter and thanked Wilkes for her time. He realized as well, that Audrey lit up at the sight of Marilyn as much as he did which signaled to him that she was not his kind. Marilyn approached Audrey and they entered into a conversation, not even noticing Quinn's departure. Quinn smiled as he fanaticized about having sex with both women at the same time. He never had been fortunate enough to have a three-some. If Wilkes was a lesbian, he would have to be alone with her to try to convert her back. With Marilyn involved with her, that might drive Audrey farther to what he considered to be on the dark side. He laughed to himself realizing that none of what he was fantasizing probably would ever happen.

Sam Lombardo was released by the authorities that afternoon. No charges had been filed and his black Dodge pickup truck was returned to him from the Frederick Police Department. He now had to make arrangements to have his truck repaired from the damage it received from the hit and run incident. The FBI and Frederick Police Department had no clues as to whom or why someone had hit Agent Thompson. Agents McManus and Walker were very frustrated that they had several unsolved cases with no sound evidence, but they suspected things seemed to point in the direction of Sean Quinn.

First Sergeant Willard Smyth called Hank Jarvis and relayed the detailed information of the three Reservists he had assigned to accompany the Wilson re-interment to their new resting place at the Arlington National Cemetery. Jarvis wrote down the names and thanked him for his information. He confirmed with Smyth that he was accompanying his ex-CO who was attending the re-interment as well. Jarvis gave Smyth a little of the details of what his Reservists could expect from Colonel Moore and advised that he should instruct the men to be at their best. Willard Smyth asked, "Hank, should I attend to ensure the strictest adherence to military protocol for this occasion?"

"No, there is no need Will. I still know how to direct and instruct men and I have enough stripes on my sleeves to enforce it. If there is any confusion from your men, I'll instruct them accordingly, that is, if it is alright with you, First Sergeant?" Willard Smyth laughed.

"That is an affirmative." Both men exchanged pleasantries and hung up.

Jarvis informed Quinn that the plan was set and re-confirmed what Marilyn had relayed to them earlier about the details she found out from the funeral director. They now had all the details for the planned re-interment. Within minutes, Jarvis had updated Moore that Quinn, Porter and he, were finished with their assignments and were awaiting the re-interment commencement on Saturday at 1000 hours. Moore acknowledged the satisfactory report and hung up.

The Bryants received a phone call from Terry informing them that if any family members planned to attend the re-interment, they needed to be at the farm on Saturday before 10 o'clock. Amy explained, "Terry, I will not be able to attend the Frederick portion of the re-interment but I will make every attempt to be at the Arlington site for the Monday morning ceremony if Bob doesn't need me. I also plan to return to Frederick after the Arlington ceremony to ask the doctors when I can get Bob back to Connecticut. I want to have him there so that both of us can finalize the banking business. I also have some information for you that might be of interest to the authorities. I'm mentioning it because it happened within the time frame of the shooting incident in Connecticut. I just learned this through a conversation with my daughter, Cora."

"Please continue," Terry encouraged Amy.

"Our alarm system at the house had not been activated during the Officer Bishop shooting. Cora remembered that during our conversation. What do you think?"

"I think we need to pass this information on to Agent Walker. Thank you for updating me." The conversation ended and

174

Terry passed that information on in a voice mail to Agent Walker a few minutes later.

John Moore wrote a memo calling a meeting in the Colony Bank's conference room for Friday at 11:00 a.m. His invitees included Attorney Audrey Wilkes and Moore's secretary, Ms. Clemens. The Colonel planned to have it on record that the Colony Bank had been as cooperative as possible in attempting to work with the Bryants to settle the foreclosure matter that was pending. He was going to mention that he made a personal offer to them for the property once he knew they were paying off the Colony's hold on the property. He also needed it on record that his employees had cooperated with the FBI on several matters concerning unsolved cases that were not germane to the Colony Bank's business. He knew he needed it on record that one of his employees was a victim of the frustration of the FBI concerning several unsolved incidents. One was that Mr. Quinn was questioned about his receiving a random speeding ticket in the vicinity of a shooting incident. Another was that he had been at a popular restaurant at the same time a particular Agent, later became the victim of a hit and run incident. A factor Moore didn't want readily known by the Bank's attorney was his meeting and several phone calls to Breen increasing his offer for the farm. He knew that was inappropriate but would react only if Attorney Wilkes found out and mentioned it.

Craig had his first decent night's rest. The pain medication allowed him to sleep through most of the night. He only awoke when the night nurse came in to take his vital signs. He managed, with the assistance of an orderly, to wash, brush his teeth, comb his hair and don a fresh hospital gown before Terry's visit this morning. He knew she had visited him daily but today, he was more awake and anticipated seeing her. He also planned to talk with Joe Walker and get updated on what had transpired at the office. He needed something to think about and he now had plenty of time to think. He also thought

175

that if he was updated on the cases that were being investigated, he could utilize his time calling on the phone and doing small tasks that always took up an agent's time. Maybe McManus would allow him to do that type of work, he thought, as he looked out the window. He turned back when he noticed someone had entered his room.

"How long have you been standing there?"

She smiled and said, "Only a few moments. I enjoy just looking at you. You are looking better and better each day." He enjoyed the flattery.

"Please, come closer to the bed." As she obliged, he reached out and pulled her close so that he could hug her. She felt a little awkward but relaxed as he kissed her neck.

"You know, you're probably the best medicine I can have to get me back on my feet again." She kissed his forehead but then realized he deserved more and kissed him on the lips.

"Here is some of the medicine you need." She then teased him.

"You know, I'd enjoy your company more if we were hugging in my bed." That statement made him blush a little but the blood in his body was finding other places besides his face. Terry moved away from his bed when she heard her cell ring.

"The office is probably calling, but I'm going to ignore it and spend another hour with you." She noticed it was from an Attorney Wilkes who had left a message. "I'm sorry but I have to listen to this message." She listened and immediately returned the call. Thompson watched her talk on the phone and occasionally smiled and winked at her as she conversed. When she hung up she said, "That was an interesting phone call."

"Yeah, I heard you talking about the re-interment of the Wilson's"

"Never mind, only attorney stuff. Now where were we in our conversation?" He pulled her close again. She didn't tell him the details of her conversation but did mentally note that she would call Walker later about what had been asked by Attorney Wilkes.

Joe Walker listened to Terry Breen's voice mail. The fact that the Bryant's daughter had failed to arm the security system was nothing tangible he could use. It only heightened his suspicion of Quinn. The puzzle was slowly and agonizingly coming together, but a few good pieces of evidence would allow the FBI to haul this group in for some serious questioning. He'd hope that something would break. He began to concentrate on Jarvis and Porter's background to look for any information he could use. He ran the tactic by McManus who cautioned him based on the run-in they had had with Audrey Wilkes earlier.

Quinn watched Walker's wife place their two year old son into the car seat in the couple's driveway. She had a few hours to get to the grocery store. Crystal Walker was attempting to complete the shopping as quickly as she could and avoid little Joe becoming too cranky before his usual 10:00 a.m. nap. She slowly backed the car out of the driveway and headed for the shopping mall a few miles from her home. All was normal except for Sean Quinn following in Jarvis's car which he had nonchalantly borrowed the keys and never let Jarvis know that morning. Crystal arrived at the grocery store and unbuckled little Joe. She held his hand as she located a cart, loaded the little boy in and pushed the cart into the store. Quinn followed and observed them while he pretended to shop. He picked up items that he never intended to buy. Crystal quickly and methodically worked her way down the aisles. Quinn actually enjoyed watching the attractive woman bend over in different positions as she tried to shop and manage a two year old at the same time. Even though he didn't like Walker, he had to respect him for the hot wife he had. Even after having a kid, she still had a real nice ass, he thought, and appreciated it as he watched her. Seeing enough to plan his next move, he parked the shopping cart half full with items and left the store. He drove by the Walker home ten minutes later. He parked the car one block away and casually walked back holding what looked to be an oversized blue gym bag he had just purchased but was really a pet tote bag large enough to fit a small child in. To a casual observer, he looked like someone ready to go to the office as he wore a navy blue sport coat, white shirt, red and blue striped tie and gray slacks. He approached their home and waited to implement his plan.

Crystal arrived almost to the schedule he had mentally predicted. She turned into the driveway with little Joe and a week's worth of groceries visible in the back seat. She removed her son and approached the front door. She never noticed Quinn, who casually cut between her house and her neighbor's home and then stood by the back door of her house. He put on his cotton gloves and picked the lock as Crystal opened the front door. He noticed the alarm but knew Crystal would disarm it as soon as she entered the home. He slipped into the kitchen, found the utility room and waited. He heard her disarm the alarm while talking to her son to sooth him as she began to walk upstairs to put him in for a nap. He listened as she reached the top of the stairs and quickly put his jacket, shirt and tie into the bag he carried. He was now in a tee shirt and slacks. He waited. Several minutes went by until finally, he could hear her return from upstairs and head out of the front door to the car to retrieve the groceries. He quickly exited the utility room, passed the front door and climbed the stairs. He quietly approached little Joe who had just fallen off to sleep in his crib. He opened the tote bag quietly and retrieved a small bottle of ether he had purchased from an auto parts store that was generally used for starting engines. He sprayed a very small amount onto some gauze he had and placed it within a few inches of little Joe's mouth and nose. The fumes were enough to deepen the sleep of the little boy while not risking overdosing or possible killing him. He heard Crystal come in the front door and put the first load of groceries on to the kitchen table. He waited until he heard her go back outside for the second trip. He figured she had three trips based on what he had observed her purchase at the grocery store. He quickly put the child into the pet tote bag alongside his clothes and descended the stairs. She was just beginning to walk back when he quickly escaped to the utility room with the child. He waited and hoped that she had no purchases to place in the

178

utility room just yet. If she did, he planned to use the ether to knock her unconscious. He hoped that he didn't need to have to do that because if he failed to knock her out quickly and she saw his face, he would need a more drastic solution to his plan. He heard her place the second load of items onto the kitchen table and left to finish her task. He relaxed and waited until she was out in the front yard before he exited the back door with little Joe. He casually walked around to the front, timing it perfectly, as she completed her task, walked back into the house and closed the front door. He walked back to the sidewalk and towards Jarvis's car. He wore his sun glasses as he exited the block carrying his small twenty-five pound package in the pet tote bag.

Crystal could smell something odd as she entered the kitchen to place her last few bags of groceries on the kitchen table. She checked her grocery bags that contained some of the kitchen cleaners she had purchased to ensure they were not damaged or leaking. She finished her chores a few minutes later. She turned on the TV but kept the sound turned down low as she always did to catch some programs she watched daily before little Joe woke up for lunch. She relaxed while she snacked and watched TV.

Sean reached the car and gently placed the pet tote bag on the front passenger seat. He slowly drove off and headed out of the neighborhood. Sean glanced at his watch. It was 10:45 a.m. He knew he needed to get little Joe to a safe place quickly since he knew he was going to be late for Moore's meeting. He spotted a Catholic church coming up and immediately parked in front of it. He turned off the car and dialed Moore's number. Moore answered in his usual tone of distaste that he had for Quinn lately. He explained quickly, "Mr. Moore, I will be a few minutes late for your meeting because there are some traffic problems." He apologized over and over again until Moore became annoyed and said, "I will wait a few minutes to allow you to get to the bank. Do not get a speeding ticket again since the last one you received has caused everyone some aggravation." Quinn laughed. "Yes Sir, I will be careful not to get one."

He completed putting his shirt and tie back on as he finished talking to Moore. Those tasks had been difficult having his cotton gloves still on. He stepped out of the car and put on his sport coat and sun glasses. He retrieved his twenty-five pound pet tote bag but remembered to remove the ether can and gauze. He walked up the church's steps and entered the church, quickly removed the sunglasses and searched for anyone kneeling or standing inside. He noticed one woman who was lighting a candle in front of a statue of the Blessed Virgin. He positioned the now opened tote bag with little Joe in it, just enough for the woman to notice when she exited, or anyone else who entered the church through the center door. Little Joe moved a little and Quinn relaxed knowing the child was fine but also became a little apprehensive when the woman began to turn in the front of the darkened church to head his way. He left quickly, returned to the car and began slowly moving away from the curb. He observed two women walking toward the church. They seemed to be in a deep conversation as he slowly passed by. He looked away just in case they decided to look his way. He passed unnoticed and headed for the Colony Bank and Moore's meeting. He glanced at his watch and observed it was 11:01 a.m. He knew he could be at the bank in about three or four minutes. He laughed out loud and said to himself as the radio played while driving the speed limit, "How are you going to like that, Agent Walker? I'm sure this will scare the shit out of you and your hot wife. Take that for fucking with me, will you."

The woman noticed the tote bag as she walked towards the holy water fountain to bless herself upon her exit from church. She had seen what appeared to be a man dressed with a tie and jacket and immediately thought he could have been the person who left it there. She blessed herself and walked over to the tote bag when she noticed that it moved. She stopped in amazement that someone had left an animal in the church. She was annoyed until she heard a cry coming from the bag. She knew that sound because she was a grandmother five times

180

over. She raced to look in the bag. She smiled at first, when she saw the little guy. He had stopped crying and was looking up at her with a curious expression on his face. After a few moments, seeing no familiarity, he began to cry again so she lifted him up and tried to comfort him. As she attempted to calm him, she observed two women coming into the church. She yelled out to both of them that one of them needed to get the pastor right away. Both women looked at her strangely until she explained that the little boy had been left in the church. The second woman reached into her bag, grabbed for her cell phone and called 9-1-1 to report the incident. It was 11:03 a.m.

Quinn entered the conference room and immediately apologized for being late. He began to explain his tardiness while looking at Ms. Wilkes when Moore cut him short and explained that they all knew why he was late. He sat down at the large polished mahogany table and looked at Moore who began his explanation for the meeting.

Father Richard Reilly quickly entered the church with the woman that was sent to fetch him. He found the other two women trying to console a little boy who was whimpering by this time. The priest could hear a siren nearing the church as he approached the woman holding the child. She explained to him that she had just found the little boy in the tote bag right where she stood. Little Joe was still upset with his surroundings and he began crying again as the emergency technicians approached with a policemen directly behind them.

Crystal Walker watched her TV program until she was interrupted by a phone call from one of her friends who called to chat. She ended her conversation with her friend a few minutes later when she looked at the kitchen clock and noted the time. She had another half hour before little Joe would be waking so she fixed herself lunch hoping that she could actually eat it before her undivided attention would be needed to feed her two year old son.

181

Moore finished up the details of the events of the last two weeks concerning the Wilson farm and now the three incidents the FBI were harassing Quinn about and asked Ms. Wilkes, "Do you have any questions concerning all the information I have given in front of everyone involved?"

"Mr. Moore, I have all the information I need to begin a harassment charge against the FBI if another incident takes place by them towards Mr. Quinn or any other person sitting in at this meeting."

"I am attending the re-interment of Captain Wilson from the Wilson cemetery, Miss Wilkes. Do you have any objection or any legal reason to council me on why I should not attend the re-interment?" He quickly added, "All of us here will be attending as Captain Wilson was part of our group in Iraq and we all want to be there to honor him."

She advised them all, "Please stand at a distance and only observe because you are not part of the Maryland Reserves who have been requested by the family to attend as honor guards. I have been informed of these conditions by Attorney Breen when I talked to her earlier this morning." Audrey then informed those present that the schedule was for the graves to be unearthed and the vaults to be lifted and placed next to open graves.

"A quick ceremony will take place where the three reservists will fire seven rounds each for a 21 gun salute. Taps will be played and the relatives, if they choose to attend, will be able to place flowers on the vaults. The family will be asked to leave so that the task of loading the vaults onto the truck or trucks that have been ordered by the undertaker can be accomplished," she said in an instructive manner. "I doubt whether the family will attend, but the undertaker has made provisions if they so desire. The trucks are scheduled to be driven to Arlington immediately and should arrive there on Saturday evening. The re-interment is scheduled for 11:00 a.m. Monday morning in which there are no restrictions as to who can attend that ceremony." Moore was pleased that Audrey Wilkes had confirmed what he and his group already knew.

Father Reilly watched as the emergency technicians and policemen took the child to the ambulance. One technician examined the child and found him to be healthy, but needed to get him to the hospital pediatric ward for a complete physical. The three women that had been at the church, were asked questions by the several other officers who had responded. The FBI office of Special Agent Jack McManus was called by the police and informed that an attempted kidnapping had occurred and that they had been requested to participate in the case.

Crystal finished her lunch and decided to check on little Joe. She climbed the stairs in anticipation of hearing him call her name as he usually did at this time when waking from his nap. She screamed when she saw the empty crib. She checked the windows in the bedroom and looked around the room including the closet for her son. She reached the phone extension in the second floor hallway and dialed 9-1-1. Within minutes, the police were at the Walker home. The 9-1-1 operator quickly connected the church incident which indicated a child had been found, and the Walker home incident, with the missing child a few miles away. It didn't take McManus long to react quickly and have Crystal taken to the county hospital where the unidentified child had been reportedly sent. Jack found Joe Walker in the central communications room sifting through background information on Moore's group. He did not indicate any details on the child until he had Walker in his FBI sedan in route to the hospital.

Quinn accompanied Jarvis into office. After they both entered, Sean closed the door and threw his keys on his desktop. Jarvis looked at him strangely but knew that grin on Sean's face meant more trouble.

"Sergeant Major, I need to tell you something."

"I hope you are going to give me good news. Lately, everything you tell me is a problem," Jarvis sarcastically answered. Five minutes later, Jarvis sat ghostly white and shaking his head at Quinn. He was too upset to even state how foolish he thought Quinn had been to take a chance and kidnap some FBI agent's kid, drop it off at a church, and attend a meeting where an attorney had been called in to protect him and the rest of the group from possible FBI harassment. Before Jarvis could vent his anger, Quinn said, "It's obvious that the local FBI agents will be looking for someone crazy. The FBI can't spend very much time on Moore's group while they are hot on this new case. Sergeant Major, a good sniper plans his moves and escape routes well in advance before he pulls the trigger."

"Quinn, go to your apartment at the end of the day and only leave there in your full dress uniform in the morning. I will tell the Colonel of your foolish act and I hope that he will deduct a considerable percentage from your cut of the money."

Quinn smiled and looked directly into the former Sergeant Major's eyes.

"Jarvis, you queer son of a bitch. You tell Moore any fucking thing concerning this little escapade I just pulled off or so much of a whisper insinuating he reduce my money, percentage or any other shit, and he'll find out about that little college boy you been corn holing and sucking off on the side. You got that?" He turned and left the office. Jarvis was sick enough to have to quickly enter the men's room to relieve his bowels. He did that too often these days when he was involved with Quinn.

Crystal screamed when she saw her son sitting on the examining table in the Pediatric Ward. She startled the child and he began to cry as she picked him up and cuddled him crying almost uncontrollably. The attending physician began to speak when Special Agent McManus and Agent Walker entered the room. McManus quickly displayed his badge to the doctor while Joe grabbed his wife and child. Crystal attempted to explain to him why she had not called him and what had happened while hugging both of them. Joe motioned for her to stop as he said, "Everything is alright now and we will talk about the whole incident later." Jack McManus waited outside the room to question and talk to both of them when they were ready.

"Crystal, they will have to investigate the incident but I can't be part of it for obvious reasons," Joe said. "You need to tell Jack everything you can remember about your day before this happened. Do you understand?" She only nodded as she continued to console her son.

Jarvis felt alone and afraid of what was going to transpire tomorrow morning at the cemetery. He needed companionship and hadn't had any for a while because of the workload Moore had given him. He called his college student to arrange a meeting before he left the office. After a few rings, the University of Maryland Senior answered. Jarvis acted casual. While he was requesting an appointment, the student cut him short. He explained what had happened to him when some deranged guy assaulted him and told him to stay away.

"Look, I don't want to get into a triangle with some crazy lover you have hanging around." Jarvis tried to act completely surprised on hearing of the incident.

"I have no lover. This must have been a mistake." The college student didn't buy the explanation.

"That crazy ass guy used your name specifically." Jarvis knew it had been Quinn but continued with his charade. He continued to deny he had any lover and pleaded with the student to agree to an appointment that night. He almost begged, even stating that he would agree to any price as long as he could spend some time with him. The art major agreed to a meeting at 10:00 p.m.

"There will be two conditions you would have to agree to. The first is that you can only be with me for an hour. I have another appointment after 11:00 p.m. with a very wealthy individual I met who really likes me." Jarvis was hurt but horny enough to withstand the boasting youth. "Secondly, the price for the appointment tonight would be $200 cash." Jarvis began to complain when the student threatened to hang up.

185

Jarvis agreed and said, "I'll pick you up at the usual time at the University's main entrance, okay?" He thanked the young prostitute and hung up.

Quinn entered the office again
"I'm finished for the day and I'll see you tomorrow morning." Jarvis never looked up or acknowledged him. He was mad at Quinn for interfering with his personal sexual life and didn't want to have him finding out that he had made another appointment. He hadn't noticed Quinn outside his door as he finished his conversation of which Quinn had heard most of. He especially noted the time and meeting place. He was going to keep Jarvis away from this little tease before Jarvis got caught and arrested which would bring more problems to the group. He knew that if Jarvis was taken in for having a homosexual affair with a college student, and some criminal charges could be rendered on him, he would sing like a canary about anything to keep from going to jail. He thought of how easy it would be for Walker, McManus or even Officer Hayes to break Jarvis in a nanosecond.

Sean rented another car to drive to College Park and the entrance to the University of Maryland. He allowed enough time to park the rental, walk onto the campus and head for the quad apartment dorm that he had visited as few days earlier to scare this guy. He waited outside in the shadows of the dimly lit area on campus where he knew the male prostitute would have to walk by. He kept glancing at his watch every five or so minutes until he noticed the handsome young man leave his dorm and head for his appointment with Jarvis. Quinn looked quickly around to see if anyone was within sight as he approached the unsuspecting youth. He first walked past him and seeing that no one was visible in that direction, turned and grabbed the student from behind. In less than two seconds, the student went limp as Quinn dragged him off the sidewalk and into the bushes that he had scoped out minutes before as a good place to store the dead body. It was a quick death for the youth. His neck was snapped expertly by the ex-army sniper. Sean

186

quickly stepped back onto the sidewalk and casually headed off campus towards his parked rental. He entered the car and waited for Jarvis's car to appear in front at the arranged campus meeting spot. On schedule, Jarvis pulled up and parked his car in anticipation of his meeting with the student and a much needed hour of bliss. He was shocked when Quinn knocked on his window. Jarvis lowered the window and began to grumble as to why Quinn was stalking him. He smiled and told Jarvis, "I would suggest that you get out of College Park quickly. In about ten or fifteen minutes, the campus police will discover a young student dead in the bushes next to his dorm." Jarvis froze and couldn't move. Quinn repeated his request. "Hank, you need to move along right now or I will move you myself."

Jarvis stared ahead and slowly put the car in gear. He left and returned to his apartment where he anguished the entire night and began his plan to right the wrongs Sean Quinn had done to him. The Campus Police were alerted of the dead student by some others who were passing by. The College Park Police and Maryland State Police began their investigation.

Saturday Morning

Mr. Thomas Atkinson of the Frederick Funeral Home led the small convoy of trucks and equipment to the Wilson farm cemetery. It was after 7:00 a.m. when his car pulled up to the family cemetery. Atkinson motioned where he wanted the trucks and the vault equipment placed. Following a few hundred yards behind, was a military sedan with three formally dressed Reservists. Atkinson motioned to them as they approached to park near his car. The driver lowered his window to hear Atkinson inform him to standby until he was ready for them. Atkinson explained that it was better for them to stay in the air conditioned car and keep cool and dry until they were needed. He also instructed them that if they were to see family approaching the area, then they were to exit their sedan and stand at parade rest to show respect for what was transpiring in the cemetery.

A few minutes later, Staff Sergeant Quinn drove into the area with Sergeant Major Jarvis sitting in the front seat. In the rear seat were Colonel John Moore and First Lieutenant Marilyn Porter in full dress uniforms. The Reservists reacted as soon as they noticed the Sergeant Major exit the car next to theirs and open the door for the Colonel. Within seconds, they were out of their car and at attention. The senior reservist, a Sergeant, saluted Moore, who quickly returned the salute. Lieutenant Porter stayed in the car and kept out of direct eye sight of Director Atkinson so that he wouldn't recognize her from her recent visit to his establishment. For approximately two hours, the military group watched as the three vaults were unearthed one by one and lifted out by chains attached to the backhoe that had unearthed them. Moore noticed that the World War One vault that had been made of steel and was heavily rusted, was still in strong enough condition for the move. Mr. Atkinson covered the rusty steel vault with a white canvas and then a 48 star American Flag. Approximately 10 minutes, later, the Vietnam era vault was placed near the first one. This vault had been made of concrete and was in excellent condition except for soil markings. Director Atkinson instructed the same type of canvas to be placed over the vault but with a 50 star American Flag placed on it. The third vault was placed near the other two within minutes. The same procedure ensued as with the previous two. This was the vault Moore was interested in. It was clearly marked with the year 2003 with Captain Todd Wilson's name on it. Quinn immediately noted that small, but significant fact he had overlooked. The replacement vault that he had hidden in the barn did not have a year or Wilson's name on the cover. That would cause a small problem when he switched the vaults. Quinn remained calm. Jarvis had not noticed the difference and had not said a word to him the entire morning. Quinn noticed the tension in Jarvis and hoped that the man would do his part to pull off the switch today but he knew he would have to keep an eye on him. He had a feeling Jarvis would try to pull something off to get back at him for eliminating his student lover. What that something was, he couldn't figure out yet, but whatever it was could jeopardize the whole operation.

The time was 10:05 a.m. and the funeral director finished putting the headstone of Jeremiah Wilson into the trunk of his car. He would place the stone in the Frederick cemetery for the Civil War Veteran in a few days. As he finished, he patiently scanned the road entering the Wilson property looking for any representatives from the family. After waiting another ten minutes, he signaled the Reservists. On cue from Director Atkinson, the Reservists came to attention with their M-16s at the ready. This signaled Moore's group to follow. The three M-16s were fired in unison seven times as the highest tribute paid to the veterans. One Reservist handed his M-16 to another and began to blow taps. Upon completion, Director Atkinson signaled for the five funeral employees to begin rigging the cables from the winch crane of the first truck to lift the first vault onto the truck. All three trucks had been lined up to receive the honored men. The first truck loading was completed and ready to transport World War One Veteran Herman Wilson to Arlington and pulled onto the farm road and

189

waited. The second truck began the task of retrieving the vault of Vietnam Veteran Arnold Wilson for his journey to Arlington. Quinn waited until the attention of the vault riggers and truck drivers were on the Arnold Wilson vault when he quietly walked to Jarvis's car, pulled out a canvas bag and approached the cable winch of the portable vault crane of the third truck to be used for Todd Wilson's vault. Quinn placed himself in a position hidden from anyone working with the funeral director and away from the Reservist Honor Guards. He pulled out a pair of heavy cable cutters from the carrying bag and applied them quickly and quietly as possible to the vault cable of the winch crane. He engaged the wire and clipped it. The cable cutters damaged the wire but he needed a second cut to make sure the cable broke with the least amount of force when it attempted to lift Todd Wilson's vault. He snipped again and this time he succeeded in severely damaging the cable. He quickly retreated to the car, replaced the instrument into the bag and took his place next to the others. He felt at ease as he knew no one saw him perform the act.

The second truck completed the task of loading Arnold Wilson's vault and moved to its location behind the first truck. It was almost 11:00 a.m. when the third truck moved into position to retrieve the vault. The vault riggers placed the cables for the winch crane to begin to lift and load the vault. It began to lift to Quinn's surprise but then snapped, to his relief, approximately two feet off the ground. The vault instantly fell, making a muffled noise on the grass to which it had landed. The cable winch stopped and the broken cable from the winch crane fell onto the settled vault. No one was injured, but the Director's face grimaced. Moore immediately walked over to him as planned.

"Mr. Atkinson is there a contingency plan for placing the vault onto the truck?"

"I might be able to position a winch from one of the other trucks." He paused as he looked over the situation. "But now that I look at it, it won't give me the steep angle I need. I won't know until I try it to see if it works." He shook his head negatively. "I'm afraid that idea might possibly damage another winch crane or even one of the loaded vaults if I don't succeed."

Quinn suggested, "Mr. Atkinson, use the backhoe."

Atkinson shook his head and said, "I know I won't be able to get the height I need to load the vault onto the truck."

"Well sir, I suggest that a new truck and cable winch crane be sent here as soon as possible to complete the task."

Thomas Atkinson looked perplexed when Moore suggested that he order another truck.

"It will probably take most of the afternoon to even find a replacement, never mind get the replacement here in time."

"Mr. Atkinson, direct the two other trucks to leave for Arlington. I will instruct my Sergeant Major to contact the Reserve First Sergeant to update him on the situation. Between the two senior NCOs, the situation should be taken care of."

Atkinson was relieved and he immediately began to complete checking the first two trucks for their road trip. Once he was satisfied that the trucks were secure and ready to roll, he instructed his assistant to take the two vaults to the National Cemetery where he would meet them later. The director returned to the damaged truck and instructed the driver to take the truck back to have the winch cable replaced just in case they couldn't get another truck and winch right away. The director knew that it would take most of the day to get the winch fixed on the truck and get back to the Wilson cemetery. Colonel Moore never instructed Jarvis to call the Reserve First Sergeant. He walked over to the three Reservists who came to attention.

"Gentlemen, you will probably have to wait on the farm property, all night if needed, until the new truck arrives to lift and place the last vault onto the truck for delivery to the National Cemetery." The three men glanced at each other immediately to the amusement of Moore. "But, I can arrange to have my two NCOs guard the vault until the new truck arrives sometime this evening or early tomorrow morning if you cannot support."

The Reservists Sergeant said, "Sir, I do not think we can support an overnight guard and we will need to check in with our First Sergeant for orders on staying or waiting for a backup." The men looked relieved and thankful when Moore also said, "I understand men. You are in a predicament and you probably have family commitments and need to return home." He instructed the Reservist that there was no need to complicate the symbolic military task by informing their superiors of the truck incident. He suggested that after he had confirmed it with the director, they were to leave and give the details to their First Sergeant when they saw him. He was sure that their First Sergeant would not object to having his old friend, Sergeant Major Jarvis, who served with their First Sergeant, be the guard for the vault.

Moore approached Director Atkinson who was busy on his cell phone trying to make arrangements for a vault truck with a crane winch to be at the farm as soon as possible. Moore stood by as Atkinson called several funeral homes that he knew very well. Quinn and Jarvis waited at parade rest near Jarvis's sedan while Porter remained in seclusion inside the dark windowed sedan. The Reservists stood by as well and waited. Approximately a half hour elapsed before Director Atkinson made contact with another funeral director. Fortunately for Moore and his team, the director couldn't be back at the farm until around 8:00 p.m. based on the information Moore surmised from what the director was saying. Disappointed, but relieved that he still would have Captain Wilson's body at Arlington before Monday morning's re-interment, Director Atkinson resigned to that schedule. Moore waited for Atkinson to finish the call and explain the situation. Upon hearing the latest information, Moore signaled his NCOs to approach him. Quickly both men stood in front of Colonel Moore and Director Atkinson to be updated with the news concerning the truck replacement timetable.

"Would there be any problem for you two to stay and assure the Director and me that Captain Wilson's vault will be honorably guarded until the Director's new truck arrives around 8:00 p.m.?" the Colonel asked.

Both men came to attention and Jarvis said, "Sir, there will be no problem."

Quinn spoke up next and said, "Sir, the Sergeant Major and I would be honored."

"I'll instruct the Reservists," Atkinson said. Moore quickly cut him off.

"No need. I'll relieve the men from their duty. I'll also instruct them to report back to their First Sergeant as soon as possible with the new orders."

"Thanks," Atkinson said as he walked over to the vault and assured himself that the flag and canvas were secured enough for the evening. Moore approached the Reservists and thanked them for their excellent support in this sad but honorable event. "Gentlemen, you are relieved. I will send a written report to your First Sergeant that you all performed with the utmost respect to these veterans. Gentlemen, these are your new orders." The three men saluted and were dismissed by Moore. Atkinson stayed until the Reservist left. He nodded to Moore as he drove his car past Quinn and Jarvis. Porter slouched and looked the other way as Director Atkinson drove by. No one in the group moved until all the vehicles had left the Wilson road and entered the highway.

Moore motioned at the two NCOs as he opened the door to Jarvis's car and waited for the two subordinates.

"We just accelerated the vault switch." Jarvis looked at him and cautioned him that it was only 12:30 p.m. and that someone from the family or from the funeral home could return at any time during the afternoon hours. He asked if they should chance this mission so early in the day. Moore looked away from Jarvis and at Quinn and said, "I'm not going to wait any longer." He ordered, "Put the stored truck in front of Wilson's vault so that anyone approaching can't readily see it until they are up close. Marilyn, as soon as the truck gets here, you are going to be in charge to watch the road for any approaching cars or trucks. I want you to stand on the flatbed of the truck. At that height, you should be the first one to see anything approaching. You will also stay there and assist when we start handing you money." He looked at Jarvis. "You are going to operate the truck winch and assist Quinn in switching the vault covers or the entire vault if necessary. Quinn, if the top comes off the vault easy, maybe we won't have to switch the vaults." Quinn didn't answer as he jogged off to get the stored truck from the barn. Within ten minutes, the truck had been driven and positioned by the vault and all four of them had changed by donning coveralls and placing their dress uniforms in Jarvis's car.

Quinn's first attempt was to see if he could move the cover off the old sealed vault with a crowbar he had stored in the truck. He prodded until he broke off a chunk of the concrete. Jarvis's face grayed and he yelled at Quinn, "Now what?" Quinn ignored him and immediately wedged the bar into another position and heard the cover move. He pried hard and could see the cover slip out of its position. He yelled to Moore and Jarvis to assist him with sliding some wood strips he brought to hold up the cover as he wedged it free. Before long, he had the cover over just enough to access the contents. The smell of stale air came out from the vault. Quinn ordered them to stop so he could unlatch the upper hatch of the aluminum coffin. He pried the lock mechanism and finally got the upper casket hatch open. He ripped the plastic bag that contained the bills and began to hand Jarvis stacks of $100 bills. Quinn asked Moore to get as close to the vault as possible and help. He also instructed Marilyn to stay on the truck and watch as the money was handed up to her to stuff the duffle bags that had been stored in the empty vault. "Place the stacks as neatly as possible in the empty bags but keep an eye on the road. Keep the weight evenly distributed if you can in each of the six duffle bags," Moore said. The process continued until all four of them were drenched in sweat from the constant movement until the aluminum casket was empty of the stacks of $100 bills and placed evenly in the bags. Quinn checked to make sure all the bills had been removed. As he tried to wedge and push the concrete cover back on the vault, it cracked and broke into two large pieces. Jarvis panicked and yelled at Quinn. He ignored him again. Moore did as well. Marilyn kept watch on the dirt road from atop of the bed of the vault truck while she loaded the duffle bags into the new vault on the truck. Moore smiled at a panicking Jarvis. Jarvis barked, "How in the hell are we going to fix this shit?"

"Shut up and follow Quinn." Quinn instructed Marilyn to get off the truck so he could replace the broken vault cover with the new one he still had on the truck. He removed a sledgehammer from the tool box on the truck. He smashed the old cover and broke it into manageable pieces that could be picked up and placed in the new empty vault a little later. First, he had to get the new cover off the truck. He instructed Jarvis to assist him while Moore policed the area for small bits and pieces of broken concrete. He rigged the new cover with the cable and guided the lifting of it off the truck and over the existing vault. The cover was then lowered and suspended within a foot of the vault by Jarvis who was in control of the winch. Quinn removed the old gasket so it would not interfere with the gasket on the new cover. Jarvis used the electric winch crane button to slowly lower the new vault cover onto the old vault. They both noticed that the aged concrete of the old vault was in sharp contrast to the new cover. Quinn started rubbing dirt onto the cover while Jarvis watched. He threw dirt at Jarvis as he yelled for him to help. Moore actually laughed as Jarvis started to help. He assisted as well.

Twenty minutes later, the cover looked almost as old as the original one. There were two exceptions they gambled on hoping that no one would notice. There was no date and no name on the new vault cover. It took another ten minutes to collect and clean up all the broken concrete pieces and deposit them into the new unused vault and next to the duffle bags full of cash. Quinn looked over at the six duffle bags, full of $100 bills totaling $11million. The unused vault was half full of concrete debris. He picked up several bags and gauged that they weighed approximately thirty-five to forty pounds each. He smiled at Marilyn and said, "Good job equaling the cash."

He covered the vault with a green army canvas he had brought and secured it with some rope. Finished with the truck, they re-installed the white canvas and American flag on Wilson's vault that the funeral director had put on earlier. They all rechecked the area to their satisfaction. Marilyn handed Quinn some chemical wipes, a bottle of water and his uniform as he jumped into the truck cab. He smiled and winked at her as he started the truck and drove it back in to the barn to conceal it again.

Marilyn Porter reached back into the bag, turned to the other two men and handed them chemical wipes to assist in removing the dirt and concrete dust from their hands and wipe the sweat from their brows. She also gave them bottled water as they removed their overalls and placed them into a plastic bag. The Colonel was pleased that all was going better than expected. Within ten minutes, the three of them watched as Quinn jogged back from the barn. He handed her his soiled overalls and she placed them in the bag with the others. All four of them were now dressed in their uniforms and besides soiled shoes, they looked presentable to the untrained military eye. The Colonel looked at his watch and it was almost 4:00 p.m. Moore figured that they still had time to get the truck out of the barn before anyone returned. He looked at Marilyn and paused before he spoke to her. "I need to get you out of here just in case Atkinson recognizes you or asks questions about you sitting in the car. He hadn't recognized you so return to the barn and drive the truck to the Wilson pond and wait there." She left as instructed. A few minutes later, the three men could hear the truck being driven out of the barn. Marilyn drove to the pond as instructed. While she waited at the pond, her mind wandered and she recalled her wine and cheese picnic with Sean. She fanaticized that there would be more picnics like that with him now that they had pulled off their plan.

Moore, Jarvis and Quinn waited near the car for the director to return. At 6:10 p.m., Quinn spotted the director's car and another vault truck approaching. It was two hours earlier then they had expected. Moore smiled, knowing he had made the correct decision to accelerate the switch. He called the group to attention and then parade rest as the vehicles approached.

Mr. Atkinson was pleased to see Moore as much as Moore was pleased to see him. Atkinson pulled up alongside the three men, stopped the car and approached them. He did notice that one of Moore's people was missing. He said, "Where is the woman you brought with you?"

Moore quickly made up an excuse and said, "Oh, my ex-military secretary. She wasn't feeling very well so I drove her home while my NCOs waited for your return." Atkinson never asked any further questions as he turned and began directing the new truck into the position he wanted it to be to load the vault. Ten minutes later, the vault was secured on the truck bed still covered with the white canvas and the American flag. Mr. Atkinson turned to Colonel Moore and gestured that he had completed his task. Moore called the group to attention and saluted as the Director's car and the truck carrying Todd Wilson's vault left the cemetery. He waited until the vehicles were on the farm road heading for the main road before he completed his salute. He ordered parade rest. He waited until the truck had disappeared when he yelled dismissed and began to laugh. Jarvis shook his hand while Quinn high-fived him. He told both of them to control themselves but laughed again. He called Marilyn on his cell phone to inform her all had gone well. He said that the three of them would be at the pond in a few minutes. Several minutes later, he instructed Jarvis to park parallel to the truck. Marilyn secured the truck and jumped out of the cab. Quinn climbed onto the truck bed and signaled Jarvis to stand next to the truck. He removed the canvas and handed Jarvis the first Army duffle bag they had stored in the empty spare vault. Jarvis began carrying each one to the sedan's trunk. In a few moments, the trunk was stuffed with four bags. Moore took the other two from Quinn and placed them into the sedan's back seat. He instructed Quinn to check thoroughly to make sure there were no other bills left in the vault.

"Jarvis," Moore called out. "Accompany Quinn to Hagerstown to dispose of the vault and to drop off the truck." Jarvis didn't answer. Quinn looked at Moore and said, "I'll take care of it alone. I don't need his help." He knew Jarvis was still upset with him.

"Colonel, he's right. He doesn't need me and I would rather go with you and the Lieutenant than ride with him anyway." Moore looked at him and then at Quinn.

"Hank, there is no room in the car now with the loaded duffle bags."

"Sean, you need his assistance." Jarvis just turned and jumped into the truck. Moore and Quinn looked at each other a little perplexed. Moore just gestured for Quinn to leave.

"Meet us at my place later when you're finished." Quinn nodded and drove away. Moore and Porter returned in Jarvis's sedan to Moore's apartment.

It was close to 7:00 p.m. and most of the apartment dwellers were either at dinner or out for the evening. Moore parked close to his apartment door and the two of them quickly began unloading the six duffle bags into his apartment. Several apartment dwellers noticed the Colonel and Lieutenant moving the duffle bags in. Moore commented to several of them that he was returning from the Reserve center with some stuff he had to store. They were dressed in their military uniforms and no one paid any further attention to what they were doing. Some even asked if they could help him and the pretty Lieutenant. He smiled and declined even though he would have welcomed the help.

Upon completion of the task, they locked his apartment door and laughed together at what they had just accomplished in full day light, under the noses of the funeral director, the Reservists and Moore's neighbors. Excitedly, Marilyn threw her arms around his neck in the apartment atrium and hugged him tightly. She then pulled back slowly and kissed him on his lips. Moore felt like superman. Perhaps now, he thought to himself, with all the money I have and her new found respect for my abilities, perhaps now I will have all of her. She teasingly brushed her tongue around his lips then slowly into his mouth. He reciprocated, but gently pushed her away and said, "Not yet

198

my dear, we still have the rest of our lives to take that up. I'm tired now and wouldn't be much of a performer. Let's get something to eat and return in an hour or so to begin our task to split up our interests" She smiled and said that she understood. Unbeknownst to him, she had hoped that he couldn't perform and was more eager to split up the cash. It was all a part of her plan. She had to keep up the act until she had her share in her hands.

Quinn drove the truck as Jarvis stared out the window. He finally broke the ice and said, "You still pissed about that college student?"

"You killed a kid. You are a cold blooded bastard and a son of a bitch." Quinn didn't say anything because he didn't want to provoke him any further while he was driving the truck. He only had about ten miles until he reached the Hagerstown Monument Company. Jarvis, intermittently, between stares out the window, called him names and threatened as to what he wanted to do to him. Quinn stayed quiet until he observed a road construction area coming up. There were several barriers partially blocking the entrance to the construction area. He managed to drive the truck between the barriers and into the construction site. Several areas had been stockpiled with concrete barriers, crushed stone, piles of old asphalt and other construction materials used for the road improvement project that was apparently being stored there. He stopped the truck behind some heavy equipment that had been parked on the site, secured it, and told Jarvis to follow him. Both men jumped onto the flatbed and uncovered the new vault that had not been used. Quinn hooked some cables around the vault and attached them to the portable crane and winch. He lifted the vault as high as he could and swung the crane out and away from the truck. He pushed a free flow button on the winch that was attached to the hanging vault. Several seconds later, the cable spun loose from the disengagement and the vault dropped. The fall from approximately ten feet was enough to smash the vault into five large pieces. Jarvis looked in amazement, wondering how Quinn thought up these ideas. Quinn handed him a sledgehammer and told him to break the vault up into smaller pieces. He secured the winch and crane while Jarvis attempted to break up the concrete vault pieces to complete Moore's orders to get rid of the vault. Jarvis was pathetic looking as he attempted to lift the sledgehammer and strike the vault pieces. Quinn became impatient as he listened to him grunt and moan as he attempted to lift the sledgehammer.

"For Christ's sake, catch your breath, stand there and watch me finish the job. You're pathetic." Sean worked quickly smashing the concrete but kept an eye on Jarvis who still was panting but irritated with him about eliminating his male lover. Quinn was exhausted by the time he finished breaking up the pieces until they were unrecognizable. He rested with his back to Jarvis as he wiped sweat from his brow but still kept aware of his movements behind him. He hadn't noticed that Jarvis had quietly removed a shovel from the flatbed's toolbox and had managed to stand behind him trying to conceal it. But Jarvis hesitated a moment too long before Quinn's peripheral vision picked up his movement. As Jarvis swung the shovel at Quinn's head, he sidestepped and ducked as it swung over him. He returned the assault with one of his own. He hit Jarvis in the chest with the sledgehammer causing him to wince in pain and loose his breath. He fell onto his knees gasping for air and moaning as the shovel fell from his hands. Quinn's second blow was to the top of Jarvis's head. The sledgehammer collapsed the top of his skull and blood and brain matter spurted out of Jarvis's nose. His eyes bulged and mouth expended a death rattle almost instantaneously. He was dead before he fell from his kneeling position to the ground. Quinn had no remorse for the man. He was pleased he had the excuse to eliminate him. He looked around for a place to bury the ex-Sergeant Major.

After stripping Jarvis naked and collecting his uniform, Quinn dragged his body into a temporary drainage ditch that had been dug at the construction storage site. He spent another half hour digging a shallow grave, laid him into it and covered the body with whatever soil, gravel and stone that was nearby. He returned to the truck, secured the tools in the toolbox and placed Jarvis's uniform clothes in the cab. As he drove along the road heading for his final destination, he checked to make sure no passing or following vehicle could witness him throwing one piece of clothing at a time, out the window, every mile or so until he had Jarvis's jacket and cap remaining. He also pulled off the ribbons and other pins and threw them out the window one at a time. He especially enjoyed throwing out the Purple Heart ribbon the most. He knew how Jarvis had earned that one. He stripped the stripes and hash marks off the jacket and threw those out over a bridge as he entered Hagerstown. He arrived at the Hagerstown Monument Company parking lot at 8:45 p.m. He parked the truck and looked for his BMW. He then looked up the number of the monument foreman he had rented the truck from and called him on his cell phone. After a few rings, the foreman answered. Quinn requested his BMW and advised that he had returned the truck. The foreman said that he couldn't possibly get back to deliver the car until the next morning. He was convinced to return to his place of employment when Quinn said that he had a considerable amount of money that would make his trip worthwhile. Quinn placed Jarvis's stripped jacket and cap into the dumpster of the monument company. The foreman returned with Quinn's BMW and parked near the truck. A half hour later, Quinn was on his way back to Frederick and the foreman was one thousand dollars richer in cash. Sean called Moore to inform him that he had disposed of the vault, dropped off the truck and that he would see him in an hour or so. Quinn ended the conversation indicating all had gone to plan. Moore didn't ask for any more details and Quinn didn't offer any.

The First Good Lead

Quinn returned to Moore's apartment and never mentioned anything about Jarvis as he entered. Moore asked, "Where is Jarvis?"

Quinn responded casually, "I'll tell you in a minute. I need to relax a bit and watch what Marilyn is doing." He noticed her counting the money and placing it in four neat stacks. Quinn couldn't resist touching the cash and began assisting Marilyn as she opened the last duffle bag and removed the remaining $100 bills to the smiles of everyone. Moore looked at Quinn and asked again, "Where is Hank?" Quinn slowly looked over at Moore while he continued to help Marilyn and explained what had happened. Both Moore and Porter looked at each other in disbelief. Quinn continued, "Hank was upset the entire day and it culminated with him trying to strike me with a shovel while we were disposing of the vault." Quinn detailed the killing of Jarvis to Porter's dismay and Moore's amazement. The Colonel remarked, "He was still acting queer until his death."

"That's no reason to kill someone. God damn you Sean. Why did you have to kill him?" Porter screamed.

Both men looked at her in amazement.

"Did you forget that he was the one that was trying to kill me?" Moore cut in, "Jarvis's portion will now be split amongst us. He smiled and said that he realized that they would have to divide another $2.75 million three ways. Porter got over her concern for Jarvis very quickly as she started separating the stacks of $100 bills on the table as he had ordered.

While Porter counted and separated the money, Moore pulled Quinn aside and asked for more details of how he had handled the situation. Quinn explained how he disposed of the body and personal affects. He also informed the Colonel of how he broke up Jarvis's relationship with a homosexual prostitute. Moore was surprised but seemed pleased that Quinn had taken care of the situation. He didn't ask any more questions as they all had just added over $900,000 to their individual wealth. By midnight, the group had separated and stacked the bills into three identical piles. Moore brought shipping boxes already marked from another room. He had purchased them for this eventful day. Each box was labeled with different titles such as dishes, pictures, china, and books. Porter and Quinn laughed at Moore's boxes but were pleased he had thought of almost everything. The Colonel looked over all that had been done and said to Quinn, "We need to get rid of Jarvis's sedan."

"Just have Marilyn return it to Jarvis's apartment parking lot. No one would know the difference. I'm heading for my apartment. I'll be in touch." Quinn knew that Marilyn would stay with Moore for the night. He also knew that she would keep an eye on him to make sure the money stayed safe.

An hour later, Moore followed Marilyn to Jarvis's apartment parking lot to drop off the sedan. They both returned to Moore's for the night. Quinn kept a good distance away but watched the entire time to make sure they both returned to Moore's apartment.

A small article in Sunday morning's Frederick News-Post reported the re-interment of the Wilson veterans. Moore caught the article by its title of, "Generations of Family Veterans Re-interred." The article gave a little history of each of the veterans. The dates and places of where they were killed were listed. It mentioned that an Honor Guard from the Maryland Reserves had attended and that the Frederick Funeral Home had been in charge of the arrangements. No photos were shown and only the date and time of the National Cemetery interment was given for the three veterans. There was no mention of the Civil War veteran. Moore relaxed as he sipped his second cup of coffee.

As he continued to read the paper, he saw another article indicating that a student had been found dead on the University of Maryland campus at College Park. It only said that the authorities were investigating the crime and there were no other details at this time. The name, class and major of the deceased were the only facts given. Moore felt confident that no one would ever suspect that Quinn had been remotely involved in this incident. He continued reading when another article caught his eye about a two year old boy that had been apparently abducted but then turned in at a Roman Catholic Church by the abductor. The article described the anxiety of Mrs. Crystal Walker who said that her child had been taken from her home while she had been occupied with chores in the household. No one could identify the abductor who apparently had lost his nerve and dropped the child off at the church. The article did mention that a parish woman said she saw a man of a particular size, height and dress in the church, holding a bag that she first thought was a pet tote bag. He became concerned when the name of the father of the child had been identified as Agent Joe Walker. Moore knew how Quinn despised Walker.

One other article made Moore's stomach turn. The Maryland State Police had been called to a roadside construction area by a security company. The story said that a watchman performing a security check on the equipment that had been parked in the construction storage area had found the partially exposed body of a naked white male. Moore read on quickly but the article said that the victim was unidentified due to head disfigurement and that the crime was being considered as a homicide. The article did state that the victim had a crushed skull. A heavy blunt object was considered the cause. No other information was available. Moore contemplated how he would handle the disappearance of Hank Jarvis. The story that Jarvis had decided to resign several days before he was found dead would not work now and would probably indicate that Moore had something to hide. He decided to go to work on Monday and by mid-morning; he would request his secretary to notify Jarvis to report to his office. He would act as if he had no idea that Jarvis had not come in that day. His secretary would be able to confirm that. He knew that he would have to play out his absence from the office day by day. He spoke to Marilyn who was busy eating breakfast.

"Marilyn, you will delay your resignation. I want Quinn to resign in about two weeks so that we can watch the investigation of Jarvis develop before he goes. If the authorities identify Jarvis before that time has passed, they will come directly to the bank looking for Quinn. He has our bank attorney's protection and will have our alibi that he was at the farm on Saturday and with you on Sunday. Even Director Atkinson can testify that Quinn was with me into the evening hours."

Marilyn asked if she needed to call Quinn and relay his instructions. He nodded and continued on reading his paper. Moore felt more comfortable now that he had all the boxes of money stacked as household items in his spare bedroom.

Joe, Crystal and little Joe Walker, spent Sunday morning attending services at their church. They realized that they had a lot to be thankful for now that little Joe was in his mother's arms sleeping while the pastor gave his Sunday sermon. Walker was tempted to get to the office as soon as possible so that he could see what had been done to solve his son's kidnapping. He was determined to watch as the case developed. He knew he was not allowed to participate in the investigation but he would be listening to every morsel of information given. He was in deep thought when his wife nudged him to hold little Joe. Her arms were tired of holding the little twenty-five pound toddler.

The Hagerstown Police had placed the John Doe into the city morgue. Several snapshots of the deceased had been taken and posted on the police database. Despite the facial features of Jarvis being distorted by the blow to the top of his head, he was still recognizable if one took the time to observe the grotesque pictures. McManus spent Sunday morning finishing up some paperwork on the dead lead on the suspected involvement of Sean Quinn with the Greenwich, Connecticut Police Officer shooting incident. He also had reviewed Walker's notes on the Thompson hit and run incident that the FBI had no leads on either. McManus wanted Walker back as soon as possible on Monday. He could take back the Thompson hit and run case but knew he couldn't assist in the investigation of his own kid's attempted kidnapping due to department policy. He yelled over to his new agent to see if he had come up with anything on the Walker kid case. Jamul Whitford said, "I have no new information to report, boss, but I am searching some new information that had just come in on known pedophiles in the Frederick area."

"I don't want you to spend too much time on the pedophiles. I have a hunch that this incident was something personal against Walker. I have another hunch of who that individual could be."

Craig was sitting up in bed when Terry walked in looking as beautiful as ever. She smiled as she walked over and kissed him. He didn't react as she expected and she sensed that the mood he was in was going to affect her visit.

"Wow, that wasn't the response I expected," she said.

He barked back, "Well, what did you expect? I'm a guy who needs a bedpan every time he has to piss or shit"

This made her upset. He immediately sensed that he had hurt her.

"Terry, I apologize. I'm a real jerk and you deserve a lot better. I really am sorry."

"Do you like me coming here?"

"Of course I do."

"If you hadn't been hurt, would you have pursued dating me?"

"Yes, but I'm stuck in this damned bed and can't do anything but wish about all the things I want to do with you." She stopped him from going on.

"Look, I care very deeply about you and I too have things that I would like to do with you as well. Don't you see that?" She rested her hand on his waist. She boldly moved her hand down close to his groin and felt his upper left thigh. He didn't move but was surprised.

"Craig, I think of you twenty-four hours a day and I am not going to let your frustration of being in this room affect our chances of being together once you get out of here. Do you understand my feelings towards you?"

He smiled and pulled her closer. This time, he kissed her long and hard.

"Now, how was that?"

"Wow, that's much better Craig."

She realized that her hand was nearer to his groin than she had intended and she could feel the arousal in her blue eyed patient. He also realized it but did not apologize as he looked directly in her eyes and said, "Thanks. Kisses like that could make me grow a third leg and get me out of this bed quicker than you think." She blushed and said, "It looks like you already have begun that." He laughed and grabbed her again but grimaced from the pain he felt in his hip.

IRAQ - The Green Zone had been quiet for the past two weeks. No injuries had been sustained by the company and patrols had been quiet except for the constant gathering of the Baghdad kids that followed the patrols looking for handouts of anything the GI's might give them. PFC Drew Watt had been in Iraq for four months now. The twenty-one year old Gary, Indiana native, walked along the street with the other members of his platoon. All seemed quiet until some shots were heard being fired from within a house several hundred feet from the direction the platoon was heading. The point man signaled for a halt and to get in a crouched position. Sergeant Russell King yelled for Watt and two others to assist the point man with searching for the shooters. Watt and the other three men entered the first floor of the house and found a woman lying face down in a pool of blood. She had had been shot through the neck but was still alive as the passing soldiers heard her moaning. Watt yelled for the platoon medic to assist the woman. The four GI's combed the first floor rooms and began to climb the second floor stairway. They reached the top of the stairs to the second floor and started down the narrow hallway that connected three small rooms. They cleared the first room and were about to enter the second when they heard the crashing of glass as the shooter panicked and tried to get out of the house. Watt entered the room and looked out the broken window to see that the man had jump from the second story window. He had landed in a small courtyard that shared a common space among the buildings that surrounded it. The fall injured the man. Watt observed him trying to get up to leave the courtyard but the pain forced him to lie in the dirty courtyard screaming as he held his leg. Watt's platoon members entered the courtyard and immediately disarmed him and yelled into the house for the medic treating the woman to come out and treat him as well. Several women peeked out from the surrounding buildings while a few children were fast enough to escape their mother's protection to get out in the courtyard and see what was happening. One older boy spit at the assailant and screamed at him in Arabic. Watt was the last one who entered the courtyard to hear some of the screaming and realized the kid was ratting out this individual for several incidents that the man had been involved with. One of Watt's comrades spoke a little Arabic and was able to translate part of the conversation that mentioned a soldier that this man had buried for money. The man was being damned by the kid, according to his comrade, because he had killed a family member who attempted to alert the authorities of that fact. Sergeant King entered the courtyard. His first instinct was to ask questions, but the man was in terrible pain and he needed to be able to stabilize the man before he got any information from him. The medic had finished attending to the wounded woman and gave a distressed signal to his sergeant concerning her condition as he approached the injured man. A few minutes later, while the medic was treating the man, the woman expired from her wounds. The injured man was taken immediately to the Green Zone Medical Dispensary.

FREDERICK, MD - The Bryants were waiting for the physician to discuss when Bob would be ready for discharge. Amy had planned to leave the hospital and meet with Bobby and Cora for the re-interment at Arlington. All three were planning to spend a little time with their relatives and then leave in two cars. Amy would return to Frederick to stay with Bob for a few more days while the kids headed back to Connecticut. Amy had decided that she didn't need Bobby and Cora around. Bob was healing well and any difficulty she encountered with him on the eight hour trip back to Greenwich she was planning, she could handle. Bob also had an appointment in two weeks with his physician to check on his leg and to finish the necessary bank paperwork to re-mortgage their house to keep the farm.

Craig was updated on the attempted Walker kid kidnapping from McManus. He also received the dead leads the agency had on his hit and run case. McManus cautioned him that he wanted his thoughts and help, but he didn't want the agent overdoing it so as not to have a relapse. The information he presented to Thompson was meant as something to keep him active but yet, not interfere with the extensive rehabilitation the agent was going to have to go through in the next two to three months.

Funeral Director Atkinson entered the Arlington National Military Cemetery administration office Sunday morning and spoke to the administrative officer. He announced that the remaining vault of the three vaults he had registered to be re-interred in the military cemetery had been delivered last night. The officer acknowledged the delivery and asked the funeral director to accompany him to the holding building where the vaults were being prepared. He explained that they had already supplied a new vault to replace the World War One vault. The other two would be reused. The officer further explained that the casket in the World War One vault would be placed in the new vault today. The vaults would be placed in the three graves as soon as the graves had been dug. He estimated that would be ready sometime in the afternoon. He wanted Director Atkinson to observe the re-interment and placement of the three white headstones that had already been prepared. Both men walked to the graves engraving area where the officer showed Atkinson the three headstones. They both checked the stones for accuracy. Atkinson asked if there would be any sort of ceremony at the site seeing that some family members would be attending. The officer explained that a twenty-one gun salute, taps and a short service by the cemetery chaplain would take place. He also explained that the military did not want to have the family endure anymore hardship. The officer said, "Mr. Atkinson, the re-interment ceremony should not take more than ten minutes to complete. The family will only observe three new white headstones with the names of their kin on them. The sod will have been replaced and to all appearances, the area will look like the men have been there since their service ended. It will be very dignified and less emotional for the family." Atkinson nodded and said that he would contact the family and update them on what they should expect tomorrow morning. He thanked the officer and departed.

IRAQ - PFC Drew Watt, along with several other soldiers, were ordered by Sergeant Russell King to stay outside the Green Zone medical dispensary while the Iraqi they had brought in was treated for a broken leg. Sergeant King entered the dispensary and explained the situation that had occurred to the security officer at the dispensary and said that he needed to question this man as soon as possible. King explained that the man was suspected of killing Iraqis as well as an American soldier.

FREDERICK, MD - Sean Quinn awoke late on Sunday morning. He relaxed knowing that in a few weeks he would be able to leave Maryland and go anywhere he so desired. He thought about taking Marilyn along for a while, but then cautioned himself against it because she had too many issues. One was her attraction to Moore. He figured he would still call her and see if she was interested in spending the day with him. He laid in bed thinking about all the things he could do to her while he had her with him for the day, but then reality set in.

He needed to behave himself, get his cut of the money from Moore and leave the old man's girlfriend alone. If she wanted to be with him she would have to initiate it, but only after he had his share stashed neatly away.

Whitford finished searching the pedophile files. He hadn't come up with anything suspicious concerning the Walker kidnapping. He buzzed through the latest crime files to see what had occurred in his agency's vicinity. He came across the file of a John Doe that had been found at a construction site just outside of Hagerstown. The picture that accompanied the file was disturbing but he printed the file. He also noted the University of Maryland murder victim and printed that file as well. They weren't related but he wanted to record all incidents that were in the geographical area of where the kidnapping took place.

Terry returned to Craig's room after receiving a phone message from Director Atkinson on the Arlington arrangements. He was sitting up in bed looking at his laptop that McManus had sent to him by one of the agents. McManus had given him permission to access FBI files to assist with several of the cases that were unsolved in their area. Thompson never looked up until Terry spoke to him. He looked a little startled because of his concentration but realized his little beauty had returned.

"My boss has allowed me to begin working again. I'm trying to give a little help in looking at some of the cases they have not been able to solve yet." Terry was interested in how the FBI searched for information. She positioned herself close enough to the laptop and Craig to get a good view of the screen he had on display in front of them. He liked having her very close to him. He especially liked the smell of her perfume. He did caution, "Some of these photographs are very disturbing so be prepared.

ARLINGTON, VA - Atkinson watched as the vaults were placed one by one into each grave in the cemetery. The

211

operation was performed with the utmost respect for the Sunday visitors. A canvas wall had been placed so the cemetery visitors would not be able to witness the re-interment. Atkinson observed the third vault being placed in its final resting place. The sealed cover to Captain Wilson's vault seemed different than he remembered. He didn't inquire since everything was moving on schedule and the vault would be covered in the next few minutes for eternity anyway. Two hours had passed and all three headstones had been placed exactly in alignment with the other headstones in the area. The sod had been replaced and the grounds attendants were racking and watering the grass to make it look like the area had never been disturbed. Atkinson was pleased by the professionalism displayed by the grounds crew and relaxed knowing that all that remained was for him to attend the Monday morning service, assist the family in any other requests and return to Frederick by Monday afternoon.

FREDERICK, MD - Amy, Cora and Bobby left the hospital Sunday afternoon heading directly for Arlington, Virginia after receiving word that the doctors felt that Bob could make the trip to Connecticut by the end of next week. They booked two motel rooms there so that they could attend the re-interment ceremony. Bob seemed comfortable enough staying in his hospital room while the family drove to Arlington.

Terry positioned herself almost parallel with Craig on the hospital bed. She continued to ask questions about the files Craig was viewing. An hour went by as he viewed the many files that had been sent to him. He took some notes as she looked on occasionally asking questions. Her interest in his work seemed to deepen his affection for her. Craig opened up some disturbing photos connected to incidences of kidnapping and murder. One photo that was extremely horrid was the picture of a naked man with his head disfigured from a heavy blunt blow to the head. Both viewers grimaced and moved on to several other photos that had been taken by the police at the crime location. As he continued on to other files, Terry stopped him and said, "I've seen that face before. Go back to it again if you don't mind." Craig looked at Terry and was about to question her when she said again, "Go back to that gross picture, please." Craig obliged and brought the picture into view. Terry studied it for a few more seconds and said, "He looks like Mr. Jarvis of the Colony Bank in Frederick." Craig looked at Terry and then back to the photo and studied it for a few more seconds. He looked at her, grabbed for the phone and said, "Good eye. I agree with you. Thanks for bringing that to my attention." He immediately dialed Jack McManus and informed him that Whitford's file divulged some interesting photos of a guy both Walker and he had interviewed only a few days ago. Walker grabbed Whitford and headed for the Hagerstown morgue.

Marilyn stood in the doorway of the spare bedroom in Moore's apartment. She was viewing all the boxes stacked and marked with a code Moore had developed for quick identification. Besides the normal boxes marked as dishes, books, clothing and other household descriptions on the top and sides of the boxes, she noted the small code written on the top corner. Moore had devised a code using a number configuration that all of them could understand. He had marked the boxes jm500k box 1 of 5 which indicated Moore had 5 boxes containing a total of more than $3.65M. She knew that each one had about $700,000 in it now that Jarvis was dead. The remaining ten boxes had her and Quinn's initials on them. Marilyn turned to Moore and asked, "They all are equal, right?"

Moore looked and smiled at her and said, "Yes, but I may hold up Quinn's until he conforms to all my instructions. I'll tell him if he disobeys orders, he could be penalized for his indiscretions. I should receive more money due to my initiation of the project and my leadership orchestrating and completing it anyway." Marilyn didn't respond to his comments.

"I have ordered a storage company to come to my apartment at noon on Monday. They will take all the boxes to a short term storage facility in Frederick. I will be the only one who has the key so I can control the events of the next two weeks." An hour later, Porter called Quinn and told him of Moore's plan to move all the boxes to an undisclosed storage facility in town.

After Quinn finished his phone conversation with Porter, he completed dressing and packed the essentials he would need to store in the BMW's trunk. He decided it was time to resign from the Colony Bank before any of the team did. He now knew that Moore had some sort of a score to settle for Jarvis's demise and the relationship he had developed with Marilyn. He figured he would end his employment on Monday morning by calling Moore and quitting. He decided that he would stay at an undisclosed location out of town until Moore sent the boxes to the storage facility. He never trusted Moore to deliver his money to an address he would have provided to him later. He had something else in mind for the Colonel. At approximately 1:00 p.m. Sean Quinn left for the outskirts of Hagerstown driving his new BMW with the top down.

Jack McManus and Jamul Whitford arrived at the Hagerstown Morgue. The morgue supervisor showed both men to the stainless steel cold storage lockers and opened one of the lockers labeled with a file number and the word 'John Doe' written in bold letters. The supervisor pulled back the white sheet as both men steadied themselves as they viewed the distorted features of the deceased man. Both agents looked for scars that had been listed on former Sergeant Major Jarvis's military medical records they had printed prior to leaving for the Hagerstown morgue. Both agents identified the bullet wound Jarvis had received in Iraq and some other identifying features that had been listed. Agent Whitford looked at his boss and said that he was 99% sure this guy was Jarvis. He mentioned that DNA testing would confirm that, but they had enough information to begin questioning some associates of Jarvis. Jack McManus was already heading out of the morgue as Whitford finished his statement. He saw McManus leaving and thanked the morgue supervisor for his assistance. He had to hustle to catch McManus, who was already on his cell phone.

Forensic Puzzle

IRAQ – The Green Zone medical dispensary had completed setting the leg of the Iraqi suspect who was being held for the murder of an Iraqi woman and under suspicion for the death and burial of an American soldier. Sergeant King and PFC Watt waited until an interpreter could be brought into the Iraqi's room. King and Watt listened while the interpreter explained that the suspect would be taken back to the area he was apprehended from and released to the people that wanted to harm him. The interpreter explained that if he divulged information that led to the identification of a buried American soldier, he would be spared that release. The interpreter also said that if the man would give information on who killed the soldier, then that would be considered in his trial to spare him the death penalty.

The Iraqi suspect was able to concentrate on what the interpreter was trying to tell him despite the anesthesia clouding his senses. His expressions of fear changed considerably every time he was told he would be released to the public if he did not confess that he had information concerning the death of an American soldier. He finally confessed that he never observed the killing but only helped with burying the American soldier for money. The interpreter paused and repeated what the Iraqi had just said. Sergeant Russell immediately sent PFC Watt to inform their CO that he should report to the dispensary as soon as possible to listen to the prisoner's statement. An hour later, a detail was sent to the location the Iraqi prisoner had said they would find a body of an American soldier. The detail sent to uncover the body, knew that there was no American officers missing but they had five enlisted men still reported as missing. Sergeant Russell led PFC Watt and three other soldiers to the location described by the prisoner. The location was a courtyard of a destroyed multi-building complex several blocks away from where the Iraqi had been apprehended. PFC Watt and one other soldier began shoveling and pick-axing the hard packed, clay courtyard. Ten minutes later, the other two soldiers took over the digging while the Sergeant continued to observe. Watt and the other soldier were drenched in sweat as they drank water, watching their replacements digging. Several minutes later, one of the soldiers uncovered the pant leg of a class dress officer's uniform with skeletal remains in it. Sergeant Russell immediately stopped the digging and notified his CO that the remains of an American officer had been found. The CO requested that an Army medical forensic team be sent to the location immediately to retrieve the remains. Russell was ordered to guard the area until the team arrived, removed the remains and dismissed them. The forensic team arrived and removed what were only skeletal remains, to start the identification process. The records for the enlisted missing men were not requested due to the fact that they had found an identifiable rank of Captain on the uniform of the skeletal remains. The forensic team was puzzled. There were no known missing captains on record for the Army or any other branch of the U. S. services. The forensic experts also noted that a large caliber bullet had entered the victim's head. The size indicated that the individual was possibly shot by a sharpshooter or sniper's large caliber rifle. The bullet was not the small caliber of an AK-47 usually used by the insurgents. The experts estimated that the body had undergone a decomposing state for three years and was a male, twenty-five to thirty years old. The skeleton was also noted to have some distinctive features that could be traced by Army medical records. One was that the individual had sustained a broken left arm as a youth and secondly, the teeth could be x-rayed and compared to the Army's dental records.

FREDERICK, MD - Monday morning was a cloudy and rain-drizzled day. The Wilson and Bryant families gathered with Mr. Atkinson at the new site that had been prepared for their relatives. Three new white headstones engraved with the family member's names, rank, unit, branch of service and the war they were killed in had been perfectly lined up. The green sod had been manicured to look like it had been in place for many years except for barely visible sod lines. An Army honor guard stood at parade rest while the family, friends and military representatives gathered to hear an Army Chaplain read scripture. The chaplain spoke for several minutes to the family members. He ended his invocation when he said that the Wilson men were now laying with the Nation's other distinguished. The commander of arms ordered the honor guard to attention. A twenty one gun salute was completed and taps played. The commander of arms thanked the family in the name of the President of the United States, and the Nation, who appreciated the duty the Wilson men had performed. The ceremony was over and the honor guard marched smartly from the site. The family viewed the headstones again, placed flowers on all three and continued to talk quietly to each other. Some members were teary eyed but thankful that the re-interment had been completed and that their uncle, son, brother, nephew or cousin had been properly laid to rest as heroes in a hero's place.

Amy Bryant personally thanked Mr. Atkinson for his services and quietly noted to him that she expected his billing to be sent directly to her and her husband. She made a mental note to thank Terry for the arrangements she made with Mr. Atkinson. She walked back to her car with Cora and Bobby. They all agreed to have brunch as a family in respect for the services they had just attended. The entire family felt that closure had finally been attained.

IRAQ – Captain Jonas Miles of the forensic team realized that matching the dental records could take several weeks if the work was performed in the United States. He had experience with the slumbering military timetable when dealing with investigations of this nature. He decided that he would request, and personally review, all records of Army officers with the rank of Captain only, who had been killed in action from March of 2003 until December 2004. Those were chosen based on the estimated time of decomposition of the few remaining body parts still attached to the skeleton. Captain Miles was pleased to see that only seven had been killed in that time frame, but he was baffled by the fact that on paper, they all had been accounted for and were properly buried in the United States. Of the seven, his research revealed that three fit the size of the skeleton found. He continued to review until he found what he had been looking for. Captain Todd Wilson had been killed in August 2003. He had sustained a fatal wound to the head by a large caliber bullet of an unknown Iraqi sniper in the Green Zone. Miles noted that his death was less than a mile away from the burial site. He reviewed the partial dental record that was in the file and noted an extraction that Captain Wilson had undergone at the Green Zone dispensary for an abscessed tooth in May of 2003. The extracted tooth area matched. Captain Wilson's records also indicated that he had sustained a broken left arm as a youth. That matched the distinctive healed area on the skeleton. The captain also noted that Wilson had been reassigned from the Maryland Reserves to work in a U.S Treasury Support Group during the initial gathering, cataloging and storing of U.S. currency found at various sites throughout Iraq. He immediately contacted his CO and reported the details he had uncovered.

FREDERICK, MD - Monday morning McManus and Whitford arrived at Quinn's apartment. McManus knocked several times and then yelled through the door that the FBI was outside. There was no response. Whitford positioned himself to attempt to break the door in. He began to move to break in the door when McManus stopped him. McManus did not have a warrant yet and it was obvious that Quinn was not at home. He planned to get a warrant by the end of the day but he first chose to call Attorney Audrey Wilkes to notify her of their findings concerning Mr. Hank Jarvis and to have Quinn available as soon as possible for questioning. Ten minutes later, Audrey Wilkes entered Moore's office to inform him that Hank Jarvis had been identified by the FBI at the Hagerstown morgue. He had been murdered. Moore immediately donned an expression of exasperation and surprise upon hearing this but deep inside, he was furious with Quinn and very concerned that he had done just enough to bring this whole operation to a quick halt. Attorney Wilkes left Moore's office to allow the bank vice-president some privacy. She recognized the signs of how upset Moore had become. He waited for her to close his office door then immediately dialed his secretary and asked her to contact Marilyn Porter and have her report to his office as soon as she got in. Meanwhile, he quickly dialed Marilyn on his cell phone hoping that he'd beat his secretary to it. He just wanted it noted that he put in the request. He caught her just coming into the parking lot and updated her on the situation.

His next task for damage control was to call Quinn. Before he could call him, he noticed that there was a message on his cell phone. He became extremely agitated when a voice message from the renegade came on indicating that he had opted to quit his job which would make him look even more suspicious. He hurriedly dialed Quinn's number. He left only a few words in the message. "Sergeant Major has been found, call me immediately." Quinn's cell phone beeped for the second time which irritated him. He'd found a small motel to stay at for a few days and decided to sleep in. He hated rainy Monday mornings and his sleep-in was being disturbed by the constant calls. He looked at the caller identification and saw that it was Moore. He was now more curious than irritated so he decided to listen to see if Moore was responding to the message he'd originally sent to him. He listened and awakened quickly. He returned Moore's call. Moore gently spoke into the phone and informed Quinn that his friend and fellow comrade had been found dead in Hagerstown. Quinn assumed that Moore must be with other people by his tone so he just listened. Moore explained that he should report to work as soon as possible. He said that the authorities were coming to question him because he was probably the last person to see Hank Jarvis alive after the Wilson cemetery re-interment. He also informed him that Ms. Wilkes wanted to brief him before the authorities arrived. "I'll be there in an hour." Moore closed his cell phone and waited.

IRAQ – Brigadier General Byron Caldwell contacted the Pentagon with the information his forensic group had reported. Within minutes, the file of Captain Todd Wilson was on the desk of Major General Thaddeus Lucas, Commanding Officer of Army Special Investigations. He ordered his staff to open an investigation on the captain.

FREDERICK, MD - McManus and Whitford arrived at Aubrey Wilkes's office.

Ms. Wilkes said, "I have been informed that Mr. Quinn is on his way into the office and will arrive momentarily." Both men declined refreshments that Wilkes offered while they waited. Wilkes's phone rang and both McManus and Whitford stared at her while she nodded and said that she understood and would ask the agents immediately.

"Mr. Moore has asked if Miss Porter or he would be required as well to be questioned again by either of you. Miss Porter is very upset at hearing the news of Mr. Jarvis and Mr. Moore would like to send her home for the day. He's planning to cut his day short as well so that he can be of assistance to the Jarvis family. Mr. Jarvis has only a sister who lives in Massachusetts and Mr. Moore is offering his assistance if she requires it," she said to both men. McManus said, "I do have some questions for both of them that won't take very long. I apologize for any inconvenience it will cause them but perhaps their answers can give us some additional insight and aid us in finding the murderer." The attorney relayed the information to Moore. Moore grimaced on the other end of the line but said he would come to the office in a few minutes with Miss Porter.

A few minutes later, Moore and a visibly upset Marilyn Porter entered Attorney Wilkes's office. McManus asked several questions concerning the last time they had seen Jarvis.

Moore answered quickly, "I last saw him when he dropped me off after all three of us had attended the service at the cemetery." While still holding Marilyn, he pinched her arm hard enough as a signal for her to continue to cry. McManus didn't ask Porter when she had last seen Jarvis based on her present condition and decided to wait until she settled down. It was what Moore was hoping would happen until he could figure out how much information McManus had on Jarvis's death.

McManus asked, "What is your relationship to the Wilson family?" Moore explained the military connection he and Marilyn had to the family. Bogus tears occasionally shed down her cheek as she continued to whimper. McManus began asking questions on the type of work that Moore did in Iraq when Wilkes cut him short and said, "This line of questioning is irrelevant to this murder case. What Mr. Moore did in Iraq is on file with the Army." Agent McManus apologized and said that both of them were leaving. Moore couldn't have been more pleased. Wilkes's timing was impeccable.

He said, "If I have any more questions for them, I will contact you, Attorney Wilkes."

As Moore and Porter were leaving Wilkes's office, Sean Quinn quickly walked in and stopped both of them and asked, "Is Hank really dead?" Porter began to sob and Quinn held and comforted her. Moore stood by and said nothing. Quinn was able to moisten his eyes enough for the agents to see, to highlight his astonishment of hearing confirmation of Jarvis's death. He released his embrace and told Marilyn that he would see her later as she left the office with Moore. He did manage to hold her hand a little too long to show their affection for each other.

Agent McManus thanked Quinn for coming in as quickly as he did and got to the point. He asked the same questions about Jarvis that he had asked Moore. Quinn gave the identical answers.

McManus asked, "Do you know of anyone who would have a reason to kill Mr. Jarvis?" Quinn thought a few seconds and said, "My ex-Sergeant Major did have some acquaintances that I did not approve of." McManus fell for the planned innuendo Quinn had just implied.

"What do you mean by that, Mr. Quinn?" Whitford asked.

"Hank Jarvis ran a little on the wild side and there were times when he would venture into relationships that were frowned upon by the military." Whitford had now fallen completely for Quinn's trap. Quinn went on to say, "Even though I respected my friend and supervisor, I didn't approve of some of his friends." McManus pushed for more information.

Quinn said, "Mr. Jarvis was a homosexual, but he covered it up while he was in the Army."

"Why is being a homosexual relevant to this case?"

"I had cautioned Jarvis about picking up strange men around town. I was afraid that Hank would get into trouble with the police and also that Moore would fire him if my suspicions were confirmed."

"Quinn, someone can't be laid off or discharged for being a gay man."

"When your boss is your former CO in the Army where homosexuality is frowned upon, things like that happen." Quinn also let it purposely slip when he said, "I'd seen Jarvis with a young man around town and I cautioned him several times at work to curb his desires for young men."

"Are you telling me that you think some gay partner of Mr. Jarvis's might have killed him?"

"Well, yes. It had entered my mind that Jarvis could have put himself in harm's way."

Whitford asked, "Okay, where can we find this man?"

"I'd check with some of the local colleges where Jarvis usually went to meet young men. I knew he had talked about friends he had at College Park." Several other questions were asked of Quinn until Audrey Wilkes said that she thought he had given enough information and that it was time to conclude the questioning. McManus and Whitford thanked Quinn and the attorney and left. On the way out of the bank, Whitford said to McManus, "There was an unsolved murder at the University of Maryland at College Park several nights ago."

"Yeah, I remember. We're going to check out the details on that student, but we'll still keep an eye on Quinn."

223

Quinn watched the two agents leave the bank.

"Mr. Quinn, I would like for you to keep yourself available for more questioning as I am sure the agents will be back," Audrey said. He pacified her and said, "I can be reached at all times at the cell phone number you have on file. Miss Wilkes, or can I call you Audrey?" He didn't wait for her permission. "Maybe the next time you need to talk to me we could, let's say, be in a more relaxing place where you could counsel me over a drink or two."

Wilkes smiled and said, "You can call me Attorney Wilkes and my office or the FBI Bureau Office is where I would desire to meet to represent you Mr. Quinn, if you know what I mean."

"I do and that's too bad," he said, smiling. He left her office knowing that she was either too straight and stuck up or too queer and had no interest. He still hoped for the former.

Moore informed Porter in a soft voice in his office, "I'm going to get the boxes out of my apartment and into a storage facility immediately. We were lucky that the agent didn't ask you when you had last seen Hank. Your excessive crying worked."

"You bruised my arm when you pinched me," she informed him.

"Sorry, but I had no choice and I hoped you would respond to my cue. You did well, my dear. I don't want him, like I didn't want Atkinson, to know you were there." He paused as another thought came into his mind.

"If he remembers to ask again, you tell him you reneged at the last minute due to emotional reasons or something like that. That will keep you distant from the three of us and put less pressure on you." He looked into her eyes, smiled and said, "I love you and want you to be protected. Plus, we both know Marilyn, you don't lie very well and this is only a small white lie that you should be able to handle." He smiled for a brief moment and told her to follow him in a few minutes. They both departed from the bank separately, but Porter kept her eye on Moore from a distance. Porter did not go to her apartment as he

224

had assumed. While she watched him get into his car, she actually felt a little moved that he had actually said that he loved her. In all the years she had bedded him, he never seriously said that to her. Then reality set in. She realized that she still didn't trust him. She knew she did not love him. Marilyn Porter had her own plan as she started her car to follow him.

She tailed Moore to assure herself that the former Colonel would not just simply load the boxes in his car and drive off. Moore arrived at his apartment where he immediately called the moving company. Marilyn contacted Quinn while at a safe distance from Moore's apartment watching to make sure he did what he said he was going to do and not leave with all the boxes.

"Good girl, Marilyn. I had a feeling that he might pull something like this. He's running scared now and I'm glad you saw it too," Quinn said.

"He's still at the apartment and hopefully arranging for a moving truck to pick up the boxes." Quinn told her to keep watch but keep far enough away so that Moore would not suspect he was under surveillance.

The movers arrived at Moore's home at the designated time. It didn't take them very long to move the forty boxes marked books, dishes, documents, kitchen items, pictures and other house hold necessities. After Moore tipped the two men, he informed them that he would be following them. He asked them to go at a reasonable speed so that he could maintain his position behind the truck in traffic. Porter stayed unnoticed in an adjacent parking area between two large pickup trucks that made it impossible for Moore to notice her in her Honda in his haste to follow the storage truck. Porter concentrated on his car for the next ten minutes until he signaled to turn off onto the road leading to the short and long term storage facility. By the time she reached the side of the road and stopped to call Quinn, he was already in his car driving to the section of the city Marilyn said they were heading to. It took him only a short while to reach them.

Quinn had already exited his car and was casually walking between the rows of the storage facility. He made sure that he kept himself out of sight as he watched the delivery truck park in front of the unit assigned to Moore. A few minutes later, the delivery men had completed unloading the boxes, closed the garage door and left. Moore was observed checking the lock on the door, looking around to make sure no one saw him and re-entered his car. As Moore left the facility, Quinn noted the storage number on the garage door and called Marilyn to meet him at her apartment as soon as possible.

IRAQ - The record of Captain Todd Wilson indicated that he had been buried on the family farm outside of Frederick, Maryland. The funeral home, family contact, dates of shipment, date of death and grave registration information seemed to be accurate except for the fact that the body in Iraq had been identified as being that of Captain Todd Wilson. Brigadier General Caldwell called the Commander of the Maryland reserves to send an investigator to review all the events that took place in August of 2003. He cautioned the commander that this investigation should be done quietly just in case there had been a mix up of who was buried in the Wilson grave. The commander understood and called in a few of his staff to begin the investigation. One of those individuals was First Sergeant Willard Smyth. Smyth stopped his commander mid-sentence when he informed his CO that he had sent an honor guard to support the re-interment of the Wilson body from the farm cemetery to Arlington on Saturday. The CO put the First Sergeant in charge to provide as much information as possible about the event by calling the Army investigative group led by Brigadier General Caldwell.

Quinn pulled up in front of her apartment and blew the horn twice. Marilyn walked quickly from her apartment complex door and into Quinn's BMW. She looked at Sean as he quickly drove the convertible down the street. After what seemed to her an eternity, he spoke.

226

"I'm going to the U-Haul rental garage to rent a small moving truck." She looked perplexed until he smiled and told her, "You will have to drive the BMW to the storage facility that Moore has rented."

"Are you telling me that we are going to empty out the storage facility. Are you out of your mind?" she asked. He just smiled and continued to drive. He pulled up to the U-Haul garage and told her, "Get behind the wheel. Follow me as soon as I get the truck." Marilyn was uneasy as she waited in the car. She didn't trust either man. She opened her purse to double check that she had her .22 caliber pistol. She re-checked to make sure it was loaded. She donned her leather driving gloves in anticipation of driving the BMW. Twenty minutes went by before he exited the rental office, smiling, with the keys in his hand. He waved for her to follow him as he found the truck he had been assigned, started it and began his journey to the storage facility. Quinn put on the lights of the rental truck as dusk began to creep in.

Moore returned to his apartment and contacted Jarvis's sister to offer his assistance in any way he could. Hanna Jarvis was a fifty-one year old single woman who had spent thirty years teaching high school English in Waltham, Massachusetts. She wasn't very close to her deceased brother she explained to Colonel Moore, but she appreciated his gallant notion and said that she would be in touch with him as soon as her brother's body had been released by the authorities. Moore gave his condolences again and said that if she needed anything, he would be there. Upon completion of his conversation with her, his cell phone rang. The caller ID indicated it was Quinn. Moore chose to ignore the phone call for a few minutes. The cell beeped and Moore realized that Quinn had left a message so he dialed in and listened. His faced turned gray and then scarlet. He yelled out loud to himself, "That son of a bitch. He's screwing with me for the last time." Moore went to his bedroom closet and searched through some of his personal items. The item he was looking for was his Officer Issue Colt

Model 1911 .45 automatic pistol. He checked the old firearm he had in his possession for many years and inserted a clip of seven shots, cocked it and slowly released the hammer. He placed several more clips in his pocket and screwed on the silencer he had obtained months ago through one of Quinn's contacts. He secured the silencer, kept the safety off just in case he quickly needed to use the pistol against him, and left his apartment. He had an appointment that needed to be kept now that Quinn was standing outside the storage facility where the money was stored. It was getting dark as Moore drove to the facility. He thought of how he would handle Quinn if the situation became ugly. He knew from firsthand experience that Quinn was an accomplished professional killer. He felt he knew him well enough to anticipate any aggressive moves.

Quinn stayed in the cab of the rental moving truck as Marilyn waited in the BMW out of clear sight since she knew that Moore would be enraged. She also wanted to stay clear of any hostilities that might break out between the two men. She realized that neither man could be trusted but she didn't mind the elimination of one of them because that would only add to her share of the spoils. She removed the .22 caliber pistol from her purse and waited to see what would transpire when the two men met.

Moore arrived in his car and immediately noticed the outline of Quinn sitting in the truck. He pulled up in front of the truck so that both front ends of the vehicles were facing each other with the lights on. Neither man exited his vehicle for several moments until Quinn made the first move by shutting off his lights and opening the truck door. He jumped down off the truck's running board and approached the car as Moore rolled down his window. Quinn acknowledged the Colonel.

"I want my cut of the money now. I'm leaving Frederick as soon as possible."

Moore laughed and said, "That would be a stupid thing to do, Quinn, because the authorities are watching you and your flight will ensure that a lot of questions will be asked by the Feds and local authorities possibly incriminating all of us." Moore ordered, "Return the truck and let the system protect you until the Jarvis thing blows over. All of us will adhere to the rules I have made and there will be no arguments concerning my orders. Now do you understand?"

Quinn barked back, "I'm not going along anymore with your rules because you changed them when you moved the money to the storage facility."

Moore became upset, "You are a fucking moron," and then paused and lowered his voice, "Do you expect me to keep that amount of money in my bedroom for the police to find? Marilyn must have told you that I had decided to move it, but she didn't know where I would be storing it at. But now, I guess she did. She's smarter than I thought. A nice ass and a smart brain as well." Quinn ignored the comment and was about to pressure Moore to open the lock when Marilyn appeared in his lights with her .22 pistol drawn. Moore laughed and said, "She looks ridiculous." She walked over next to Quinn as Moore, ever so slightly, began preparing to use the pistol he still had stored under his right thigh. He slowly removed the Colt so that he could position it on his lap and closer to the open window.

Moore smiled as he looked at Marilyn and said, "Well, well, Marilyn. I can see that you have switched allegiances again. You do it quite well with all the different men you've been screwing. One thing I can tell you though, is that I have never lied to you. Maybe I have failed to tell you everything but I have never lied to you." Marilyn said nothing as she positioned herself closer to Quinn. Moore looked over at Marilyn and realized he needed some advantage to make her hesitant and possibly side back with him as he moved the Colt closer to the window. He elevated the stakes.

"Marilyn, did Sean ever tell you how he shot and killed Todd in the Green Zone? He blew his head half off with a sniper rifle" The remark sickened her as she looked directly at Quinn. He could see her stare in his peripheral vision as he slowly anticipated drawing his pistol to shoot Moore who had moved a little during the conversation, alerting his instincts. Quinn made the mistake Moore had anticipated when he glanced over to Marilyn to defend the accusation and tell her that Moore had ordered the killing. For that split second, Quinn the teacher was overcome by Moore the student. Moore drew his Colt and shot Quinn in the stomach as he tried to draw and move at the same time. The silencer Quinn had on his pistol restricted his ability to get the pistol out quickly. He was thrown back several feet by the force of the bullet from Moore's Army Colt. Before the pain could overtake his senses, he fired back twice with the new .10 mm pistol still clutched in his right hand. The bullets found their marks in Moore's face and forehead with two small red holes. The exiting wounds took a third of Moore's brain with it. Quinn found himself on his back and unable to move his legs. He realized, in absolute terror, that he was paralyzed from the waist down and losing a lot of blood. Marilyn stood frozen with her pistol still clutched in her hand as she witnessed the scene. She regained her senses and slowly moved to the right side of Moore's car. The sight of the Colonel with a third of his skull and brain exposed and lying across the front seat sickened her. She moved around to the rear of the car and looked over the trunk to see Quinn quickly weakening from the blood he was losing. He never made a sound or asked for her help. She looked to see if anyone was visible in the storage aisle they were in. She realized that Quinn was partially hidden by the rental truck and that no one could see Moore lying across the car seat. The storage facility was only lit by a few lights in the aisles and by the fence perimeter. The lighting in her aisle was much dimmer except for the lights of Moore's running vehicle. Marilyn waited several more moments staying by the rear of Moore's car. She knew better than to approach Quinn just yet, for he was a master of deceit and she was still afraid that he would attempt to kill her to keep all the money. She walked back around the right side of the running car and around the back of the rental truck. She approached Quinn from a different angle to see if he had moved or showed any indication that he was playing possum. With her .22 caliber pistol pointed at his head, she approached him. He never moved as she kicked the pistol from his hand. She looked at his eyes and noticed that he had a blank stare. He never blinked and she knew he was dead. She expected someone to investigate the shots fired with the two vehicles parked with one set of lights on in the storage facility parking lot but no one came, much to her surprise. She stored her .22 caliber pistol in her purse and moved back to Moore's car. She slowly opened up the driver's door and searched his pockets for some type of keys needed to open the storage facility. There weren't any keys to be found. She retched a few times at the sight of Moore's open skull. The sight sickened her but she could not find any remorse for the man. She forced herself to concentrate and checked the chain attached to the keys in the ignition and found the two keys she had been searching for. She shut off the car and removed the keys. She then removed the storage keys from the key ring. She reassembled the key chain and restarted the car and left it running with the car's lights on. She moved to the garage door and unlocked it. She pulled open the door and the storage boxes were stacked in front of her. She knew Moore's code and found the boxes that contained their initials. She also found the two extra boxes that Moore had used as bait for her to stay with him as well. She smiled to herself and figured that she was probably going to get caught anyway, so she chanced taking the time to load all the boxes into Quinn's rented truck. After emptying everything, she double checked to make sure and locked the garage door and deposited one of the keys in Moore's pocket. She climbed into the rented U-Haul truck and then slowly drove out of the storage facility fearing that she would be stopped any moment by the authorities. She drove cautiously while checking her side rear view mirrors constantly for flashing lights of police vehicles coming for her. There weren't any and she was back at her apartment a half hour later.

She parked the loaded truck in her apartment parking lot and just sat there. The mental picture still stuck in her mind of Moore's exposed brain and Quinn sprawled out in a pool of blood. She retched as the vivid scene played over and over again in her head. As she regained her composure, she looked into the side rear view mirror of the truck to check herself before she exited. She smiled as she thought that she was the only one left of the four who had been able to ship the largest amount of money out of Iraq without the Army or anyone knowing that the money was gone. She thought about how many times Moore took advantage of her and had constantly belittled her. He did it tonight until Quinn blew part of his head off. She quickly thought about Quinn. Too bad he was killed, but she knew there would never have been anything between them except good sex. She also knew that he was capable of anything and she was pleased that he would never have the chance to turn on her as he had on Wilson, Jarvis and Moore. She never even thought about Hank Jarvis as she exited the truck. She looked around and saw another rental truck parked in the lot. She laughed realizing she had parked the truck in a place where many people moved into and out of the apartment complex daily. Who would think any different of the truck she just parked. Marilyn thought about Quinn's car. It had her fingerprints all over it. She laughed when she realized that she still had her driving gloves on. She amused herself realizing that they would find Quinn's car at the storage facility with most of his fingerprints on it. She surmised, that being Quinn's girlfriend, she could talk her way out of why some of her prints were in his car as she walked to her apartment thinking, at any time, the authorities would be waiting for her there. She arrived back at 8:30 p.m. and checked her messages. There were none. Porter continued on her lucky streak she felt she had and decided to go to dinner so that she had half an alibi. After quickly freshening up and changing, she casually left her apartment and walked to her car. She drove her Honda to the opposite side of town to a small restaurant she visited when she wasn't with Moore. She ordered dinner a little after 9:00 p.m. and said to her waiter that she would be expecting her boyfriend in a few minutes.

Major General Thaddeus Lucas, Commanding Officer of

Army Special Investigation received a call at his home at 9:10 p.m. His chief of staff informed him of four facts that the general needed to know before making any decisions on this case. One, was that Captain Todd Wilson had been confirmed by Army forensics as the officer found in the shallow grave in Baghdad. Two, was that the captain had just recently been re-interred at Arlington National Cemetery by his family. Third, was that the captain had been working for the Treasury Department collecting and counting currency hidden by the Hussein Government. And fourth, was that contact with the FBI indicated that they were in the process of an investigation of the finance group that Captain Wilson had served with in Iraq. Major General Lucas ordered the grave of Captain Todd Wilson at Arlington be exhumed. He also ordered his chief of staff to find the closest Army legal officer and get the proper paperwork in motion.

Rookie officer Thomas Perkins was on routine patrol when he noticed a car with its lights on in one of the storage facility aisles. He thought it was odd for a car to be sitting there with no one loading or unloading anything into the open storage facility. He passed by and decided that he would check the facility on his return in fifteen or twenty minutes. He began to concentrate on his driving when he caught the sight of a BMW parked on the other side of the parking lot. He decided to investigate since he would never park a car like that in a twenty-four hour storage facility parking lot. As he slowly pulled down into the storage lot and passed the BMW, he noted the license plate and called it in to his dispatcher. He continued around to the aisle where he had noticed the car lights and stopped the black and white. The dispatcher informed him that the BMW was registered to a Sean Quinn with a local Frederick address. The car had not been reported stolen. Perkins felt relaxed as he exited his car and walked toward the lights. He walked close to the opposite line of storage facilities and away from the direct glare of the car's lights. When his eyes adjusted to the glare of the lights, he observed a person lying on his back. He drew his automatic pistol and approached cautiously with his flashlight. As he approached the car, he saw a man flat on his back in a pool of blood. Before he called in backup and the license plate of the running car, he concentrated first on the person on the pavement. Seeing the man on the ground was obviously dead, he switched his attention back to the running car. He approached and yelled in the direction of the car. He gave his identity and waited for a response. He cautiously approached the right side of the car and flashed the light inside. His light illuminated the red and pink tissue of a man with a massive head wound. He immediately called in for backup and two ambulances. He moved around the car and approached the first man he had seen flat on his back. He observed the pool of blood under the man's torso. He touched the neck of the victim and confirmed he was also dead. He searched the premises for the possibility of finding other victims. He was relieved that there were none and began to relax as he waited for backup and the ambulances to arrive.

Five minutes later, Officer Dan Hayes arrived at the scene. Hayes looked in, and quickly away, as he noticed the gruesome condition of the man in the auto. He called in the license plate and waited for a reply as he walked over to the person on the pavement. Hayes did a double take and realized he had seen this man before. He remembered that this guy had been the victim of a stolen car incident but also had been questioned by the FBI for being a suspect in a shooting of an officer somewhere in Connecticut. Hayes pulled the man's wallet out from under him. He carefully opened the wallet to check the cards and papers inside. The man was identified as Sean Quinn. Hayes remembered the FBI Agent's name and called his dispatcher to contact Agent Joe Walker or his office and inform him that Sean Quinn had been murdered. Hayes handed the ID of Quinn to Officer Perkins, who had regained his stomach enough to pull the wallet from the victim in the running car. Hayes paused to listen to what Perkins called into the dispatcher. The license matched what the dispatcher confirmed a few moments later. It was John Moore with a local Frederick address.

Agent Jack McManus received a call from the FBI office as he drove from visiting the University of Maryland at College Park, that the Frederick Police had found the bodies of Sean Quinn and John Moore at a storage facility. As he hung up his cell phone, he turned to Whitford.

"Damn. Quinn and Moore were just found shot to death. It looks like an apparent gun fight based on the preliminary report from the officers on the scene." Agent McManus returned to the office with Whitford.

"Notify Thompson and Walker immediately that Quinn and Moore are dead. I'm going over to the Frederick PD to get all the details. After that, I'll be at the city morgue."

Joe Walker received the news while he was at home. He immediately headed for the FBI office to assist in the investigation. Craig was lying in his hospital bed with Terry cuddled next to him half asleep. They had already been warned that she had over extended her visiting time and should have left the hospital an hour ago when visiting hours ended. The bedside phone call woke Terry as Craig answered, listened and nodded. He turned to Terry and said, "They just found John Moore and Sean Quinn shot to death, it looks like some sort of gun battle at a storage facility."

The Interrogation

Marilyn returned to her apartment but sat in her car for a few minutes with the worst case of heartburn she had ever had. She surmised that the light salad and broiled chicken dinner she had didn't settle well as she continued to reflect on the events she had witnessed at the storage facility. Those events, along with her fear that the authorities were ready to apprehend her at any moment, contributed to the acid and bile building up in her stomach and esophagus. She observed the rental truck in the apartment parking lot as she remained in her Honda. She noticed one of her neighbors exit his car and wave at her as he quickly passed by the rental truck on his way to the entrance to the apartment complex. She made a mental note to remind herself that he had seen her. That was the beginning of the alibi that she would need to keep clear and concise if she would have to tell the bank's attorney or any authority figure that questioned her on where she was during the shooting of Moore and Quinn.

All seemed normal to her as she glanced at her watch. It was 11:05 p.m. She had seen no police, FBI or anyone of suspicion following her or waiting for her in the apartment complex parking lot. She tried to relax as she exited her Honda and headed for her apartment. She knew she would have a long restless night before she performed the biggest charade she would ever have to act out in the morning. She entered her apartment and checked for any messages. There were none. Relaxing a little, she undressed, showered and prepared for bed. She watched television until she fell asleep sometime around 1:00 a.m. She awoke, startled from the noise of the remote hitting the wood floor of her bedroom. She quickly got out of bed and glanced out her apartment window and could see that the rental truck was still where she had parked it. She quickly dressed and prepared to report to work as usual.

On her way into work, she called Moore's office. She knew that his secretary would be at her desk to take the call. Her plan was to ask her if Mr. Moore had arrived. She said that she had some questions for him concerning a task he'd asked her to perform. Her real reason for the call was to see if the secretary had been informed of Moore's death. On the fourth ring, Moore's secretary answered.

"Good morning. Colony Bank. This is Ms. Clemens speaking. May I help you?"

"Good morning Ms. Clemens. This is Marilyn Porter. May I speak to Mr. Moore, please?"

"I'm sorry Miss Porter, but Mr. Moore is not in his office yet. Is there a message?"

"No, I'll just talk to him when I see him this morning. Is his calendar open first thing? I only need a few minutes." She waited a few moments for the secretary to answer. "Miss Porter, his schedule is open."

"Good, I'll see him as soon as he comes in. Thank you." Marilyn was surprised that no one in the office had been informed of Moore and Quinn's death.

As she prepared to stop by the hospital for a ten minute visit, Terry received a phone call from Mr. Atkinson of the Frederick Funeral Home.

"Miss Breen, I just received a call from the Arlington administrative office that the body of Captain Todd Wilson has been scheduled for exhumation by order of the Army forensic headquarters. I know you are the representing attorney of the Wilson and Bryant families and I want you to know about the exhumation. I will be attending."

"For what reason is the body to be exhumed?"

"The Army has reason to believe that the wrong body is in the casket. This is a delicate matter and I am cautioning you about telling the Wilson and Bryant families until there is confirmation that a mistake has been made."

"I agree with you Mr. Atkinson. I'll wait for your call for confirmation before I inform the families. Mr. Atkinson, I have received news that both Mr. Moore and Mr. Quinn have been killed and under the circumstances, until all is known, this is the other reason I am delaying telling my clients."

"Miss Breen, I had no idea. I have a very uncomfortable

feeling about what is developing. I will call you as soon as I know more."

Marilyn reported to work at 9:00 a.m. sharp. After hanging up her coat and storing her purse in her office, she walked directly to Mr. Moore's office. As she approached the office, she found Ms. Clemens very upset and noticed that she had been crying. "What's wrong?" she asked, as she stood near Ms. Clemens's desk. She immediately saw FBI Agent McManus come out of Moore's office. He looked directly at Porter and asked, "Where were you last night?" Looking perplexed as she had planned, she replied, "I was home until 8:30 p.m. or so and then I went out to dinner before 9:00 p.m. I had a dinner date with Sean Quinn, but he never showed nor called to cancel." Marilyn stopped and asked, "Why are you here and in Mr. Moore's office, Agent McManus?" She changed her expression and asked, "Do you have information for us on the investigation of Mr. Jarvis?" McManus looked at her very suspiciously and said, "You have not seen either Mr. Moore or Mr. Quinn this weekend, Miss Porter?" Marilyn steadied herself because she was about to tell the biggest lie of her life and she knew she had to be especially good at it since Moore often told her she didn't lie well.

"Agent McManus, the last time I saw Mr. Moore was when you interrogated us about Hank's death with Attorney Wilkes present." McManus remembered something he'd missed asking her then and said, "Didn't you accompany him to the re-interment on Saturday?" She was surprised that he asked it now that he was investigating the deaths of Moore and Quinn. She realized that this man was shrewd. She remembered John Moore's little white lie. She also remembered what he said to her. McManus waited for an answer and said, "Ms. Porter did you…"

"No, at the last minute I reneged. I didn't want to go through that again," she said.

"Then when did you see Mr. Quinn last?" he asked.

"I saw him over the weekend several times. I talked to him

yesterday when we arranged to meet for dinner at 9:00 p.m. We didn't see each other much over the weekend. He attended the re-interment and he had some more work to do for Mr. Moore," she said while looking McManus directly into his eyes. McManus paused.

"Miss Porter, sit down and listen to what I have to say." Marilyn became slightly indignant and asked, "What is it this time Agent McManus?" She also remembered that Audrey Wilkes's office was several doors down from Moore's but she hadn't seen her yet and hoped that she would come in soon. Marilyn looked at Moore's secretary who was still sitting at her desk in a state of shock.

"What is wrong here? What is going on that you have this woman crying?" The FBI Agent looked at Marilyn for a few moments longer than anyone would normally do in a conversation before speaking, and said, "Miss Porter, I have very bad news for you so please sit down as I had asked you before." She found a seat quickly and braced herself to put on her best dramatic performance ever.

"Miss Porter, last night the Frederick Police found, what looked to be, a double homicide at a storage facility in the city. Two men apparently shot and killed each other. The victims were John Moore and Sean Quinn." It was easy for Marilyn to add to her charade. When she initially saw McManus, the liquid in her stomach quickly bubbled. Now it was time to release the fluid. She forced her eyes to get as wide as they could possible get and gagged a little to release what looked to be vomit.

She screamed, "Oh my God!" as she continued gagging then crying hysterically. No tears came at first so she pushed her lower eye lids into her eyes with her fingers so that her mascara would make them tear. It worked very well and the tears came streaming down. During her performance, she said a silent prayer that it would be believable. McManus was very surprised at her reaction and thought about consoling her but decided he would observe a little more to make sure her reaction was genuine and not a cover-up. He hadn't trusted her since he met her for one simple reason. She went with Quinn, who he perceived as a smart ass and sneaky son of a bitch. He felt that if she could be with someone like that then she had to have some of the same qualities. He thought that she was pretty, smart, and could get someone better than Quinn.

Audrey Wilkes came through the office door and immediately said, "Why are you here and why had I not been informed of your visit?"

McManus simply said, "Ms. Wilkes, I didn't really need to inform you this time. This is a homicide investigation now and I have not charged any of your clients, nor do we have any suspicion of your clients."

Wilkes froze in her tracks as she comprehended the word homicide. A few moments later, she composed herself and said, "I will be representing anyone in this bank that is under suspicion."

McManus said, "There aren't any under suspicion at this time, Ms. Wilkes, but I want to question a few more people at the bank concerning why Moore and Quinn would turn on each other in a remote parking lot of a storage facility." Wilkes was stunned. She had no idea that two of the bank's employees had been murdered. She managed to compose herself enough to ask, "How? When?" McManus would only say that it's all under investigation.

"Ms. Wilkes, I am simply asking questions of people that might be able to aid my department in the ongoing murder investigation of Mr. Moore and Mr. Quinn."

Marilyn had put on a good act. Agent Whitford had to supply her with water and some paper towels from the men's room. McManus had a few more questions.

"Do you know of any recent hostility between the two men?" She shook her head negatively.

"What about your relationship to Quinn?"

"He's been my boyfriend ever since we started at the bank."

"How serious was your relationship with him?" She looked at him and began to cry. McManus didn't ask any more questions. He wasn't sure about her but he chose not to push anymore until he had more information from the forensic lab.

He told Wilkes, "Please inform all the bank employees that they should make themselves available as there will be more questioning from my office as the case develops." Both agents thanked those present and left. Marilyn burst into tears again as they were leaving and hugged Wilkes. She actually enjoyed the hug as she had no remorse for Moore or Quinn, but did have feelings for Porter. It actually disgusted her thinking that Quinn had sex with her. Wilkes fantasized many times, thinking that she could satisfy Porter's sexual needs a lot better.

Director Atkinson stood by and watched the back hoe complete the digging. A green canvas had been draped around the area that encompassed the three headstones. Several cemetery workers attached cables to the back hoe and signaled for it to begin hauling up the vault containing the casket of Todd Wilson. The vault was secured on the grass next to the pile of dark brown dirt. Two cemetery workers removed the cables and unsealed the vault. The back hoe was hooked to the vault cover and it was slowly removed. Several minutes later, the aluminum casket was opened and nothing was found in it. The officer in charge took pictures of the open aluminum casket while several of the workers looked on. The officer instructed the men that this was a confidential matter and that they were bound to national security regulations. He turned to Director Atkinson who nodded in agreement. Atkinson approached the casket and looked inside. He noticed what appeared to be a piece of currency stuck in the folds of the partial remains of the padded cream colored casket upholstery. He reached in and pulled out the torn piece. The officer in charge snapped a photo of the piece in Atkinson's hand and then confiscated it for evidence. The officer immediately called the chief of staff of Major General Thaddeus Lucas to inform him of their findings. Within minutes, the General was informed and he called the Director of the FBI to initiate an investigation.

McManus and his group were informed of the Wilson grave

investigation within an hour of the findings. He immediately got a court order to investigate the accounts of John Moore, Marilyn Porter, Hank Jarvis and Sean Quinn at the Frederick Colony Bank. He called Audrey Wilkes and told her of his court order. He instructed her to inform Miss Porter that she was to surrender to the authorities as soon as possible for additional questioning.

Wilkes asked, "What is the intent of the FBI? Do you intend to arrest Miss Porter? If so, what are the charges?"

"She is not under arrest, but she is a prime suspect in the death of Captain Todd Wilson and for possibly being involved in stealing money from the U.S Treasury. Also, she may possibly be involved, or knows more information, concerning the murder of Hank Jarvis. And now, may I add Ms. Wilkes, the shooting deaths of Moore and Quinn." Wilkes acknowledged his instructions and said she would escort her to the FBI's office.

Marilyn was about to head out of the bank to return home and plan her next move when Wilkes entered her office to inform her of the intent of the FBI. Marilyn composed herself, but when she saw Wilkes, she prepared herself for another emotional outburst to keep up her charade. Audrey approached her, touched her shoulder, and then held her hand while she informed her of the instructions that Agent McManus had just given her. Porter immediately began to act upset. Inside, she was nervous that the whole charade would come down around her. She buried her face into Audrey's shoulder. Audrey caressed her hair and said, "Everything will be alright." Marilyn sensed the affection from Wilkes and responded enough to keep the woman close to her. She continued to fake a cry while she blurted out half sentences.

"I can't believe what has happened between Sean and my good boss." She continued to babble saying, "What am I going to do?" and "The FBI is being unreasonable."

Wilkes hugged her even harder as she fantasized about making love to her.

"Marilyn, you have rights and I am going to be your attorney for now. We need to find out more of what the FBI has in mind. I know an excellent attorney friend who is the top criminal lawyer in Baltimore. I will make contact with her as soon as we both know what we're up against."

Porter relaxed a little and withdrew her face from Wilkes's shoulder. She gently kissed Wilkes on the cheek long enough for her to feel that she was more than just thanking her for her support and advice. Wilkes glanced into her eyes looking for a sign that she was interested in her. Porter returned the eye contact with a soft smile and continued to look directly at Wilkes until she looked away. They gathered their possessions and headed for the FBI office downtown to begin, what both women felt, would be an interrogation.

Terry was informed by Director Atkinson that the casket was empty.

"Miss Breen, I'm telling you this as a courtesy to you because you represent the Wilson family. The Army will contact you with information concerning the missing body. Please act surprised when they contact you. Just be prepared to divulge the information to the Wilsons when the Army says it is the appropriate time. Captain Wilson has been identified in Iraq and will be soon arriving stateside for interment at Arlington. I caution you that the Army is embarrassed and that there are other issues at stake. This information is confidential." Terry understood.

"I assure you Mr. Atkinson that I will not relay any information to my clients until I am instructed by the Army." Terry closed her cell phone and looked at Craig. She explained what Atkinson had said. Thompson immediately informed McManus who was preparing his questions for Miss Porter along with Whitford and Walker. All three agents waited for Miss Porter and her counsel to arrive.

Craig surmised that Moore, Jarvis and Quinn were involved in the death of Todd Wilson. He sat in his bed and made a list of facts he knew about the case. Terry stood by as he wrote them down. The list included the relationship of all three men during their service years and employment at the Colony Bank. Thompson recorded their joint interest in the Wilson farm and Moore's insistence on being at the re-interment of Todd Wilson as indicated by Terry in the statement she gave. Terry cut in and said that Moore also offered to pay for the re-interment costs for the Wilson family. Thompson smiled as his beauty contributed to his analysis. He also listed Quinn's record as a sniper, his Special Forces experience, and his time spent under Moore in the Army's group to assist the Treasury Department. He looked at Terry and surmised out loud, "That son of a bitch could have killed Wilson in the Green Zone. He had the sniper experience to pull that off just like he had the experience to shoot that cop in Connecticut." Thompson looked at Breen and also said, "I wonder if he took a chance on trying to knock off your clients as well."

"Now you're speculating, Craig," Terry said as she stood with her hands on her hips. He laughed a little.

"I expected that answer from a lawyer. I'm pretty sure that Quinn drove his Mustang into your client's car now that I start looking at all the connections. I never believed that Quinn's car was stolen."

Terry listened to her man speculate then realized that what he said so far, could hold more truth than conjecture. He changed his tone a little when he started wondering if this guy could have killed Jarvis.

"This guy could have been involved with the killing of that college student in College Park also. The kid was a known homosexual and Jarvis had been known to visit the campus according to the statement Quinn gave to my boss. He could have been trying to lead us away from him by informing us that Jarvis was a known homosexual. I believe that this bastard could have killed Jarvis as well," Craig said. Terry said that even though he was probably onto something, the FBI, Frederick Police or the Army hadn't proven any of that yet.

"The guy is dead now. Who can verify any of your theories?" Thompson looked at her while he called McManus. He reached his boss and relayed his theory. Thompson faced lit up as he smiled listening to McManus. He slowly hung up the phone.

Terry asked, "What did he think of your theory?" Thompson reached for her hand as he pulled her closer to his bed and said, "All the agents agree with me and they hope, in a few minutes, Marilyn Porter will be able to shine some light onto it."

Terry moved close to her blue eyed companion and let him kiss her neck and right ear until the ward nurse entered the room to take his vital signs.

Porter and Wilkes entered the office of McManus. The two attractive women had to walk past Whitford and Walker who observed their beauty. Both men got up from their desks and walked to the viewing area of the interrogation room. Neither agent was going to be able to question Porter. They planned to take notes. That had already been decided by McManus who felt that Whitford was too inexperienced and Walker might be too aggressive causing the attorney to pull Porter out of the questioning session as he liked to call it. They all knew that they did not have any proof Porter was involved in the business matters of the three men. McManus also said earlier, that he would be the lead interrogator because he figured that Quinn was somehow involved in the abduction of Joe Walker, Jr. Walker and Whitford did have the recourse to stop the session by pushing the button for a small red light in the room to light up. It was strategically positioned so that only the interrogator could see it. This would indicate they felt that McManus should stop the questioning and leave the room to listen to some fact or idea they had.

McManus didn't say a word to Porter initially and only addressed Wilkes. He informed her of the reason he called her client in for questioning and relayed that this was an informational session and not an interrogation. Wilkes reminded him, "Agent McManus, if the informational session becomes ugly in my estimation, I will withdraw my client and walk out of the room. In order to stop me, you will need a warrant for her arrest. That is my intent. Do I make myself clear?" McManus nodded and just motioned to the open door leading to the interrogation room. Marilyn was ready to vomit again due to her nervousness. She realized that she had one shot to convince the FBI Agents that she was innocent. She smiled inside knowing that if she pulled this off, Moore would have been very surprised. But Moore was dead now and couldn't witness her attempt to conceal her involvement with the group of dead men.

McManus, Wilkes and Porter took their seats at the interrogation table. The agent pushed a button on the table that led to the audio and visual recording camera mounted on the wall. He pointed to the camera and informed Wilkes and Porter that the session was being video recorded. Marilyn glanced up at the camera to see a red dot glowing above the lens. She made it a point to remind herself not to look at the camera, but look directly into the eyes of Agent McManus.

McManus began with the usual questions concerning her name, address, occupation and other standard information for the record. He began with her involvement with Sean Quinn and asked personal questions about their relationship. Several minutes went by and he pushed a little more than Wilkes felt comfortable with. Before she could protest, Marilyn stopped her and said she didn't mind the questions. She answered that she was only dating Quinn and that their relationship had not gotten very serious. McManus pushed a little too hard when he asked, "Did you have sexual relations with Mr. Quinn?"

Wilkes cut him off, "What does her personal intimate business have to do with this investigation, Agent? I think I heard enough of this line of questioning. Marilyn, we should leave now." Marilyn put her hand on Wilkes's and spoke up and said, "If you mean was I fucking the man, then your assumption is correct agent. That didn't mean I loved him, it meant that I enjoyed the sex."

Wilkes and McManus were taken aback by the boldness of her answer. McManus finally moved onto other questions. He asked about her involvement with Todd in which Marilyn indicated that she was never romantically involved with the man.

"Captain Wilson was my direct superior officer in Iraq. As part of my duties, I was involved in counting and shipping currency back to the United States."

McManus crossed the line again when he asked, "Was Captain Wilson anything else to you besides your superior?" Wilkes stood up and instructed Marilyn, "Okay, that's it, please follow me out of the room." Marilyn calmed Audrey and pulled at her hand to sit down.

"My relationship with Captain Wilson was strictly professional. I knew from my conversations with him that he was planning to be married upon his return to Maryland. I never met his girlfriend, but I respected their relationship. And besides, Colonel Moore frowned upon such things in his command that could jeopardize our mission. You know, Agent McManus, Colonel Moore had a very high standard of ethics and romantic relationships among his officers were not encouraged."

McManus asked about her relationship with Mr. Moore. Marilyn started to cry but managed to say, "I had the utmost respect for him. I am very upset that he's been killed." Marilyn managed to cover her face for a few moments to indicate she was wiping tears away but her main motive was to push the heavy eye liner into her eyes again to start the tears flowing. She managed to accomplish enough irritation to her eyes to convince the interrogator, and her attorney, that she was visibly upset about the man's death. She had all praises for her former boss and even was able to fake being choked up. Whitford and Walker observed, but neither indicated to each other that they were suspicious that she was not telling the truth.

McManus asked Porter, "Did you know about Jarvis's sexual preferences?"

"Yes. Sean had indicated that he was gay, but I didn't really care about his sexual preference the way they did. Women have different feelings about people's sexuality." She looked at Wilkes while she explained to McManus, "Jarvis was probably gay, but he treated me with respect and did a very good job for the unit I was assigned to and for the bank."

McManus pushed Porter when he asked, "Had Quinn said anything to you about him having to caution Jarvis about his homosexual activities?" Marilyn just shook her head negatively. She was asked about Moore's obsession with the Wilson farm. She stopped the agent and asked, "What makes you think that Mr. Moore was obsessed with the farm?" McManus went into some detail of Moore's conversations with Attorney Breen and his offer to Amy and Bob Bryant for the farm. Marilyn brushed off the question.

"Mr. Moore would never do anything unprofessional like that." Her attempt to make her seem distant from Moore's plans was working. She was getting tired since she had been at this intense questioning for over twenty minutes. Her stomach was very upset so she swallowed air which caused her to belch and fake vomiting again. She worked on the swallowing for a few more minutes as McManus continued with his barrage of questions. Some were repeated, hoping to catch Marilyn giving conflicting information, but Attorney Wilkes screened those and made sure to point out that her client had already answered those questions. McManus asked about her trip to Boston with Quinn and the traffic ticket he received in Greenwich, Connecticut.

"Do you really think that the authorities will believe that you were asleep in the back seat of Quinn's car with a blanket thrown over you?"

Marilyn paused for a few seconds. She looked directly into McManus's eyes and said, "You are correct Agent. McManus, I wasn't sleeping in the back seat. I was awake the whole time but I was embarrassed that the officer who gave Sean the ticket would realize that I had not only my skirt off but my underwear as well. I had just finished screwing him while we were driving down I-95. There was no one on the road and apparently my thrusting caused Sean to exceed the speed limit. Do you realize how embarrassing that would have been for me to have to get out of the car with no underwear and skirt on with semen running down my leg?"

McManus and Wilkes stared at Porter until McManus finally looked away. Whitford and Walker smirked to each other in the observation room. Whitford commented, "Wow, she is a hot number." Walker put his finger over his lips indicating for him to be quiet. He agreed with him and he also believed her. McManus waited for the red light from his agents to alert him that they didn't believe her descriptive excuse, but no light came on. He changed the questioning and asked if she knew anything about the Wilson farm foreclosure. She looked him directly in his eyes and said, "Can I have a glass of water? Before Agent McManus could order someone to bring her a glass of water, she said, "Sure I do. I did all the research on the farm, the brothers who owned it, the Bryants who planned to pay off the mortgage and live in it. I know all their finances, net wealth and the attorneys that represent them. You need to know that when you work in a bank as the loan officer and assistant to the Vice President. It's my job." McManus didn't push the point since it would not divulge any wrong doing on her part to know information of that nature. He poured the water that had been brought in by Whitford, into a cup, and made one more try to connect Marilyn Porter with any one of the four murders. He asked her if she was at any meetings where information could have been exchanged between Moore, Quinn or Jarvis that seemed odd to her. Marilyn knew he knew that she had been seen by Breen and Walker at the restaurant meeting Moore had called.

"Mr. Moore hardly ever called any meetings concerning work except two times that I can remember." She took a sip of water from the cup and looked at Audrey Wilkes and said, "Mr. Moore had called me into a meeting where he assigned Attorney Wilkes here as counsel for me if the FBI continued questioning Sean and I concerning a shooting incident in Connecticut somewhere. I don't remember the town's name. He'd also taken the group out to dinner once as appreciation for doing good work that earned him a salary increase."

Audrey Wilkes looked at her watch and said, "Agent, you've

had my client's cooperation for well over forty-five minutes now. I think that is enough for now. Unless you have sufficient evidence to arrest her, I am calling this informational session closed." She looked at Marilyn and motioned for her to follow. Marilyn began to rise from the seat when McManus tried one more time to break Marilyn.

"Ms. Porter we have reason to believe that Colonel Moore, Sergeant Major Jarvis and Staff Sergeant Quinn killed Captain Wilson in Iraq, buried his body in an undisclosed area in Baghdad, filled his empty coffin with probably a large amount of money, real or counterfeit, and smuggled it into this country in the empty coffin of Captain Wilson. We believe their actions over the past several weeks, and their deaths, were directly caused by this act. We believe that you know more than you have indicated and it would benefit you to cooperate with us since we will report that cooperation to the proper authorities when sentencing is considered in this case." Marilyn burst into tears and gagged, forcefully vomiting a little of the water she had stored in her mouth.

"That's it Agent McManus, we are done. If you need to speak to my client again, get a warrant. We are leaving."

With that, Wilkes and Porter left the room and walked out of the office. McManus waved at the mirror for Whitford and Walker to leave the viewing room and enter the interrogation room. He waited until he saw Wilkes and Porter leaving the outer office.

"Well, what do you think?" he asked. Both agents said that she couldn't be that close to them and not know something was going on. McManus said that he had obtained search warrants for the agents and the Frederick Police. They are searching all the residences as we speak. He informed them that he felt something would turn up once the search was completed.

Agents Morse and Hemingway, with the assistance of the Frederick Police Department, had completed a thorough search of Moore's apartment. No evidence had been found linking him to any of the theories that Agents McManus, Thompson and Walker had surmised. Agents Bowling and Baginski had searched Quinn's apartment as well and found nothing incriminating. Cell phone records indicated calls to each other prior to the killings and Porter's calls to Quinn checked out to the time frames she had given when she last either talked or left a message for him. Porter's several phone calls to Quinn were on record for times past the estimated time of death set by the forensic investigators. Quinn's cell phone was analyzed and found that he never answered Porter's calls from the restaurant. All credit cards for Quinn, Porter, Moore and Jarvis were researched. The only purchase found indicating a tie to the shooting was Quinn's purchase of a .10 mm pistol from a gun shop in Hagerstown. All the information had been given to McManus within an hour of Porter's questioning. Only one bit of information was concrete. It was the fact that Jarvis's was a homosexual. The forensic team had found semen and blood in Jarvis's car. Both were from him except one spot of blood that was found that was O negative. The question was; was it the blood of the college student murdered on campus? Jarvis's apartment was clean of any evidence and McManus realized it would take a few more days for the DNA testing to be completed to confirm whether it was the student's blood. The fact that Jarvis was a homosexual didn't solve anything but could possibly have some meaning concerning the kid's death. The autopsy on the student indicated that his neck had been snapped by a professional. The only one who fit that description was Quinn who was on record for being in the Army Special Forces and a known martial arts expert.

The two agents with McManus looked at the picture of the piece of currency found in the casket of Captain Wilson. Whitford said, "The three of them must have had money stored in the casket." Both of the other men agreed, but McManus spoke up and asked, "Is Porter the fourth one? She has to be the fourth one. If it isn't Porter than who is it?"

McManus ordered a twenty four hour tail on Porter hoping to prove that she was, or, get lucky and find another member who would surface. He assigned Agents Morse and Hemingway for the first watch.

251

Audrey drove Marilyn back to the office to pick up her Honda. She told her that she would pick her up in the morning if more questioning was requested at the FBI office or worse, a warrant had been issued for her arrest. Marilyn remained quiet on the ride to get her car. Wilkes pulled in next to her Honda where Marilyn began to thank her for what she had done for her during the interrogation. Wilkes blushed.

"It was nothing to thank me for. It's my job."

Marilyn disagreed and held Audrey's hand.

"Would you like to follow me home and come up to my apartment for some tea or anything else you desire? I could use a stiff drink." Audrey declined. She handed one of her business cards to Porter.

"Marilyn, you can reach me at any of these numbers." Porter made sure to hold Wilkes's hand a little longer to show appreciation for what she had done for her at the FBI Office. She exited the car and made sure she showed enough of her slim legs and thighs for Audrey to get a good look. She then inconspicuously dropped the card on her exit out of the car. She bent over a little more than necessary, and exposed the roundness of her buttocks. Audrey could not help but observe. Marilyn fumbled a little longer so Audrey could relish the sight. All Marilyn could say was, "I am so clumsy at times. Audrey, thank you again."

She watched Wilkes drive off and then entered her Honda. She was home in a short time and observed the rental truck had not been disturbed as she passed directly by it.

Attorney-Client Relationship

Marilyn rushed into her apartment and changed immediately. She checked her purse to make sure the keys to the rental truck were still where she had put them. She needed to get the truck out of the parking lot before any agent or policemen became remotely suspicious that the truck was hers. She also knew the federal agents would be tailing her as soon as possible. She feared they could already be watching her, so she decided to take a jog around the streets in her area. She exited the apartment carrying the keys, her license, Audrey's business card and some cash. She put them in the inside pocket of the jogging suit. She stretched a few minutes while observing her surroundings nonchalantly. Satisfied that there was no one yet watching her, she began her jog and circled the parking lot continuing to look for any car or person of suspicion. She jogged up and down both sides of the street looking for any sign. Once satisfied that there were none, she returned to the truck, donned her jogging gloves, opened the door and started it. She slowly moved out of her parking lot and turned down the street. She noticed a black sedan in her side rear view mirror pulling over into her parking lot. Her adrenaline surged thinking that they could be agents that were assigned to watch her. She laughed as she thought about that. If they were agents, then they had not seen her driving the truck and she had at least an hour to find a place to store the boxes. She remembered Quinn's comment that there were other storage facilities in the area, so she headed in the direction she figured she would be able to find one of them.

"There's Porter's Honda. She's still here. This should be an easy assignment," Agent Hemingway said. Agent Morse just smiled. He shut off the sedan and pushed the seat back to relax.

Ten minutes later, Marilyn located a storage facility on her side of town. She pulled in and parked the truck away from the office window. She walked the hundred feet or so to the window and waited for the attendant, who was on the phone, to notice her. She noticed that he was around seventy years old and had a hard time doing more than one thing at a time. He seemed unorganized and extremely busy talking on the phone while shuffling through a stack of papers. When he finally hung up the phone, she asked where she could store some household goods. The attendant rummaged through some more papers then shoved a chart at her indicating the different sizes of storage areas available and the price ranges. As she looked over the chart, his phone rang again. She needed an angle. Seeing how unorganized this man was, while he was still on the phone, she showed him her license but managed to keep Audrey's business card over it enough hoping that in his confusion, he'd mistakenly register the account in Audrey's name. He hardly glanced at the license as he yelled into the phone. Marilyn put the cards back into her purse and settled on a small storage space, signed her name as Audrey Wilkes, and paid the attendant in cash for a one month rental. The attendant handed the keys to Marilyn and mumbled, "Thank you Ms. Wilkes." She knew her little trick had worked. She smiled back and said, "No, thank you sir."

She jogged back to the truck; put on her jogging gloves again, entered and started the truck, still looking to spot any tail on her. There wasn't any as far as she could see. She drove the truck to the designated storage room. She could feel her heart pounding as she unlocked the garage door and lifted it up to find some crushed empty boxes left from the previous renter. She unloaded the boxes quickly and stacked them neatly in two sections. The boxes marked clearly as only house items were separate from the ones marked similarly but with Moore's special coding on them. Satisfied that she had pulled off the most devious crime to date, Marilyn closed and locked the storage room. Her heart was pounding a little less now as she entered the truck and started thinking of ways to get rid of it. As she contemplated her next move, she noticed the rental slip that Sean had left wedged in the driver's side sun visor. It was a copy of the original rental slip he was given when he rented the truck. Porter read it and began to laugh and said out loud, "That devious shit head." The name on the rental agreement was John Moore's. Porter realized that Quinn had stolen the Colonel's bank credit card somehow and used it to rent the truck. She checked the return date and realized the truck was due. With that known fact, she returned to the truck rental agency and parked the truck next to others in the lot. The place was still open and there was only one attendant waiting on a customer. She was pleased that the place was nowhere as busy as when she waited for Quinn to rent the truck. She saw another truck pull into the lot. She observed the driver get out and walk over to what looked like a night deposit box. The person deposited his keys into it. She looked around for any cameras that could identify her returning the keys. She couldn't observe any. She pulled up the hood of her jogging jacket, jogged over and deposited the keys into the return box. Just to make sure, she double checked to make sure the attendant was still busy with the customer apparently renting a vehicle. She surmised that as long as the keys were deposited into the key return box on time, no one would care. If there was something missing or something wrong with the truck, then Moore's card would be charged. She laughed as she began jogging towards her apartment.

Several miles went by when Marilyn realized she was still four or five miles away from her apartment. She knew she wasn't in good enough shape to jog that many miles and she wanted to be home before it got dark. She found a pay phone and dialed Audrey. She answered on the second ring as if she anticipated a call from Marilyn.

"I'm sorry to call you but I went jogging and I ran and ran until I couldn't run anymore. I was trying to undo the stress I had from what happened to me today. Audrey, I really need a lift home. I'm so exhausted and don't want to walk home in the dark. Please, Audrey, can you come and pick me up?" Audrey bought the whole story and couldn't wait to pick her up.

"Stay where you are. Give me the directions. I'll be there as soon as I can." She fantasized about saving the maiden in distress. Within ten minutes, Wilkes had Porter safely in her car and on the way back to her apartment.

"Audrey, I noticed a black sedan when I was exiting my building to begin my jog. I wonder if they are agents instructed to watch my apartment."

"Don't worry, I'll check it out if it's still there and run down the license plate with a police officer I'm friendly with."

Porter wondered if the officer was a woman acquaintance.

They arrived at Porter's apartment complex and Wilkes noticed the black sedan with two men sitting in it. She recorded the license plate and called her police friend. They stayed in the car for several minutes until Wilkes received the information she had requested. The plates were registered with the Government. She closed her cell and looked at Marilyn.

"You were right. Janet, my friend, confirmed it. The plates are registered with the government." Marilyn knew the officer was a woman now which confirmed in her mind that Audrey was probably a lesbian. Porter decided to use that to her advantage.

"Audrey, please come in with me. I want to invite you for dinner as gratitude for picking me up."

"Look Marilyn, you don't have to compensate me for picking you up." Marilyn insisted.

"The least I can do is fix dinner for my new friend and attorney." Both women entered Porter's apartment at 7:45 p.m. as observed by Agents Morse and Hemingway.

"I don't remember her leaving with Wilkes. Do you?" Agent Morse asked. Hemingway continued to watch the two women enter the apartment.

"We must have gotten here after the two had left. No big deal. We know where Porter is now. Call into the office and give the update."

"Audrey, do you mind if I take a quick shower before I prepare dinner?"

"Marilyn, you don't have to go to all that trouble to prepare dinner. How about we both go out for a quick bite?" Marilyn emphatically refused as she began undressing in the doorway to her bathroom.

"I want to return the kindness that you have shown me as my attorney and now as my new friend." Audrey could not take her eyes off of her. She had stripped down to her sports bra and panties. She smiled and said, "I'll be out in a few minutes. I just want to sweeten up a little bit." The statement stirred Audrey's desire for her even more. Marilyn left the door ajar enough for Audrey to witness her strip completely naked and then casually closed the door exposing enough of her body for Audrey to remember.

Audrey regained her composure and began looking around the apartment and then out the window occasionally, to check on the agents. After a while of browsing, she noticed pictures of Moore in combat fatigues with Jarvis, Quinn, Porter and another gentleman she did not recognize. She turned over the picture to the read the writing on the back. "Iraq '03." No names had been written so the identity of the man was not available to her. She heard Marilyn say behind her, "That was taken in Iraq in 2003."

"Who's the other guy, the good looking one standing next to you?"

Marilyn played it cool and said, "Oh, that's Captain Todd Wilson. He was killed shortly after that picture was taken. We were all very upset about that. He had a fiancé at home waiting for him, too." Audrey just acknowledged the statement and never asked anymore about it.

"By the way, that was a quick shower," Audrey remarked.

"I didn't want you to have to wait long," Marilyn said and smiled. Audrey noticed that she was wearing only a terry cloth bathrobe and her hair was up in a towel wrapped to dry it.

"Ok, what would you like to eat? I make a great ham and cheese omelet. How's that for a light dinner even though most people consider it breakfast."

Audrey just smiled and said, "I'll help you." They finished quickly. Audrey could not take her eyes off of Marilyn throughout dinner. The tragic news about Sean and John was brought up, but Marilyn kept sidestepping and inquiring about Audrey and her life up to their meeting. Audrey finally took the bait and explained her college days at Georgetown, Law School at Harvard, and her failed marriage with a law

schoolmate that lasted only three years. "I haven't been very lucky with men since that time."
Marilyn sympathized. "I haven't been very successful with men either."
Audrey picked up on that and laughed. "With a body and looks like yours, I would think every dick in town would be waiting in line for a chance to bed you."
"Aren't you sweet, but on the contrary, I find it very difficult to find a man that can really please me. I need gentle, not bravado. Sean was like that if you know what I mean." She pushed her chair back from the dinner table as if relaxing but had managed to separate her legs enough for Audrey to get a glance at her firm thighs. Both women bantered a little more about experiences with men until Marilyn suddenly switched gears and executed her plan to set Audrey up.
"I had my first real orgasm in college with my roommate."
Audrey listened intently now.
"She was a closet lesbian but finally came on to me a few times. I evaded her for a while but eventually, I said, what the hell, and I tried it. If I must say, I enjoyed my senior year the most. I would spend weekends with some of the jocks, but I had the pleasure of weekdays with her in the privacy of our dorm room. I guess you could say that I was bi-sexual then. I haven't been for a long time but the thought enters my mind."
Audrey stood motionless and almost speechless after hearing Marilyn's last sentence.
Marilyn stopped and said, "I'm sorry. I hope I haven't made you uncomfortable by divulging some of my inner secrets."
Audrey smiled. "You can tell that I'm a lesbian, right? "
"Yes, I can and you are a very attractive one at that Marilyn said, smiling."
She opened her legs a little more to expose her most private part. Audrey stood up and moved towards her. Both beauties stood face to face and began to kiss and caress each other. Within a few minutes, Marilyn broke off the engagement and took hold of Audrey's hand and led her from the table. She led the brunette beauty into her room where she had already

prepared the bed.

Audrey smiled and said, "You had this planned all the time, didn't you?" Marilyn laughed as an admission of guilt. "Guilty as charged." They both laughed at her statement. She undressed Audrey completely. As she dropped her panties to the floor, Marilyn commented, "You are so beautiful Audrey." Audrey reciprocated and gently guided Marilyn to the bed. She began kissing her from her head to her toes but stopping long enough to spend time on each breast. Marilyn moaned as Audrey worked both of them with her tongue and mouth. She continued down Marilyn's body until she reached her most private area. She separated her legs and began to tongue and nibble until Marilyn's moans of pleasure became accelerated until she climaxed and shuddered in Audrey's face. The women reversed positions and the process began all over again. Each woman was pleasured continuously for over an hour until Marilyn pleaded for Audrey to stop.

"Audrey, I am too weak to continue but I promise you I will increase my stamina the next time we make love." Audrey laughed. "I'm glad you stopped me. I couldn't last through another climax as well." Both women laughed and cuddled until Audrey fell asleep.

Marilyn knew she had this woman where she wanted her and laughed to herself that Quinn would have enjoyed a three way with them if he hadn't been so stupid to get himself killed. She looked at the alarm clock. It was now 10:00 p.m. She stirred enough to wake Audrey who realized that she must leave and prepare for tomorrow if the authorities came for her newest client and now lover.

She reminded Audrey to look to see if the agents were still watching the house. Audrey smiled and said, "I hope they weren't looking through your bedroom window."

"It was only your way of prepping me for the next go around with the authorities," Marilyn said as they hugged and kissed.

"Thank you for a great night. I look forward to seeing you and making love to you again."

Agents Morse and Hemingway observed Attorney Wilkes

leaving Porter's apartment at 10:10 p.m. Wilkes carried her purse and briefcase as she entered her car parked in the parking lot. Audrey casually looked in the direction of the agents, and then away, as if she had not seen anything. She made a mental note to herself that the agents were still watching her client.

The autopsies of Jarvis, Moore and Quinn were inconclusive. The only contributing fact that did emerge beside the massive blow to Jarvis's skull was that of his health. He was in the early stages of HIV. John Moore had one third of his skull missing from the .10 mm bullets that Quinn had put into his skull, but he also had the onset of liver disease. The physician that performed the autopsy estimated he had about two years before he would have felt the effects of the disease. Sean Quinn was a very healthy individual until the bullet from Moore's Colt .45 smashed into his number one lumbar spinal bone and severed his spinal column. It would have rendered him a paraplegic for life, except the bullet ricocheted and severed a large artery leading to his left kidney and caused him to bleed to death.

Jack McManus, Joe Walker, and Jamul Whitford gathered in McManus's office the following morning to review the information they had compiled that implied Moore, Quinn and Jarvis had been partners. Their task was to review the facts so that they were comfortable that they could convince the Federal Prosecutor to begin a case against Marilyn Porter who was the only remaining suspect they had. On the speaker phone in McManus's office, was Craig Thompson who had been invited to listen in and participate in the review. McManus was under pressure from his supervision to solve the cases. He explained the reason for the meeting was to review all the data and make some conclusions about what had transpired over the past three weeks. He began with the sequence of events and encouraged all the agents to contribute as he spoke.
"Officer Jake Bishop is shot by an unknown assailant in Greenwich, Connecticut on August 23rd. The investigation revealed that a weapon was discarded in a roadside truck stop

outside of Philadelphia, Pennsylvania. The weapon was identified during ballistics testing, to be the pistol used to shoot Officer Bishop. Bishop identified the car and part of the license plate. That led to the identification that it was a Maryland plate. The sorting that was done by the Maryland Motor Vehicle Department, and handed off to this office, narrowed the search down to Sean Quinn who was ticketed in Greenwich, Connecticut within an hour of the shooting in Greenwich. Interrogation of Quinn and his supposed girlfriend, Marilyn Porter, revealed that she was banging Quinn on his way to Boston when they were stopped. It took several sessions with Porter to get that out of her, indicating she is either full of shit, or really was with Quinn. I believe we all think the former."

"Cora Bryant remembered that she did not put on the alarm at the home of her parents the same day Officer Bishop was shot two houses away from the home. Amy and Robert Bryant were away and in the process of buying the old Wilson farm property," Walker said.

McManus continued, "Good point Joe. The Bryant's were run off the road by a black Mustang GT convertible which happened to be registered and owned by none other than Sean Quinn. He was questioned and had a good enough alibi to keep us from arresting his ass. He also had the balls to buy a new BMW after he reported that his Mustang had been stolen. The Wilson farm went up in smoke between the time Quinn lost his Mustang and when he bought the new BMW. We checked all the rental car company records for that period and found that Quinn had a car during the period from when his car was supposedly stolen but after the old farmhouse burned to the ground. Every time we look for Quinn, he is either out of town on bank business or with Marilyn Porter who, we all agree, would be someone to spend the night with. Well, maybe not you Walker since you are a happily married man." Everyone laughed.

He continued, "Moore was always protecting Quinn to the point that he made himself look suspicious. We were planning on bringing him in for some one on one questioning, but he avoided our meeting permanently by getting his head blown off by the guy he was constantly protecting. But what were they fighting about? Somebody had to be there at that storage facility the night they blew each other away. We looked up credit card hits during that time frame and came up with two from Moore. One was that he had some movers come to have some household boxes moved to a storage facility. The movers report said he signed for forty some odd boxes of stuff that were marked dishes and shit like that. Our guys checked the storage facility and found nothing. Nobody knows where the boxes went. The second hit was for a delivery truck rental which was dropped off several days later. The rental company said that they never saw who dropped off the truck and their surveillance cameras were not turned on until after the place closed. So whoever returned the truck did it during normal working hours, after the shooting at the storage facility. Porter was either at her apartment, or with Wilkes, during those times, according to Hemingway and Morse who were watching her. They did report that they were surprised when Porter and Wilkes arrived at her apartment because they never saw them leave. I think that was insignificant but it's still something I wanted to bring up."

Whitford cut in, "Maybe by the time you gave the order for Morse and Hemingway to tail her, Wilkes had picked her up. They said they saw her car in the lot when they first arrived. They probably decided to go out to dinner or something."

"Yeah, I figured the same thing but I still wanted you all to hear the facts."

Thompson said, "The guy who owns the truck that hit me, has been investigated and cleared. The truck was apparently stolen the same night that I saw the Moore group at the restaurant. The forensic guys found out later, during our investigation, that the truck had been hotwired. Lombardo is a diabetic and couldn't have functioned with the amount of alcohol in him that the forensic lab guys found in the truck."

McManus thanked him and continued, "Yes, Quinn had another alibi that he had been to dinner, and then, spent quality time with Miss Porter. Moore started really protecting both using the bank's attorney, Audrey Wilkes. She seems clean right now, but we understand that she and Miss Porter have spent some time together. Maybe she was counseling her last night. We still do not have a strong enough case against sweet Marilyn yet for some one on one questioning again."

All the agents in the room smiled at their supervisor for his chauvinistic comment, and he continued, "The most interesting point of all of this which makes me believe that they must have snuck in something of value into the country, was their collective pressure on the Bryants, who were in the process of buying the Wilson farm. Moore was too inquisitive and too accommodating to Attorney Terry Breen. She is the one who alerted us to Cora Bryant's admittance that she screwed up not putting on the security system at her parent's home the same day Bishop was shot. She was also the one who pointed out the group to Craig during his dinner date with her."

McManus stopped and spoke into the speaker phone, "By the way Craig boy, how did that evening go before you got clocked by that Dodge truck?" Thompson could be heard laughing a little.

"Boss, be careful, Miss Breen is visiting and she is listening in now."

Terry Breen spoke up, "Special Agent McManus, the dinner and subsequent evening went well until the hit and run incident. But, as fate would have it, the incident also created a nice relationship between this blue eyed cutie and me." The agents all erupted into laughter to the embarrassment of Agent Thompson who just shook his head at Terry.

"Miss Breen, I am pleased you are listening in and please feel free to add anything."

"Thank you Special Agent, I will if something is pertinent."

McManus continued, "The Bryants were probably the victims of Quinn's attempt to eliminate them from the equation. Whether Moore sent him, or he acted on his own, remains to be uncovered. The Mustang was identified and proven to be the instrument of the accident that sent the Bryants to the hospital.

Lucky for them, it wasn't more serious. Quinn was real cocky when he was questioned about the Mustang being stolen. I'm sure he fabricated the whole story about the car being taken with the keys in it and all. He was way too smart to do anything like that. The most interesting event of all is the uncovering of a body in close proximity to the Green Zone in Iraq that turns out to be that of Captain Todd Wilson who was supposedly buried on the Wilson farm. He was an officer under the leadership of one Colonel John Moore. He knew Lieutenant Marilyn Porter, Sergeant Major Henry 'Hank' Jarvis and our sniper, Special Forces and decorated killer, Staff Sergeant Sean Quinn. I wonder who really killed Captain Wilson in Iraq. Was it the Sunni insurgents or one of the Army's own? I think and suspect, the latter, but I am sure, based on what I hear is developing at high military levels in the Army, they will deny that. I read the incident report supplied by the Army. Sergeant Major Jarvis was wounded in the sniper attack. I wonder whether Quinn was trying to make the incident look real by wounding his top sergeant as well during the suspected assassination of Wilson. That is a stretch, I know, but possible. He sure didn't like Jarvis very much. He revealed to us that Jarvis was a homosexual for all the years that he knew him and that didn't sit well with Quinn. I think Quinn used that as a way of covering up the murder of the college kid. I'm sure Quinn killed the kid to keep Jarvis away from him during whatever they had planned. I also think Jarvis must have approached Quinn outside of Hagerstown about the killing and got killed himself. I don't know why either of them would be up there right after the re-interment. Well, I know Jarvis was. I can't prove anything else, but the way Jarvis was killed and then hidden, indicated some serious thought by someone to keep Jarvis from being found. They must have finished whatever they had planned and Quinn, or whoever, eliminated Jarvis."

McManus paused to sip some coffee that was going cold on his desk. He'd been talking continuously for twenty minutes. He continued, "Funeral Director Tom Atkinson found a piece of a bill which later turned out to be a piece of a $100 bill in the

264

empty coffin of Captain Wilson. So gentlemen and lady, these guys had smuggled some cash into the U.S. using the coffin and death of Maryland's hero Captain Todd Wilson, as a cover. Captain Wilson was dishonorably interred in a shallow grave in Baghdad while his entire family attended a full military honors funeral twice. These fucking guys even attended the funerals. They had some balls to do that."

McManus realized his language and apologized to Miss Breen for his outburst. She replied that she did not take offense and that she could not have said it any better. All the agents laughed while McManus regrouped his thoughts.

"How they were able to remove the contents of the coffin is astounding. They managed to get into the Wilson vault due to a malfunction of one of Atkinson's vault trucks. According to Atkinson, Moore, Jarvis and Quinn, along with three Maryland Reserves, attended the re-interment at the Wilson farm. Atkinson didn't remember Porter, but did say a woman attended. When Atkinson had to leave, he said that Moore's group sent the Reservists home because of the delay of moving Wilson's vault and casket. Instead, they said they were honored to guard it themselves. What took place is only known to the woman that was present which I'm sure was Miss Porter. When Atkinson returned, everything seemed in order according to his statement. He did mention the woman again because he asked about her as she was gone when he returned. He was told by Moore that he drove her home. He said Moore never told him her name as far as he could remember. I have already contacted Attorney Wilkes to have Miss Porter here at 11:00 a.m. for further questioning or I will issue a warrant for her arrest at 11:01 a.m. if she doesn't show."

He sipped his cold coffee, made a face in disgust and continued, "Atkinson said that he remembered later that the vault cover was a different one than the one originally supplied when he viewed it at Arlington. He remembers that Wilson's had his name on it while the one dug up at Arlington did not. The piece of currency explained enough for me that there was a smuggling job accomplished by this group. The Colonel, Mr.

Moore, was disciplined for a similar incident under his command that cost him a star. He also had some monetary problems before he was stationed in Iraq. It makes sense to me that he pulled off this job to live happily ever after, but he ran into some .10 mm bullets that stopped his retirement plans. We need Marilyn in here to finish up the puzzle and find out where the money is. How much, is another story. Our Treasury friends said that you could fit about $9 million in a casket in $100 bills; more, if you had ripped out the upholstery of the aluminum casket as was observed by Atkinson and the Army. That would push the amount up another million or two. You all remember seeing some of those CNN pictures of rooms full of stacked $100 bills?" he asked.

He looked at his watch and said, "It's 10:15 a.m. and Miss Porter will be here in 45 minutes. We'll just sit and wait. We will question her if it takes all day until she gives us something. There has to be a fourth person and I believe it's her. Perhaps she is the keeper of the funds. She has to know a lot more than she said when we questioned her."

He excused the agents in his office and relayed his best to Miss Breen who was still on the line with Thompson. After a little joking, he hung up and grabbed another cup of coffee. His coffee had grown very cold during his lengthy synopsis of the multiple crimes that all lead to Miss Porter who was alive and well and on her way to his interrogation room again.

Marilyn Porter dressed for her eleven o'clock meeting with Special Agent McManus while talking to Audrey Wilkes on her portable phone.

"Marilyn, I'll be picking you up in a few minutes. I'm on my way now."

"No, just meet me there. I have some errands to run before we meet with them." Wilkes could not believe what she was hearing from her newly found lover.

"Marilyn, I need to coach you prior to the meeting. This is a very serious meeting you are about to attend. I have also reached a tentative agreement with the criminal lawyer that I mentioned to you before. She has agreed to take your case."

"Thank you very much Audrey but I will breeze through the questioning just like I did the previous day when you were there representing me."

Wilkes cautioned her and said, "Marilyn, the FBI must have new information regarding the autopsy reports on Quinn and Moore and probably other information that neither you nor I are not privy to."

"Look, there is nothing on my end that has changed and I have nothing to hide." She repeated, "I'll meet you at the FBI Office ten minutes before our scheduled meeting with McManus. Audrey, thank you again for a nice evening and I'll see you very soon." She hung up the phone before Wilkes could argue with her anymore.

Marilyn finished dressing in an appealing blue dress she had recently purchased for an evening with Quinn that never materialized. She looked over her makeup and hair, adjusted her gold bracelet that Moore had given her, and smiled at herself in the mirror. Her stomach ached but she knew she would either be in jail in an hour or so or free to lay low and wait until the right time to remove the boxes of cash from the storage facility. She laughed inside when she calculated that she had a lot of years to spend $11 million. She realized that a girl could get spoiled on that kind of wealth. She also dreamed up a plan that if she was caught and was sentenced for so many years in prison, she would rely on Audrey to place the boxes in a safe place. She would have to figure out a way to sway Audrey into hiding the boxes of cash but $11 million was a lot of temptation even for a Harvard degreed lawyer. Marilyn realized she was thinking like Quinn. The bastard had infected her. She also thought that too much of her time had been spent with Moore who had also influenced her. She changed the contents of her purse and realized she had the key to Moore's storage facility still in it. She made a mental note to throw that key away. She also had the keys to her storage facility. Those, she decided, had to be kept safely. She went into her computer desk and retrieved a padded envelop used for shipping small items by mail. She placed one of her storage keys in the envelope and addressed it to Wilkes at the bank. She put her name on it in the lower corner that read 'RE: M. Porter. She scribbled a short note and placed it in with the key and sealed the envelope. She left the apartment, looked to see that no one was looking, stooped down and quickly pushed Moore's storage key into the loose black soil that surrounded the manicured flowers and plants in front of her apartment complex. She then got into her Honda, placed her other storage key into her glove box, and headed directly to the Frederick Post Office. She mailed the envelope and headed for the appointment with the FBI. She knew this session would probably last until she either broke down during the interrogation because they had incriminating evidence or cried enough to convince them that she was innocent. If she broke, she decided she would turn the situation around that she was a victim of some high stakes crime that her bank associates had committed without her complete knowledge and that Moore had insinuated that she would be harmed if she didn't go along with the plan once she figured out some of what was going on. It was a long shot, but she figured the worst that she could get if she broke and turned in evidence was seven to ten years which could probably be reduced with good behavior. She might even get a better deal with the Baltimore lawyer Audrey was arranging to defend her. She would always maintain the story that she was never told what the amount of cash was and where it was hidden after the group removed it from the vault. That information went to the grave with the three who knew.

Marilyn concentrated on the type of questions McManus and the others would likely ask her. She convinced herself that her main objective was still to keep all the events clear in her head and claim her innocence, protesting that she didn't know what Moore and the others had in mind. No one knew she was screwing Moore except those who were dead, so they wouldn't ask her if he divulged any information to her. They knew that she was doing Quinn, but she thought that she could convince them that Quinn never divulged any of his actions to her. She adjusted her rear view mirror so that she could look at her facial expressions while she practiced answering the kinds of questions she assumed that they would be asking her. Unfortunately, she failed to keep her concentration on her driving.

While traveling north on North Bentz Street, Marilyn failed to see the stop signal at the intersection at West Patrick Street. A FedEx Delivery truck never had time to slow down as it slammed into the driver's door of Marilyn's Honda. She never even saw the truck before it hit her. The impact caused her neck and head to jerk violently enough to snap her spinal cord, killing her instantly before the side and frontal air bags could deploy. The force of the collision caused the Honda to crumble under the force of the truck which pushed it a hundred feet or so before resting on the other side of the intersection. Several other vehicles were damaged when cars following the FedEx truck, slammed into the rear of the truck or swerved to avoid the accident. There were no serious injuries that occurred except that of Marilyn Porter.

The first Frederick Police officer on the scene checked and noted the license plate and called it in to his dispatcher while requesting an ambulance. He checked her for any vital signs and found none. He searched for any identification in the purse he observed on the floor of the car. He recorded her name and waited for the dispatcher's report to confirm the same information he now had. The call he received, matched his information he had compiled. He then called for the Fire Department to secure the area which smelt of fuel, and to assist the ambulance attendants if needed in removing Miss Marilyn Porter from her twisted, crushed and steaming vehicle.

Audrey Wilkes looked at her watch. It indicated that Porter was now five minutes late for her appointment. Special Agent McManus noticed her waiting outside in the lobby of the FBI Office. He approached Audrey and said, "Ms. Wilkes, I have just issued a warrant for the arrest of Miss Marilyn Porter. I have also put out an all-points bulletin to apprehend her upon sight and bring her into the closest jail."

"Agent, maybe she was detained in traffic or is having auto trouble."

"Or maybe she just left town."

"If she was going to leave town, she should have done it hours ago. I just finished talking to her at 10:30 a.m. Special Agent." McManus was about to make another wise crack when Jamul Whitford called him.

"Boss, after I put out the all-points bulletin, we got a response from the Frederick PD that Porter was involved in an accident at the intersection at West Patrick and North Bentz. The officer on the scene reported one fatality. It was Porter."

"Holy shit," was all McManus could utter as he looked at Wilkes who stood silent and had just turned gray. Audrey found a bench in the lobby and sat before her legs gave out from under her. McManus was gentlemanly enough to instruct Whitford to get some water for the attorney as he sat next to her not uttering another word.

The Key

The FBI and the Frederick Police Department searched the residences of all four of the suspects again for several days. Audrey Wilkes had to obtain counsel to insure her attorney-client rights were respected as well. She had to sustain several interrogations with the FBI in that two day period that followed Marilyn's death and had to stand by while several forensic technicians combed her house for anything to tie her to the Moore group. Audrey assumed that she was being considered a suspect now that Moore's entire group was dead. She realized they thought she retained information based on attorney-client relations. She was allowed to maintain her position as a legal representative for the Colony Bank but she was asked to leave by the Bank's board of directors once the investigation was concluded. She heard from some close colleagues, but could not prove, that her reputation in the Maryland Bar Association was damaged. The Bank President and Board Members had said that they wanted the bank to distance itself from any employees that had been considered suspicious. The offices of all four were also searched during that period for any evidence of collusion, but no new evidence had been found. The only thing the FBI had was conjecture, four dead suspects, records of some credit card purchases, cell phone calls and a piece of a $100 bill.

The Wilson family was never informed that Captain Todd Wilson had been killed by a suspected Army Special Forces Staff Sergeant and buried in an unmarked grave. Major General Thaddeus Lucas ordered his staff, Brigadier Byron Caldwell and his staff, Captain Jonas Miles of the Army Forensic Team in Iraq and Sergeant Russell's team in a secret memo, that the disclosure of this hideous killing and suspected crime would be an embarrassment to the United States Army. It further said that it would cause further grief to the family of Captain Todd Wilson and tarnish the reputation of four honorably and decorated discharged veterans. The memo further reminded all the recipients that despite suspicion from the FBI, there was no proof that anyone of the four veterans was involved in the incident. He emphatically ordered all the addressees that they were bound by secrecy concerning this unfortunate matter and could be prosecuted under the code of military justice if they divulged any of this information. He further said that the Federal Bureau of Investigation had closed the case based on his recommendation that it be held as secret for one hundred years. Special Agent McManus informed Terry Breen, Audrey Wilkes, and Funeral Director Thomas Atkinson of the Army's position on the Wilson case and advised that they were bound as well.

Staff Sergeant Sean Quinn was buried in Baltimore with full military honors. His death was listed as an apparent dual homicide due to a personal argument with another civilian. A few of Quinn's distant relatives attended. One non-family participant was Agent Jamul Whitford who had been sent by his supervisor to observe the funeral and those that attended. Colonel John Moore was also buried in the same cemetery as Quinn on the same day with the same military honors. His ex-wife and children did not attend.

Moore's flag was given to a cousin who was one of eight people who attended. Agent Joe Walker was there to observe the participants. Marilyn Porter's funeral was held several days later in her hometown and attended by her parents and approximately fifty other mourners. Her death was listed as an accident and only two of those attending ever knew she was a suspect in the monetary heist. Those two individual were Audrey Wilkes and Jack McManus. Audrey stayed far away from McManus, who she despised for attending, during the funeral. Hank Jarvis was the last one to be buried. His body was returned to his family plot that his sister had finally made the arrangements for. She tried many times to contact Colonel Moore, until the FBI contacted her to have Jarvis's body removed from the Hagerstown morgue and informed her that the Colonel had been killed.

One week into the two week notice Audrey Wilkes had been given to vacate her office and leave the bank's employment, John Moore's ex-secretary, Ms. Clemens, placed an envelope in Attorney Wilkes's in-basket on her desk. When Audrey returned from a session with the bank's Human Resources representative concerning her 401K account and medical benefits, she saw the envelope in the basket she had emptied earlier. Marilyn's name in the corner sent a chill down her spine and an ache in her heart. The 'Re: M. Porter', written in Marilyn's handwriting, confused her as she stared at the envelope. She sat down and opened it. A key dropped out onto her desk as she removed a small note. She read it and immediately cried. It read, "I will probably be in only one of three places; with you, in jail or with God. Take this key to the place and number indicated. It is the key to my heart, Love, Marilyn." She put the note and key back into the envelope, composed herself enough to gather her purse and told Ms. Clemens, as she passed her desk, that she was finished for the day and could be reached by cell if anyone needed to contact her.

She cried all the way as she drove her car and returned home and contemplated what Marilyn had left for her and what the key would open. She changed and took a walk around the neighborhood to insure the FBI had finally convinced itself that she was an innocent party to whatever the Moore group had done. She rounded the block several times at a fast walk looking in every direction for anyone looking suspicious. She felt sure that she was not being observed and returned home. At dark, she left her apartment and walked around the neighborhood again. There was no indication that she was under any surveillance. She returned home to use her car. She left and drove directly for the storage facility. She took a few side roads to ensure there was no tail on her. She relaxed a little realizing that she had become too paranoid over the last several weeks. She found the facility and slowly drove to the storage area that the key had indicated.

There were several cars and trucks loading and unloading

boxes and different types of furniture, but none were close to the one she needed to open. She exited her car and casually walked over to the door. She inserted the key in the lock and it opened with relative ease. She pulled up the garage door which immediately engaged a soft light for her to observe two stacks of boxes marked as household items. She read the writing on the boxes, but then focused on the smaller writing that indicated initials and numbers that were piled separately. The first one she observed was marked "MP – 1 of 5". She looked further to observe "MP – 5 of 5" written on another one then "SQ – 1 of 5". She then found the entire set of five with SQ written on them. She then observed "JM – 2 of 5. She froze and realized the initials were Marilyn's, Quinn's and Moore's. She confirmed her observation when "JM – 4 of 5" was observed. She didn't stay at the storage facility very long and forced herself to take the box marked "MP – 1 of 5". She was too scared and nervous to open it up in the facility. She put the box in her car, locked the storage room and returned home.

She drove at the posted speed limit and still continued to look for any indication that she was being watched. She disciplined herself to make the proper signals, observe all the traffic signs and get home as inconspicuously as possible just to make sure she wasn't pulled over for some traffic violation. She didn't know what she was carrying in her car but, until she knew, she had to be overly cautious.

Upon reaching her apartment, she locked her doors, closed the blinds and walked around the table where she had placed the box in her living room. She picked up the box and shook it. There was no sound of movement. She expected to hear some glass clinking because the writing on the box indicated that it contained a variety of glassware. She began to open the box but realized that the packer had used heavy clear tape to seal it. She got a cutting knife from the kitchen and began to cut the sealed tape. Within seconds, Audrey Wilkes was looking at the most money she had ever seen in her entire life. She lifted one stack of $100 bills in marked $10,000 amounts and became nauseous. She emptied the contents and counted that she had

$654,800 in cash on her coffee table. She sat at the table and tried to comprehend the amount of money she was looking at. If each box contained approximately the same amount, there could be several million or maybe more in that storage facility. She became mad but resisted from screaming her disgust when she said out loud, "Marilyn, you cunt, you lied to me. You were no different than Quinn or the others. You were in it the whole time. You bitch!" She cried hysterically for several minutes looking at the cash and thinking how she had given herself to Marilyn when all the time Marilyn had other reasons and was just baiting her to believe that she loved her. Wilkes read Marilyn's note again, "I will probably be in only one of three places; with you, in jail or with God. Take this key to the place and number indicated. It is the key to my heart. Love, Marilyn." Audrey crumpled the note and threw it across the room. She cried a little more but then composed herself. She wondered what she should do. The obvious thing, thinking as an attorney, would be to turn in all the cash and explain how she came upon it. She talked to herself out loud, "Would they believe me? Would they prosecute me for being an accomplice? Would they add murder to the charges? Everyone was dead. Except for Marilyn, everyone was killed under suspicious circumstances. Could I be the other suspect that McManus always referred to? That fucking pig would love to shove this case down my throat so he would get credit for solving it." She continued to think out loud to herself as she paced back in forth in her living room, "If I keep it… but no, that's wrong," she chided herself. "Besides that, it's a crime punishable by a lengthy stay in prison. But if I do keep it, who would be hurt by my decision? Wilson had been killed for apparently not going along with the plan. Marilyn was probably going to share the spoils with me I think, anyway. Why else would she send me a key? She didn't expect to get killed and I would have followed her anywhere." She immediately felt lonely. She stopped pacing around the room and sat down. Audrey thought of that beautiful woman rotting in her grave even though she had deceived her. She didn't care about Moore, Jarvis and especially that cocky chauvinistic killer Quinn, who probably even murdered that innocent gay college kid. Quinn deserved death based on his disgusting disregard for human life. She packed up the box as best as she could and resealed it. She kept out $10,000 and stored it in her trial brief case. Audrey returned to the storage facility an hour later and re-deposited the box as she remembered finding it. She made a mental note to re-new the storage fee the next day. She also realized the coding was Moore's and he probably was about to short change Quinn based on the changed notations on a few of the boxes. She spoke out loud as she laughed, "That sneaky son of a bitch. Even in the end, he tried to screw his partners." She needed time to think through the implications of Marilyn's gift and she realized that she now had that time.

Her ride home and her constant thoughts made her even more paranoid. She thought of how the FBI had searched all the credit cards and phone calls of all their suspects. She realized Marilyn couldn't have used her credit card to rent the storage facility. She must have had to pay in cash. She must have also used another name on the rental agreement. The FBI couldn't trace every place in Frederick where Marilyn paid cash for services, especially using another name, she surmised. As an attorney, she knew identification was needed to rent a storage facility for contract and insurance issues. She also knew she would have to renew the storage area through the storage facility office. She needed to find out how long Marilyn rented the storage area. When she presented the storage number, she would find out whose name it was rented in.

Audrey continued to ponder how Marilyn could have accomplished all of it. She retraced everything she could remember about her. The talks, the love making, the interrogations and anything else she could remember in detail. Then she remembered and said aloud, "My business card. She must have used the business card I gave her when she registered for the storage unit. That's how she got enough information. The tricky bitch". She laughed to herself again.

Audrey remembered the day she gave Marilyn the business

card and some personal information written on it. She continued to drive and remembered that she would be out of a job in a week, had only two weeks of salary coming, and what she saved in her personal bank account. She smiled to herself as she also remembered that she had an additional $10,000 in her brief case at home in $100 bills. She began to cry again on her way home. She couldn't decide whether it was happy or sad tears, but she cried about her friend Marilyn. She composed herself by the time she exited her car in the apartment parking lot. Audrey glanced towards her mail slot as she entered the apartment atrium. She noticed through the glass door that she had mail. She opened her purse, drew out her mail box key and opened the mailbox. She quickly shuffled through several utility bills, credit card bills and advertisements until the letterhead on one of the envelopes indicated it was from the Maryland Bar Association. Her stomach turned as she opened the envelope to read its contents. The letter informed her that a letter of reprimand had been entered into her Bar Association record for not fully cooperating with the Federal Bureau of Investigation and the United States Department of the Army. The letter further indicated that she could appeal the letter of reprimand and gave her the procedure to initiate the appeal. It said also that if she, on her appeal, convinced the FBI and the Army that she did not overextend the use of the attorney-client relationship privilege, the letter of reprimand would be removed from her file. It further explained her rights and the contacts she could make if she so desired to appeal. She re-read the letter again as she stood in the apartment atrium. Her first response, as her stomach turned, was professional embarrassment. It soon turned to hurt. She realized her professional career had been tarnished. She also knew that, until the letter of reprimand was removed, her chances for employment at any firm, never mind a prestigious one, were slim to none.

As she contemplating seeking professional counsel to combat the accusation and the letter of reprimand, she became more irritated. The amount of time, the expense, the trudging through the Moore group investigation again went through her mind. The more she thought about it, the madder she became. Was it worth it? She realized that she had the money. But someone might ask how she was able to afford a top notch law firm to defend her for probably a lengthy time. Someone might check. McManus was still out there and she didn't need to be on his radar again because she was sure that he would be called in by the Bar Association. Again she asked herself, was it really worth it? She crumpled the letter and talked to herself while gritting her teeth and said, "They screwed me real good, the bastards."

Epilogue

Audrey Wilkes realized the letter of reprimand from the Maryland Bar Association was going to affect her ability to have an active practice in the state. It was going to be very limited, if not career ending. She made her decision and returned to the storage area the day after receiving her letter of reprimand. She found out that Marilyn did register her as the renter when she renewed it. She returned a few more times to the storage facility after that and over a few weeks, completely emptying it.

FBI Agent Craig Thompson fully recovered from his injuries and eventually proposed marriage to Attorney Terry Breen. She was also made a full partner after the retirement of Attorney Edward Manning. Special Agent Jack McManus never reached Chief Agent due to his inability to solve the Wilson case. He continued on serving with distinction as a Special Agent in the Frederick, Maryland office. Joe Walker was promoted to Special Agent and reassigned to the Baltimore office. His wife Crystal became pregnant and delivered twin girls. Four year old Joe Walker, Jr. began pre-kindergarten which gave his mother a little extra time to deal with the twins during the day. Jamul Whitford left the FBI to pursue his Doctoral Degree in Criminal Investigation at Georgetown University.

Amy and Bob Bryant returned to Frederick and built, what looked like from the outside, a replica of the original Wilson farmhouse. The Geo-Thermal heating and cooling system, the electrical solar panels on the south side of the home and the windmill generator, were the only signs that the homestead was completely modern. The continual improvement of the interior of the homestead became Amy's full time job when she was not editing Bob's written speeches. Bob Bryant continued to write speeches for notable politicians in the Washington area.

Cora and Bob, Jr. moved into the homestead and both began teaching in the Frederick school system. Cora met and married John Kramer who grew up on a dairy farm just twenty miles away from the Wilson farm. He manages the two hundred and fifty dairy cows on the very productive, and still called, Wilson dairy farm. Cora became pregnant with the Bryant's first grandbaby. Bob, Jr. just recently became engaged and is planning to marry within a year. Amy's dream of filling the farmhouse with grandkids will become a reality. The Wilson relatives meet several times a year at the farm for holidays. Thanksgiving has the largest attendance.

Audrey Wilkes continued to search for employment, but her involvement in the Wilson case and the letter in her file caused considerable doubt in the minds of potential employers and continued to damage her career. After a year with no success of finding a firm that would accept her, she moved from Frederick to Annapolis; found, and purchased an old cottage remotely located on the banks of Chesapeake Bay. She spent a fair amount of money to make the place perfect. She always paid her contractors in cash with a little extra in tips to keep them discrete each time she needed their services. They have always been very responsive when she required any new renovations to the place.

Audrey eventually found a teaching position at the United States Naval Academy at Annapolis due to her brief letter to Major General Thaddeus Lucas, (US Army Ret.). She wrote that she felt her inability to practice law was due to a letter of reprimand that had been inserted into her file by the Maryland Bar Association concerning her attorney-client status to one of the suspects in the Wilson case, and that it was unfair.

She informed the retired Major General that she contemplated writing a book as a teaching instrument for law students about reasons to challenge the interpretation of the Maryland Bar Association, the Federal Bureau of Investigation and the United States Department of the Army, concerning attorney-client privileges. She informed the Major General that she planned to call the book, "Dishonorably Interred," emphasizing external pressure being instituted by the government in State civil cases like the Wilson Investigation. She also said that she has now considered teaching history and political science at the college level because of her inability to practice law. She also mentioned that she had applied for a civilian professorship position opening at the United States Naval Academy.

She never pursued writing her book due to a verbal promise she made to Retired Major General Lucas in a phone call she received from him concerning the professorship she mentioned in her letter. She now enjoys her associate professorship at the United States Naval Academy.

One of the renovations to the cottage that Audrey had recently completed was an extensive library of legal and personal books she collected. Behind one of the shelf sections that slides away, is a jeweler's safe full of Marilyn's love for Audrey and instructions for her personal representative, when she dies, to divide whatever cash remains in the safe amongst the several organizations and families she has listed. One particular family that she lists is to receive fifty percent of her remaining money. That fifty percent is to be divided equally amongst the living descendants' of the Bruce Wilson, Benjamin Wilson and Amy Wilson Bryant families.

The End

About the Author

Thomas Michael Coletti has lived most of his life in the Norwich, Connecticut area. He has been married to Donna Jean for 38 years. He has four grown children and two grandchildren. Jennifer, his illustrator, is married to Paul Harren. They have two children, Katie and Sean. Kimberly, Crystal and Michael, completes his family,

Tommy graduated from Norwich Free Academy in 1967. He enlisted into the USAF in 1968 and spent four years as a medic. He was honorably discharged in 1972 and went to college on the G.I. Bill. He received an AS from Mohegan Community College, Norwich, in 1974, and a BA from Eastern Connecticut State University, Willimantic in 1976.

He applied and was accepted to law school but declined admission to work one year at the Electric Boat Shipyard (EB) in Groton, until his wife gave birth to their first child. He remained there as subsequent children were born. He has been there for 35 years and plans to retire in August of 2011.

CPSIA information can be obtained at www.ICGtesting.com
Printed in the USA
BVOW031948031011

272214BV00007B/7/P